REA

ACPL ITE̶M̶
DISCARDED

ALLEN COUNTY PUBLIC LIBRARY
3 1833 03615 11

W9-CSX-222

MAR 1 5 2000

The
Final
Fabergé

BOOKS BY THOMAS SWAN

The Da Vinci Deception
The Cézanne Chase

The
Final
Fabergé

THOMAS SWAN

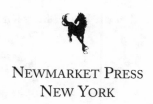

NEWMARKET PRESS
NEW YORK

Copyright © 1999 by Thomas Swan

This book is published in the United States of America.

All rights reserved. This book may not be reproduced,
in whole, or in part, in any form, without written permission.
Inquiries should be addressed to Permissions Department,
Newmarket Press, 18 East 48th Street, New York, NY 10017.

10   9   8   7   6   5   4   3   2   1

Library of Congress Cataloging-in-Publication Data
Swan, Thomas.
The final Fabergé / Thomas Swan.
p. cm.
"A novel of suspense."
ISBN 1-55704-382-5 (hardcover)
I. Title.
PR6069.W344F5   1999
823'.914—dc21   99-34408
CIP

QUANTITY PURCHASES
Companies, professional groups, clubs, and other organizations may qualify
for special terms when ordering quantities of this title. For information,
write Special Sales Department, Newmarket Press, 18 East 48th Street,
New York, NY 10017, call (212) 832-3575, or fax (212) 832-3629.

Manufactured in the United States of America.

With all my love to Barbara,
the best and most patient
research assistant in the world!

Author's Note

The events and characters in this book are fictional, except for those persons who were or are genuinely real and who inspired much of the story. Peter Carl Fabergé was a brilliant goldsmith and jeweler. Grigori Rasputin is the stuff of legends; his true role in the government of Nicholas II and relationship with Alexandra will be endlessly studied.

. . . O God, how many thorny paths there are in life!
—Grigori Rasputin

Chapter 1

On the table was a box. Not one made of ordinary pine, but of a fine-grained wood that had been cut and pieced perfectly together. The wood was holly and had been stained a pale brown, brushed with several coats of shellac, then rubbed to a rich luster with a powder made from pumice and cigarette ashes. The box was eight inches high, the same as the cut glass and silver pitcher that was next to it. Beside the pitcher were figurines made of semi-precious stones, jeweled mantel clocks, cigarette cases, snuff boxes, necklaces, jewelry, carved stone sculptures, and other samples of the work produced by a hundred craftsmen in the house of G. Fabergé, 16 Bolshaya Morskaya Street.

Seated at the table was a balding man with a dense white beard, blanched skin, and steel-rimmed glasses that had slipped low on his nose. Dignity showed in an intelligent face lined with the wrinkles of seventy years, and in eyes that held the glint of youthful good humor. In all, there was the appearance of a wise and immensely creative man. He opened the box and took out an object shaped like a large egg. The man was Peter Carl Fabergé, the jeweled object was an Imperial Easter egg for which Fabergé had become world-famous, and which was intended as a gift for Czarina Alexandra Feodorovna.

Fabergé placed the egg on a swatch of deep blue velvet and nudged it toward the man who sat across from him. "In spite of the war, we found nearly all the materials we had planned to use. Except for gold. That we used sparingly."

The Imperial egg stood upright and was held by a pair of delicately sculptured hands which seemed to reach up from a round, white onyx base. On top of the egg was a little basket made of delicately woven gold strips. Inside were flowers made from either a diamond or sapphire, their petals individually enameled in pinks and white. The egg had been covered with a thin layer of pure silver that had been hammered, engraved, polished, and finally overlayed with a fusion of glass and metal oxides to produce a translucent enamel surface. The blue color was as intense as a pure summer sky, testimony to the fact that nowhere was the technique of guilloche ground so well executed as in the shops of Peter Fabergé. Two half-inch bands of silver circled the egg and on each were clusters of rubies and emeralds. The onyx base was encircled with a stripe of blue enamel over which gold leaf tips and rosettes had been applied.

Fabergé placed a finger against the largest of the rubies in the silver band. The pressure released a spring lock and the upper third of the egg opened to reveal a pocket lined in silk the color of cream. In the pocket was the "surprise." The surprises found in Fabergé's other Imperial eggs ranged from a precise model of the royal yacht to a chirping ruby-encrusted cockerel. The surprise that rested on the silk was an enameled portrait of the Czar and Czarina, and a tiny easel on which to show it off.

The design of this Imperial egg was especially different from the previous Easter gifts commissioned by Czar Alexander III and his son Nicholas II. Instead of just one surprise compartment, there were two. The second compartment in the egg held by Fabergé was so cleverly concealed it was likely to be discovered only by cutting apart the egg.

And this Imperial egg was also different in that it had not been commissioned by Czar Nicholas as an Easter gift to his wife, but by a man of dark intrigue and power, a man who many conjectured was as powerful as the Czar himself, and who now sat across from Fabergé. The hands that held the egg, turning it over slowly with long, bony fingers, belonged to the peasant monk Grigori Efimovich Rasputin, forty-five years old, heavily bearded, with long, curling black hair and eyes set deep under thick brows. His voice was thin, nearly inaudible.

He glanced up at Fabergé, his head tilted. "You have made a very beautiful gift for my friends." Rasputin closed the egg and ran his finger over the silver and stones, searching for a way to open the second surprise compartment.

"How do you open it?"

Fabergé took the egg. "Here, on the inside, is a circle of twelve pearls.

All, that is, except for one." He pointed to a perfectly round sapphire. "If you think of it as the face of a clock, then the sapphire would be twelve o'clock. When I push three of the pearls, in a specific order, the second compartment will open. Just so—"

Fabergé carefully pressed against three of the pearls, he knew the ones. Each was minutely different from the others. He twisted the lower half of the egg at the silver band, separating the egg. With his fingernail he pried up a tiny door revealing a hollowed-out compartment the size of a walnut.

Fabergé smiled. "Good enough?"

"It's like a toy," Rasputin said with a grin. "And I have a name for it. I will call it *The Egg of Eternal Blessing*." From a pocket in his voluminous pants he took out a leather pouch. He opened it and took two stones and placed them in Fabergé's outstretched hand. One was blue, the other a pale yellow. "These will make it a true surprise."

Fabergé put a loupe to his eye and studied the stones. First the blue stone, a cut cabochon star sapphire. He pronounced that it had excellent color and that the star was nearly perfectly formed. He set it aside and put the diamond under the glass and studied it for several minutes, murmuring his fascination aloud.

"Most strange color . . . rare cut . . . over fifteen carats. Where did you—"

Rasputin had come around and stood behind the jeweler, beyond the bright light in a pool of his own darkness. "It was a gift from Madame Alikina," he said. "She was the grand-niece of Count Orlov and it had been handed down from her father, who had been given a box of precious stones when his father died. I helped the old lady over her sickness, but she was eighty-five and before she died, she gave me the diamond. Is it valuable?"

It seemed incredible to Fabergé that the wily and reputedly clever Rasputin could not know how valuable the diamond actually was. He weighed it: 18.7 carats. "It has the yellow of pure sunlight," he said slowly, with reverence. "Never have I seen one like it." He peered at the monk's dark face, into the black sockets where thin rims of fire glowed.

"Valuable?" he finally answered. "In normal times it would easily sell for a hundred thousand rubles."

The two stones were put into the second surprise compartment, but only after Rasputin asked Fabergé to show him the pearls and the order they must be pressed to open it.

Rasputin said, "I must write down the numbers in the correct sequence."

Fabergé gave him pen and paper. Carefully, Rasputin wrote the numbers and folded the paper, slipping it into the leather pouch. At Rasputin's urging, Fabergé returned the egg to its box and wrapped it with brown paper.

"I am going directly to Prince Yusupov's home and there's no need to raise suspicions."

"To a soiree?" Fabergé asked, knowing of the monk's proclivity for carousing and his notoriously insatiable appetite for women. "The prince will show you a good time."

Rasputin shook his head as he all but disappeared beneath a huge coat of beaver and fox. "Felix has insisted on this evening. I'm very tired, brother Fabergé, but I've been promised that Irina will be there with her friends." Irina was Yusupov's recently acquired wife, a distant cousin of Czar Nicholas and a beauty who had confided privately that she was anxious to meet the infamous monk.

❧ ❧ ❧

It was after ten o'clock when Rasputin reached Yusupov's palatial home on the Moika River, where music blared from a distant room, a gramophone playing "Yankee Doodle." A house steward, a young, bearded man, gathered in Rasputin's heavy coat and reached for the box he carried under his arm.

"I should keep it with me," Rasputin said.

"Nonsense," a small man said, approaching. "It will be safe with Nikolai. You don't want to spend the evening clutching some bit of shopping you brought along."

Felix Yusupov was short and slight with a high-pitched sibilant voice, but assertive nonetheless. He took the box, instructing Nikolai to take it and fold the great coat over it and take both to the master's bedroom.

"There now, we will go downstairs for a while, then I will take you to meet Irina."

Downstairs was a room the size of the ballroom above it, furnished with heavy pieces from Paris and rugs from Ankara. One wall was covered with big and small icons and in direct contrast, the adjoining wall held the strange works of a young painter named Picasso. It was a room befitting every ruble of the Yusupov fortune. Even though young and small, Prince Felix Yusupov Sumarokoff was someone to reckon with. His family represented prominence, prestige, and power. He seemed to be studying Rasputin, eyeing his velvet pantaloons, silk blouse, and thick yellow cross that hung from a heavy chain. Rasputin had shown his friendship on recent occasions, aware perhaps that Yusupov had made complaints about the monk's continuing influence over Czarina Alexandra Feodorovna.

"The wine has a fruity flavor," Yusupov said, offering a glass to his guest. "It's from my cousin's vineyard near Yalta. Or would you prefer vodka? Or brandy?"

Rasputin took the glass and it seemed he quickly crossed himself before he drank nearly all of it. He sighed heavily, finished the wine and sat in an upholstered chair overflowing with fat cushions. Yusupov refilled Rasputin's glass, then took his own to a chair next to his guest. "Have you had news of the war?" he asked.

Rasputin shook his head and answered slowly, "There should be no war."

Rasputin had long been rumored as sympathetic to the Germans, and had been accused of persuading Nicholas to wait dangerously long before moving into action. Yusupov also knew that Rasputin had a deep influence over Alexandra. Now the "little man" had invited Rasputin into his home for a soiree, a late evening entertainment with Irina and her friends.

"Chocolate or cream?" Yusupov asked, proffering a tray filled with sweet cakes.

Rasputin stared blankly at the desserts, then put up a hand and declined.

"But you must," Yusupov said, popping a chocolate cake into his mouth, watching Rasputin carefully, waiting patiently and moving the tray closer. Rasputin drank the second glass of wine, then accepted one of the cakes, eating it immediately. Yusupov smiled. The music from the floor above grew louder; another American song.

Rasputin said, "They are dancing." It was half a question, half a statement, as if he knew that Irina's guests were drinking and enjoying a party. He added, "We should join them." Then, almost absently, he took another cake and held out his glass. "I like your brother's wine."

Yusupov went for the wine bottle and stood by the table while Rasputin ate the sweet. He poured a fresh glass and returned with it, handed it to Rasputin, and stared closely at the monk's eyes and hands. After eating two of the cakes Rasputin showed little change from when he first appeared, and in fact seemed to be in an even lighter, happier mood.

Yusupov knew that should not be.

Little more than an hour before, the room in which Rasputin was now sitting had been a scene of frantic activity. Yusupov and four associates, Vladimir M. Purishkevich, Grand Duke Dimitri Pavlovich, Anton Sukhotin, and Dr. Feodor Lazovert, had been gathered for the single purpose of planning the assassination of Rasputin. Purishkevich was a flamboyant politician known for his public disavowal of the Czar and open hostility toward Rasputin. Pavlovich was his obsequious protégé and held similar views. Sukhotin was a military officer and would be a link to high-ranking and sympathetic members of the army. Because Yusupov retained the right to determine how Rasputin would be killed in his own home, Dr. Lazovert, a neo-revolutionist, had been recruited to secure and implant potassium cyanide crystals in the dessert cakes. Lazovert had declared that he had brought sufficient poison to kill Rasputin several times over. "A single cake should do it," he had said confidently. "However, if you encourage him to have two cakes, there will be no question the cyanide will do him in."

When Yusupov offered the tray of dessert cakes again, Rasputin all but pushed it out of his hand. He drank the wine, then got unsteadily onto his feet and went to the door leading to the stairs and up to the music.

"It's getting late, little one," Rasputin said. "Let's go to the party with the music and women. There is no party here. Only those sweet cakes and the wine that tastes like berry juice."

Having said this, Rasputin doubled over, nearly falling to the floor. Yusupov started toward him, certain that the poison was taking hold, afraid it would be a painful death, one he hadn't the stomach to watch. It was also distressing that he would soon see the most famous monk in Russia writhing in pain, staring up with his black eyes, damning him, and threatening a terrible revenge.

But as quickly as it seemed he had collapsed, Rasputin straightened, took a guitar from a shelf next to the door, and suggested that Yusupov play a tune. Yusupov took the instrument and ran for the stairs, taking the steps two at a time, shouting back to Rasputin, "Stay there! I'll find Irina."

Purishkevich met him at the top of the stairs and they were immediately joined by Dr. Lazovert, who stared expectantly at Yusupov, waiting for the proclamation that Rasputin was dead. Instead, Yusupov screeched the words that he had escaped from a fiend: "He's not human! Two cakes with the cyanide and he thinks only of when he can join Irina's party. He asked me to play this damned thing!" Yusupov dropped the guitar and began breathing so rapidly that Lazovert feared he would hyperventilate.

Purishkevich said, "We'll go with you. I have a revolver."

"This is my responsibility," Yusupov said, and went to his study, returning with a pocket Browning. He continued noiselessly down the stairs and slowly went into the room where he found Rasputin standing at the table on which were the cakes and wine. The monk had filled his glass again. He turned and faced Yusupov.

"You're back, little one," he said cheerfully. "That is very good. Let me fill your glass, and after we've had the wine, we will join Irina." He filled a glass and offered it to the little man.

Yusupov now stood less than ten feet from Rasputin. In his left hand was a bronze crucifix, his arm extended and rigid. "Say a prayer, Grigori Efimovich. You must do that."

Rasputin stared wonderingly at the cross, then at the barrel of the gun Yusupov had brought from behind his back and pointed directly at the monk's chest. A word formed in his mouth, then the gun exploded, a loud snapping noise that echoed with rapid reverberations off the walls. Rasputin crumpled, then fell. Yusupov took several tentative steps toward him, looked down at the body, then ran like a frightened schoolboy back up the stairs to the waiting conspirators. This time they were all gathered, all talking at once, asking if Rasputin was dead and where he had been shot, demanding to know how many bullets Yusupov had fired.

"I killed him!" Yusupov said. "For the good of Russia." He clutched the gun with both hands, his body shaking, his face white and wet from sweat. He said, his voice high and shrill, "I never killed anyone before."

The others, led by Purishkevich, pushed past him and went below and into the room where they found Rasputin had fallen onto his back and lay sprawled on a bearskin rug. Dr. Lazovert bent over him and put his hand beside the growing splotch of blood high up on Rasputin's chest. He pressed fingers against the monk's neck, searching for a pulse, and apparently not finding one, looked up to the others and nodded.

Purishkevich took control, ordering Sukhotin to personally report
Rasputin's death to the military command, and for Pavlovich to go forward with the plan previously agreed to for the disposal of Rasputin's
body. To Lazovert he said without a shred of conviction, "You've done
your work, go home," making it plain that the good doctor had botched
his assignment. Purishkevich edged closer to the prone body, lit a cigar,
and spat out shreds of tobacco on Rasputin. He turned and said, "I must
use the telephone."

Alone, Yusupov sat in a straight-back chair, facing the body, eyes
fixed blankly on Rasputin's face, lips forming words to a childhood
prayer. Then he saw an almost imperceptible movement in the dead
man's face. Not possible, his nerves playing tricks, he thought. It had
been like a twitch, and then it happened again. One eye opened.
Yusupov scrambled to his feet, searching for his Browning, sick with the
fright that Rasputin was not dead. Now both eyes were open and the
monk rolled half a turn and struggled to his feet and was coming at
Yusupov, roaring in anger, blood trickling from his mouth.

"Felix! Felix!" he screamed with a mad voice, saying only the name
over and over. "Felix! Felix! Felix . . ." He locked an arm around
Yusupov's head, but the smaller man wriggled free and ran upstairs,
finding Purishkevich in his study.

"He's alive, God save us!"

Purishkevich ran quickly, making his fat short legs move with unac-
customed speed, tugging his own revolver from his coat pocket. The
basement room was empty, and he hustled back to the main floor, and
out to the courtyard, where he found Rasputin stumbling over the
banks of snow, shouting, "Felix, I'll tell the Czarina!"

Purishkevich fired twice, missing, then moved closer and put a bullet in Rasputin's back. He moved closer and aimed more carefully. The
last bullet tore through the monk's neck and once again he lay sprawled.
Purishkevich went to him and kicked him fiercely in the head.

Yusupov came into the courtyard, his steward, Nikolai, next to him.
The steward bent down over the body. "I think this time he is dead."

"Get his coat," Yusupov ordered. "We'll wrap his body with it, then
put him in my car. Later, when the streets are empty, you will take it to
Petrovsky Bridge and drop it in the water."

Nikolai Karsalov did as he was commanded. It was proper for him to
obey orders given by every member of the powerful Yusupov family. He
retrieved the coat and as he draped it over his arm, the package that had

so concerned Rasputin fell to the floor. Nikolai hesitated, then tore away the wrapping and opened the box. He held the *Egg of Eternal Blessing* in his hand, dazzled by the jewels and shining blue enamel. He could not guess its value, nor in that brief moment did it occur to him that the infamous monk may have put a curse on the egg. But he was aware that in all the excitement, Felix Yusupov would not remember that Rasputin had appeared with a package under his arm. He put the egg back into the box, wrapped it, then ran to his room and took a high boot from the bottom of his armoire and crammed the box inside it.

Chapter 2

Someone had fixed the first day of the siege by the German North Army, which included the 56th Motorized Corps of the 4th Panzer Group, as August 10. After 128 days, Petersburg, as the stalwarts called it, had all but run out of food, fuel, and most other basic necessities, and was encountering one of the cruelest winters in memory. Cold and death; no conversation went without mention of either word, no radio broadcast—erratic as they were—failed to pile horrifying statistic upon chilling detail, and no one escaped the miserable piles of bodies that could not be buried in the frozen, concrete-hard earth. Rations were officially posted but meant nothing when there was no power to heat the ovens to bake a bread made from rye, flax, wood cellulose, and skimpy portions of wheat flour. Many citizens would argue over when the siege actually began, but the hard fact was the city was strangling and upward of ten thousand men, women, and children died every day from the appalling conditions, an unalterable fact no matter how much quibbling over when the siege began.

Nikolai Karsalov hugged his son tightly and inched forward in the line before the bread shop, his mittened hand cradling the small head, pressing his cheek against the boy's cheek to keep him warm. Two weeks earlier Marie Karsalov had stood in the same line with her nine-year-old daughter, Nina, who had been giddy with delight that on the very next day she would become ten. It had been a rare, sunny day before the dreaded cold had come when mother and daughter had gone happily to collect bread and a meat ration and a birthday gift Nina would select from one of the few shops that somehow had remained open and sold recycled household items and a paltry selection of books.

10

Darkness had come as it would in winter—in mid-afternoon—and as they returned home, a roving pair of young thugs waited, demanding food, and when they were denied, surrounded Marie and drove a knife deep into her chest. She was stabbed again and thrown to the snow, the bag of food and the ration cards in her pocket taken. Nina had tried to help her mother but had been severely beaten and left lying limp across her mother's body, a pink-covered package beside her. An hour later Karsalov had gone to find them and it was he who discovered his dead wife and desperately injured daughter. That Nina was alive was a miracle; she was one of the fortunate who had received hospital treatment and though she had lost toes on both feet from the cold, she was making a determined recovery.

Finally, Karsalov jostled his way into the bread shop, gave two coupons, then grasped whatever it was that was pushed out of a dark opening in the wall onto the grimy counter. Each piece was the size of a fist and no longer resembled bread, but was nearly black, without aroma, and hard like dried wood. He dropped the black lumps into a sack, looked about for someone to complain to, but a voice said, "Keep moving . . . move ahead . . . keep moving." A woman standing between two uniformed militia repeated the instructions in a bored, dull voice. Clearly, complaints would be ignored.

It was shortly after eight in the morning, the time when Karsalov took his son, Vasily, to fetch bread and go on to the edges of Gorodskoy Park, where he was usually able to buy several logs and kindling. On this day he was followed and when he had collected the wood and had put it into a sling to carry home, he was greeted by a gruff, yet pleasant voice: "You are comrade Karsalov?"

Karsalov was a reluctant comrade, and played the part grudgingly. "Yes, and you?"

"Pavlenko. I have done plaster work in the galleries. Remember?"

Karsalov studied the man, seeing an unusually healthy specimen, ruddy and full-faced, with particularly uncommonly clear, wide-open eyes. He shook his head. "No. When would this have been?"

"Before all this. Two years, a little less perhaps. In a gallery of Chinese art—there was water damage. You were there, I saw you."

"I apologize," Karsalov said. "I don't remember."

"It's no matter," Pavlenko said. "I am in a new business, no more plastering."

Karsalov nodded. "I'm happy for you. No call for plasterers in these times." He pulled on the ropes to his son's sled and started to walk. "My son is cold."

"My new business may be of interest to you, comrade Karsalov. Where can we talk?"

Karsalov stopped and looked again at Pavlenko, computing he was younger by ten years, dressed in a handsome beaver-lined heavy coat, well fed. Then he asked himself why he had been chosen.

Karsalov said, "I prefer not. My daughter is still in the hospital and when I am not at my work or on errands, I have no time for my son, or for myself." He spoke temperately, as he had been trained to treat people with respect, whether friend or stranger. "But, thank you."

"Let me come tonight to your home. I promise I will not take too much of your time. And after your son is in bed." He stared hard at Karsalov. "It is important."

Karsalov hesitated, then curiosity drove away his reluctance. "All right," he sighed. "Come before nine o'clock. I live at—"

"I know," Pavlenko interrupted. "You are at 68 Petra Lavrova, off Liteyny Prospekt." He put both hands on his black wool hat and pulled it down over his ears and walked quickly out of the park.

🐜 🐜 🐜

The apartment was on the third floor in a turn-of-the-century building, large for a nonprofessional, but Karsalov lived only in the kitchen, the other rooms sealed off to conserve the small amount of heat generated by the every other day's fire built in an ancient cast iron stove. Little Vasily had not been able to keep down his tiny meal and by early evening the three-year-old was having severe chills and crying without a pause. Karsalov prepared a mixture of sour-tasting vodka and warm tea, put him to bed, then crawled beside him to help keep him warm. Finally, at a few minutes before nine, the youngster fell into a troubled sleep.

Punctually at nine, Pavlenko arrived and was let into a tiny hallway that led past closed doors to the kitchen. He emitted what seemed to be the warmth of a July sun, and had also brought with him a heavy paper sack and from it he took a bottle and package and offered both to Karsalov. "A small gift," he said cheerfully.

In the bottle was a pepper-flavored vodka and in the package a portion of sausage, more meat than Karsalov had seen in four months. "I don't want your food," Karsalov protested. "We don't know each other, and I . . . I can't repay you."

"There's no obligation." Pavlenko grinned widely, brushed past Karsalov into the kitchen where he found glasses, and poured the yellowish liquid. He handed a glass to his baffled host. "Let's toast a new friendship."

Hesitantly, Karsalov raised his glass, then took a deep sip, then more. It was superior vodka, with flavor, and strong.

Pavlenko went to the bed where Vasily lay in a small lump under blankets, a gentle wheeze rising up from the little one.

"Do you have enough food?" Pavlenko asked, his hand about where the little boy's shoulder would be, patting it.

"No one has enough," Karsalov answered bitterly.

"I am sorry about your wife," Pavlenko said kindly but without any deep feeling. "They took her ration card—and your daughter's. I know."

"Is that your business? To know who died and who lost a ration card?"

"Not precisely." He turned back to Karsalov and nodded. "Yet, you might say that food is part of my new business."

"To look at you it must be," Karsalov said. "Our rations were cut again, no butter today, no fish, no meat."

"This comes at the right time," Pavlenko said, pointing to the package of sausage.

Karsalov said somewhat irritably, "Explain why you're here. Why me?"

Pavlenko unbuttoned his coat, reached inside for a cigarette case, opened it, and held it out to Karsalov, who looked first at the broad smile on Pavlenko's face before he took one and lit it by the match Pavlenko was holding in his other hand. Pavlenko sat in a straight wooden chair next to the table and crossed his legs comfortably. He also lit one of the cigarettes, inhaling the aromatic smoke and blowing it out in a steady stream. He held out the cigarette case to Karasalov. "Do you know what this is?"

"A cigarette case, of course," Karsalov said sharply, and lowered himself into the chair across from his guest.

"No doubt about that," Pavlenko said. "But do you know who made it?"

Karsalov took the case and looked at it carefully. He had seen cigarette cases like it before, when he had been in the service of Prince

Yusupov, when all the gentry and high government moguls had carried a snuff or cigarette case as grand as the case he was holding, its heavy silver skillfully chased with a military scene. He turned it over. On the back was imprinted G. FABERGÉ. Karsalov said, "Expensive . . . when it was new," and gave it back to Pavlenko.

"It's still worth a good deal, not because it's a Fabergé, but for the silver and gold. Not now, not in this city. Nothing has any value except food."

Karsalov savored the cigarette, tasting the smoke and allowing the sting of it in his throat and lungs to grow more intense as the tobacco burned hotter. It made him dizzy but it was so different a feeling from the boring discomfort of cold and hunger that he didn't want it to stop. He consumed nearly all of it, until the hot ash burned his finger. Then, reluctantly, he put the remains in a tin and let it smolder. When the last bit of smoke was gone, he looked up and said, "You haven't answered my question. Why have you chosen to come here?"

Pavlenko sat back, his right arm resting on the table, his hand holding the cigarette case, which, very gently, even tantalizingly, he tapped on the table every several seconds with the insistent precision of a metronome.

"I'll explain," he began. "Petersburg is under siege and if Hitler has his way, the Panzers will crush every one of us. There are no means to bring large quantities of food or fuel into the city, no trains, the highways are blocked, and only when Lake Ladoga freezes over can our truck convoys deliver supplies. Even then the German air force may destroy that hope. So the trick is to survive, and to survive we must have food, good food. The bread you got today was made from substitutes . . . wood dust and tree bark." Pavlenko reached for the bottle of vodka and poured a generous helping into each glass. He raised his for a toast. "To your son." He waved his glass in the direction of Vasily. "May he be warm and have a full stomach."

Karsalov sipped from his glass, then he drank it all in a gulp. He was immediately warmed by the strong drink, and looked enviously at the cigarette case. Pavlenko snapped it open and offered it to Karsalov, who took a cigarette and immediately struck a match.

Pavlenko turned over the case and pointed to the name. "Does G. Fabergé mean anything to you?"

"It was one of the best shops in Petersburg. Expensive, I couldn't afford to go there."

"But you do have something that was made by Fabergé. Isn't that so?"

Karsalov inhaled again. "No," he said softly.

Pavlenko poured more vodka into the glasses. He smiled and said, "Let us drink to an improvement in your memory." They both drank and Pavlenko continued. "Near the end, the man who employed you— Felix Yusupov—invited the crazy monk to his house. You saw him, Rasputin. Remember?"

Karsalov looked away and said softly, "I knew nothing of what went on. Not until they took him away."

"Rasputin came that night with a package. Correct?"

"A gift for Yusupov, perhaps."

"No. It was something Rasputin had picked up earlier from Fabergé, something he planned to take home with him, but—" Pavlenko drank the rest of his vodka. "—he never left the house alive."

"That part is true, but it was twenty-five years ago, I have no memory of the rest." He stood, "Thank you for the vodka, but take what is left, and take the sausage, too. I must ask that you leave now."

"Please comrade, I think you will want to hear what I have to say."

Karsalov stood with his back to the stove, arms crossed with hands high, the cigarette in one. "Quickly, then."

"In the package was an Imperial egg that Rasputin had ordered from Fabergé himself, a gift for the Czarina. You took the package to your room. A house cleaner saw you do it, she had come down from her bed after she heard the shooting."

The cigarette again. Karsalov drew heavily on it. "Who tells such wild stories?"

Pavlenko smiled. "I was told all of this ten days ago. That was when I learned of your wife's death and that sad news helped me find you. After all, there are others with the name of Karsalov in Petersburg, but only one Nikolai Karsalov."

"Who said all these lies?"

"Someone who knows, someone with a long memory."

"Even if this was true, how is it your business?"

"Your Fabergé egg has no value, comrade Karsalov. Go on the street and offer it for a loaf of bread and they will laugh. Yet in spite of that, I will buy it."

Karsalov put the vodka and sausage in the paper sack and pushed it in front of Pavlenko. "Take it and go."

"I will pay you with food. Food enough to keep you and your son well fed until the ice road opens."

"Do I look like a complete fool?" Karsalov pushed his chair away noisily. "I've asked you to go."

Pavlenko's smile was unconvincing. He tapped the cigarette case twice more on the table, then reached inside his heavy coat as if to put it away. When his hand reappeared it was holding a long-barreled revolver. It was Russian-made, heavy and menacing.

"Comrade Karsalov—"

"Don't call me by that fucking word."

"*Mister* Karsalov," Pavlenko said with oily politeness. "I have offered to take the Czar's egg in exchange for bread, meat, and sugar . . . food enough to keep you and your son alive until the Germans are driven away."

"I heard your damned offer," Karsalov said, "but I don't have the Czar's egg, or anything else that belonged to him."

The room was lit by an electric light in a frosted globe suspended over the table, and another, dimmer bulb in a floor stand next to the bed. Pavlenko got to his feet and went over to the bed. He pulled away the blanket and pointed the gun directly behind Vasily's ear.

"Put the egg on the table or I will save your son from the agony of starvation."

"You won't shoot a helpless child," Karsalov said.

"Two thousand children die every day in this city. Another one?" He laughed. "It's quite simple—squeeze slowly—"

"It's here, I'll get it!" Karsalov yanked open a cupboard door and reached in behind a stack of bowls and brought out the box, now wrapped in newspaper, tied with a heavy cord. He put it on the table.

"Unwrap it," Pavlenko said.

Karsalov began to untie the cord, doing it slowly, his eyes on Pavlenko and the revolver. "I was saving it for the children," he said, visibly shaken. "It belongs to them. I promised my wife they could have it when the war was over, when it would be worth something again."

"Hurry," Pavlenko said, watching impatiently. He edged toward the table.

Karsalov took the last of the paper away. "Don't take it, please, I don't want your damned food."

Pavlenko said, "Open it."

Karsalov opened the box and took out the Imperial egg. He glanced at Pavlenko, then put it on the table and stepped back.

Pavlenko came forward, the revolver in his right hand, his left reaching out to take hold of the Imperial egg. He turned to Karsalov, "Show me how it opens, I—"

He twisted his body sharply, trying to become a small target, desperately bringing up the gun he had failed to keep trained on Karsalov. But too late. Karsalov shot twice, putting two bullets through Pavlenko's magnificent coat and into his chest. It was Felix Yusupov's pocket Browning, the pistol that had failed to kill Rasputin. Karsalov had resurrected it after his wife had been ambushed and killed. He had cleaned it and put new shells in the cartridge and had been carrying it with him, tucked under his belt.

Later, Karsalov draped Pavlenko's arm over his shoulder, then, half carrying, half dragging, took the body onto the street and lay it in the doorway of a bombed-out apartment building. Pavlenko's death was likely to go unnoticed, remembered only by a survivor if indeed there was one to notice he was missing. Karsalov wrapped himself in the warm, heavy coat. In one of the pockets he found an envelope stuffed with food ration cards. He took two of them. They would replace the cards that had been stolen when Marie had been murdered.

No question about it. In the agony of old Petersburg's starvation, Pavlenko had gone into the food business.

Chapter 3

TALLINN, ESTONIA, NOVEMBER 23, 1963

An early morning wind rushed in from the Gulf of Finland, blowing icy gales over the capital, auguring a day of sleet and supreme darkness in a city the sun would not visit frequently until April. But to Vasily Karsalov, the bleak weather could not spoil his high spirits, and he walked briskly from his post at the naval station to the hospital and to the maternity ward, where at the fourth partition along the outer, windowed wall, he pulled away the curtain and found his wife nestling their hours-old son, born a few minutes past midnight, exactly two hours after the sensational announcement that John F. Kennedy had been assassinated. Vasily bent over his wife and kissed her, then knelt to better see the tiny infant that he had decided on his walk to the hospital would be named Mikhail.

"He'll be handsome, like you," Anna Karsalov whispered. She was no more than twenty, her skin soft as the babe's, her hair a pale yellow, her pretty face in happy repose. Vasily Karsalov kissed her again, his breath hot and strong from too much celebration brandy. Anna was right, her husband was handsome, with light brown hair, a wide, strong face, determined mouth, and eyes that no matter how magnificently blue they were, were set a trifle too close to each other.

"I want to call him Mikhail," he said. "You like the name, remember?"

"Not Nikolai, for your father?"

"I carry my father's name, that is enough." He rubbed the baby's cheek, and said, as if to end the discussion, "Let Mikhail Vasilyovich Karsalov start fresh."

"What was all the excitement last night?" Anna asked. "I don't remember much . . . just the pain, then this one came. The nurse must have given me something."

Vasily smiled. "They killed President Kennedy. In Texas, I think."

"That's funny?"

"Kennedy wasn't our friend. Last year when I was with the fleet in Cuba, we were forced to back away." He shook his head. "That wasn't good for us."

"You want to play at war all the time."

Vasily ran his fingers across a row of ribbons on his chest. "I'm a navy man. It's boring to do nothing but wait."

Anna patted his arm indulgently and nodded. Then her eyes closed and she said, "I'm very tired."

He kissed her again, on her lips, then sat back and stared at mother and baby until he was certain both were asleep. A final kiss, then he slowly backed away, and left the hospital.

Even before he reported to his station, it was obvious to Vasily that there had been a massive reaction to the assassination of the American president. The Baltic Fleet had been put on alert, security had been tightened to maximum readiness, and ships with six weeks' provisions were under way to join other naval contingents in the North Atlantic. Vasily Karsalov's immediate orders were to assist in provisioning three Krivak Class destroyers which had been placed on emergency standby. He had graduated from the Naval College in Leningrad in 1960 and following a year at sea had returned for training as a supply officer. Anna and he had been married two months before his transfer to Tallinn. His father, Nikolai Karsalov, was now a pensioner, and though not yet seventy, was in failing health, and living in Leningrad. His sister, Nina, had married and was living in Moscow. From outward appearances, Vasily was a model naval officer; hardworking and dutifully loyal to the ideals of Soviet supremacy. There was a dark side to Vasily Karsalov, however. He was a budding alcoholic and had had frequent bouts of drunkenness that occasionally erupted into brawls and outbursts of a vicious rage that went uncontrolled during an alcoholic blackout. There had been warnings and he was, at the ripe old age of twenty-three, in jeopardy of disciplinary action or discharge if his behavior did not change.

The new father was in no mood for good conduct, but rather for a good time. He would host a small party in his miniature apartment and celebrate the birth of his son and the death of the criminal American president.

❧ ❧ ❧

Vasily invited two fellow officers, Lieutenants Leonid Baletsky and Oleg Deryabin. He had also asked Sasha Akimov and Artur Prekhner. Akimov, at thirty-eight, was the oldest and held the rank of *starshiy michman*, or chief warrant officer, and was a veteran of the Soviet-German war. He was a small, round man, surprisingly agile, with an agreeable disposition. Akimov had become Vasily's mentor, teaching him the fundamentals of procuring basic staples as well as going to extreme measures to find luxurious provisions for the higher-ranking officers and the steady flow of gray-suited officials whose only role in life seemed to be to travel from one military base to another and fill out endless forms and eat Scottish beef and drink American bourbon.

Artur Prekhner was the only civilian in the party of five, and had come from Leningrad at Vasily's urging. Years before, Prekhner and Vasily had been neighbors, and though Prekhner was ten years older, a close friendship had developed between the two men. At the time, Prekhner was a mid-level functionary in the vast bureaucracy that was responsible for supplying food and clothing to the state-owned shops and markets. From the same commissaries, supplies were shipped to military bases in the region. Into the naval base in Tallinn, Vasily brought in frozen meat, powdered milk, sugar, and American liquors. The list would grow, they agreed. Just weeks earlier, an order for fifteen hundred pounds of beef never left the food lockers, yet payment was made. It was an oversight, but Prekhner saw it, and so did Vasily. They had stumbled onto a way to divert valuable foodstuffs for their own purpose. All that was needed was for Vasily to approve the invoices and order additional quantities to cover the shortages. Prekhner knew where to find willing buyers.

While they had worked together for only six months, Vasily Karsalov, Baletsky, and Akimov had become a team and were good friends. Leonid Baletsky, somewhat older at twenty-eight, was a pleasant, easygoing sort. The same could not be said of Oleg Deryabin, a recent transfer and somewhat of an enigma.

Deryabin was twenty-four, though he seemed older. He was a man of medium height, thick through the chest and muscular, with reasonably handsome features and deep-set eyes that were dark and inquiring. He wore a small smile at all times, as if only he had caught the humor of a story or knew the answers that no one else could supply. He had a rich, resonant voice, and had a sharp wit to go with a sharp tongue. He had made himself popular with his fellow officers in quick order. But with a reservation. He could be, and often was, intimidating. Perhaps it was the man's supreme self-confidence. Or the occasional flash of a wickedly strong temper. Even so, he could be good company.

A seemingly endless round of toasts began, each man finding some insignificant wrinkle to drink to; all related to the fact that Vasily Karsalov was a new father, that his son's name was to be Mikhail, and that Anna was a beautiful mother. When those subjects were exhausted, new toasts were proposed to celebrate Kennedy's death, including rumors and suggestions of rumors surrounding conspiracies to shoot the young president by the Cubans, Chinese, Israelis, and a coalition of Italian-American mafiosi.

To a man they agreed that the Kremlin had overreacted to the assassination, though none would express surprise if there had been Soviet influence (to which they also drank). As the liquor and wine flowed, the toasts grew more frivolous: a salute to the memory of Lenin's mistresses, or to Stalin's death from syphilis. Finally, Vasily proposed a toast to end the toasts and begin a game of cards.

Briefly, there was no further drinking, and they began to play preference, a game at which four usually played with one sitting out on each hand. The stakes were nominal and an even flow of wins and losses kept the players in a relaxed mood, the emphasis more on good-natured bantering than on competition. It went along that way for half an hour until Vasily challenged Baletsky over a hand he was certain he had won. Both had started to drink heavily again.

"I should have won," Vasily repeated, his words slurred.

"Do you think he printed the fucking cards?" Deryabin challenged.

"Play 21 if you think I'm cheating," Baletsky said. "You were opening a bottle when you should have been watching."

Vasily tossed the cards to Akimov. "Deal, old man."

Akimov laughed. "Old man? I'm not forty but I can still whip your ass on the wrestling mat."

"Deal," Vasily repeated, downed his vodka and poured another.

The game changed to poker and everyone played. When the deal had gone around the table, Deryabin had won three of five hands while Vasily had been shut out. After the next round, Deryabin continued to be the big winner, Vasily the only loser.

Artur Prekhner cautioned his friend. "Take a break, Vasily, you're in a bad run of cards."

Vasily waved his hands impatiently, signaling for Akimov to deal, then he emptied his pockets, putting all of his money beside a fresh drink. Another round was played, Vasily did not win. But on the next hand, he won a small pot and jubilantly raked in the kopeks. "Who's having a bad run?" he chided Prekhner.

But for the next half hour, Vasily, aided by his own sloppy play, proved that Prekhner had been correct. With his money gone, he sat disconsolately, grumbling that his poor luck had started when he had been cheated out of a winning hand two hours earlier. The others continued, warming to more spirited competition, the stakes growing inevitably larger, rubles replacing kopeks on the table. All were drinking, all except Deryabin, who was content to keep a glass of wine next to his growing stack of rubles, sipping only occasionally from it.

A half hour past midnight, an intense feeling of nausea drove Vasily out of his apartment. The cold air might set him right, and indirectly it did, as he felt no constraint to hold in the rumbling sickness, and he vomited a huge volume of food and vodka, mercifully and tentatively, denying his bloodstream any further rush of alcohol. Immediately he considered himself sober, a preposterous surmise, but he was emboldened to return to the cards and redeem his losses. It was a fatal judgment, one from which he would never fully recover.

Resuming his seat at the table, Vasily put his wristwatch in front of him and announced that it was worth forty-six rubles, but he would accept forty. It was passed around and the highest offer was twenty-eight rubles from Leonid Baletsky, who said he made the offer in good faith and to prove he had honestly won the disputed hand. The fact that Baletsky was approaching complete inebriation may have had some additional influence on his offer. Vasily accepted the money, and Baletsky put the watch on his wrist, mumbling something to the effect that his old watch was broken and he had been saved the bother of buying a new one.

To everyone's surprise, Vasily won the next three hands; none were large wins, but wins were wins and good for a damaged ego. The next hand—they were now playing straight five card draw—was a large pot, more than forty rubles, and won by Deryabin. Vasily was back to the money he'd been paid for his watch. Then, in less than five minutes, he was reduced to four rubles. Perspiration gathered on his forehead and above his mouth. He filled a large glass with wine and drank it all in one voracious gulp.

It was Deryabin's deal. Vasily was dealt five high cards that caused his spirits to soar and his hands to shake. He drew two cards, making four jacks. All five remained for the first round of betting, Prekhner dropped out on the second, and Baletsky on the third. Vasily's money was gone, but he continued, taking rubles from the pot and piling them up in front of him, accounting for all of his wagers. Akimov dropped out, leaving Deryabin and Vasily. They continued to raise each other, until, finally, Deryabin said Vasily could no longer continue to bet unless he proved he could settle his debt to the pot in the event he lost. It was a challenge that Vasily took as an affront to his honor.

"*If* I lose, do you doubt I'll pay up?"

The usual little smile was on Deryabin's lips, but there was no humor in his voice. "You may be ordered out of here tomorrow and we'll never see each other again. Gambling debts are paid with rubles, not with words."

"First, you have to win."

"Are you calling for my hand?"

"One more raise. Twenty rubles."

Deryabin's smile vanished. "I'll bet the twenty . . . after I see your twenty."

Vasily looked into the eyes of the others; his asking for help, theirs refusing. He stood and stared down at Deryabin. "You'll see the twenty, and twenty more." He disappeared into an adjoining, tiny bedroom. Baletsky stared at the others, muttering that it was time to go home. Then he staggered from the room, saying he was going to take a piss. Akimov began to sort the money in preparation for counting it. Prekhner lowered his head and shook it sadly. Deryabin stood, fidgeting nervously. Then he sat again. He swept all of the discards into a pile, shuffled them, then stacked the cards neatly. Prekhner watched. Vasily returned with a package wrapped in old newspaper.

"My father gave me this, it was owned by—" He stopped abruptly, then went on. "Two men have died because of it." He tore away the paper and put the box on the table. He opened it and took out the Imperial egg and set it in front of Deryabin.

"What is it?" Deryabin asked.

"An Imperial Easter egg," he said, the words slurred, "made by Fabergé for Czarina Alexandra Feodorovna."

Deryabin cradled the egg in his hands, eyeing it skeptically. "If it was made for the Czar, how did your father get hold of it?"

"That's not important. It belongs to me now."

"What's it worth?"

"Hundreds . . . thousands. You can see there are diamonds and two rows of rubies and emeralds, and inside there are pearls." Vasily took the egg and opened it. "Two dozen pearls, and this—" He took out the enameled portrait of Nicholas and Alexandra. "The frame and easel are made of gold."

"Remember to count the rubles in front of Vasily," Deryabin reminded Akimov.

The others watched as Akimov separated and sorted the notes by their amount, recording numbers on a piece of paper. "Two hundred and eighty-six rubles," he announced.

"That's three months' wages," Baletsky said.

Vasily placed the egg squarely in front of Deryabin. "There are my damned twenty rubles. Where are yours?"

Deryabin had been the only winner, but now all of his winnings and nearly all the money he had brought with him was on the table. To lose meant he would live frugally for the next month. He studied the Imperial egg for several minutes, then, holding his cards inches away, looked at them once more with the careful concern of a banker. Two ten-ruble notes came from a pocket.

"Let me see your cards," he said crisply.

Not since he picked up his hand ten minutes before had Vasily Karsalov smiled. Now a grin broke and widened as he put his cards on the table, first a king, then four jacks. The others, except Deryabin, seemed to relax, the tension broken.

"Very good," Deryabin said. "But—" He flipped the three of diamonds to the side, then lay four queens next to Vasily's four jacks.

There was utter silence, as palpable as the tension had been seconds before. It was broken when the chairs scratched over the wood floor as Baletsky and Akimov pushed back from the table. Prekhner got on his feet, sobered by what he had seen, his eyes wide. He looked at Vasily, held out his hand and tried to speak. But nothing came. He put on his coat. So did the others and they left without a further word.

Deryabin took the stack of ruble notes and divided it equally. He put a half in each of his coat pockets. Next he put the Imperial egg back in its box, closed it, then cradled it in his left arm. He reached the door, paused, then turned and went back to the table. Vasily had not moved, his eyes still staring blankly at the cards that lay face up on the table.

Deryabin said, "It was a good bet, Vasily Nikolaiyvich, but you went too far." He took fifty rubles from his pocket and dropped them on top of the four jacks.

"For your son." His little smile had never faded. "For Mikhail."

Chapter 4

"Mike's a lucky bastard," the driver of the polo green Cadillac said to the man beside her, pushing away strands of hair of an indefinable color though red might come first to mind. Under the hair were eyes that contact lenses made bulge slightly, eyes that were alert and moved quickly, that were highlighted by a skillfully applied razor-thin line of dark brown. She was attractive, not pretty, but might have been, now forty-something.

"The weather's perfect," she said as if it were a fact she didn't want to admit, "and the radio said it would stay that way all weekend."

The man, even in the big car, seemed squeezed into the passenger seat. He was long, nearly six and a half feet long. He was also in his early forties and beginning to lose hair on the very top of his head. As if to compensate, he was cultivating a new mustache that he constantly rubbed as if it itched. He wore glasses but they were usually dangling from a gold chain around his neck. He said, "Is he always lucky about picking opening dates?"

"Always," the driver said, her voice a two-pack-a-day Marlboro kind, husky and filled with the sounds of New York, of Brooklyn leavened with a tincture of the Bronx. "Mike picks dates out of his scrotum for grand openings and never fails to have great weather. Never!"

The driver of the brand-new Seville STS knew about this because she had planned the PR and advertising strategy for seventeen grand openings in seven Eastern states over a four-year period and in that time it had sprinkled once, on a Saturday afternoon when the food, soft drinks, and customers were about to run out at the same time.

"There's the LIE," the man said.

The car turned smoothly onto the ramp, circled around, and merged with trailers headed east on the Long Island Expressway.

"What's this Mike guy all about?" The man exuded an air of super-ciliousness, as if whoever he talked to or about was a couple of degrees

26

beneath him. He fished out a small tape recorder from his shirt pocket. "Mind if I use this, Patsy?"

"Go ahead."

Patsy was Patricia Mulcahy Abromowitz, product of a fiery Irish mother and a staid Jewish father who claimed the blood of a thousand accountants in his ancestry. Patsy was blessed with the best of both, particularly the same pretty skin of her mother, the same feistiness, yet tempered by her father's calm.

"First off, you call him Mr. Carson when you meet him, even though he's younger. And, Lenny, if he likes you, he'll ask you to call him Mike."

Leonard Sulzberger, no relation to the famous *Times* family, had been with the *Bridgeport Post Telegram,* then the *New York Post* and now was freelance, commissioned by Patsy to write a profile on the man who pulled the dates for his grand openings from deep inside him, and who had become one of the most successful automobile retailers in the United States at an incredibly young age. He was an all-American success story: hardworking, good-looking, even celebrated his birthday on November 22 when much of the country commemorated the tragic death of JFK. He was nearly too good to be true, but it was true that Mike Carson was a Russian who had emigrated to London when he was fourteen years old armed with a vocabulary of exactly seven English words. There were other bits of information about Mike Carson in the three closely printed pages Sulzberger scanned.

"This says his name is Mike Carson. That it? Just plain old Mike . . . not Michael?"

"He was born Mikhail Vasilyovich Karsalov. Ran off to London when he was fourteen, and after he had learned to speak English without a trace of a Russian accent he changed his name. Someone told him that Mike had an all-American ring to it, so Mikhail became Mike and Karsalov became Carson. Vasilyovich means 'son of Vasily,' but Mike will have nothing to do with his father. He once told me he thinks his father was in the navy, was booted out, and sent off to some dreadful place near Mongolia. Doesn't know if he's alive or dead."

"His mother?"

She shook her head. "Mike's mother was sick when he was a kid. I don't know if it was physical or mental. Both, maybe. Whatever it was, she wasn't well, and then she was gone. Just like that . . . out of his life. He's never told me much more than that."

"A little weird, right?" Lenny said.

"Hm, yeah. But Mike's a normal guy. You'd never guess his background. He has an uncle, mother's side, in London who he likes, and that's all I know about his family, and more than you need to know." Patsy gave Lenny Sulzberger a stern glance. "Don't ask about family, it's not part of the Mike Carson story."

"Brothers, sisters?"

"You're not paying attention, Lenny. No family."

"I'm asking you, not him," Lenny said testily. "The better I know him, the better I can write about him."

Patsy Abromowitz accelerated into the fast lane. "Okay, he's an only kid. That better?"

"You said he speaks perfect English. You don't mean that, do you?"

"I do mean it and I think you should make something out of it. I've got eighteen years of school but talk like a sixth grader in the Bronx. Mike Carson sounds like he grew up in the middle of Oxford University. And he's not the first to do it. Robert Maxwell, the English publisher, did the same. I heard one of his speeches, couldn't believe he'd been born and raised in Czechoslovakia. He had a voice like Laurence Olivier."

Lenny considered what he had heard. "Mike Carson was sixteen when he arrived in Brighton Beach . . . the late 1970s. How come Brighton Beach?"

"That's where the Russians went. He had been brought up Orthodox if he had been brought up anything, but here he was in America in a Jewish community. Actually he went to a Catholic church when he first arrived. To meet people, not for the religion. I'm not sure he has any religion, though he seems ethical enough." She paused, then added, "He's damned ethical."

ᚕᚕ ᚕᚕ ᚕᚕ

Carson Cadillac & Oldsmobile occupied a glass-enclosed building that, from a distance, resembled a luxury greenhouse not quite the size of the Pontiac Silverdome, and was situated in a row of automobile dealers on Northern Boulevard near Roslyn, and convenient to the upscale communities that lined that part of northern Long Island. It was dealership Number 24, a number Mike Carson considered lucky, but then Mike had learned when he opened his first used-car lot on Coney

Island Avenue consisting of a half-acre lot, six bare bulbs, and a hand-painted sign that the number he assigned each of his dealerships was a lucky number. Now, Carson Motors Inc. had showrooms in Boston, Washington, Atlanta, Jacksonville, and St. Petersburg, Florida, selling Ford, Dodge, Jeep, Chrysler, Oldsmobile, Buick, and Cadillac. There were six car-rental franchises and three truck-leasing operations to round out the privately held company that in the previous year had grossed slightly less than a half billion dollars. Not bad for a man about to be thirty-five who didn't go to school in this country until he was sixteen, who finished high school two years later, then got a bachelor's from Long Island University in three years, and all the while holding down two jobs.

Banners and metalized streamers glistened in the late-May afternoon sun, creating the kind of loud, glitzy show that had somehow been institutionalized by American car dealers, as if a display in quiet, good taste might fail to attract attention, or heaven forbid, send the wrong message to potential buyers. And so there was hype and bright lights, with pigs-in-a-blanket and Swedish meatballs next to a bar where the strongest drink was Coke Classic. It was American all right, that fabled love affair with the automobile continuing, but an anachronism nonetheless. In the showroom were Cadillacs and full-sized Oldsmobiles with prices beginning at twenty thousand and going up to sixty-five-thousand-plus for the Cadillac Fleetwood that weighed in at nearly two tons and could be propelled from 0 to 60 in 7.8 seconds by a 295 horsepower Northstar engine.

Patsy Abromowitz's Seville had dealer plates, which meant she was waved into VIP parking. Lenny's eyes took in all the sights, then his ears were assaulted by the Top 20 hits blasted over a dozen speakers and interrupted by the rapid-fire voice of a local radio DJ broadcasting live from the showroom floor, urging everyone (eighteen and older) to enter the giant sweepstakes that promised a grand prize of a week at a deluxe motel in St. Petersburg, Florida, free airplane tickets, five thousand in spending money, and an Oldsmobile Cutlass Supreme convertible which the lucky winner would claim at Carson Olds & Pontiac, located a hundred yards from the motel.

A pair of clowns, one female and one male, watched over the kiddies while mother and dad were shown the newest in automotive luxury. In the evening, the New York commuters came in larger numbers, the ones who lived in Glen Cove and Oyster Bay, the ones with the real money.

Patricia's advertising agency had scouted the territory and mailed expensive invitations to homes in the correct zip codes; the research department predicted, based on previous history, that 2,734 adults and 3,411 children would visit the showroom during the three-day grand opening.

Patsy grabbed hold of Lenny's arm and ushered him past young men and women dressed in the Carson uniform, gray slacks or skirts and maroon blazers, each wearing a badge with name and title, all smiling broadly as they handed out grand opening packets that contained product literature, service specials, and sweepstakes entries. Then the two went by a Cutlass Supreme convertible that overflowed with balloons and gift boxes wrapped in gold and silver, and with a sign suspended over it that said the car was the Sweepstakes Grand Prize. Flanking the car were two stunning models wearing dangerously brief bathing suits, one in Carson gray, the other in Carson maroon. Lenny was momentarily dazed by the immensity and cluttered noisiness. Patricia's expression was watchful, searching for mistakes, of ways to do things better the next time.

"Over there," she said, pointing to the escalator that connected to a mezzanine. Her badge contained her photograph, and the word "Executive" across the bottom assured entrance past a huge man wearing a size 50 extra-long blazer. Dennis LeGrande had recently retired from his position as defensive tackle with the New York Giants, and though he was in training to become a Personal Transportation Consultant, his assignment during the grand opening was as a kind of marshal. He was anchored at the foot of the escalator to keep the kids from running up the down steps, and vice versa.

Patsy said, "Mike's waiting for us, and remember, it's Mr. Carson."

On the mezzanine, eight clusters of desks, chairs, and low cabinets surrounded the communications center, each work station separated by leafy plants or small trees in pots. Along the inside wall were private offices, none large, except for one that had a commanding view of the showroom below, and in the doorway to that office stood two women and two men in their company blazers talking animatedly. They gave way to a man who came out of the office, paused briefly, then seeing Patsy, walked toward her, one hand held high, waving to her.

"Let's go." Patsy smiled broadly and waved back. "There's your man."

Lenny studied the man as he walked toward him, a surprised look on his face, as if the man he saw was not what he expected. But what had he expected? Did Mike Carson look too ordinary? Was his hair receding, or was his hair an early gray or very blond? Were his teeth crooked or was there a gap to one side, a small but noticeable gap? Did he look younger then thirty-five as Patsy said he would be on the 22nd of November?

"This is Leonard Sulzberger," Patsy said efficiently.

Mike Carson's smile was still in place. "Welcome, Mr. Sulzberger, Patsy told me you were a good writer." His hand went out.

"Hi, Mr. Carson," Lenny said with a firm voice, certain not to make an immediate mistake. "I'm very happy to meet you." His hand caught hold of Mike's and he shook it affirmatively.

There was too much about Mike Carson's background that did not comport with the way he came across in the flesh. In every respect he seemed regular or average, nothing at first meeting glistened or stood out. The thinning hair Lenny thought he saw was, in fact, a heavy thatch of blond, the kind most women would kill for. Then his face, his features. All standard except when looked at individually were better than average; strong nose, alert, solidly blue eyes, an expressive mouth with even a tiny cleft in the chin. And yes, there was a small gap in the teeth on his left side, but a minor flaw. He stood five eleven, no flab at the waist. His voice was solid, and if there was any accent at all, it was Rochester, New York, or was it Ogden, Utah? This, in spite of having spoken only Russian until he was fourteen? But something else. A supremely confident aura surrounded Mike Carson. He seemed relaxed and mature, traits that usually came from a secure and well-provided environment, not from a broken family, or from a youngster who had emigrated on his own terms when he had barely reached his teens.

Mike's hand went to his side. "I'll call you Leonard, and you call me Mike. Okay?"

"Okay, but make it Lenny. That's what everyone calls me. Can we talk now? Is that good for you?"

"Whatever Patsy says."

Patsy said, "Sooner you get started, the sooner it will be over."

"Before we do anything, let me show you the store. It's our newest design, something you might use in your story."

They were about to go down to the main floor when a loud squabble broke out at the bottom of the escalator. Dennis LeGrande and a small, balding man were jawing at each other, the man obviously frustrated in his attempt to make himself understood, but unable to find English words to help his cause.

"What's the problem, Denny?" Mike looked curiously at the man, who started to scramble up the steps toward him.

The man broke into an enthusiastic smile. "*Mikhail! Mikhail Vasilyovich—myenya zavut Sasha Akimov.*"

For a split moment Mike Carson was confounded, then greeted the newcomer warily. "Akimov, it's a surprise to—" He didn't complete the sentence, instead, he took hold of the man's arm. He called over to Patty Abromowitz and Lenny Sulzberger.

"An old friend of the family. It shouldn't take long."

Sliding glass panels completely covered one side of the office that was Mike's when he visited the dealership, an office with a conference table, and a view past the floor-to-ceiling glass to the showroom immediately below. It was there that Mike took his unexpected guest, repeating that he was surprised by the visit.

Akimov said, in Russian, "I am not good with English, will you speak in Russian?"

Mike nodded his grudging reluctance. Akimov spoke rapidly, spilling out a polite and more formal greeting, one he had probably rehearsed during the long journey, moving all the while to the wall of glass, where he stared intently down at the growing crowd. Mike watched, amused.

"Are you expecting someone?"

Akimov said he was not, then retreated to the table where he produced a package out of which came a bottle of vodka. "A toast, Mikhail?"

"I am not Mikhail," Mike said forcefully. "I am called Michael. Mike Carson . . . not Karsalov, not Vasilyovich."

Akimov took two glasses from the tray on the conference table and poured vodka into both and handed one to Mike. He proposed a toast to their reunion and drained his glass. Mike sipped. Akimov was a surprisingly small man, smaller even as he had aged. His body was no longer stout, but more like that of a young boy, and covered with a dull, wrinkled gray suit that was brightened by a row of military ribbons pinned above the breast pocket and a necktie that lay against a shirt with frayed collar and cuffs.

He refilled his glass and toasted to Mike's success, then said, "Please, you sit, and allow me to tell you why I have come to New York. And please, also, allow me to call you Mikhail, as that is the name I knew you to have, even on the night you were born." He gave a warm, paternal smile. "You will be Mike when I go away."

Mike glanced quickly at his watch, then at the door to be certain it was closed, and sat back and sighed, the merest hint of an ironic smile on his lips. "Mikhail," he whispered to himself.

"I knew your mother also," Akimov continued. "Anna was very pretty, and very proud of you. But there was a bad feeling between your mother and father, so deep it caused them to fall away from each other. Do you know?"

"My father was never good to her, always forgetting and getting drunk, spending money. There was nothing I could do."

"Too much of this." Akimov lifted the bottle of vodka, then set it down noisily. "Do you know what happened to your father?"

Mike's eyes strayed from Akimov. "He was sent away, I never knew why. To a Central Asian country I recall."

"To Uzbekistan. And for what reason? You know?"

"I never wanted to know. Whatever little scraps of memory I have about my father I have tried to erase. He never knew I was sent to an orphanage, and that's where they put me when I was eleven." He turned back to Akimov. "I was in four of them until I ran away, and I kept running until I found my mother's brother in London. I was fourteen. Did you know that?"

Akimov nodded. "Yes, and much more. Shall I tell you?"

Mike had picked up and put down his glass a half dozen times, and now took a long sip from it. The vodka burned going down and seemed to ignite into a ball of fire when it hit his stomach. "Tell me, Sasha."

"When you were about eight, a group of us were transferred to Petersburg. I was assigned to the same department with your father, but within half a year, he was working strictly by himself, including the paperwork that I had been responsible for. I discovered he had been parceling out a portion of each shipment of food received at the commissary, then transferring it to a warehouse in the city where a partner, a local merchant, sold it. They had been stealing meat, liquor, and cigarettes, selling to whoever paid the highest price, always in dollars. Your father was never caught, not for stealing food." Akimov shook his head slowly. "They arrested him for murder."

Mike didn't like what he was hearing. "Murder?" he said, disbelieving. "I was never told that. Who did he murder?"

"Your father had made a lot of money, but he couldn't mix any better with money than he could with vodka. I don't know what happened between your father and his partner. I suspect the partner was cheating. Whatever it was, he was found with his throat cut, and your father was accused of murder. He was drunk when they arrested him. They say he confessed, but I never believed it. There was a military trial, secret as always. A week later I learned he had been given a lifetime assignment to a military department in Uzbekistan. It was like exile. I saw him briefly after the trial, and he would say nothing except he was innocent. Then he was gone."

"My uncle never mentioned this."

"What could he know?" Akimov looked carefully at Mike. "He hated your father. Your mother told me that."

"How is it that you know so much about my family?"

"Your mother and I are both from Sochi, on the Black Sea. Our families had been friends and it was easy for her to talk to me. I think she liked that. It is also the reason I knew your uncle, though we only talked on the telephone. When the trouble between your mother and father began, she could not deal with matters, and spent days closed off, alone, talking to herself. The navy doctors tried to help and finally she was sent to an institution."

"My uncle never told me what sickness she had. Only that she had been sent to a good place."

"You were young. He was being kind."

"She is my only link to Russia that matters. I haven't tried to find her and I'm not proud of that. I was afraid of learning the truth. That she had abandoned me."

Akimov got to his feet and fished out a pair of smudged eyeglasses from a pocket and put them on, and from another pocket found an envelope that he placed on the table. Then he buttoned his jacket and inhaled deeply. Each movement was deliberate, as if he were about to present a solemn salutatory.

"I am not here to trouble you with the past, Mikhail, but it is important that you understand the relationship I have with your family." He took a small piece of paper from the envelope and handed it to Mike. "Here is where you can find your mother if you wish to see her or perhaps write to her. She is not an old person, and perhaps the doctors have helped her."

Mike looked at the address, then folded the paper neatly and tucked it into his wallet. "I suppose you have another piece of paper with my father's address on it?"

Akimov nodded. "I have an old address. If you write to him, they may send your letter to where he is living now."

"Then, he's alive?"

Akimov nodded his head once more. "Very possible. You will write to him?"

"I may. I don't know."

"I will leave the address. Then you can decide. Your father once owned something that should be of special interest to you."

Mike folded his arms across his chest. "What would that be?"

"On the evening of the day after you were born, your father invited four of his friends for a celebration. Two were lieutenants, as he was. I was a chief warrant officer. The fourth was Artur Prekhner, a civilian. As you would suspect, we drank, and heavily, too, as we played cards and began to gamble. We drank toasts to you and your mother and your grandfathers and grandmothers and Khrushchev and to the assassination of John Kennedy." He lowered his glasses and said solemnly, "Were you ever told of that night?"

Mike shook his head.

"That night your father drank heavily. I have said it was not unusual for him, but in addition to being drunk, he had a poor run of cards. He lost all of his money including a wristwatch that he sold for less than it was worth. But he wouldn't give up, and kept playing. In the last hand he was certain he could win and get back what he had lost. Only one other player stayed in the betting. He was an officer like your father. Your father bet all he had and began to borrow until he was challenged to prove he could pay all the rubles he owed. Your father put a box on the table and took out of it a jeweled egg that he claimed had been made by Fabergé for Czar Nicholas. Your grandfather had given it to your father, and your father had planned to give it to you. While none of us knew what it was worth, we knew it was worth far more than all the money bet on that last hand. Your father was stubborn and foolish, and he lost."

"And so you've come to tell me my father lost an egg with jewels on it—that he drank too much and was stubborn?"

"Patience, Mikhail." Akimov continued: "I remained in the navy, always able to stretch my active status until I was past fifty and then forced to retire. But for eight years I had no employment, then, four years ago, I was introduced once again to the same person who won the Fabergé egg from your father. He had started businesses under the new freedom of Perestroika. He owned an import and export business, very profitable when the timing was right and the correct products were traded. A very clever man, but with a single fault, he had no feeling for money. He would spend it quicker than he could earn it. But at the time it was a good match for both of us, as I had experience in truck and ocean transportation. And, also, I was bored with a pension that was buying very little comfort.

"I was paid with dollars, as much as twenty thousand dollars when the business was good." Akimov paused. "In Petersburg, that was a fortune."

"I'm sure that it was, Sasha." Mike glanced at his watch, showing clearly that he wanted the unplanned interruption to end quickly. "They'll be expecting me any moment."

"A few minutes longer, Mikhail." Akimov again went to the glass panels, where he studied the crowds both inside and outside the showroom, then came back to his position at the table. "Ten days ago, I was told that I was no longer needed, that it was time I enjoyed retirement. I was invited to the private office of this man I had known for so long. It was an office with leather chairs and a television and a rug from India. It was late in the afternoon and we were alone. On his desk was a bottle of vodka. This is the man who rarely will have vodka, but on that day he had more than two glasses. He wanted to talk and he asked if I remembered that night in your father's apartment when we played cards and if I remembered how your father had had too much to drink, and how he promised he would cover his bets with the Fabergé egg. I said I remembered, that—"

"But you've told me this, Sasha," Mike said, his patience approaching its limit. "Please—"

Akimov put up a hand. "You must listen, Mikhail. There are two things you must know."

Mike held up two fingers. "Only two?"

"*Dah*. One is about the Fabergé egg, the other is the truth about your father's trial for murder."

Mike sighed. "I want to hear what you've come to tell me, Sasha, but later, when there will be time to talk."

Akimov refilled his glass yet again. "*Vahsheh zdahroveh!*" He drank it all. Mike smiled, able to understand that Akimov had toasted to their good health. He took the bottle, poured a tiny amount, and drank it. Then he sat back, resigned to hear what the little man had come to tell him.

"I was asked if I remembered what cards your father held and what cards won the game. I remembered that your father had four jacks, but he lost to four queens. Imagine! I said that the odds of two hands out of five receiving four jacks and four queens were one in a million."

"Very interesting, Sasha, but please hurry."

Akimov continued. "Then I was asked if there had been anything else I remembered about the evening, especially, he asked about that last hand of cards. I said again that I would never forget the four jacks and four queens. Then he gave me an envelope. I opened it. I thought he had given me a lot of money, but it was in dollars and deutsche marks and Swiss francs and only later did I discover he had given me less than two thousand dollars. For all I had done for him, it was very little.

"As I was about to leave, he asked me if I recalled any of the details that surrounded the murder charge against your father. I said I did not, and he asked me a second time and I said no again, then I took my envelope and went home to my apartment. I packed a small suitcase and went to the rail station where I waited for the morning train to Moscow. I found a hotel near the air terminal and I stayed there for three days, putting the little bits of my personal affairs in order. I made telephone calls to London and New York. And I bought a ticket on Aeroflot to Copenhagen. From there I came here."

Something in Akimov's ramblings stirred Mike's interest and it showed. He had leaned forward and was listening to every word, every Russian word that was no longer strange to him.

Akimov went on. "The Fabergé egg belongs to you. It is worth many millions of dollars. Mikhail, you must reclaim it."

Mike was genuinely perplexed. He got up from his chair and looked across the table to Akimov. "You say the Fabergé egg belongs to me, but you also say that my father lost it in a poker game. So, it is not mine."

"I will explain. This person I have been telling you about has become a powerful man in Petersburg. He brings medical supplies from Switzerland into Petersburg, where they are put in new packages and sold in Kiev and Moscow. He was the first to bring videotapes to Petersburg, then in his factories he made copies and sold them for the original. He has a chemical laboratory that can duplicate the expensive perfumes and they are sold in packages exactly like the genuine products. The laws don't stop him. He says he is a trader, a businessman."

Akimov laughed. "He used his connections with the Party and built a syndicate. He was the *vor*. You know what that is?"

Mike said he didn't know.

"It is the *vor v zakonye* and means Godfather of a crime gang."

Mike rubbed his face thoughtfully. "You've told me everything but his name. So, tell me that, Sasha. Who is the son of a bitch?"

Akimov put down his glass and moved to the edge of the table. "I will tell you, but first—"

The door opened, and the music and noise from the throng below surged into the room. Mike and Akimov turned to see a young woman in her maroon Carson blazer close the door and take one step toward them. She was pretty, though overly made up, with short blond hair and a figure that scored a perfect ten. Her eyes made a fast inventory of the room then settled on Akimov.

Mike said, "Hi . . . I'm sorry I don't know your name, but we're nearly finished." He stood. "Tell the others I'll be with them in a minute."

Then, as if it had happened with mirrors, there was a gun in her hand pointed at Akimov. Mike reacted by throwing the nearest object he could get his hands on, the vodka bottle. It hit her arm just as the gun fired. Akimov spun and fell, and Mike lunged toward the woman, but she fired again toward Akimov, then pulled open the door and ran. Mike chased, yelling for help, "Stop her, Dennis. That one . . . coming at you!"

Mike's shout was barely audible above the music, but the former Giant saw the woman pushing her way past the others on the escalator, and he saw Mike struggling to catch her. Lenny Sulzberger heard the commotion and watched the blond woman run off the escalator into the arms of the huge football player. Dennis clamped a powerful hand on her shoulder and as he did, his head jerked up and his eyes widened in disbelieving pain and surprise. He groped at his right side, several inches above his belt, where his fingers found the fat, knurled handle of a knife. Then he lurched and fell.

Little children saw the blood leaking from him and screamed, and when their parents saw the side of the giant turn crimson, they backed away in horror. Then bedlam. In the confusion, two figures made their way to a car in customer parking and drove away.

Chapter 5

Boulevard Plaza Motel wasn't much. A two-story red-brick affair that probably had looked out of date the instant it was built. Location was its strong suit; twenty minutes from Kennedy Airport on Rockaway Boulevard in the heart of what was known euphemistically as South Ozone Park. Its commercial rate, half that of a room in Manhattan, made it popular with commission salesmen, good, too, for anyone catching an early morning flight.

Boulevard Plaza was also a motel listed by New World Travel, a Western style travel agency, part of a growing conglomerate that had recently moved to an office on Nevsky Prospekt near the Gostinyg Dvor metro station in St. Petersburg, Russia. The manager was Feodor Puserov, an ash-white man of fifty-two with early symptoms of emphysema and an abhorrence of the sun; a man who had spent twenty-seven years with Intourist, and who had capped off his government career by being named director of the Leningrad office precisely fourteen weeks before the Government Travel Authority was consigned to permanent obscurity. Puserov had reserved a twin-bedded room for three nights, and had prepaid in dollars through the National Bank of Finland. Reservations were in the name of Viktor and Galina Lysenko from Kiev. The couple were in room 12, their rented car, its hood still warm, parked outside their room.

Galina Lysenko stood in front of a mirror, looking intently at her reflection, her stunning face expressionless. Fingers tipped with a discreet red polish brushed over the embroidered Carson Cars logo on the breast pocket of the slightly oversized blazer which she now took off and dropped onto the bed. She removed a scarf tied to resemble a necktie, then her blouse. After she let the skirt fall to the floor, and still staring at herself in the mirror, a small smile of approval began to show. She was wearing black bra, panties, and stockings, and heeled shoes that increased her height to three inches less than six feet. Her shoulders were broad, her waist nipped in naturally, her breasts full and firm, as was proven quite magnificently as she unhooked the bra and let it fall away. She began breathing heavily, then her body quivered as her smile disappeared and her eyes closed. In front of her, on the dresser, was a neat little Semmerling pistol, four inches of deceptive firepower that held five rounds of 124 grain 9mm Luger cartridges. Her fingers wrapped around it and she lifted it, holding it high in both hands as if it were an offering. She inhaled its faint odor of oil and burnt powder, then put the gun back on the table. She ran her hands vigorously through her tightly combed hair, loosening it, letting it fall softly so it touched her shoulders.

The little smile returned as she saw, reflected in the mirror, the door to the bathroom open and a man come into the room, rubbing a towel over his naked body. She watched him come toward her and felt his presence immediately behind her. Viktor Lysenko's eyes were on a level with Galina's, his slim body only slightly heavier than hers. There was an incredible similarity between them, their hair and eyes the same color, their features so alike it might be they were brother and sister. Twins, perhaps. Both had high foreheads, full arched eyebrows, large, brown eyes, small noses, expressive mouths with full, sensuous lips, strong chins, and long, slender necks. For a minute they continued to look at each other in the mirror, then Galina turned and put her arms around Viktor, and they pulled each other tightly together. They kissed. A long, passionate kiss.

Abruptly she pulled away. She spoke in Russian. "Twice I fired at him, but the other one, Karsalov, threw a bottle. I . . ." She stared into Viktor's eyes. "I am not positive Akimov is dead."

He put a finger on her lips. "You told me all this. You saw blood on his neck, you saw him fall." He shook his head slowly. "You don't miss."

Her expression did not change. "I always know when the hit is . . . right. This time, I do not know."

"Tomorrow, Galina. Tomorrow we will know."

Chapter 6

There was something about hospitals that held a strange fascination for Mike Carson, and the North Shore University Hospital was no exception. Perhaps it was an elusive childhood memory of a time when he fantasized that he might someday become a doctor. He looked at his watch and saw that it was merely four minutes since he had last looked at it. Two after midnight. It had become Saturday.

"It's taking too long," Mike said.

"It's a good sign," Patsy Abromowitz replied. She was sitting on a hard plastic chair that she was certain had been contoured for a hunchback, but all the chairs in the stuffy waiting room were that way, so she curled her legs under her unsatisfactorily. "If they had come right out, they would have said he was dead. It would have been all over."

Mike grunted his agreement and went to the doors, a pair of swinging doors with large windows in them. He stood motionless, staring down the length of the long corridor, at the green and yellow signs above the doors and at the red exit sign a hundred feet away.

"You said you hardly knew him, that you were a kid when you last saw him," Patsy said, watching him carefully. "You care what happens to him, don't you?"

"I want him to live, of course." He looked at his watch again, turned and went over to where Patsy was sitting. "I tried to rush him along but he insisted there were two things he wanted to tell me. I was trying to get away, but I said go ahead. But then I began to hear things about my mother and about a Fabergé egg my father once owned. And something about my father . . ." His voice trailed off. "He was going to tell me about my parents and suddenly I wanted to hear more. Then this woman came into the room. She was wearing one of our uniforms. I'd never seen her before, but I'd know her in a second if I saw her again."

41

He stared at Patsy. "She shot Akimov. What the hell was that all about?"

He took the chair next to Patsy. "Look, this happened in my office, in my building. Akimov came to see me. I'm responsible."

"No, Mike," Patsy said with a lawyer's firmness. "Whoever shot him was damned clever . . . *they* were damned clever. There's no way it's your fault."

"You're sure Dennis is all right?"

"They were transfusing him and said they'd know for certain once that was done. The doctor didn't seem too concerned, except that he'd lost an awful lot of blood."

"Poor bastard looked like a wounded hippo."

One of the doors swung open. A police sergeant held it, waiting for a man who was not in uniform to follow him into the room. "Mr. Carson?" the sergeant said.

Mike acknowledged that he was.

The plainclothesman produced a wallet and identification which showed his name was Peter Crowley, his rank was detective, and he was attached to the 6th Precinct of the Nassau County Police. He recited the information in an indulgent tone that carried the suggestion that Mike Carson couldn't read. He went on to say, "I've got to put something in writing about the shit that happened this afternoon in that new showroom of yours. Mind if I ask a few questions?"

Mike glared at the young detective. He had learned to detect the glimmer of superiority that shone off people of real or imagined authority, the same way some self-proclaimed elitist Americans looked down on poor souls so unfortunate as to have been foreign-born. It was clear to Mike that Detective Crowley had crammed a bunch of oversize prejudices into an average-size body. His cheeks were blotched with acne scars and the kind of little red sores that seemed to never go away.

"Can we do this tomorrow?" Mike said.

"We can, but I want to do it now." Crowley stood in front of Mike, and with his eyes, signaled for the police sergeant to stand next to him. His mouth twisted into a smirk. "Let's do it now, Mr. Carson, then we won't have to do this same shit again."

Mike glanced from one to the other, then, speaking softly, described to the two police officers how a young woman wearing a Carson Motors uniform had come into his office, produced a gun, shot Sasha Akimov, and ran away.

"How old was she . . . was she tall, skinny, red hair . . . ?"

"She was nice-looking, I can't say how old—it all happened quickly. She was tall. Blond hair."

"Nice-looking? My aunt's nice-looking. What do you mean, nice? Pretty, beautiful—?"

"She had a beautiful face. How's that?"

"Built? You know what I mean?" Crowley said, putting both hands on his chest.

"I said it happened too quickly for details."

"It's a detail most men notice," Crowley said as if he had made a profound observation. "Did she say anything?"

Mike shook his head. "No. The only noise she made was with the gun. Two shots at a man standing twenty feet away."

"You're certain it was two shots? Not three, not one. Two. You're sure?"

"That's what I said," Mike answered.

"Was she an employee of yours?"

"Of course not."

"You said she was wearing a company uniform."

"Two of my salespeople were found in the used-car sales office. They had been tied up and their mouths taped shut. I'm sure your people know that."

"Mr. Carson, I don't know what other people know or don't know. My job is to start at the beginning and gather as many details as possible." Crowley fussed with another cigarette that he didn't light. "Tell me about this Akimov person."

"Tell you what about him?" Mike said.

"Is he a friend, a customer, a business acquaintance, that kind of shit."

"That kind of what?"

"Excuse me, Mr. Carson," Crowley said acidly. "I'll try again, very simple. Did you know this guy Akimov?"

"Yes. When I was very young."

"He's Russian?"

Mike nodded.

"You're Russian, too, right?"

"I'm an American citizen."

"But born in Russia?"

"Does that matter?"

"Mr. Carson, I don't really give a shit where you were born, I'm merely trying to make a little sense out of what happened in your office this afternoon. Let me try again. What do you know about Akimov?"

Mike stared hard at the young detective, noticing the yellow stain on the fingers of his right hand and imagining that Crowley was dying for a cigarette, concluding also that he was the exception that proved the rule; most of the police Mike had come in contact with, including detectives, were civil, reasonable people.

"Sasha Akimov knew my parents," Mike said.

"Did he come to see you on business?"

"You could say that."

"What kind of business?"

"Personal."

"Do you think your personal business had any connection with the fact some good-looking broad busts into your office and shoots him?"

"If I knew who she was, who sent her, then I might find a connection."

"You said you hadn't seen him since you were a kid, then he shows up after all these years. That's kind of strange. Agree?"

Mike chose not to answer.

"Hey look, Mr. Carson, you gotta admit it's pretty damned strange this guy comes all this way to pay a visit, then gets shot right in front of you. Maybe if we know why he came to see you, then maybe we'd have an idea."

"I'll think about that," Mike answered.

"Well, ain't that great shit. You'll think about it." Crowley fumbled for a cigarette, got it halfway to his lips, then angrily shoved it back into the package. "So, after you've thought about it, are you going to let me know, or what? Call a news conference?"

Patsy Abromowitz's eyes rolled up, then closed, and she pursed her lips as if words were about to come out. None did, and instead, she smiled, Mona Lisa–like.

A man in a surgical gown came through the double doors, his mask and cloth cap hung loose from his neck. There was a weariness around his eyes and a day's growth of a dark beard and he spoke without looking up from a piece of paper he held. "Is one of you Mike Carson?"

Crowley pointed a thumb at Mike. "I'm Pete Crowley. County police."

The doctor turned to Mike. "My name's Kaplan. I was making rounds when I was paged to emergency. We've done what we could for Mr. Akimov, but there's considerable damage in his throat. In fact I'm surprised he's alive, and he wouldn't be except the bullet missed the carotid artery and didn't shatter his spinal cord. Another miracle."

"He'll live?" Mike asked.

"If the tracheotomy holds, he should make it."

"Will he be able to talk?" Patsy asked.

Kaplan sighed wearily. "He needs a laryngoplasty—a reconstruction of the larynx. With luck, and a lot of therapy, he'll be able to squeeze out some sounds. I can't say more right now."

"He's visiting," Mike said. "He's Russian."

Kaplan nodded. "They told me. They've got good people over there, but he couldn't tolerate a long trip."

"Suppose he doesn't go back. Where can a larynx— whatever it is, where can it be done?"

"Here . . . any good hospital, it's not like open heart. What's important is to have someone with experience do it. There's also the cost."

Mike said, "I'll cover it."

"It's an involved procedure," Kaplan said. "Expensive."

"I said I'd cover it," Mike repeated with finality. "How's LeGrande . . . the big guy?"

Kaplan showed animation for the first time. "He's okay, except for a high fever we're not too happy about. Everyone recognized Dennis. At least the Giants fans did."

"Fever? What's that about?"

"He lost a lot of blood, and they put a lot back. Sometimes that causes it. Or he picked up a bug, or he was coming down with something. They're watching him."

"And Akimov. They're watching him, too?"

"He's in intensive care where he's monitored continually."

"Not good enough," Mike said. "I'll put one of my people with him."

"Not unless we say you can," Pete Crowley said. "You got a problem with hospital security?"

"Somebody was clever enough to get into my office wearing one of our uniforms and shoot Akimov. That somebody wants him dead. I want him alive."

Chapter 7

Outside was a prototypical London day complete with fog and raw dampness, and inside, on the fifteenth floor, in the corner office of Elliott Heston, Deputy Assistant Commissioner, Operations Command Group (OCG), New Scotland Yard, the air was thick with the deep emotions of old friends arriving at a minor crisis in a long relationship. It was mid-afternoon, on Saturday. But that wasn't a consideration; personal matters are given attention, whatever the day. Heston let his tall, lean body slump back in his chair.

"You promised to give this more thought and I'm sure that if you had, you would have changed that damned stubborn mind of yours." He brushed away the hair that had strayed across his forehead. "It means of course that it's unlikely we'll ever go fishing together." He let the words hang in the air for a moment, then added a touch of the martyr in his voice, "like old times."

Detective Chief Inspector Jack Oxby had taken a position by the corner window and was leaning against the sill, his arms crossed over his chest, his head cocked slightly in that reflective way one cocks the head to hear more clearly, or on occasion to create the impression of listening intently. He wore an Oxby smile, the one that was disarming or misleading, depending on his purpose, a smile that spread over his face to a pair of blue-gray eyes that were capable of expressing humor or compassion, eyes that were trained to see beyond the obvious, that at times could intimidate or taunt. He stood five nine but he seemed taller. A rather long nose was a noticeable feature though not one that detracted from his agreeable good looks. He was blessed with a rich voice, one that he had put to good use when he dabbled in television after graduation from Cambridge University. By then, and with the help of his parents and the considerable time he had spent on the Continent, Oxby could speak French with the ease of a Parisian and Italian with the singsong fluency of a Florentine. He could detect and he could mimic the infinite ranges of accents throughout the U.K., a not inconsiderable talent that would prove useful in the career he finally chose when he joined the Metropolitan Police Service.

"Fishing is what our relationship has come to?" Oxby said, pronouncing the words slowly. "Is that what you're telling me? That I'm expected to plan, provision, select your hooks and flies, then clean any bloody fish you should be so lucky to catch? Are you saying that if that doesn't happen, our friendship is out the window?"

"Don't go on with all that rot," Heston said. "You know perfectly well I can choose my own flies and clean every fish that I'm very well likely to catch." It seemed he wanted to go on about fishing because it was a sport that gave him infinite pleasure. But his tone changed. "It's what's needed around here that I'm anxious about. Your experience and the way you train the young guys." Momentarily his eyes strayed from Oxby's, as if hoping the argument he was about to make would go unchallenged.

"Look, Jack, once the other shoe dropped and the changes were announced, morale around here went to hell and some of the best people—you most of all—opted to bail out."

"Other shoe? Elliott, what dropped was a fifty-pound jackboot. They've eviscerated the Arts and Antiques Squad in the name of the holy Es: Efficiency and Economy."

Heston sighed. "You know how they're always tinkering."

"Good word, Elliott. It's time I did some tinkering for myself. I'm all paid up, I don't have any obligations."

"So your mind's made up?"

"Pretty much. I've accumulated five weeks' leave and may run up north and be with old friends. Might play some golf."

"Oh, Christ, not golf. Bad enough you're leaving the service, but you can't be serious about that godawful game." He pronounced *golf* as if it were a deadly contagion.

"Why not? With a little practice, I'd be good at it. I can golf and fish if I want." He smiled a little evilly. "You might join me for a few days."

"You know I can't get away, not until I've put this reorganization behind me." Heston got to his feet and circled around his desk, then sat against it, facing Oxby.

"I know you feel that they downgraded the squad, but it's happened before and we always brought it back." He reached behind him for an envelope marked confidential. "In the meantime, this is my authorization to move you up to Detective Superintendent."

Oxby glanced skeptically at the envelope. Then he opened it and took out letters and memoranda and forms with official stamps on them; in all there were a dozen sheets of bureaucratic file fodder. Oxby read a few of the pages, then put all the sheets back in the envelope and placed it on Heston's desk.

He looked squarely at the Assistant Commissioner and shook his head. "I've been with the Yard for fifteen years and liked every one of them. Even being shot at, knifed, and scared half to death. But before I no longer like it, I'm stepping out."

"Forever? You talked about leave time. Good! Get refreshed, then come back. You've got a new spot with more responsibility, more money."

"I've made my choice, Elliott. All I want is for you to wish me good luck."

"Good luck," Heston shot back rapidly and retreated to his chair. "What happens after you play golf? Write an exposé of all the deep, dark secrets you uncovered in historic Scotland Yard?"

Oxby smiled. "Hadn't thought of that, but I might." He pulled away the chair in front of Heston's desk and settled into it. From his shirt pocket he took out a business card and put it in front of Heston.

"Ring a bell?" Oxby asked.

Heston reacted immediately. "Of course. Christopher Forbes is the son of Malcolm Forbes. I knew the father slightly. Met him at the time he bought Old Battersea House." Heston grinned. "The old boy enjoyed a good time. Rode motorcycles, began going out with Liz Taylor. What are you doing with Chris?"

"Kip, as he likes to be called, wants me to find an egg."

Heston ran a finger slowly down the length of his nose and made a wry face. "What sort of an egg?"

"Start with the fact that Kip helped his father accumulate the largest private collection of Fabergé Imperial eggs in the world."

"I didn't know it was larger than the Queen's, but answer my question. What egg does Kip Forbes want you to find?"

"An Imperial egg commissioned by Grigori Rasputin."

A disbelieving frown erupted on Heston's face. "That's preposterous. Who thinks there's such an egg?"

"Apparently, quite a few people. It's one of those delicious rumors that's been around since Rasputin was assassinated. It was given new life a short time ago when a newspaper article appeared in Schaffhausen, Switzerland. Forbes sent me a copy of it. It seems that a ninety-four-year-old spinster died without heirs or a will. When the court examined her little estate, they found a trunk containing records belonging to her father, a man named August Hollming. Hollming had been an assistant workmaster in Fabergé's shops in St. Petersburg at the time of the revolution."

Oxby handed a copy of the newspaper clipping to Heston. "You read German."

"Passably," Heston said.

"You'll see that Hollming exchanged notes with other workers in Fabergé's workshop. One of the notes refers to Rasputin."

Heston read the clipping. He said, "Fabergé must have known that Rasputin was a charlatan. Hell, the man was a drunk, and a womanizer."

"Not to Alexandra. The Czarina thought he was a saint. She believed he'd saved her son's life more than once. Besides, women liked the scoundrel and gave him jewels or gold. That's how he could pay Fabergé, and rather well, I imagine."

"On the basis of this paltry piece of news from, where the hell was it—Schaffhausen? You're going to leave the Yard and a future—?"

"Elliott, don't be redundant. We've covered that ground."

"But you've got to have more to go on than a newspaper clipping."

"I have." Oxby produced a second piece of paper, unfolded it, and showed it to Heston.

"It's a handwritten note by Henrik Wigstrom to August Hollming in November of 1915. They were both Finns, so it's written in Finnish. Forbes came on to it somehow through his contacts in Geneva. At that time, 1915, Wigstrom was the head workmaster for the Imperial eggs. I can't read Finnish but I'm told the note merely confirms a detail concerning the construction of an Imperial egg. All I can make out are three numerals: 2, 11, and 9."

Heston took the memorandum, glanced at it quickly, then gave it back to Oxby.

"I'm not impressed."

"I didn't think you would be."

Heston shook his head, then sighed heavily and said, "So you're going on an Easter egg hunt?"

"It looks that way. First I'll confirm that Rasputin gave Fabergé a commission. Then, and I don't expect it will be easy, I've got to be convinced that the bloody thing still exists. That it wasn't blown up or melted down in the war. If it all checks out, then I go hunting."

"Be worth a bloody fortune, I suppose."

"In dollars, it might bring five million. If Rasputin is part of the provenance, it will be worth even more."

Heston's frown grew bigger. "If the fool thing hasn't popped up after eighty years, what makes you believe there's any chance you'll find it?"

Oxby grinned. "That's the challenge, Elliott. That's what I like about it."

"And I think you're going on a wild goose chase."

Oxby smiled. "God knows I've been sent on plenty of those around here."

Heston hunched forward, both arms resting on his desk. "You're being paid, of course. Plus expenses."

Oxby nodded. "First class. But I might need your help, Elliott."

"Go to hell," Heston said, glowering. "You've never been to Russia. It will take even you a month to learn the damned alphabet. You won't like the food and they make their wine from prunes."

"You're positively crazy about the country, aren't you?"

"Just want you to know what you're getting into."

"I've got a good friend in St. Petersburg. In fact you know him. Yakov Ilyushin. He's agreed to be guide and interpreter."

"Yakov's an old man," Heston said.

"Seventy doesn't make him an old man. You'll be lucky to do as well when you are his age."

Heston seemed finally resigned to Oxby's inevitable departure. "When do you go off on this crazy chase?"

"I leave on Tuesday. Forbes is in Paris. I'll go on from there."

Chapter 8

IBM Sales & Service was on the third and fourth floors. Business for the American computer giant had been expanding and the director of the office, a local boy in the process of making good, was planning to expand. The building, on Majorova Prospekt, was a Stalin-era design of straight lines and yellow bricks and was about to go through yet another metamorphosis. IBM would move into the first and second floors once a half dozen tenants were relocated.

On the top floor, the fifth, were the headquarter offices of a Russian company. Walk off the elevator and one was accosted by a huge outline of post-Soviet Russia with the words NEW CENTURY emblazoned across it. Incorporated into the flamboyant logo were the names of seven subsidiaries. Double doors opened into a reception room, the carpet, lighting, and furnishings executed in a rich medley of copper, gold, red, and a warm brown.

Mirrors covered the walls and nearly half the ceiling, and gave the square room a feeling of spaciousness. Visitors announced themselves to a receptionist who sat behind an opening in the mirrors. Seated less than ten feet away was a large man wearing a gray suit, white shirt, and vintage Countess Mara necktie. A folded, unread newspaper rested on his lap. One hand held a cellular telephone. The man, or one exactly like him, was present throughout the day.

Visitors never entered the inner offices unless accompanied, but when they were admitted they found offices that were large by Russian standards and equipped with the same stylish furnishings as were in the reception room. Computer screens beside every desk glowed either with a work in progress or the soundless animation of animals that turned into flowers, then into gyrating geometric designs.

There was an air of activity accompanied by the sounds of electronic machinery; soft clicks of the keyboard, rapid whooshing of printers, xylophonic chimes of phones and fax machines. And a feeling of tension,

51

too, that grew out of the relentless high speed and seeming impatience of the myriad machines, and from the people who stared at the work before them.

Every door in sight was open, save for one. Another man wearing a similar gray suit, and looking remarkably like the guard encountered before, stood in front of the closed door. His arms were folded across his chest and his head turned slowly from side to side. A wire ran from inside his jacket to a tiny earplug. He was connected.

A corridor led to a suite of rooms. First was a windowless sitting room of medium size, then a room that looked all the world like a fine bedroom with private bath. The third room, in a corner location with windows on two sides, was a large office. In contrast to the contemporary design motif encountered earlier, the office appeared as it might have looked in the final years of the Romanov dynasty. The furniture was made of oak and walnut and was massive. In a corner opposite from the desk stood a huge charcoal-fueled heater covered with white and blue Delft tiles. Next to it, nearly indiscernible, was a door that opened into a private conference room. On the wood floor were heavy carpets, hundreds of years old, still thick, the colors unfaded. The wall sconces held fat candles in hand-blown globes and were flanked by a variety of large and small icons; brilliantly painted pictures on sheets of silver depicting Mary, the Christ child, or St. George the dragon slayer. Two of the museum-quality icons measured four feet in length and dated to the fourteenth century.

On shelves, on occasional tables, and in one cabinet were displays of jewelry boxes, perfume flasks, picture frames, vanity cases, and a particularly spectacular collection of cigarette cases. Every piece was in mint condition and each carried a mark that distinguished it as having been crafted by the House of Fabergé.

Angled into the corner, near the windows, was a desk of great proportions. It was truly wide, long and high, and made of woods that had been stained and polished to a dark and shining finish. It was covered with more of Fabergé's production; a silver ink stand, picture frames, and a collection of animals carved from quartz, jasper, nephrite, and black onyx. On top of round bands made of silver and gold were brightly painted porcelain Easter eggs.

On the desk in front of two visitor's chairs was an oval-shaped silver *kovsh* embossed and chased with the Russian Imperial Eagle. The ceremonial drinking cup contained business cards on which was emblazoned the New Century logo and beneath it the name: Oleg Vladimirovich Deryabin. On his desk was an out-of-focus photograph of Deryabin with a pretty young woman. It was the only suggestion of a family; no pictures of children or family pets, or even of the family *dacha*.

The view from Oleg Deryabin's corner office was out to St. Isaac's Cathedral, a summer sun reflecting dazzingly off its immense, gilded dome. A glance down to the street and one saw the red awnings of the Astoria Hotel. Farther south was a statue of Nicholas I, and just visible, perhaps a half mile distant, was the top of Yusupov Palace, where a piece of history had played out on a winter night in 1916 when young prince Felix Yusupov put a bullet into the back of the infamous Grigori Rasputin. Deryabin knew of the incident, and cherished it in a maudlin way. For it added a novel touch to the history of the most valuable piece of Fabergé art in his collection. Stashed away in its own hiding place in a wall safe behind one of the icons was the Imperial egg that he had won in a poker game on the day after John F. Kennedy was assassinated.

The office was quiet, except for the din from the traffic that poured past Isaakiyevskaya Square directly below. Deryabin got up from his desk and walked to the door that connected with his conference room.

It was a square, brightly lit room, and equipped with phones, fax, and another computer that was up and ready for use. In the middle of the room was a long table covered with leather that was tooled with a gold leaf design that encircled New Century's corporate logo. Nine chairs surrounded the table. There were four chairs on one side of the table, three on the other. The chair at the head of the table was bigger and higher-backed and upholstered in a heavy tapestry cloth in reds and golds. It was where Oleg Deryabin sat when he led the occasional meetings that were attended by the division managers of the corporation. There was another chair at the foot of the table, one that would be occupied by Deryabin's counselor. A shelf ran the length of one wall, a built-in bar at one end, a refrigerator and microwave oven at the other.

Above the shelf was a large, rectangular-shaped white board and a tray with felt pens and erasers. Beside it, and nearly as big, was a surface of cork on which were pinned architectural renderings of buildings, each a different design for an automobile showroom. Deryabin stood in front of the drawings, studying each one as he had done many times before. He took down one, then another, until his final choice remained. He pinned it in the center of the board, stepped back, and stared at it.

The little grin that seemed at times as if it had been tattooed to his face stretched into a satisfied smile.

Next to the drawing he pinned a photograph of another automobile showroom. The similarity between the two was unmistakable. The photograph showed the banners and streamers that heralded the grand opening of Carson Motors' newest showroom in Roslyn, New York.

At the top of the cork board was a banner with the name KOLESO printed on it. Koleso, the Russian word for wheel, was the newest division in the galaxy of New Century subsidiaries. At present, Koleso provided limousine and overnight package delivery service to Moscow, Kiev, Novgorod, and Helsinki. Before the year was out, Deryabin planned to open a glamorous showroom that would offer a selection of late-model American Cadillacs and Oldsmobiles.

And, while Deryabin would announce that the Koleso showroom in Petersburg would be the first of a chain to spread across all of Russia, there were no plans to actually go forward with such an aggressive program. The cost would be prohibitive, the competition fierce, and the economy unprepared. Boris Berezovsky, one of Russia's wealthiest businessmen, had pioneered with the Logovaz chain of car dealerships.

Deryabin had another reason to be in the business of selling Cadillacs and Oldsmobiles. Out of every ten cars he planned to import from America, three would be sold in Petersburg, and seven would be put back on a cargo ship and and sent to Nicosia, Cyprus. Concealed in each car headed for the Mediterranean would be a small cylinder containing a substance worth twenty times the value of the automobile.

Deryabin, as he approached sixty, was losing the hardened look of the athlete he had once been. His dark hair was graying and thinning and he had a round spot in the back of his head that looked from not far away as if he might be wearing a pink yarmulke. His skin was a pasty white, and over his cheeks and nose were flecks of tiny bursted capillaries. He had a fighter's nose, broad and bent slightly, and beneath his eyes was a fresh crop of tiny lines. His lips moved constantly as if he were speaking and would part from time to time to reveal teeth that were stained from a lifetime habit of heavy smoking. A canine tooth was covered with gold and behind it was an empty, black hole.

Even though the edges of Deryabin's mouth curled up and his eyebrows arched, there was rarely genuine mirth in his face. Those who knew him or worked for him were aware that his cold, perpetual grin served to mask an unbridled temper that put dread in the heart of many a subordinate.

Oleg Vladimirovich Deryabin was a complicated man who had learned that success in the restructuring and struggling Russian economy came to those who had survived the old system, had learned to act decisively and boldly, and were well connected to the new bureaucracy. In his office, in silver and enameled frames, were photographs of Deryabin with men he worked alongside in the navy and later in the KGB when he was attached to the Soviet embassy in Paris, followed by two years in Baghdad, where he made significant friendships and gathered important IOUs. Then a final three-year assignment in Washington.

During each tour of duty his official title was communications officer. His true role had been as a member of the First Chief Directorate, the espionage branch of the KGB. He had distinguished himself by ferreting out two Soviet counterintelligence agents suspected of doubling back on Mother Russia. One perished in his car, a suspected suicide, and the second died from an extreme case of food poisoning. In each case, Deryabin had assumed direct responsibility and had been the executioner, as well.

He had spent twenty-seven years in the navy and with the KGB, and the range of experience and positions held had taught Deryabin how to sacrifice others for what he had deeply believed was for the common good; the valiant cause inspired by Lenin. But loyalty to a dead cause was out of fashion. The cause that now inspired him was the accumulation of personal wealth. It was sufficient for Deryabin to constantly remind himself that real power was no longer achieved inside the government as it had been for seventy-five years. Money was power, not party recognition, not advancement up the labyrinthine trail of what had become a discredited political philosophy.

Deryabin was also proving the wisdom of a new adage that was gaining popularity: old KGB officers don't die, they go into business and become capitalists.

There were demerits in Deryabin's résumé if one were ever to be accurately written. He could be cruel, dispassionately and indiscriminately, as demonstrated by the failure of his one abbreviated marriage. Blessedly, he never attempted another. In spite of what appeared to be a spotless military and government record, Deryabin's penchant for revenge had become legendary by the time he returned to civilian status. With Deryabin, it wasn't an eye for an eye, but two eyes for one eye.

But most damning to a man who craved to be admired as a Russian Renaissance man was his complete inability to handle money. While he had never been trained in economics or banking, he lacked even the most basic talent or ability to shepherd resources wisely and keep his books in balance. While he worshipped money and excelled at devising ways to obtain it, he would spend without discipline, then vent his notorious temper if he were dunned with an overdue invoice.

New Century, for all its glitz and sparkle, sat atop a shaky financial foundation. It was held together, however tenuously, by the one man who had Deryabin's unswerving confidence. He was also the only person who knew the dark secrets that Deryabin tried so desperately to hide.

Deryabin pulled a chair away from the table, sat, and pressed a button on a panel set into the table. The door opened and he was joined by a tall, thin man who took the chair on Deryabin's left. He had a long neck and narrow face with high cheekbones and full brows. He wore glasses framed by a rim of thin steel and frequently carried a second pair in his left hand. He might wear the spare glasses during a negotiation to obscure his eyes behind lenses that had a deep, bluish cast. His voice was gentle and unhurried. He was older by four years, more fit, perhaps, and his name was Trivimi Laar. Trivimi Laar was listed on the roster of the company as simply an aide to the chairman. He would be spotted entering or leaving the building, but only a select few had actually been introduced to him. It was generally known that the tall man could see Deryabin any time he chose. Some had heard the two arguing, their voices rising until it seemed the next noise from behind the closed doors would be a pistol shot. To most New Century employees, Trivimi Laar was known simply as the Estonian.

The two men had a relationship that went back to the time they were in their mid-twenties in Estonia when Deryabin was stationed at the Soviet naval yards in Tallinn and Laar was a government clerk. Later, showing rare diplomatic skills, Laar rose through the tangle of departmental officialism and at a time when the Estonian government was under the thumb (and heel) of Moscow. Their paths crossed again during Deryabin's tour with the KGB. A unique friendship ensued and eventually grew to where Deryabin brought Trivimi and his special skills into New Century.

Deryabin spoke first. "I sent the Lysenkos to put an end to Akimov.

They failed." He got up from his chair and thrust his hands deep into his pockets. "I don't tolerate incompetence. Tell me everything."

The Estonian also stood, his feet apart, his head lowered, to put him level with the shorter Deryabin.

"Galina did not catch up with Akimov until he was in Mikhail's office. She doesn't know how long they had been together. She found them standing beside a table, each holding a glass. There was a bottle on the table. Mikhail spoke to her but she paid no attention. She aimed at Sasha's chest—she's a crack shot and doesn't miss at that range. But Mikhail threw the bottle. It hit her arm just as she fired."

"She uses a Semmerling double-action that holds five bullets," Deryabin said impatiently. "She's been trained to kill. Why didn't she?"

The Estonian shook his head. "I don't have an answer. Mikhail may have charged at her. She may have tried again. I'll get a report. She swears they will learn what Akimov said to Mikhail."

"Where did the bullet hit Akimov?"

"In his neck. It tore up his larynx. If he survives, in time he will be able to write—"

"No! He won't live to hold a pen again. What did Viktor tell you?"

"He estimated that Akimov had been with Mikhail for ten minutes. Even less time than that, he thought."

"He thought, he thought. That's bullshit, Trivimi. How long were they together? Five minutes? Eight minutes?" Deryabin shouted. "They were sent to stop Akimov *before* he got to Mikhail."

"It would have been a miracle. They tried."

The anger subsided. "When did you talk with Galina?"

"Early this morning. It was after midnight in New York."

"What were your instructions?"

"To learn what Akimov said to Mikhail. They know that he was spreading false rumors about you and New Century." Trivimi added solemnly, "I told them that Akimov was not to leave the hospital alive."

Deryabin nodded, then returned to his chair and lit a fresh cigarette from the old one. "He would talk about the Fabergé egg, and tell Mikhail that I should give it to his mother. The simple ass was saying foolish things."

"Why would Akimov suggest that you give the egg to Mikhail's mother?"

"Because he was like a brother to Mikhail's mother. Anna Karsalov and Akimov were from the same city. From Sochi."

"Yes," Trivimi said. "I'd forgotten." He walked slowly around the conference table. "You have a very fine collection of Fabergé, your office is filled with them. But the Imperial egg is locked away. Why not put it out for everyone to enjoy?"

"Because I prefer not to," Deryabin said, as if closing off any further discussion.

"Have you thought more about putting it into auction?"

"I don't want to discuss it." He stared at Trivimi, the smile missing. "Understood?"

"No, I don't understand. You agreed the market was ripe for a sale. There's new interest in Fabergé and particularly in the Imperial eggs. I think you should sell it."

"It's not your fucking decision," Deryabin said angrily.

"You're still afraid of it, aren't you?"

Deryabin drew heavily on the cigarette, then shook his head. "That's my affair. Not yours."

Trivimi sat in the chair next to Deryabin. He shook his head slowly. "I don't agree. It might be my affair also. You claim you've told me everything about the egg. Perhaps I've forgotten something, Oleshka." He had spoken softly and called Deryabin by his familiar name. "Tell me again."

Deryabin crossed his arms over his chest. He drew on the cigarette and with his eyes fixed on a point beyond the Estonian, he began. "Fabergé made Imperial eggs under commission from the Czars. Easter gifts for the Czarina or the Czar's mother. Grigori Rasputin asked Fabergé to make one. As a gift for Alexandra, it is supposed. The mad monk had money. I don't know how it happened, but Mikhail Karsalov's grandfather got the egg at the time Rasputin was murdered."

"I remember you telling me this, but what proof do you have that the egg is authentic? It's possible that it's a forgery. "

"The crossed anchors and scepter marks of Fabergé are on it," Deryabin replied. "So is the date and the initials of the designer."

"Then the card game and you won it from Vasily Karsalov. Except you didn't actually win it. You stole it."

Deryabin bristled. "We swore a blood oath to keep the confidence of what we have told each other."

"I have told no one about the egg. I have kept my side of the bargain."

Deryabin caught Trivimi's eyes. "And so have I."

"But now you want to do business with Vasily Karsalov's son?"

"If Akimov spread his lies, there is a problem. But if Viktor is correct, Akimov had ten minutes or less with Mikhail before he was shot. First he would talk of old times, of Mikhail's mother, of Petersburg and how it has changed. All that before he would begin to spread his lies."

"Tell me again about the card game."

"There were five. Vasily Karsalov, Sasha Akimov, Artur Prekhner, and Leonid Baletsky. Of course, I was the fifth."

Trivimi studied his hands. "You were playing draw poker, I believe it is called. And you won the Imperial egg with four queens."

Deryabin nodded. "I have told you that several times."

The Estonian smiled. "Four queens? Very strong. And no wild cards the way the Americans play."

"I told you there were no wild cards. Why do you bring it up?"

"Because you held four queens, and Vasily held four jacks. Without wild cards, the odds are incredibly high."

"It was damned unusual. I have always said that."

"But when Vasily got up from the table to get his precious Imperial egg, you only held three queens. Is that so?"

Deryabin bit on his lips. "I told you that."

"And in the cards that had not been dealt, you found the fourth queen?"

"Why are you digging this up again? I've told the story before, and I don't have to go over it again for no reason."

"Oh, there is a reason, Oleshka."

"What fucking good reason do you have?"

"I want it all in front of us one more time. You won Vasily Karsalov's Imperial egg by cheating. That was thirty-five years ago and you've done nothing with it. Never shown it to the museum, never let anyone see it in your office. And, of course, you've never sold it."

"What are you getting at?" Deryabin asked.

"I'm getting at why you felt it was so terrible for Akimov to go to New York and tell Mikhail that his father lost a Fabergé Imperial egg to you in a card game. Is that a reason to have him killed?"

Deryabin screamed his response, "I told you the bastard Sasha would tell lies about me."

"What lies, Oleshka? What lies would be so terrible that you wanted him killed?"

"I don't know which ones . . ." Deryabin seemed at a loss to explain.

"But whatever he might say could destroy my plans to bring Mikhail Karsalov into our new venture."

"But not because of the Imperial egg. Even if Sasha told Mikhail you cheated to win the Imperial egg, you would have a chance to explain."

"I hired Akimov when he left the navy. His pension was a laugh and he needed work, so I took him on. But he thinks I was unfair to him, that I cut him off for no reason. He would tell Mikhail anything to get revenge over me."

"He was an old friend. It was a mistake to turn him out. And a mistake to send the twins to kill him."

"I don't make mistakes!" Deryabin roared. "The lying bastard would say anything against me. He was acting like a crazy old man."

The Estonian moved his chair so that he was squarely in front of Deryabin. He was silent for a moment, and when he spoke his words were hushed.

"There is something in this Akimov matter that is puzzling." A bemused look covered the Estonian's face "The Fabergé egg? An expensive bauble and frankly, I don't give a damn how you came to own it." The Estonian wrapped his long fingers around Deryabin's arm. "But, remember, Oleshka, there is trust between us." He squeezed the arm gently. "Tell me about these 'lies' that you were afraid Akimov would say about you."

Deryabin glared and pulled away from the Estonian. "Damn your fucking trust. I told you Akimov was losing his senses. He was inventing wild stories about me."

"He came to me, Akimov did, after you told him he no longer had a job. He was angry because you made him go back to his paltry pension. He said there was bad blood between you and Vasily Karsalov."

Deryabin flinched and glared wildly at Trivimi. "What bad blood was he talking about?"

Trivimi shook his head and shrugged. "He never found the words."

"Sniveling bastard never found the courage. Besides, what of it? He'll soon be dead."

"What was he going to tell me, Oleshka?" Trivimi hardened his tone. "Tell me what Akimov has on you."

"Not a fucking thing, you Estonian bastard."

"Not as bad as Russian bastards. That's what you are."

"Leave! Get your stinking ass out of here!" Deryabin was on his feet, pointing fiercely at the door. "Go!"

"I'm going nowhere until we talk this through."

Deryabin grabbed the phone and began jabbing numbers, but the Estonian pulled the phone away from him. He said calmly into the phone, "Everything is all right." Then he clicked off.

Deryabin glowered. "You're pushing too far."

"Not far enough," Trivimi said firmly. "It's time you come clean with me."

Deryabin's face was flushed, and his eyes darted from the Estonian to the ceiling to the door. He put a match to another cigarette while fussing with the one still smoldering in the ashtray. He swept up a red felt marking pen from the table and went hurriedly past the drawings of the proposed Koleso showroom to the long, white writing surface. In block letters two inches high he wrote a name: Artur Prekhner.

He turned and faced the Estonian.

"Prekhner and Vasily were old school friends. They started a business while Vasily was at the naval base in Tallinn, and Prekhner was a clerk in the commissary in Petersburg. That's where I met him. It was a small operation, just the two of them. Part of each shipment never got to Tallinn, but ended up in a warehouse in Pushkin. Then they shipped the meat and liquor to the black market in the Petersburg region. I hadn't seen Prekhner in over a year, then, in September of 1972, I met him at a wedding party for a mutual friend. He asked if I could meet with him two nights later, said he was having a problem and wanted my advice."

Deryabin drew hungrily on his cigarette. He inhaled deeply, then swallowed as if to keep all the smoke inside him. When he spoke, little gray wisps escaped from his mouth.

"We met for dinner, then he asked me to go with him to his office. It was his apartment but he worked out of it. He told me he was having trouble with Karsalov, that he was drinking heavily again. I gave him my ideas and thought that was that. Then a young couple came to the apartment."

Deryabin looked across at the Estonian. "It was a complete surprise. There was vodka and good whiskey and food you couldn't get anywhere unless you had a top government position or were a goddamned ballet star. For a couple of hours, I didn't mind being there. There was strange music, I remember, and a sweet odor. You might think the lights would be small and dim, but they were bright and different colors; yellow and orange and purple.

"The couple danced and kissed, then they undressed each other, sitting on a blanket in the middle of the floor. Then they began screwing. Prekhner joined them. Three of them were screwing each other. Man and woman, man and man. Then a second girl came. She had big tits and a solid ass and said I could do anything I wanted with her. She liked to fuck. We did. I was smoking marijuana. Had never done that, so I didn't know what to expect. I didn't feel differently, not until they showed me how to take cocaine. That was a big change. I wanted the feeling to last forever.

"I looked for Prekhner and he was gone. It was a small apartment, a few tiny rooms. But I couldn't find him. I guessed that he'd gone for more food and I paid no attention whether he was there or not. The high I was on didn't last long and when it went away I got sick. But sober, too. Then, Prekhner was back, like he'd never gone away."

Deryabin rubbed his mouth. "I got out and went back to the navy base."

The Estonian had listened, amused by Deryabin's embarrassment as he recounted his long-ago experience. "Why do you tell me about Artur Prekhner and his orgy?"

"You say there are no secrets between us?"

Trivimi Laar nodded. "No secrets."

"I once described to you the way Prekhner died. A knife here, in the neck." Deryabin planted his hand on his own neck.

Trivimi said, "You told me that during an argument, when Karsalov was drunk, he stabbed Prekhner."

"It's true there was an argument and a knife. But I am the one who put the knife into Prekhner."

"You?" Trivimi said, uncertain and surprised.

"A week after his party, Prekhner was waiting for me at the entrance to the General Staff building. We got into his car. He handed me a photograph album. I had no recollection of doing what I saw in the pictures."

"Blackmail? What did he want?"

"Prekhner knew that I was being trained for an assignment in the First Directorate and wanted my help on a wild scheme he had put together. He made it very simple. Either I cooperate, or he would send photographs to my superiors. He said he could send one a week for three months."

"And so you—"

"I told him I would need time to think over what he had said. Two days later I called him and said I was going to go along with him, but I wanted to talk about the details. There were so many, I couldn't remember all of them. Then, I set my own trap." Deryabin's smile lengthened. "I suggested to Prekhner that we meet in his apartment. He liked the idea, even joked about having his young friends join us. It was essential that Vasily be present. When he arrived I gave him a bottle of vodka. I didn't have to encourage him to drink it. In an hour he was drunk and I put him in the bedroom and told him to sleep it off. To be sure he slept, I gave him a sedative."

The Estonian listened intently, never taking his eyes off Deryabin.

Deryabin said, "I took my own knife and pistol, but found a heavier knife in the kitchen. I hid it in my sleeve."

Trivimi leaned forward in his chair. "He never suspected?"

"No. I told him that his scheme had too many complications. He insisted he had worked through the plan and got rid of extra details. I told him he was wrong, baiting him to argue back. He did. Then I tore his plan apart and said he'd have to make changes. It made him furious. After another minute we were shouting at each other. It was exactly what I was hoping for. I wanted his neighbors to hear a loud argument come from his apartment. It was eleven o'clock and I figured they had come home from wherever they had been."

Deryabin stepped to the table and picked up a cigarette and jabbed the air with it as he continued. "We were standing a few feet from each other in the middle of the room. I slipped the knife from my sleeve and when he saw it in my hand it was as if he turned to stone. I remember that the only feeling I had was whether his blood would get on my clothes. I struck him twice. The first was in his chest. I aimed the second thrust lower, at his heart."

Trivimi had not budged, his gaze still riveted on Deryabin's face. "Had you done that before?"

Deryabin said he had not, but said that during officer's training he had been taught to strike twice. The first to inflict pain and neutralize the opponent, the second to kill. Then he explained, as dispassionately as if he were describing the fundamentals of rowing a boat, how when the heart stopped beating, the blood stopped flowing.

"Prekhner fell against a chair and when I pulled it away he rolled onto the floor. Then I went into the bedroom for Vasily. I carried him out and put him next to Prekhner's body. I put the knife in his hand and closed his fingers over the handle. I bloodied his arms and shirt. Then I went to the bathroom and cleaned the blood off my shirt and hands."

"Did you find the photographs and the negatives?" Trivimi asked.

Deryabin was relieved to have told the story, and finally lit the cigarette he had been holding.

"Prekhner's work area, his 'office,' was in his kitchen. There was a desk and typewriter, a telephone and a file cabinet. I found two sets of the photographs and the negatives in a desk drawer. I learned I wasn't the first to be sucked into Prekhner's blackmail business. There were other photographs and negatives. Enough fucking and sucking to fill twenty pornographic magazines."

"Akimov suspected that you killed Prekhner? That's why you wanted him eliminated?"

"I told you there were five of us in the card game." He printed four more names on the board in the same big letters. He called out their names as he did.

"As I said, in addition to Prekhner, there was Sasha Akimov, Vasily Karsalov, Leonid Baletsky, and myself. These three," he drew a line under Akimov, Karsalov, and Baletsky, "stayed together in the navy. First in Tallinn, then in Petersburg where they were transferred in 1970. They were all friends, including Prekhner."

"I'll ask again. Did Akimov suspect you killed Prekhner?"

"I didn't think any of them knew about it. Then, a few months ago, Leonid Baletsky appeared out of the blue. He was waiting at the entrance to our building. I hadn't seen him in all those years and didn't recognize him. But he knew who I was. He told me that after he left the navy he lived in Moscow with his wife and son. Then his wife died and he moved back to Petersburg. He said he had read about New Century and me, and did I have a job for him. He said he had talked with Akimov. About the egg and the poker game. And about other things, too."

Deryabin stared at Baletsky's name. "He was nervous and couldn't look me in the eye. He blurted out that he remembered the card game and that I had cheated Vasily out of the egg. I asked him why he didn't call me on it right away. He said he didn't know about it until recently. He said he wanted five hundred dollars and he would forget everything."

"Baletsky threatened you?" Trivimi said.

"I asked who told him. He wouldn't tell me. I asked if he knew if

Vasily Karsalov was still alive. He thought he was, that he was still in Uzbekistan. I said that what he had learned about the card game was old history, that I had regretted the way I had won the egg and realized that I was not entitled to keep it. I told him I had given the egg back to Vasily before he was brought to trial and sent away. He was surprised, but I think he believed me. Then I gave him money, a hundred dollars, I think."

Deryabin gave the Estonian a knowing glance. "If he makes trouble for us, we can silence him for much less five hundred dollars."

"Perhaps I should pay him a visit?"

"Have him followed. We should keep track of him for a while."

He stared at the names. He spoke in a whisper. "Sasha Akimov. I thought we'd become friends, but he deceived me. I made a mistake when I let him get away. But he won't talk anymore."

"And so they all knew what happened in the card game?"

"One of them knew, and spread it to the others. My guess is it was Akimov."

"Do they know it was you and not Vasily who put a knife into Prekhner?"

"There's no way for them to know. Except that Vasily claimed he was innocent and swore vehemently at his trial that he was passed out and could not have done it. He accused me, but because I had put together a good service record and had been chosen for an important position, the court was pressured by the KGB to ignore his testimony. Then they changed it to a charge of self-defense and gave Karsalov a lifetime assignment in Uzbekistan."

Trivimi went to the board. "Prekhner is dead," he said flatly, and drew a line through his name. "Akimov? He can't talk, and he, too, will soon be dead." He drew a line through Akimov's name.

Next, he put a question mark after Vasily Karsalov's name. "Is Vasily alive? If he is, where does he live?"

Deryabin said, "I will give you names and phone numbers of people who can get that information."

"That leaves Baletsky," Trivimi said. "I will personally learn what he knows." He added a question mark after Baletsky's name.

The Estonian returned to the table. He sat, bolt upright, his hands clasped tightly. He looked at Deryabin and waited for him to sit across from him. Then, with a measured voice, he spoke.

"I strongly believe that the Fabergé Imperial egg is at the heart of your relationship with each man whose name you wrote on the board. Certainly that is true with Karsalov. Because of him, you became involved with Prekhner. I pick Akimov as the one who knew about the card game and the final hand when you claimed the egg unfairly. While it may have taken many years, it was Akimov who told Baletsky what had happened.

"I also believe that in some unexplained way, they have strong suspicions that you killed Prekhner. That Vasily was innocent."

Deryabin lowered his head. He rubbed his fingers over his face, concentrating on what the Estonian had said.

"Why not reconsider selling the egg?" Trivimi asked. "It's quite valuable. And, though you won't admit it, you desperately need the money."

Deryabin said, "I am not superstitious, but neither am I a fool. I believe it is possible that Rasputin put a curse on the egg. The mad monk called it the *Egg of Eternal Blessing*. Vasily's father told him."

"That doesn't sound like a curse."

"I believe Rasputin cast a blessing over the rightful owner. But for any other person to profit from it there could be unpleasant consequences."

Chapter 9

Left over from the grand opening celebration that had festooned Carson Cadillac & Oldsmobile's showroom were the helium balloons that had floated up to where they looked like giant M&Ms glued to the ceiling. The shooting two days before had received the usual local television coverage over the weekend, replete with twisted presumptions about the mysterious Russian victim and even wilder speculations concerning the gun-wielding woman masquerading as a Carson employee. The publicity, grudgingly (though secretly) applauded by Patsy Abromowitz, had generated far more traffic into the showroom than even her most optimistic projections.

One potential buyer was looking at Oldsmobiles shortly after 10:00 A.M. He passed the coupés, and sedans and settled behind the wheel of an Oldsmobile Bravada, a chunky sports utility colored medium red metallic on the outside with fresh-smelling graphite-gray leather on the inside. The man was in his early thirties, casually dressed in jeans, sweater, a Mets baseball cap, glasses, and appeared to be a quintessential yuppie father complete with a mortgage and 1.8 kids. Viktor Lysenko had been trained for the role, as well as others, and there was zero chance that he would be identified as the man an eyewitness saw next to Dennis LeGrande, who had run off with the woman who shot the Russian up there on the mezzanine in the office with all the glass.

A Carson sales consultant with dirty-blond frizzy hair, and outfitted in the company uniform, approached the driver's side door, her hand extended.

"Georgia Gradowski," she gushed in a rich accent straight out of Atlanta. "That's a great piece of machinery you're sittin' in."

Viktor nodded and waved a hand at the interior space. "I need something bigger. For the family." His English was barely marred by an accent.

"Give it a test," Georgia said helpfully. "Bring the family and you'll see they fit just fine."

"Perhaps," Viktor said. He turned to Georgia, his face a picture of innocence. "Was someone shot here on Saturday?"

"You can bet that someone was shot right up there. Right in that office where I'm pointing at." Georgia's finger was aimed up to Mike Carson's office on the mezzanine.

"Was he killed?"

"He was shot pretty bad, but he's alive. That's the good news. But Dennis? That big old football player is the one we're all worried about. I was standing not ten feet away when he was stabbed right here —" She put a hand on her side. "I got to say, it was horrible. And such a nice man." Georgia pronounced "man" as if it had two syllables. "Mr. Carson said that Dennis lost a powerful lot of blood."

"Is Mr. Carson here today?" Viktor asked.

"Heavens no," Georgia said. "He was just here for opening day. He has a big office somewhere. And he works in his home. He works all the time, that man does."

"He lives in the city?"

"Now, just a minute," Georgia said, smiling supremely. "I'm the one supposed to be asking the questions . . . like do you want to take that Bravado for a spin . . . and do you have a car to trade?"

Viktor laughed, too, but there was something more that Georgia saw. Something in his eyes that frightened her.

He stepped out of the vehicle. "I'll take one of the brochures and show it to my wife. Maybe she will want to see it."

"You ask for me." She plucked a business card out of a little wallet. "Now, don't forget, you come back!"

Viktor pocketed her card, then slowly made his way past the brightly polished Cadillacs clustered at the front of the showroom. He paused, glanced up to the mezzanine a final time, then pushed open the double-glass doors and walked off.

Georgia followed him with curious eyes until he disappeared in a virtual sea of automobiles surrounding the dealership. "Goll-ee," she said quietly to herself.

⁂ ⁂ ⁂

Viktor Lysenko sat in the Taurus, a powerful, collapsible telescope on the seat beside him. He had driven out of the parking spot and was now parked alongside a row of Oldsmobiles, from where he had an unobstructed view into the showroom. A cellular phone came with the rental car. He touched the numbers. He asked the motel operator for Mrs. Lysenko and let the phone ring ten times before hanging up. Galina was not in their room.

It was eleven o'clock and clouds blew in from the southwest, bringing a light rain. Shortly after noon the rain intensified and made the inside of the car a safe haven. He called the motel again. Galina answered.

Viktor said, "Akimov is alive. He is in special care, and under guard. I am at the showroom. Carson is not here."

"The Estonian called," Galina said. "Oleg said we must learn what Akimov said to Mikhail. He's angry that he's still alive, and wants—"

"Damned fool," Viktor interrupted. "Oleg doesn't know what a miracle it was that we found Akimov at all."

Viktor held the phone with one hand and with the other he panned the telescope slowly across the faces in the showroom. He said, "Before Akimov arrived last Saturday Carson was with a man and a woman. The man was tall. The woman had red hair."

"I remember," Galina said impatiently. "I was there. But why does it matter who he was with—"

"Because I'm looking at a tall man right now. The same one."

🦗 🦗 🦗

Georgia Gradowski was standing at the foot of the escalator. "We met on Saturday," she said. She had regained her big smile and was beaming it up to Lenny Sulzberger, who towered over her. "I'll never forget that day as long as I live. You're Mr. Saintsbury. Right?"

"Sulzberger," Lenny corrected.

"Ooh, I'm sorry." She blushed. "I've been practicing all those tricks for remembering names, and I thought I had yours. You came with Patty Abromowitz, and you were going to meet with Mr. Carson. Now, you tell me if I have that right?"

"You do. I was going to interview him, but the Russian came. Then the shooting."

"And the stabbing. Don't you ever forget that. It happened right where we're standing and I was this close." She pointed to the carpet at Sulzberger's feet. "They cleaned up the blood and you see they didn't get it all." She winced. "It was the most terrible thing I ever saw."

"Yeah," Lenny said. "I'm sure it was. Did you see the woman who did the shooting?"

"You mean could I tell you what she looked like? Awful pretty I can say. Not the kind of face that goes around shooting people." Her eyes widened, her head began to shake. "Would you believe she was dressed just like I am? Can you ever imagine that? Truth is, I don't remember anything else about her."

"Lot of excitement," Lenny said, understanding Georgia's confusion. "I was hoping to find Mr. Carson. Is he here?"

Georgia's smile expanded. "Lord, love a duck. Somebody else was asking for him." She shook her head. "Mr. Carson is not here and I do not expect he will be here. Like I said to that other man . . . " Her voice went silent and she peered past the showroom windows to the steady rain.

Chapter 10

Lenny Sulzberger lived in a loft apartment on the north side of North Moore Street in New York City's TriBeCa neighborhood. He shared the space with another writer, a Japanese woman who at one time thought it would be a good idea to marry a New Yorker with a name like Sulzberger and be instantly absorbed into the Manhattan mainstream. But Sheri Ono was having second thoughts and was on her way home to be with her father in Japan where she could "sort out" her relationship with Lenny.

"Why not sort it out with me, for God's sake," Lenny said aloud, as if Sheri were still somewhere in the vastness of the loft apartment. Sorting out personal problems with Lenny was not easy because Lenny's ego was liable to soar to heights about as tall as he was. Strange, how he managed to encapsulate a little man's pomposity in a big man's body. It wore off, too, witness the fact that Lenny generally made a positive first impression, but subsequent encounters invariably resulted in flat rejection. His résumé showed that he had been with a dozen blue-chip publishing and PR firms over the same number of years, then for the past couple of years he could do no better than a grab bag of assignments with third-rank outfits that paid little and usually paid late. In spite of all, Lenny was a damned good writer with a knack for putting punch and energy into his profiles of successful businessmen and women. Patsy Abromowitz knew Lenny's dark side, respected his talent, and still liked him, disagreeable disposition and all.

But the assignment Patsy had given Lenny was about to fizzle, his deadline for the profile article now only three days away. He had failed to catch up with Mike Carson, and the response that came back to him was simply that Mr. Carson was not available. Compounding his personal diminution, Sheri had gone off, at least tripling his feeling of abandonment. Along with Sheri's departure went half of the money necessary to pay rent and all the bills coming due for the utilities and maintenance. He tore up Sheri's note and let little pink shreds fall from his hand as he walked to the middle of the huge center room. He thrust both arms over his head and shouted, "Fuck! Fuck, fuck, fuck!"

It was a catharsis, cheap and fast. He was saved from worrying how long the spell would last because the phone rang. Patsy Abromowitz had worked a small wonder and if Lenny wanted one last crack at an interview with Mike Carson, he'd have to act damned fast.

"I tried, God knows," he complained. "I waited so long in that show-room I smell like the front seat of a goddamned Cadillac Deville. Besides, it's after nine o'clock."

"Tell me about it!" Patsy said sharply. "I know he keeps crazy hours, but if you want to see him, get your ass over to Fort Lee before ten-thirty."

"Where's—"

"The Jersey side of the George Washington Bridge."

"I know where Fort Lee is," he said impatiently. "What's his address?"

"One-five-two Palisades Avenue."

🐦 🐦 🐦

The cab ride went as Patsy said it would. At 10:15 Len reminded the driver to wait. He had negotiated a round-trip flat rate and didn't want to be left stranded by an impatient Indian with a red circle impressed into his forehead. "One hour. Any longer and you get extra. Okay?"

The high rise was one in a row of apartment buildings on the scenic side of Palisades Avenue in what was known as the Gold Coast. Buildings put up after the war were gone, replaced by taller, more modern designs. Mike Carson lived in the Atrium Palace, eighteen floors of condominiums priced from a half to over a million dollars and nestled between the Colony and the Plaza. The lobby was empty, except for a uniformed guard with a badge on his chest that read Carlos, and who was seated before a bank of black and white monitors, a switchboard, and a radio tuned to the Mets–Pirates game. Carlos spoke into the phone, nodded, then said "18 South" and pointed to the elevators.

Mike answered the door. He was dressed in jeans and T-shirt and guided Lenny past unopened cartons spread throughout high-ceilinged rooms. The furniture was covered with drop cloths and paint cans were arrayed over the floor. Wide, gray-tinted windows faced east and south to a spectacular view of the Hudson River. Immediately north, and as if one could reach out and touch them, were the towers and cables of the George Washington Bridge. Directly across the river were the northern reaches of New York City, and to the south were the twin towers of the World Trade Center.

They stopped in a small room lined with bookshelves, and a desk on which were several stacks of letters and folders, two phones and a combo fax/printer. Beside the desk was a personal computer.

"Excuse the clutter," Mike said. "Any more and I'll have to move." He motioned Lenny into a chair and sat behind his desk. He smiled, genuinely. "As I remember, you like to be called Lenny."

"Yeah," Lenny said, "good memory. You know, *Playboy*'s going to run the story and they're big on photographs. Maybe that sales gal in your new showroom. Georgia?"

"She's a sales consultant," Mike said evenly.

The mild rebuke went right past Lenny. "Yeah," he said, nodding. "Okay if I send a photographer here? Good idea to show you at home."

"Home is a mess. Talk to Patsy about photographs. In fact, talk to Patsy about everything, except the interview. She can't do that. I'm sorry about Saturday. That wasn't a good day for any of us."

"She gave me a file on Carson Motors, and a little bit on you, but not enough to do a profile. And I want to ask questions about the shooting."

"You can ask, that's why you're here." Mike sat back, relaxed. "But let me warn you that there might be questions about the man who was shot that I can't discuss. Fair enough?"

"Fair enough," Lenny said. "Nice apartment. You live alone?"

Mike nodded. "I do now. Had a friend, but she was getting impatient. Wanted kids. A bunch of them. You know how that goes."

"Yeah," Lenny said. "I damned well know how that goes. Had the same situation. No kids for me, not now. Don't know if that was the issue, but she took off. Going to sort it all out, she said."

"You were married?"

"No. It didn't get that far."

Lenny balanced his notebook on a corner of the desk. "I asked because I don't see any pictures."

Mike opened a desk drawer and took out a silver frame and handed it to Lenny. In it was a photograph of Mike and a young woman. They were on board ship and wearing evening clothes. "I kept one, just in case."

Lenny made a low whistling sound. "She's beautiful."

"I know. Everyone felt the same way. Problem was, so did she." Mike put the photograph back in the drawer. "But you're not here to talk about an old girlfriend."

"Yeah." Lenny began with his questions. They were succinct and flowed in a natural progression, never prying for dark secrets, always slanted to keep Mike involved, even interested in searching his memory for obscure, interesting details.

Indeed, Lenny was a pro and in thirty-five minutes he filled twenty-five pages with a fast pen that wrote squiggly big letters in a weird scrawl, plus his own bastardized shorthand.

"That pretty much takes us up to last Saturday," Lenny said, turning to a fresh page. "The media are trying to figure out what happened." He glanced up. "And you've gone under cover. What can you tell me about the man who was shot? We know he was Russian, but who was he?"

"You talk as if he was dead. He's not." Mike rubbed his hands together. "He is someone I knew when I was very young."

"Can you tell me his name?"

"Sasha Akimov."

"How old were you when you last saw him?"

"I don't know exactly. Just a little guy, maybe seven or eight. He was a friend of my parents."

"So, it's been twenty-five or more years since you last saw him?"

Mike nodded.

"After all this time, why did he come to see you?"

"I never found out. I think he was about to tell me, then—" Mike's hand went involuntarily to his throat.

"How long had you been together before he was shot?"

"Ten minutes, but that's a guess. I didn't expect him, but I was expecting other people. Then, he began telling me about my family."

"Was he a close friend of your parents?"

"He and my mother came from the same town. It's on the Black Sea. He was in the navy with my father."

"They're still friends?"

"They went separate ways. It isn't something I want to discuss."

Lenny turned a page. "Akimov came from Moscow?"

"St. Petersburg."

"You said you were a kid when you last saw him. Where would that have been?"

"St. Petersburg."

"Is that where you always lived? When you were in Russia?"

"I was born in Estonia. My father was in the navy and stationed in Tallinn. I was just a little guy when we moved to St. Petersburg."

"Was Akimov in the navy?"

Mike nodded. "And he was transferred to St. Petersburg, too."

"So, after all these years, he showed up in your showroom? Pretty good for a guy who doesn't speak English. Why did he want to see you?"

Mike shrugged. "He started by telling me that my father had a party the night I was born. He wanted me to know that my father invited his navy buddies to celebrate the fact he was a new dad and also because President Kennedy had been assassinated."

"That's an interesting headline," Lenny said. "Mike Carson born the day John Kennedy died." His pen flew across a page. "So, there was a party—"

"With a lot of drinking and gambling."

"The old Soviet Union wasn't crazy about Kennedy, and I suppose your dad and his friends thought they had a couple of reasons to celebrate."

"Akimov said that."

Lenny smiled. "He told you about a party that took place more than thirty years ago? Must have been some hell of a party. What else did he say about it?"

Mike looked down to the keyboard and tapped on the keys, causing the cursor to dance across the screen. He tapped again and the word Fabergé appeared.

Mike said, "My father had too much to drink. He did that a lot, I remember. But that night he lost his money, his watch, then . . ." He deleted the words on the monitor and turned to Lenny. "It's all kind of personal from there on."

"Yeah," Lenny said, clearly disappointed. "Can you describe the woman who shot Akimov?"

"She was tall, had short, blond hair, and damned good-looking." Mike paused for several seconds, "That's not much of a description but that's what I remember."

"Is it possible this good-looking assassin was trying to shoot you?"

"I hadn't thought of that." Mike smiled weakly. "I don't think so. She wasted no time putting her gun on Akimov."

Len paused and rubbed his hand across his chin. "What else can you tell me about Akimov?"

"I can tell you he's a little man. Seventy or a little older. I don't think he has a family." Mike shrugged and added, "I said he was alive, but I'm afraid he's going to die."

"That bad?"

"I'm not sure how much fight he's got in him. And he's alone in a strange country. In fact, I'm having him transferred to a hospital in Englewood. That's right next to us. I'm also looking for someone to stay with him. Someone who speaks Russian."

Lenny made a final note and put his pad away. He thanked Mike Carson for his time and at ten after eleven was back in the cab.

🚲 🚲 🚲

Across from the Gold Coast on Palisades Avenue was the rest of Fort Lee; small homes and duplexes on typically suburban side streets. One such street, Slocum Way, was directly across from the circular driveway in front of the Atrium Palace, and where the yellow cab was parked. A gray Ford Taurus was parked close to the intersection. From it the driver could observe the entrance to the apartment. Viktor Lysenko had driven with all his skill to stay close to the cab on its race through red lights up the West Side Drive to the bridge. He had lost sight of it when he reached the New Jersey side of the bridge. But the yellow taxi was like a moving beacon as it reflected the bright lights that flooded over the ramps and toll plaza. He had caught up to the cab and had followed it to the Atrium Palace.

Viktor watched Lenny Sulzberger get into the cab. It immediately drove off. He picked up the phone and spoke into it.

"They are coming. Forty-five minutes and they will be at Sulzberger's home on North Moore Street."

🚲 🚲 🚲

It was a few minutes before twelve when Lenny's cab stopped in front of 68 North Moore Street. The driver had computed the elapsed time for the round-trip, "Two hours and fifty-eight minutes. And four dollars for the bridge."

"You agreed to a hundred bucks, tolls included," Lenny said. "But here's another ten for keeping me awake with your recipe for curried lamb and fermented eggs." He handed the driver a wad of fives and tens. "I'll skip the eggs."

Lenny took his keys from his shoulder bag and went up the worn marble steps. He was about to turn the key when he was overwhelmed by the frightening sensation that he was not alone. He turned.

Standing on the step below him was a woman. She wore a black raincoat over a stocky body, a scarf covered her hair and was tied under her chin. Her face was colorless and featured a broad nose and thick eyebrows.

"Are you Mr. Sulzberger?" she inquired in a faint, accented voice.

"Lady, you scared the hell out of me. Yeah, but who are you?" Lenny looked behind the woman, searching for others in the sidewalk, or in one of the cars parked across the street.

"I am Katya Mirova. I know about the man who was shot in the automobile place."

"It was in the news. A lot of people know about him."

"I mean to say that I have met him. His name is Sasha Akimov."

Surprised that a stranger would appear at midnight to tell him that she knew Akimov, Lenny pulled the key from the lock, then stepped down to the sidewalk. "Why have you come at this hour to tell me that you know Sasha Akimov?"

"I am sorry that it is late, but I am flying from New York in the morning. Are you not writing about the Mr. Carson who owns the place where Akimov was shot?"

"You seem to know quite a bit about me; where I live, that I'm a writer. How the hell do you know all this?"

"I will tell you, but you must tell me what you have learned about Akimov. Is there a place," the woman gestured suggestively to the door, "where we can talk?"

Lenny looked up to the windows of his apartment, then turned. He said, "There's a restaurant a block south that's open. We can go there."

Yaffa's was at the corner of Greenwich and Harrison, a bar and eatery that was gaining recognition as an institution for the newly burgeoning TriBeCa neighborhood. Its aged-wood bar ran nearly the length of the front portion of the restaurant and had a back bar made from dark walnut and stained oak. Odors wafted up from a kitchen in the basement. A few young people, Wall Street and ad agency types, were finishing a late supper. Lenny led the way to a table that could be made private by pulling a stained maroon curtain. He asked the waitress for two bottles of Evian, a lime and a knife to slice it.

"I thought my day was over," Lenny said, unzipping his shoulder bag and taking out his notepad. "But, if you've got something to tell me about Akimov, I'll be happier 'n hell to listen."

The café, while not large, was illuminated by the dull power given off by 25 watt bulbs scattered on the walls. Small candles in round globes were meant to supplement the light, though the flame in most had died hours before.

Lenny started to write. "Katya Mirova." He spelled her name aloud as he wrote. "Did I get it right?"

He glanced up. Even in the warm light her face was pale and certainly plain enough. But there was a hint of past good looks, and somehow she seemed younger than her stocky body and graying hair signaled. She carried a cloth bag and put it on her lap when she sat down. The water came and she drank half a glass.

"You spelled it right." She nodded. "When you met with Mr. Carson at his apartment, did he tell you why Akimov had come to see him?"

Lenny stared hard at the woman. "How could you know I was there? You were at my loft building as soon as I—"

"I don't wish for it to be a mystery, Mr. Sulzberger, you must trust me. Akimov is wanted by the MVD."

"Look, Katya, I'm not up on current events in Russia, except what I read and some of that stuff hasn't been very good lately." He scribbled the letters. "What's the MVD?"

"The government people say it is the Ministry of Security, but it is the old KGB with a new name. The police. Including the secret ones."

"Are you part of it?"

"No. But they have agents in America."

"Then what are you connected to?"

"I have been hired to follow Akimov. To know where he is at all times."

"Right now he is in a hospital at all times."

"The one in Long Island. Called North Shore Medical Hospital."

"Right again. But it looks like he may be moved to one in New Jersey."

"Then you know the hospital?"

Lenny fanned the pages of his notepad. "Yeah. It's in here someplace. I don't remember things like that when I'm interviewing. Tough enough to ask the right questions and get all the stuff written down. Sweat the details later."

Katya sawed a slice of lime and pinched it into her water. She didn't look up. "What did Akimov say to Mr. Carson?"

Lenny twisted his long body in the chair. "He said damned little. He was shot, you know."

Katya nodded. "But he came for a reason and I thought you may have learned what reason it was."

"You have to understand, Ms. Mirova, I'm a journalist. That means I treat all my sources as confidential and unless I have permission to discuss what I learned during an interview, that information stays with me. Besides, I told you I don't really know all the details I wrote down." He smiled. "I surprise myself with what I find."

Again Katya nodded. "But did Akimov tell Mr. Carson why he came this great distance to see him? You don't have to tell me what he said, only if Akimov explained why he'd come so far."

Lenny leafed through his notes, then suddenly folded the notepad and put it in his jacket pocket. "It's almost one in the morning, and this is a school night for me. I've got to do twenty-five hundred words in two days and I want every one to be a goddamned pearl. All I can tell you is that Akimov talked about old times, and then he was shot."

Katya put her glass on the table and cupped her hands around it. "Will you tell me more about your interview?"

"What's going on here?" Lenny said, his voice raised. "I've told you more than I have any right to discuss. All I've learned from you is that Akimov is wanted by this MVD of yours and you haven't told me why. It's your turn to give me information."

"I told you I am here to watch Akimov. The police want him, and others, too."

"What others?"

"His enemies. There is much crime in Russia today, like the Mafia in your country. Akimov pretended to help pensioners hold on to their little apartments. He was, we say, a *makler*. He would buy their rooms for thousands of rubles less than they were worth. He said they could live in their apartments until they died, but Akimov would not wait for them to die. The old people would die mysteriously and Akimov would sell the rooms at a huge profit. There are many who do this. Akimov is not the only one."

"Not a very nice guy." Lenny uncurled his legs and got up from the table. "If you don't mind, I'll pay the tab and get on home. Like I said, I have to work tomorrow."

"The name of the hospital where Akimov is going. You are not going to tell me?"

"Yeah, I'm not going to tell you." He patted the pocket where he had put the notepad. "It's here, someplace, but it's privileged information. See you around." He went to the bar, paid the bill, and continued out to the street.

Katya looked at her watch, waited exactly half a minute, then followed. The streets were deserted, only a single car was moving south on Greenwich Street. She saw the tall figure a block away turn the corner onto North Moore Street. The car passed and Katya began to run. She moved like a sprinter. At North Moore she saw Lenny Sulzberger cross the street and approach his loft building. Katya immediately crossed to the same side of the street and quickly closed the gap between them.

When Lenny reached the outside door he had his keys ready and inserted one of them into the first lock. As he turned the key, he heard a loud pop and at the same instant felt a terrible burning sensation in the back of his right thigh.

"Shit!" he yelled and reached a hand to his leg.

Then a second loud pop and the same pain erupted in his left buttock. Lenny collapsed, writhing, screaming for help.

Katya ran up the steps and knelt beside him. She put the barrel of her pistol against his cheek. "I could put another bullet here, but then you would be dead and all the pain would be gone."

She took the notebook from his pocket. "Wait until you can't bear it anymore, then yell all you want."

"You bitch. You lousy, fucking bitch," Lenny said, breathing hard, unable to control tears of both pain and anger.

But Katya was gone. She had jumped down to the sidewalk and was running east toward Hudson Street. The Taurus was parked near the corner. As she opened the door the engine started. She slipped in next to Viktor and waved Lenny's notepad.

Chapter 11

Both phones in Mike Carson's home office were ringing. Mike punched the hold button on one of them and said hello into the other.

"Has anyone told you what happened to Lenny Sulzberger?" It was Patsy Abromowitz.

"No. Seems like he was just here." Mike pressed a few keys on the computer and his calendar popped on the screen. June 2—8:04 A.M. Then, into the phone, "Patsy? He walked out of here nine hours ago. What happened?"

"He went home after his meeting with you and got mixed up with a woman who said her name was Katya. They had a talk in a neighborhood restaurant, Lenny went home, Katya followed and shot him. Shot the poor bastard two times. He's in St. Vincent's Hospital and so am I."

"How bad is it?"

"He was hit in the right thigh and left ass," Patsy said without hesitation. "Right now he's flat on his stomach and so damned pissed off he'd bust out if he could."

"I feel sorry for him, but there's nothing I can do. Or is there?"

"Not really. Apparently this Katya woman wanted to know what you told Lenny about Akimov. Lenny claims he didn't tell her anything, so she shot him and took his notebook."

"Lenny saw her? Did he describe her?"

"He told me she was a plain-looking forty-five-year old, on the heavy side."

"That's not the one who shot Sasha."

"What do you suppose she wanted from Lenny?"

"I haven't any idea. Lenny took a lot of notes, but I really didn't tell him very much. Sasha talked about my family, and that's off limits for Lenny or anyone else."

"That may be, but I think whoever's behind all this wants to know

81

what Sasha came all this distance to talk about. More'n likely they figure it wasn't idle chatter about your mom and dad. I think this, Mike:
if they don't find what they're looking for in Lenny's notebook, they
might pay you a visit."

Mike thought a moment. "I think they're looking for something
Sasha never had a chance to tell me. Hell, I'd like to know what it was
myself."

"I'll stay with Lenny until they get him leveled out."

There was a moment's silence before Patsy continued, "You know,
Mike, your Russian friend brought bad luck with him. Like there's
three people in the hospital? I'd hate like hell to see you make it four."

Chapter 12

I t came as a stroke of good fortune that Christopher—Kip—Forbes would be in Paris on business at the very time Oxby was planning his flight to St. Petersburg. Kip phoned the news, suggested they meet in the family's château in Balleroy, a few miles west of Caan, in the Normandy region. The 360-year-old château had been purchased by Kip's father in the early 1970s. Oxby knew the magnificent old château's history, knew about its library of ancient manuscripts, that its walls were covered with historic paintings, and most especially knew that the area surrounding the château was the venue for the annual Forbes International Balloon Meet, held each year on the second weekend in June. Oxby was meeting Kip a week before the festivities. He had not made the guest list (a very short one), because he neither a) owned a balloon, nor b) was a world-famous celebrity.

Kip Forbes, a handsome young man with a strong resemblance to his unpredictable father, was at the door to the château when Oxby alighted from a pure white Citroën. They were about to have their first face-to-face encounter since Kip challenged Oxby to search for and find the Rasputin Imperial egg.

"I hoped you would send a balloon for me," Oxby said.

"The wind is wrong," Kip answered. "But I might send you back in one."

Oxby insisted on a tour and Kip obliged. They talked about art and old books and about French Provincial cabinets and chairs. After that they talked for hours about Fabergé's Imperial eggs.

"My brothers think I've gone off the deep end with this one," Kip said, smiling.

"I've got one of my hunches," Oxby said with total candor. "I'm going to find it."

ǝ҉ ǝ҉ ǝ҉

To avoid a long layover in Stockholm, Oxby ticketed himself on Air France to Frankfurt and Aeroflot flight 656 to St. Petersburg. The Russian TU-134 was similar in design to a Boeing 727, and despite Oxby's premonitions of delay or worse, the plane departed on time. The pilot took advantage of the bright, clear weather and circled north over the Baltic Sea, over Helsinki, then turned to a southeasterly heading over the Gulf of Finland, and finally over St. Petersburg. Seen from the air, cities have a distinctive personality, no two alike, and there was no danger that the city beneath the descending airplane would be an exception. At eleven in the evening on this June 3, two weeks from the beginning of the White Nights, thousands of lights burned unnecessarily under a sky that was as bright as mid-morning. Still the lights reflected off the shimmering sheets and ribbons of water that were everywhere surrounding the city; the canals, the wide Neva River, the bay, and Lake Ladoga. It was a rare picture that Oxby would not forget, one he savored until the plane was on the ground.

They landed at Pulkovo II Airport, a surprisingly small international terminal located less than a mile from the highway that connected St. Petersburg with the town of Tsarkoye Selo, or the village of the czars, and renamed Pushkin by the Soviets.

Perhaps it was the lateness of the hour, but the ritual that usually elongated the process of passport inspection and appraisal by security police moved with unusual speed and Oxby was able to claim his suitcase in less than twenty minutes after deplaning.

For fifteen years Oxby had devoted his life to recapturing, even saving, great works of art. And he had been a student of that vast world of visual and decorative arts. Yet, he had never before ventured into one of the truly great art centers of the world, an omission that was about to be corrected. Oxby would have as his host and guide a man as Russian as a country *dacha*, and as native to St. Petersburg as the infamous czar who founded it.

Yakov Stepanovich Ilyushin was waiting immediately outside the cramped arrivals hall. The two spotted each other, and simultaneously raised an arm and waved to the other.

"*Privyet*," Oxby called out, hurrying past the final barrier. "*Kak dela?*"

Yakov's smile broadened and he responded in rapid-fire Russian that was too fast and too colloquial for Oxby to comprehend.

Assuming Yakov had answered positively to his simple greeting, Oxby said, "We had better talk in English for a few days. Or in French. I can handle that."

"English. I need practice." Yakov took Oxby's arm and half pulling, half guiding, led the way out of the terminal.

Yakov Ilyushin might have been an inch or two taller than Oxby, but he was slightly stooped because the left leg below the knee had been amputated when he was eleven. He had lost it during the siege of Leningrad when he and thousands of others lost fingers and limbs in the record cold winter of 1941. Yakov had a narrow face with high cheekbones. His eyes were fully rounded and colored a warm brown and over each were wispy, gray eyebrows. A quite normal nose seemed large in his drawn-in face. His mouth was a circle made up of full lips, and his teeth were yellowed with here-and-there spots of gold or silver. His stringy hair, long and gray, fell over his ears and touched the collar of his jacket.

Now, barely seventy, Yakov was retired from his position as senior curator in the Russian Museum. Although not as famous as the Hermitage, the Russian Museum held the largest collection of Russian art in the world, outstripping even the Tretyakov Gallery in Moscow. The Oxby-Ilyushin relationship had been forged by their common interest in art, particularly decorative arts, which was at the center of Yakov's academic career. He was an acknowledged expert in Russian iconology, and a collector to the extent his modest salary permitted. Oxby had called Yakov to London on two occasions to provide expert testimony on cases involving stolen art objects. Their most important collaboration involved a valuable icon painting by Andrei Rublyov that showed up at a Sotheby auction. Yakov testified that the painting had been stolen by a German army officer during the war, and somehow Yakov had uncovered the official sales records and established an unassailable provenance for the painting.

Yakov had been recruited by Oxby to direct all his skills toward discovering whether or not Rasputin had commissioned Fabergé to create an Imperial egg or if it was merely a persistent rumor that might, at last, be put to rest.

Yakov's car was a four-door Lada sedan of indeterminate vintage due mostly to the fact that all Ladas of a certain age are exact copies of all the others. Like rings in a tree, the age of a well-preserved Russian car could be determined by the layers of its paint. Few, however, contained the accumulated detritus of academia as littered the interior of the car Oxby climbed into.

"Push it aside," Yakov said. "Probably junk but I can't throw away anything." Oxby would hear the same plaintive comment every time he entered the cluttered relic. Despite appearances, the engine started up immediately and within minutes they had driven off the airport grounds and turned onto the M20, traveling north toward St. Petersburg. Though a veteran traveler, Oxby felt the keen exhilaration that invariably accompanied a new experience. He observed the landscape, the cars, buses, and trucks on the highway, and the surprisingly few buildings they passed. Just then they went by a new Coca-Cola bottling plant, sparkling in its bright red and white colors.

Oxby broke the brief silence, "I hadn't any idea what to expect, but . . ." He made a sweeping gesture." Except for driving on the right side of the road it looks to me like an approach to any one of our big cities."

"Petersburg is Russia's second largest city and this is our main highway. When you drive into London from Heathrow Airport, it is a hundred times more exciting than this uneventful drive."

"Inhaling the exhaust from a thousand lorries isn't my idea of excitement. Frankly, I prefer this."

"No more complaints," Yakov said. "I won't spoil your first trip to Petersburg."

"Since we talked," Oxby said, "have you had any luck with your search to find the Rasputin Imperial egg?"

"I've accomplished one thing. This rumor, this seventy-year-old rumor, has new life, thanks to me."

"Why is that?"

"I wrote a brief story about Rasputin and Fabergé and put it in one of our newspapers. I chose *Nevskoye Vremia*." Yakov pulled a folded newspaper page from his pocket and handed it to Oxby. "It is in Russian, of course, but it has caused several old people to write to me. And my friends in museums call to joke and ask if I am ready to pay rewards for any person who can find Rasputin's egg."

"That's it? No response worth a follow-up?"

"Not thus far. But I am encouraged to put the story in our other newspapers. A friend who knows about computers will put it on what I think you call the Internews."

"The Inter*net*," Oxby corrected. "I'm sure it's the same in Russia."

Yakov laughed. "My computer is old and was given to me by the museum. I think it is more decoration for my home than to make my work more easy."

"Do you believe the Rasputin rumor?"

"I wish to say to you that I heard long ago these rumors about Fabergé and Rasputin, rumors that many of us wanted to believe. Then came the war and rumors of such things were not important." Yakov swerved to avoid a minivan that cut in front of him. He leaned on the horn and swore in English for Oxby's benefit. "The young ones. They think only of themselves."

"They do it in London, too," Oxby said, and reached anxiously for the seat belt that wasn't there. He turned to his friend. "You haven't answered my question. Do you believe the rumor?"

Yakov replied, with a wince, "You know that Rasputin was demonized so much you could not recognize who he was. Just now he is being rediscovered for being a simple and holy man with mystic powers. Not so sinister, or evil."

"You are not answering my question. Do you believe Rasputin asked Fabergé to make an Imperial egg?"

"If it is true," Yakov replied, evading a simple yes-or-no response, "it is also possible he cast a spell over it."

"A curse, you mean?"

"Not as you mean a curse. Not to cause harm or evil to another person. *Blagoslovennyi*, I wish to say, a Russian word that has positive meaning . . . as blessed. Imagine that this egg has power over evil. That you would say is blessed." Yakov glanced at Oxby. "Can you believe that?"

Oxby thought for a moment. "I suppose. Here in your country there are spirits and supernatural beings. Is that what you mean?"

"We have no more spirits than in England, or Greece, or, I would think, America. Remember there is no doubt that Rasputin had his wicked moments, but wicked in matters of the flesh, and in social ways. His sexual appetite was you say gargantuan." He winked. "And alcohol was a problem. That was true, we know. But in Russia, that can be a sign of his manhood."

They slowed and merged with traffic entering a wide street. Yakov said, "This is the Nevsky Prospekt, our most important avenue. Farther east are shops and beyond is our Neva River and Hermitage. I live a few minutes from here. Not in that large building ahead, I am afraid."

"It's monstrous," Oxby said. "What is it?"

"It was many things, like the other old palaces in Petersburg. Now it is called the Youth Palace, but it was originally the Anichkov Palace, named for a captain whose regiment built it. But Anichkov never lived in it."

The name and the little bit of history that went with it meant nothing to Oxby and he smiled indulgently, knowing he had heard the first of many mini-lessons his scholarly host would deliver in the days ahead. If he were to ask who had lived in the palace, Yakov would tell him. And much more and all of it would be interesting, but easily forgotten.

"This is Liteyny Prospekt where we are turning," Yakov said. "Go straight and you come to Bolshoi Dom. It means large building and was where KGB offices were until the breakup. They call it by other names, but it is old KGB."

Again Yakov turned, "This is Belinskogo Ulitsa. *Ulitsa* is street and *Prospekt* means avenue. Okay?"

Oxby nodded with a smile, thankful for the language lesson.

It was a narrow street and immediately Yakov turned into a dirt-and-cinder-topped parking area. He stopped. "This is where I live," pointing to the building on the corner of Liteyny and Belinskogo. "I have made maps for where you will want to go. There," he pointed, "three hundred meters, is the Reka Fontanka, the Fountain River. You will see it. There are buildings and apartments along the embankment. Some are very pretty.

"From here, even I can walk to the Russian Museum, though I do it rarely. There are shops along Liteyny Prospekt and it is five minutes to our metro that is surrounded by food kiosks."

Yakov's apartment was on the first floor, in the rear of a stone and brick building that had been constructed in 1877, the year Russia declared war on Turkey. The historical note was another small lesson passed on by Yakov. A corridor ran from the entry hall back to Yakov's apartment, a distance of twenty-five feet, and had a stone floor. The stuccoed walls were painted in a color that was becoming familiar to Oxby; one he labeled industrial yellow. But Oxby was only able to see the color of the walls for the first few feet. Beyond, the corridor was in complete darkness.

"I am sorry, Jack," Yakov said. "They steal my light bulbs. I try, but I cannot stop them."

"Who steals them?"

"Perhaps Makarova in apartment 11, or Krasikov in 16, or the

Skokov children in 19." He shrugged. "I put in new ones and before you blink, they will be gone."

It was clearly not an unexpected inconvenience because Yakov took out a pocket flashlight and shone a light on the floor for Oxby's benefit. As they approached the end of the corridor, Yakov raised the light and it shone on the door to his apartment.

On the door was a large, bulging envelope, held there by strips of bright orange duct tape. "You have a present, Yakov."

"*Nyeht*," Yakov said and pulled away the tape. "I don't get packages this way. Someone is playing a joke."

Yakov turned a key in two locks and opened the door. The apartment was as black as the corridor they had just passed through, except for little orange and green lights that glowed from a clock or from what Oxby assumed were Yakov's accumulation of electronic devices. Yakov said, "Stay where you are until I put lights on."

The flashlight shone on a lamp. Yakov switched it on, and quickly turned on another. Oxby entered the apartment and found he was standing in a small room, tiny actually, and square-shaped. There was a door in three of the walls, and in each door were panels of painted glass. There was also a table and a bookshelf that ran from floor to ceiling. In the fourth wall were two narrow doors, one to a tiny room that contained the toilet, the other to a room with sink and small shower/tub. The doors were closed but little bits of light came through the colored glass.

"I will give you our grand tour and find drinks for us, but first this package."

Yakov placed it on a table. With his pocketknife he cut away the tape and paper to reveal a dark green box approximately five inches in each dimension, and neatly tied with a pale green ribbon. Taped to the box was a business card.

"You may have guessed correctly," Yakov said, with a semblance of a smile. "I wish to say it is a strange way to send a gift." He handed the card to Oxby. "It is from the Fabergé shop on Bolshaya Morskaya Street."

Yakov slipped off the ribbon and opened the box. Inside, wrapped in tissue, was another, smaller box. He opened it and took out a papier-mâché Easter egg painted in bright colors. The egg was three inches high and held together with two rubber bands. Yakov turned the egg over in his hand, studying it.

"Strange," Yakov said. "It is in pieces, but is held together with rubber bands."

"Unusual gift, if that's what it is," Oxby said. "Open it."

Yakov placed it on the table and when he took away the rubber bands the egg came apart into five pieces. The egg contained yet another package that was two inches long and an inch around. It was wrapped in cloth. Oxby began to unravel the cloth, pressing gently with his fingers, feeling that whatever was inside was in two pieces. When the last of the cloth was removed Oxby was holding a painted, lacquered doll, the kind found in Russian *matryoshka*, or set of nesting dolls. The head, that of a circus clown, had been torn loose and was crushed.

Yakov took the two pieces and joined the neck to the body. Clearly, he was puzzled. He turned the pieces over and over, searching for an identifying mark, but not finding one. Inside the doll's body was a folded piece of paper. Gingerly he removed it, unfolded it, and read the brief message. His face paled and he stared with frightened eyes at Oxby. The note slipped from his hands onto the table.

"What is it, Yakov?" Oxby asked, looking at the unfamiliar swirls of the Cyrillic alphabet.

"They warn me not to look for information about Rasputin's egg. *Assteregaisya*! they say—Look out! Or your head will be crushed like the doll."

Oxby grimaced. He gathered the contents of the package in front of him; the tape and Fabergé box, the pieces of the egg, the cloth wrapping, and finally the broken doll and the note he could not read. All of it was evidence. On the job at home, he would package it in plastic bags and hand it to SO-10, who would photograph and examine it, then send it to Lambeth for a workover by Scotland Yard's great forensic labs.

"Is there anything here that suggests who might have sent this to you? Could a friend be playing a joke?"

Yakov shook his head. "Nothing. The note is printed by typewriter on plain paper. And my friends are not so clever, or so cruel."

"I don't know about Russian dolls. But somewhere there is a nest of dolls that is minus this little man." Oxby glanced at Yakov. "All we have to do is find it."

Chapter 13

The Lysenkos' persistence paid off. Viktor and Galina had pored over Lenny Sulzberger's notebook, struggling to make sense of a strange form of shorthand that defied interpretation. Their training had not prepared them for pages of hieroglyphics laced with Yiddishisms and homemade notations probably picked up from his recently departed Japanese roommate. It wasn't that Lenny had devised a personal language for secrecy purposes, it was just his way. But Viktor spotted an opening. Mixed in with all the gibberish were simple abbreviations, which when plucked out, could be understood.

Lenny had headed his notes with the capital letters MC, an apparent reference to Michael Carson, and throughout his notes had used a capital M for Michael. And similarly he had found it easier to write ENGLWD-RX, than render it in an undecipherable scribble. Using this information, Galina and Viktor began to make phone calls to Patient Information in the North Shore University Hospital and to the Englewood Hospital and Medical Center. After hours of continuous telephoning, on June 3 just before noon, Viktor learned that Sasha Akimov would be transferred by private ambulance to Englewood Hospital and Medical Center in Englewood, New Jersey, on the following day, June 4, at 9:00 P.M.

Now Viktor and Galina could set in motion the plan that they had created even before they knew the name of the hospital where Akimov would be transferred.

The Estonian had doggedly maintained twice-daily communication and had flashed the words of Oleg Vladimirovich Deryabin: "Any failure by the Lysenkos in dealing with the Akimov matter will not be tolerated. In such event, they will no longer be needed."

"What Oleg means," Trivimi explained, "there will be no excuses and no discussion. You will be . . ." He had paused before finishing the sentence. "Let go."

Deryabin's message was thinly veiled and ominous. It meant both he and Galina would be hunted down and killed. Destroy the evidence.

The threat had angered Viktor. "We shall see who is needed and who is not."

᠀᠀ ᠀᠀ ᠀᠀

The Ford Taurus Viktor had rented was gone and in its place was a black Grand Am with red stripes. Do not hold on to a rental car for more than three days was one of many commandments he had learned during his training. Though he had been cautioned to stay with popular American models, the kind that were like so many others on the road, Viktor's personal taste in automobiles favored power and maneuverability. He stretched the rules and chose the Pontiac with a big engine and a dashboard reminiscent of a jet airplane. The catechism further required a change of address every three days or every other day if there was the slightest chance he and Galina might be under surveillance.

While Viktor shopped the rental agencies for his car, Galina took on the job of finding a new place to stay. She chose a small hotel, the Adria, centrally located in Bayside on Northern Boulevard. It was accessible to the major expressways, thirty minutes to Kennedy Airport, out of the way, and had an enclosed parking area

Without consulting Viktor, she phoned an old friend from St. Petersburg, the only person in New York that she knew. Pavel Rakov had left Russia in January of 1994, two years after the Union of Soviet Socialist Republics went out of existence. He had gone directly to New York and lived where he told Galina he could see the big river. They had been introduced by Viktor, who later complained that Pavel could not be trusted. But Galina knew that it wasn't a matter of trust. It was because Pavel had warned her that Viktor was jealous. Even more threatening, he had said that Viktor was an impetuous human time bomb.

Galina needed Pavel's help. She had brought the little Semmerling pistol with her, carefully packing it in two pieces so that it escaped detection. There had been three bullets in the gun when she packed it, and she had brought additional ammunition in small, oddly shaped tin boxes that would show as a compact or lipstick when her cosmetic case was put through the X-ray line. But mysteriously, or because at the last minute she failed to pack them, extra ammunition had disappeared. Pavel was not anxious to oblige her, but after much imploring, he agreed to bring a quarter of a box of Remington 9mm Luger 88 grain cartridges. They met briefly at an Exxon station a half mile from the motel.

At 10:35 on Wednesday morning, June 4, Mr. and Mrs. Gustav Cernik from Prague signed in at the desk of the Adria Hotel. Their clothes and makeup had converted them to a middle-age couple, average in the usual categories. To all the world, they were a typical husband and wife on their every-other-year visit to America. Mr. Cernik, who walked with a slight but noticeable limp, had asked if passports were required. When told they were not, he had slipped the Czech passports back into his wallet along with a Visa credit card. He said he would pay in U.S. dollars.

Their room was an improvement over the Boulevard Plaza Motel, though minimally. The bed was king size and took up a third of the room. In front of the window was a table and two chairs and running the length of the inside wall was a low built-in unit that combined a set of drawers, a desk, and a surface on which the television had been placed.

∎ ∎ ∎

Early that afternoon, the Lysenkos, separately, and appearing in their new roles, entered Englewood Hospital. They agreed to meet in the cafeteria at 2:15. Viktor arrived first, bought a cold drink, and went to an empty table. Several minutes later, Galina joined him. They met as strangers. They exchanged pleasantries, and spoke quietly to each other.

"Akimov will be taken into an examining room in the emergency department," Galina said. "I went there. The nurses wear white. Some are in blue, but most in white and they wear a sweater that has colors, like the one over there." She pointed to a nurse wearing a white cotton sweater with a print of small flowers in pastel colors.

Viktor said, "Security is not tight. They have cameras, but in the usual places. Entrances, stairs, one at the ambulance ramp. No one patrols. I have the number for the pay telephone that is in the corridor outside the waiting room. Everyone wears a name badge and has other pins on their uniforms." Viktor stood. "I'll meet you in the car." He stopped for a newspaper on his way out of the hospital.

In the town of Paramus, a short drive from Englewood, they had found Irene's Uniform Center in one of the shopping malls. Viktor had parked and waited while Galina selected her uniform.

Irene was a pleasant woman who listened sympathetically to Galina's tale of woe, a story that was told with a rush of strangely accented words that were completely unintelligible at times.

"My husband will be angry," Galina had said, genuine tears flowing as she described the contents of her lost suitcases.

"But your husband will understand. It was the airline's fault, not yours."

Galina shook her head, sobbing. "He is very strict. But I must have a uniform. I begin early tomorrow."

Taken by Galina's plight, Irene helped her choose pants and a blouse or basic scrub as Irene called it, a kind of overblouse. And sneaker-style white shoes. Irene recommended that she buy two pairs of scissors, a pocket flashlight, and a pen with a chain and clip. "My customers buy their own stethoscope." Galina asked Irene to select one.

"Maybe you have a badge I could put my name in?"

Again, Irene proved helpful and had put a boxful of pins and badges on the counter; big and little, gold-plated and enameled. Galina chose a pin commemorating Blood Donation Week, and a red ribbon AIDS pin. She also found a badge with ENGLEWOOD HOSPITAL AND MEDICAL CENTER embossed at the top and snatched it up.

"That's one of the old ID badges," Irene had said, grinning, "and I think it looks better than the new ones. They wear both."

For less than two hundred dollars cash, Galina had acquired a nurse's uniform, complete with the basic tools of the trade and an all-important hospital badge. After a few purchases at a stationery store, Viktor would be able to fashion a clip-on ID pin that would look from six feet away like all the other ID pins worn by authorized personnel in the hospital.

❦ ❦ ❦

Galina studied herself expertly in the mirror. She was wearing the nurse's uniform. She scowled. "It looks too new." She smudged her fingers on the bottom of her shoes and rubbed little dark spots around the pockets of her pants and blouse, then she put tiny streaks of face powder on the collar of the blouse. After several more minutes she had aged her uniform and it no longer looked brand-new. She brushed out a wig of brown hair speckled with gray, and then put it on, carefully tucking her own hair inside it. Her scowl disappeared. Galina had transformed herself into a woman of fifty-five, reminiscently attractive, only barely so now. She had used more care with the makeup than when she had surprised Lenny Sulzberger two days earlier. And for good reason. In several hours she would be under close scrutiny.

There was one final detail and Galina concentrated her full attention on it. In a zippered case was a hypodermic syringe and an inch-and-a half-long stoppered vial that contained a clear liquid.

🦋 🦋 🦋

A critical asset in the Lysenkos' scheme was their unswerving dedication to carrying it out with professional skill and efficiency. They each knew their assignments, and as was usual, each was capable of carrying out the other's role.

They knew that they could not allow themselves to be overwhelmed by the immensity of New York: its vast network of highways and city streets; its rivers, bridges, and tunnels; its relentless, heavy-thumping rhythm. And so they concentrated on two locations: the North Shore Hospital in Manhasset, New York, and the Englewood Hospital in Englewood, New Jersey. It was as if all the thousands of other sights and attractions in the great city did not exist.

Viktor had computed the direct air distance between the two hospitals at slightly more than sixteen miles, and the most direct route by car, at 20.6 miles. The ambulance that would carry Akimov might make the trip over one of a dozen different combinations of roadways and bridges, but the most direct and most likely route would take the ambulance via the Throgs Neck and George Washington bridges.

Success would also hinge on Galina's ability to become part of the Englewood Hospital receiving team. She would have to establish herself as a nurse on assignment to the wounded Russian by the time the ambulance carrying Akimov was backed into one of three positions at the emergency receiving dock.

The plan was simple, as good ones usually are. Galina would enter the hospital at 7:30 in the evening and familiarize herself with the layout of the emergency wing as well as learn who held and dispensed authority. She would announce to the duty nurse in the triage station that she had special training and allow a heavy Russian accent to add authenticity to her claim. She would say that her name was Iyrena Petrenkro, the name on her badge. She would tell one of the roving security guards that she was awaiting the arrival of Sasha Akimov from another hospital. At 8:00 P.M. she would venture into the staff cafeteria and have a dessert and cup of coffee. At 8:30 P.M. she would go to the car that she had rented earlier in the day and wait for Viktor's call on her own cellular phone. The call would come at 8:45. Viktor would describe the ambulance that was transporting Akimov to New Jersey. He would give Galina an estimated arrival time.

After talking with Viktor, Galina would inspect herself in one of the small rooms reserved for doctor-family conferences. While there, she would take from her sweater pocket a hypodermic syringe and load it with a lethal dose of sodium pentobarbital.

When Viktor called, he said that the estimated arrival time for an ambulance marked TRANSCARE was 9:25.

& & &

A white Transcare ambulance with orange and red trim turned into the Englewood Hospital and Medical Center at 9:39. Waiting was a receiving team comprised of a male nurse in blue scrubs and white Nike shoes, a security guard with phone in hand plus two beepers and handcuffs dangling from a wide black belt, and Galina Lysenko.

The driver's assistant, a paramedic, opened the double doors in the rear of the ambulance and went inside to help a nurse who had accompanied Akimov during the ninety-minute drive. They released the clamps that held the stretcher in place, then quickly eased it out of the ambulance and extended its legs. The IV unit was reattached and an additional blanket laid over Akimov's body. He was awake, his eyes moving slowly to take in the mystery of another strange place. Then he heard familiar words . . .

"*Dobriy vehcheer.*" The greeting came from a new face that suddenly appeared close to his. "You are in New Jersey," the voice continued in Russian. Galina leaned nearer to him, speaking slowly.

They were inside now. Experienced hands reached under Akimov and with barely a jostle moved him onto a hospital gurney and transferred the IV bottle. The team from Transcare ambulance service followed the gurney into the emergency room and acknowledged that the patient had been successfully turned over to the team from the receiving hospital. They returned the stretcher to the ambulance, then went off to attend to the paperwork.

The gurney was pushed ahead through automatic doors and into a large square room with a nurse's station in the center surrounded by small rooms and stalls partitioned from each other by gray-colored curtains. Half were occupied with patients who waited for whatever treatment their emergency required.

Sounds ranged from mechanical noises to the hissing of air under pressure to the soft moans that came from behind a curtain where the wounds received in an automobile accident were being cleaned and sutured. Akimov was wheeled into a room that bristled with chrome and bright lights and the accoutrements needed to deal with emergencies ranging from broken bodies to a heroin overdose. A young woman physician appeared. She was accompanied by a nurse who exuded considerable authority and maturity and who was clearly the senior-ranking ER nurse. The doctor leafed through the medical report that had been faxed from North Shore Hospital. She examined Akimov, then added her own notes to several of the pages. Watching, one at each side of the bed, were the male nurse and Galina. The doctor looked again at the wound under the thick dressing that covered his neck and upper chest. Akimov's half-closed eyes were on the doctor, watching with silent curiosity.

There was a stirring of voices at the nurse's station. A man had appeared, unannounced, asking for the patient who had been transferred from Long Island. Mike Carson insisted he had come to register his Russian friend, and that he would be responsible for all charges.

Mike was directed to where Akimov was undergoing the intake procedure. He introduced himself to the doctor, spoke tenderly to Akimov, trying in his unfamiliar Russian to comfort the old man. Pleased that the transfer had been successful, Mike Carson acknowledged the help of the staff, then went off in the direction of the registration office.

It was decided that Akimov would be placed in overnight isolation where he could be monitored closely, and where the surgical team would have an opportunity to determine how soon they might schedule the procedure. The doctor wrote out her instructions and discussed them briefly with the senior nurse before going on.

The male nurse was in his early forties and had a full crop of prematurely white hair. He said to Galina, "I'm Nick. Kind of a fixture around here." He frowned. "This poor bugger needs all the help he can get. You know about him? He's the one that got blasted at that car dealer a week ago. Long Island. Funny he shows up in Jersey."

Galina replied quietly in Russian.

"Where you from?" Nick asked. "Tonight's the first time I've seen you."

"I have come for special assignment," Galina said with a heavy accent.

Nick released the brake on the gurney and backed it out of the examining room. "You coming with us?"

Galina nodded. She moved beside Akimov, and as she did, she put her right hand into the pocket of her sweater and gripped the hypodermic syringe. The IV was clipped to the sheet next to Akimov's shoulder and the tube followed his arm down to an angiocath that was taped to the back of his hand.

Nick began to push the gurney ahead. Galina looked back at Nick, whose attention was drawn to the lights at the elevator thirty feet ahead of them.

Galina cupped the IV tube in the palm of her left hand, and at the same instant took the hypodermic from her pocket with her right hand. Expertly and swiftly, she punctured the tube with the needle and quickly discharged 12 cc of sodium pentobarbital. It was done in less than twelve seconds. The dose was more than needed and most likely not all of it would enter Akimov's body because the man's heart and circulation would simply cease to function.

Galina estimated that it would take several minutes, less than ten, to reach the intensive care unit. She knew that in fifteen minutes, Akimov would be dead. She slipped the empty hypodermic syringe back into her sweater pocket, then leaned over and spoke to the Russian. She continued to speak to him as Nick pushed the gurney onto the elevator and the door closed behind them. Galina looked up to Nick.

"He is asleep. That is good."

Nick smiled. "That's good. Means we probably won't have any problems with him."

❧ ❧ ❧

The instant Akimov was turned over to the ICU staff, Galina retreated to the stairs next to the elevator and down to the emergency department. But she turned to a door that led to the main lobby of the hospital. Four minutes later she was standing in the driveway. A Pontiac Grand Am came to a stop in front of her and a door opened. She got inside and the car went off.

Galina slipped off the wig and loosened her hair. She said, "Sasha Akimov is no longer a problem."

Viktor nodded. "As it should be."

Chapter 14

It was a few minutes before 7:30. Mike Carson loaded his briefcase and was about to go off for a morning of meetings in Manhattan when his phone rang. He stared at the instrument for several long seconds, then lifted the receiver.

"Mr. Carson, I am calling from the Englewood Hospital Center. My name is Karen Woo."

"I was going to call the hospital from my car. Everything all right?"

"I'm afraid not." There was a pause, then Karen Woo said with great solemnity, "Mr. Akimov died sometime during the night. I don't have all the details and because we have only sketchy records for him, we're not exactly certain what caused his death."

"But he was all right when they brought him in last night."

"We're sorry, Mr. Carson. He had been badly injured, and, well, I'm calling you because you'll have to claim the body."

"I'm not sure I know what to do. He wasn't a relative, and just barely what you'd call a friend." Mike sat at his desk and sighed heavily.

"But your name is on the records, Mr. Carson. You authorized treatment, including surgery. And you guaranteed payment for all expenses."

"That's true," Mike said. "I'll come over and work things out."

"Ask for me. I'll take you to the right people. One last question. It isn't essential that you authorize an autopsy, but it will facilitate matters. Do we have your permission to go ahead?"

"Is it necessary?"

"I'm afraid so. Because of the circumstances, we must report Mr. Akimov's death to the police. They will want positive assurance that death was not assisted in any way."

"Assisted?" Mike asked. "How could that be?"

"I don't make the rules, Mr. Carson. But it is possible."

❦ ❦ ❦

It was 6:52 A.M. in Bayside, Queens, New York; 3:52 P.M. in St. Petersburg, Russia. Galina was sitting on the edge of the bed, a towel draped loosely around her naked body. Viktor stood beside her, holding the phone to his ear. He was listening, his lips pressed tightly together, his eyes closed in concentration. His mouth opened, as if he were going to speak, then he pulled the phone away and stared angrily at it.

"Son of a whore!" he said into the mouthpiece, then let the phone dangle from his hand.

"Oleg would not talk to me."

"He knew you were on the phone?" Galina asked, rubbing her hair with the towel. "Or did the Estonian lie and say he was not in his office?"

"Oleg was there. I could hear him telling Trivimi what to say. The bastard expects us to report every word that Akimov said to Mikhail."

"We'll tell him," Galina said. "He won't know if it's true or not."

"Oleg won't be easy to fool."

"We'll do it. We're a team."

Viktor moved in front of Galina and put his hands behind her head, then gently pulled her face toward him. Her lips touched his taut stomach, then she reached up and kissed the tiny swelling of his breasts. Her tongue swirled over his nipples and she suckled him gently. Then she lay back on the bed and pulled him on top of her. They lay quietly for a minute, then made love; gently at first, then more vigorously until their passion exploded into a rapturous pleasure each could excite in the other. Then they lay together, arms entwined, silent. After the quiet period, Galina pulled away and sat on the edge of the bed.

She said, "I don't like it here. How soon can we return to Petersburg?"

"It is the only good news from the Estonian. He has reserved our seats on a flight tomorrow evening."

"*Choodyehsniy!*" Galina said happily and fell back against Viktor once more.

Chapter 15

After two days it became painfully obvious to Jack Oxby that he would have to make an immediate and concerted effort to speak and understand Russian. He needn't master it (his natural inclination), but he must quickly learn how to make himself understood, ask questions, and comprehend—at least adequately—the answers. With Yakov's patient help, he took the first and essential step of learning the Russian alphabet.

It was an hour of intense concentration, but he succeeded, even to his friend's complete surprise. Lying in bed, a phrase book and dictionary on his belly, he began to build a vocabulary. He was tired, but stayed awake until after 2:00 A.M. when sleep finally overtook him. In the morning he woke with the opened book by his side.

He greeted Yakov in the kitchen. "*Dobrah eh ootrah.*" The words came slowly as Oxby began the torturous process of speaking in Russian. His "good morning" greeting came a few minutes before 7:00 A.M. as he joined Yakov Ilyushin in the tiny kitchen for a breakfast of hot cereal, yogurt, and toast. Yakov had brewed a pot of strong tea, unaware that Oxby was the rare Brit who had an aversion to the beverage. But, good guest that he was, Oxby added spoonfuls of honey to the tea and sipped it as if it were nectar. The table, barely large enough for two, was crammed between a small gas cooking range and a porcelain sink stained a deep brown from years of water that ran with the effluvium of rust, iron, and other mysterious impurities. In addition to its use as a kitchen, the room, a scant three meters square, served as a space for dining, simple entertaining, and television viewing.

Yakov had insisted that Oxby sleep in his bed while the host made do on an uncomfortable sofa in a room only slightly larger than the kitchen. The room also contained a desk and chair, and the walls were covered, floor to ceiling, with bookshelves that sagged under the weight of Yakov's splendid literary and reference collection. Scattered about were photographs of Yakov's family; most especially of his wife, Valentina, who had died nearly six years previously. So it was that both men had suffered the loss of a wife, and nearly at the same time. A sadness that helped bond their friendship.

Oxby had put the doll, now taped together, in the middle of the table as a constant reminder that others were interested in Rasputin's Imperial egg, and whoever it was, had a grisly turn of mind. He had also placed on the table the clipping from the Schaffhausen newspaper and the handwritten note that Kip Forbes had given him, the one that had been exchanged between Henrik Wigstrom and August Hollming, two of Fabergé's most skillful workmasters.

"I've been remiss," Oxby said. "I meant to show you the clipping and the note long before now. Do you read Finnish?"

"I learned them all—Swedish, Finnish, Estonian, Lithuanian, and the others when I was young. You learn one, the next ones come easily."

Yakov read the newspaper clipping in half a minute, but spent considerably longer on the note. It was brief, barely covering half the small sheets of yellowed paper.

"Do you have a problem?" Oxby asked.

"A little one. I wish to say I can read the handwriting, but there are a few words I don't know. I think they have technical references."

"It's two short paragraphs, it can't be about much. What's it about?"

"The one who is writing the note, he is saying that a spring must be a certain size, and with a specific tension. Those are the words I can't translate. In the second paragraph he says: 'We should choose one even number and two odd numbers. I recommend two—eleven—nine.'"

"What do the numbers mean?"

Yakov shook his head. "He doesn't say."

Oxby closed his eyes, as if he were in the process of putting the information Yakov had given into a special compartment in his brain. "Three numbers," he murmured. "Put together they add up to twenty-two." He shrugged. "Mean anything?"

"I am sorry. I wish I could be more help."

"But you've been a great help, Yakov. A very great help."

"Good. I am pleased."

Yakov collected the plates and took them to the sink. "This morning, we go back to our Hermitage. You will like that."

"Yesterday I spent two hours inside that incredible museum, and it was as frustrating as being limited to five minutes in the best salmon stream in Scotland." Oxby buttered a slice of sour, brown bread, and took a bite of it.

"You'll have time to go through a few galleries. But what is most important is the chance for you to meet Iouna Botkin. I've told you she has more knowledge of Russian decorative arts than any person in Petersburg. Or Moscow." He glanced slyly at Oxby, "What do they know in Moscow? About art, they come to Petersburg to learn."

"I hope you're right about Iouna." Oxby nudged the box toward Yakov. "The only response to your newspaper story was a warning to stop meddling and the crushed doll's head."

*   *   *

Yakov drove slowly so that Oxby could take in the wondrous bronze statues at each corner of the Anichkov Bridge that spanned the Fontanka River.

"They were buried during the siege," Yakov said. "I remember as a boy how we worried the Germans would bomb the bridge and blow up those great horses. But one day I walked over the bridge and they were gone."

Yakov kept up a steady commentary as they drove along the Nevsky Prospekt, each one punctuated with a personal touch, each giving Oxby a novel insight into Petersburg and its trove of architectural wonders.

Yakov's old Lada had a red and blue sticker on the windshield that allowed him to park in restricted zones. Ten years earlier, during the waning days of the Soviet Union, he had cajoled a sympathetic bureaucrat in his district to issue a certificate that entitled him to the same privileges accorded disabled veterans. Survivors of the great siege held unofficial recognition and the fact he had lost part of his leg helped qualify him for special consideration.

It was a brilliant, sunny day. And cool. They walked through Palace Square to the front of the Winter Palace and the main entrance that overlooked the Neva River.

Two older women—*bahbooshkah*, Yakov called them—stood behind the ticket counter and one of them scooped up Oxby's rubles like a trained croupier. He received an admission ticket and a small amount of change that was put in front of him without a nod or even a faded smile. Yakov flashed a card that worked with the magic of an open sesame, and he led Oxby toward the opulent Jordan staircase with its wide steps of marble and carved granite and light standards trimmed with gold. But before they reached the steps, a man approached Yakov.

"*Pozhaluista*," was his hushed greeting. "I know you are Yakov Stepanovich. I must talk with you."

Yakov stopped and sized up the man, who appeared to be about sixty-five and dressed plainly, with a single military ribbon on the lapel of his coat. He was bald except for a thin ring of white hair that circled the back of his head. His face was deeply lined and ruddy and he wore thick glasses that exaggerated the natural bulge of his eyes. The expression on the face was slack, and in his eyes was a hint of fear.

"*Dah*. I am Yakov Ilyushin. You are—"

Oxby eyed the stranger, stepped away from both men, then scanned the great hall through which they had just walked, searching for others who might have accompanied the man who had intercepted Yakov. Hundreds had entered the museum, the buses were emptying their loads of tourists. The man was alone, Oxby concluded.

"I am Leonid Baletsky," the man said to Yakov, and handed him a folded piece of newspaper. It was the story that had appeared in *Nevskoye Vremia*. "I have information about the Fabergé egg." The man paused, as if searching for his next words, then said, "But you must pay for what I tell you."

Yakov translated for Oxby. Yakov shook his head and said, "I have no money to pay a stranger."

"He must have followed us from your apartment, and he looks frightened enough to melt into butter. My hunch says he's playing square. Ask him how much money he wants."

"*Skolka?*" Yakov asked. The two Russians talked animatedly for a minute, then they shook hands.

"A hundred dollars," Yakov said.

Oxby was both surprised and amused. "Only a hundred?"

"You forget what a hundred dollars can buy in Petersburg. He tells us he is a pensioner, that he needs money, and that he doesn't sell information for a living. He has marked a gallery in our museum guide. We can meet there."

Yakov nodded and made a gesture. For an instant it appeared that Baletsky, anxiously looking at the growing mob of tourists, might bolt for the exit. But he began walking, taking short, choppy steps to the Grand Staircase and up to a wide landing. He paused there before continuing up another flight of stairs. Then he was gone from sight.

Yakov studied the floor plan. "We will meet him in gallery 250, a room that contains a ceramic collection."

ஃ ஃ ஃ

Leonid Baletsky was alone in a small gallery, standing next to a display case that contained ceramic masterpieces. In an instant, Oxby realized he was in a room filled with the distinctive blue and white colors of Delft serving bowls, dishes, and vases. It was a collection of magnificent quality, all produced centuries before in Holland. During his years with the Arts and Antiques Squad, Oxby had encountered Delft forgeries and was somewhat of an expert in sorting out the fakes. But never had he seen such an extensive display of the great Delft producers, particularly from the shops of Hoppesteyn and Frederick Frijtom.

Though they were alone in the room, Baletsky looked furtively beyond the door to the endless corridors and numerous galleries that lay beyond. Then in a whisper he asked for the money.

"The money," Yakov said.

"Tell him he will get half now, the balance after he has given us his information."

Yakov explained the terms, which at first confused Baletsky. Then he nodded his agreement. Oxby handed the Russian two twenties and a ten.

It was obvious to Oxby that Baletsky had become more agitated, more apprehensive than when they first met. Oxby said, "Ask him if he thinks he's been followed."

Yakov repeated the question and Baletsky explained that he was embarrassed, but that he badly needed money. "My son is gone and I live alone. There is no work for a man my age." Though the gallery was small and they were the only ones in it, Baletsky looked anxiously into the shadows.

"Tell him he has nothing to fear from us," Oxby said. Yakov spoke reassuringly and after a minute of soft and gentle prodding, Baletsky relaxed.

"Remind him of the newspaper article. Then ask what information he has. Don't interpret for me, I understand a little, and you'll tell me the rest."

Yakov closed his eyes and grimaced, straining it seemed, as if to bring into clear focus all the information he had put into the newspaper article that prompted Baletsky to follow him. Finally, he opened his eyes and smiled. He began talking. Slowly, easily. He was setting a scene, helping Baletsky bring his thoughts forward.

After a minute, Baletsky began his story. Oxby listened intently, able to pick out a few words, but sensing the rhythm of the language. Occasionally a recognizable name popped out: Rasputin . . . Fabergé. Then others, each repeated several times. Karsalov and Kennedy. Yakov wrote notes on a museum folder, twice asking for clarification of a detail. In five minutes a small volume of information passed between them. Finally Baletsky shrugged and his expression said he had no more to say.

"I have learned some things," Yakov said. "I wish to say that this man claims to have seen a Fabergé Imperial egg in 1963 on the day after President Kennedy was assassinated. He does not have proof that the egg was connected to Rasputin, but swears it is the one."

"Does he know where it can be found?"

"He says there are two people who may know. He has told me one name, but will not say the name of the other."

"We need more than a name. Ask for an address or a phone number."

Yakov asked Baletsky for more details.

"He tells me one of the names. Vasily Karsalov. They served together in the navy. Karsalov owned the egg but lost it gambling, but he tells me it is possible that it was given back to him."

"Pin him down," Oxby urged. "Does Karsalov have it or doesn't he?"

Vakov prodded Baletsky, but apparently was unable to get a definitive answer. "He says to find him and ask ourselves."

"Where do we start? Petersburg?"

"He tells me he was sent away by the military. To Tashkent."

"But Tashkent is in—"

"Yes. Uzbekistan."

"When was he sent there?"

"Many years ago. Twenty-five, maybe more."

Yakov fired several more questions at Baletsky, who gave terse responses and showed renewed apprehension.

"There was a trial and after it, Karsalov was sent away. It was, he tells me, like an exile."

Oxby's expression was one of intense concentration. It was difficult enough to think of a logical line of questioning, let alone convert his questions into Russian.

Oxby said, "Karsalov could be dead. Does he know?"

"He thinks not, but cannot be certain of it."

"Then the other person. Who is that?"

Yakov relayed the question. "He says he cannot tell us the name."

"Would he give us the name for more money?"

"No. He wants only his remaining fifty dollars."

"Vahlootoo," Baletsky said, and turned to Oxby, his hand extended, palm up. *"Dollahri!"* he insisted.

Oxby looked at him sternly. "Tell him, Yakov, we want the other name."

Yakov interpreted.

"Nyeht!" Baletsky said resolutely, then rambled on excitedly.

"He is unhappy and will say no more. But he demands that you pay the other half of his money."

Oxby extracted several notes from his wallet and gave them to Baletsky. "He's frightened out of his wits over something, and I'd bloody well like to know what it is. Explain to him that there is more money if he will give us the other name. And if he can tell us where we can find the egg, I'll pay him five hundred dollars."

Yakov made the translation and Baletsky's response was to shake his head and storm from the room.

Yakov started after him but stopped before reaching the gallery door. He looked at Oxby, who had moved in front of another display case, a smile spreading over his face.

"There is something to laugh about?" Yakov said.

"I'm not laughing, not exactly, but I do find it amusing that for one hundred dollars we have learned, assuming Baltesky can be believed, that there is an Imperial egg with connections to the notorious Rasputin. Though we don't know exactly where to find it, we have the name of someone who might have the answer."

Yakov said, "It is like an old Russian saying. 'In Russia everything is a secret but nothing is a mystery.'"

Leonid Baletsky walked as quickly as his arthritic legs would allow, taking some of the steps two at a time as he descended the Jordan staircase to the first level of the Winter Palace. He paused next to a column that rose nearly thirty feet to a painted ceiling. He gathered his money from two pockets and put it into an old leather wallet which he put into the inside pocket of his suit jacket. He looked carefully at the faces of the growing throng, then slipped in among them and proceeded to the exit.

Behind him was a tall, slender man wearing a tailored suit and tinted blue glasses. Trivimi Laar checked his watch and wrote notes in his small notebook.

Chapter 16

Scattered fog caused an airport delay in Helsinki and the Finnair flight from JFK to Petersburg arrived two hours late. Not until nearly 2:00 P.M. were Galina and Viktor inside the terminal and queued in the line designated for nationals. The tourist lines moved at an agonizingly slow pace, but the dozen or so Russians passed through passport control quickly. The Lysenkos claimed their luggage and set off for the exit.

They heard the voice before they saw the Estonian.

"He is waiting."

Viktor scowled. "Where?"

Trivimi Laar ignored the question and proceeded through the lobby and out to a cream-colored Mercedes. Its windows were tinted a smoky gray. Eyes inside could look out, but could not be seen by those looking in. A door opened.

"In here," a voice grumbled.

The big car had been stretched to limousine length. Oleg Deryabin sat on the soft leather seat and motioned for the Lysenkos to sit in the jump seats that faced him. They climbed into the car, each clutching a carry-on shoulder bag, both showing their irritation, both sensing the tension that inevitably surrounded Oleg Vladimirovich Deryabin.

The Estonian got into the driver's seat, closed and locked the doors, and started the engine.

"Give me your report," Deryabin said, his first words unaccompanied with a greeting, or a smile, or a handshake.

"We are happy to be home, Oleg," Viktor said.

"Put your sweet sayings up an asshole," Deryabin said. "Your performance was not satisfactory."

"What do you know of the problems we had?" Galina leaned forward. "What the Estonian tells you?"

"Trivimi tells me precisely what you say to him. He does not write

110

fiction." He lit a cigarette. "So, now we face each other, separated by, what . . . a cloud of smoke?" He wore a stone-rigid expression. His deep voice was flat and unmodulated. "Your report," he demanded again.

Slowly, Viktor began to recount each detail of their mission. Galina offered details where needed, never apologizing, never making an excuse or exaggerating the complexity of their assignment. Viktor said, "We did everything possible to stop Akimov from meeting with Mike Carson—"

"Call him by his correct name," Deryabin snapped. "He is Mikhail Karsalov." He drew heavily on the cigarette and blew the smoke directly at Viktor. "I don't agree. You should have found Akimov easily. He could not speak English, and he moved like a tired, old man. You had every opportunity to intercept him."

"Understand that Akimov did not fly to New York from Russia," Viktor said. "We could not trace him on any airline, and our best hope to catch him was to wait for him at the showroom. But there was a mad celebration. Big crowds, loud music, and police everywhere directing traffic. Two of the salespeople went for a cigarette and we followed them. We took their uniforms, then tied them together and put them in the back of a car."

"They saw you? They could identify you?"

"No," Viktor replied. "We knew better than to let them see us. We came up behind them. Galina took the woman and I took the man. They were young and frightened."

"But you didn't stop Akimov from meeting with Mikhail." Deryabin blew another stream of smoke into Viktor's face. He said, as if pronouncing a death sentence, "That is where you failed."

Viktor pleaded, "We didn't fail, Oleg. We saw Akimov as he was going up to Mikhail's office. We couldn't run after him. Too many people. And the police. Galina followed him as quickly as she could. It was no more than ten minutes, less I think, until Galina was inside Mikhail's office."

"My first shot should have killed him—"

"Fuck the should have," Deryabin cut her off.

Galina said, "He is dead, Oleg."

"Too late he is dead, goddamn it!" Deryabin shouted.

Trivimi interceded. "The writer," he said. "What did you learn from him?"

"His name is Sulzberger. He went to Mikhail's apartment to interview him. We hoped he would tell us what Akimov and Mikhail talked about."

"But you shot him?" Deryabin said.

Galina explained how she had waited for him, and about their brief meeting in the restaurant, and how he stubbornly refused to talk, but that his notebook might contain the information she wanted.

"There was no other way," Galina said. "We agreed that if necessary, I would shoot. I use a small gun and can put my shots where I want. It's better sometimes to cause pain than to kill. I have done this before." Galina's eyes widened, and she glared forcefully at Deryabin. "I hit him here—" She slapped low on her backside.

"You crippled him? Only that?"

"Only that was needed."

"He's still alive, and can talk about it," Deryabin said. "He can recognize you."

"No, he will remember a plain-looking, gray-haired woman who caused him a great amount of pain."

"You have his notebook?

Galina unzipped her shoulder bag, found the notebook, and gave it to Deryabin. "You see that it is written in a code or shorthand. But were able to learn the name of the hospital where Akimov was sent."

Deryabin flipped the pages, then dropped the notebook on the seat next to Trivimi. "We will send this to an old friend who is now with Internal Affairs. She will break it down."

Then silence that stretched for several miles, and broken when Deryabin said, "There is another man in the city who has had a sudden urge to talk about old times. His name is Leonid Baletsky, a friend of Akimov. He came to see me a short time ago. After we met, I hoped not to hear more from him. But we have learned that his memory is playing tricks, and he has started to talk to people about me."

"How do you know this?"

"Good things can happen from a coincidence. We have been watching the movements of a former teacher at the Academy, a pensioner who lives alone. He was also a curator at the Russian Museum. His name is Yakov Ilyushin. He met an Englishman at the airport and took him to his apartment."

"Who is the Englishman?" Galina asked.

"We suspect he is a detective with the London police."

"Scotland Yard?"

"That is possible. I will know for certain in a day or two." Deryabin smoked his cigarette and watched a stream of smoke disappear in a round hole that drew the stale air from the car.

"Yesterday, Trivimi followed Ilyushin and the Englishman to the Winter Palace. They were met by Baltesky in the reception hall. From there, they went to an obscure gallery where the three men talked for fifteen minutes."

Deryabin crushed out his cigarette. His smile broadened. "Trivimi can be very resourceful. He waited for Baletsky to leave the meeting, then followed him down the stairs. He caught up with him and said he was a visitor from Tallinn and would he take his photograph inside the Hermitage. Baletsky did, and Trivimi said it was his turn to take a picture. Then he asked for his name."

Both Galina and Viktor knew not to be dissuaded by Deryabin's smile, yet they knew when he was pleased and when his creative mind was whirring. They knew, too, how Deryabin enjoyed pitting one subordinate against another.

Deryabin produced a photograph and handed it to Viktor. "Recognize him?"

Viktor studied the face, then handed the picture to Galina. Neither could identify the man.

"That is Leonid Baletsky."

The limousine was approaching the Smolenskoye district, an area of small factories and apartment buildings. The car made two turns and came to a stop.

The Estonian said, "Directly ahead is Zagorodny Prospekt. The building on the corner, on the fifth floor, is where Leonid Baletsky lives."

Deryabin said, "Take two days. No longer. This time there will be no mistakes."

Chapter 17

During the evening of that same day when they encountered Leonid Baletsky, the two men had had a spirited discussion on whether they should make reservations on the next available flight to Tashkent. Oxby's contacts in British diplomatic circles were not powerful enough to initiate a search for an obscure Russian naval officer, and Yakov's contacts were of even less promise. The decision rested solely on information Leonid Baletsky had given them, and Oxby's indomitable optimism.

Hunch and hope aside, there were questions neither could answer, including: Was Vasily Karsalov still alive? Had he moved? Does Karsalov have the egg? (After all, he had lost it once in a poker game.) What had all the years done to his memory? Most worrisome was whether they could find him in a far-off city not known to either man.

"Even if you put aside those questions," Yakov said, dispiritedly, "You won't enjoy Uzbekistan. It will be very hot. I am told that Tashkent is not a friendly city. The food is—"

"Inedible. Right?" Oxby reached across the table and patted his friend's arm. "I'm willing to take the gamble. Besides, the trip is on me, or more accurately, my client. I have a hunch that something is stewing underneath all this. First the surprise package, then Baletsky materializes out of the air in the Hermitage." He stood and stretched. "Sometimes we have to go a long way off before we can see what's going on under our noses."

In the end, they agreed to chance it. A phone call revealed that there was a direct connection between Petersburg and Tashkent, but it departed on Saturday, and they had missed it. The alternative was to take the evening flight to Moscow the next afternoon, Sunday, then transfer to a TransAero flight from Moscow's Sheremetyevo No. 2 airport. It would leave at ten past midnight.

"Midnight?" Oxby said, disbelieving. "When does that get us into Tashkent?"

"Six-fifteen Sunday morning. But there is a two-hour time difference."

By noon, Oxby had canvassed half a dozen bookstores hoping to find an English language guidebook that might give him a glimpse of the city where he would soon find himself, though he would settle for one in Russian or French. For all his effort, he was only able to find a ten-year-old gazetteer with missing pages, one that had been published by Intourist. While Oxby canvassed the booksellers, Yakov searched his district library for references to Uzbekistan. He came up with a German guidebook with a few pages on Tashkent, and half a dozen magazine articles covering subjects that ranged from irrigation and fertilization, to gold mining technology, to the paucity of locally produced television programming.

During the four-hour flight to Tashkent, Oxby made a determined attempt to extract at least some useful information from the meager references he and Yakov had gathered. He pestered Yakov for definitions, and separated hard facts from the dry pap that the Soviets fed to foreign reporters and tourists who ventured into Tashkent before that city regained its status as the capital of an independent country.

Oxby learned that five of the former Soviet republics that had been spun off from the old Soviet Union in 1991 were now known collectively as Central Asia, or Turkestan. Uzbekistan was the third largest of the five, yet had the largest population. He also learned that one didn't travel two thousand miles to the hills of the Chatkal Mountains in search of gourmet food or luxurious hotel accommodations. But Tashkent was where they hoped to find Vasily Karsalov and move a giant step closer to uncovering the secret to the Rasputin egg.

🐝 🐝 🐝

0632. Tashkent, Uzbekistan.

A rush of hot air swept over the passengers even before the aircraft was on the ground. Then it thumped down, came to a halt, and slowly taxied to a position about one hundred yards from the terminal. There it stopped, with no further activity for endless minutes as the temperature inside the plane rose ominously. Finally, gloriously, the doors opened and the passengers filed out and down the steps of a ramp that had been wheeled against the plane. Oxby gazed up warily at an early morning sky filled with a dusty haze and felt the intense heat rising up from the cement. He took Yakov's arm and they fell in line behind others waiting to board a yellow box on wheels hitched to a small tractor that would pull it to the terminal.

Once inside they faced the ordeal of passport and visa inspection by a young man with an expressionless face and wearing a black tie pulled loose from a soiled white shirt. The officer had no difficulty with Oxby's passport, but turned his visa over and over, mumbling so indecipherably that even Yakov could not make out what he was saying. The standoff seemed headed for a stalemate until Oxby remembered the all-purpose curative power of a crisp twenty-dollar bill. Promptly a rubber stamp crashed against the visa and it was handed to a very relieved Oxby.

"*Spahseebah*," Oxby said, aware that saying thanks might be taken as an excessive show of civility.

"*Nyehzahshtah*," came the surprising response, accompanied by a wave of the hand inviting Oxby and Yakov to continue on to a room where luggage was passing by on a conveyer belt. They picked up their bags and were sped through customs and on to the stark, poorly lighted central hall of the terminal. Ahead were doors leading to the street, a neon red taxi sign above one of them.

Yakov evaluated his choice of taxis and chose the one with the oldest driver on the assumption the man spoke Russian as well as Uzbek and would be amenable to accepting an offer to serve as both guide and driver. The driver's name was Hoja and he would have to consider a price for his services. He was perhaps fifty-five, with toughened skin and a pair of glinting eyes. He wore dark pants and a sleeveless shirt opened at the collar. Atop his head was a frayed, embroidered skullcap, a sign the driver was probably Uzbek and a Muslim.

Hoja's taxi, an old Lada with bicycle-thin tires, was not airconditioned, nor, Oxby immediately surmised, was any taxi in all of Tashkent. London cabs aren't air-conditioned, he reasoned, but even a hot June day in London could never compare to the oppressive Tashkent heat. Hoja pondered the matter of price and asked for payment in dollars, adding that he could convert dollars to sum, the national currency, that his brother was in the exchange business. A city map might be a problem, his was in shreds and a new and accurate map would be difficult to find, but he would try. He claimed to be familiar with the old Soviet military installations.

"After the Independence," he said in a blend of Russian and Uzbek that Yakov was able to understand, "and the Russian soldiers were gone, we found we had the same president as before and the KGB was called

National Security Committee." He turned and smiled, exposing a mouthful of gold-covered teeth. "You hear that we do not like Russia—but we are just like them."

Yakov showed Hoja the address of the apartment he had miraculously been able to rent as a result of calls to his friends at the University of St. Petersburg. He remembered how each spring there would be listings made up from teachers throughout new and old Russia who made their homes available for rent while the owners took a holiday or found summer work to supplement their low wages. A married couple, Russian expatriates who taught at the university, occupied an apartment in the Frunzensky Torgoviy center—primarily a residential district. Yakov had been instructed to stop in the owner's apartment for a key and drop off an envelope with the rent money.

It was now nine in the morning and the sun's aureole was a hot amber, the sun itself a golden circle of intense heat that had raised the temperature to 100 degrees Fahrenheit and would inevitably send it higher still. It was an arid heat that Oxby found to be tolerable, more so than a rare 85 degrees in humid London. Now they entered a densely populated section of the city, and were on a wide avenue with plane trees, their thick, white-painted trunks emerging out of the cement and bricks. Hoja leaned forward so that he could identify the street, often marked by a sign in Russian on a building at the end of a street. He made a hard right turn onto a narrow street and followed it for several blocks before turning again into an alley only wide enough for one car. The car stopped and Hoja pointed to an opening in an apartment building. Near the door was the rusted front end of a small truck that had been chopped in two.

Oxby got out of the car and inspected the neighborhood. Yakov came beside him. "Remember Jack, don't judge the inside by what you see on the outside."

Apartment 2 was smaller than Yakov's little home in Petersburg. The teaching couple had, with their meager professor's wages, furnished it with imagination and good taste. A Bukhara rug covered nearly all of one wall, and against another stood a glass-fronted cabinet in which were treasures of porcelain and decorative arts from Kazakhstan and Afghanistan. There were photographs and paintings on the walls of mosques and other religious buildings that were stunning in their color and design. The telephone was in working condition, except the call Oxby made to the English consulate was interrupted by other voices before he succeeded in registering his presence. An affiliation with New Scotland Yard helped smooth the process.

"I believe it will be more successful to go directly to the military base," Yakov said. "To telephone and ask for a meeting will give someone reason to start a flow of paperwork that will only block our way."

Hoja helped with the luggage and volunteered to get food from the kiosks and little shops on the street. The heat had chased any thought of food from Oxby, and while early in the day, there were exotic odors in the air that most likely came from the food cooking on braziers outside the neighboring apartment buildings. In a corner of one room—there were four tiny rooms in all—was a range, a miniature refrigerator, and a sink. Ample for breakfast, Oxby contemplated. He was not prepared to set up housekeeping and cook meals in a land where lamb might turn out to be from a young goat, or more likely, an old one.

Hoja returned with two plastic bags filled with fruit, bread, and a few eggs. He also had a victorious glint in his eyes because he had found a map, used by appearances, but of recent printing and listing many of the recently renamed streets.

"It is here, you see, what is called Uzbekistan Pentagon." He smiled, as if making a small joke. "I know these buildings."

Soviet architecture is notoriously uninspired and dull. But in Tashkent, following a devastating earthquake in 1966, new structures were added to the old military complex. Ignored, unfortunately, was the influence of the uniquely beautiful Islamic mosques and seminaries found in Central Asia. Less than three hundred miles distant in Samarkand were the great works inspired by the ruler Tamerlane in the fourteenth century. But not a breath of the freshness of those edifices could be found in the dark, forbidding administration building Jack Oxby was about to enter.

Soldiers in fatigues, rifles held casually at their sides, had moved from the hot afternoon sun into the shade a dozen paces from the entrance. None was of a mind to challenge, and watched, sullenly, as Oxby and Yakov opened the heavy doors. Inside, they spotted a woman officer posting notices on a bulletin board.

Yakov greeted her with a broad smile, one that was not returned. "We have come from Petersburg to find someone who was sent here many years ago."

The officer was young, likely a lieutenant, Oxby judged. "Call her captain," he whispered.

Yakov repeated the purpose of the visit, and when he called her captain she turned quickly to face him, protesting the sudden promotion, but unable to conceal the pride it brought her.

"I am not a captain," she said, pulling at the emblem on her collar. "If you have questions about where our people are assigned, and you have credentials to ask such questions, then you must go to the offices on the third floor." She pointed. "The elevator is at the end of this corridor."

Oxby nodded and said *spahseebah*. Yakov also thanked her, profusely it seemed. They went ahead, leaving behind a new friend. They exited off the elevator into a dimly lit hall. Ahead, through a wide opening, was a large room with windows along each side. Rows of desks faced a wall at the front of the room on which was a large clock and a magnificently framed painting of Islam Karimov, once First Secretary of Uzbekistan's Communist Party and then its first elected executive president. The painting, in the style of old Soviet poster art, captured Karimov wearing some kind of quasi-military uniform.

A stocky man hurried to them, eyes wide with curiosity, sweat trickling down his neck onto a wet shirt collar that was still uncomfortably buttoned. His upper body was that of a weightlifter and he was an officer of middle rank with the demeanor of someone who was, and would probably remain, second in command.

"What is it you want? Do you have authorization? Why was I not informed?"

There were many more questions he would ask but Yakov interrupted and applied his charm. He said that he had been told by someone whose name had suddenly slipped his memory . . . "a general whose name you would know . . . and excuse my impatience, but what is your name?"

"I am deputy assistant of our personnel section and my name is not important." With that he took both Yakov and Oxby by the arm, and with surprising force, began to usher them toward the elevator.

Oxby pulled away and began to speak in Russian, his words coming slowly. "We must find someone. There is money," and he held up his hand and rubbed his thumb over his first two fingers.

"Money for what?" the officer demanded.

"Explain it to him," Oxby said.

Yakov and the officer exchanged words for half a minute when, suddenly, the subaltern released Yakov's arm and invited his surprised guests, as he now called them, to come into his office. Framed awards on the wall said the deputy's name was Y. Sergeev. A small fan tried vainly to move the hot air in the tiny office. "Our air conditioning is broken again. Tomorrow, they always say."

Yakov put a piece of paper on the desk. "There is the name. Karsalov was transferred to Tashkent in 1973. We do not have a date. He had been in the navy, but was sent here."

Sergeev studied the name for several seconds, as if he might remember it. Then he took the phone and barked out an order. Oxby plucked only Karsalov's name from the deputy's torrent of words, but could easily detect the universal "I am the boss" tone of voice.

Sergeev sat back, his elbows resting on the arms of his chair, and his hands folded beneath his chin. He looked pleased, as if positive results from his phone call would inevitably materialize. There was one other chair in the room and Oxby insisted Yakov take it. They waited, in silence, in the pitiless heat.

The phone rang. Sergeev answered and listened, scribbling and occasionally grunting or nodding. Finally, he signed off and put the phone down.

"Vasily Karsalov was transferred to the military hospital in December of 1990. Our records show he was still there, in the psychiatric unit, until 1997. With the change of government, the records are not complete."

"Is he alive?" Yakov asked.

"I cannot answer. The Uzbek military command issued new regulations concerning Russian personnel, therefore we have no way of knowing what has happened to Karsalov. Possibly he is in the hospital, or he may have been sent to his home," Sergeev glanced at his notes, "to St. Petersburg."

Oxby tapped Yakov's arm. "Ask him where we will find the hospital."

Sergeev raised a hand and pushed himself away from his desk. "I understand your question," he said, then turned to face Oxby, and continued in his competent English. "I will show you."

Oxby glared a little admiringly at the perspiring, grinning officer. Don't assume a bloody damned thing, he thought.

"First, you will need this," Sergeev said. "No one will ask for a pass, but it is good to have in case someone decides to do their job." He stamped a couple of pieces of paper and handed them to Oxby.

Sergeev then led the way into a large room that was filled with the noises of old typewriters and ringing telephones. The air, suffused with human smells, was sucked and pushed by fans with blades big enough to lift a helicopter. Sergeev continued on to a row of windows.

"There," he said, pointing at a desultory building, "is where Vasily Karsalov was sent."

Oxby looked through the unwashed windows to a blocklike building made of dark red brick and gray stone. The windows were narrow, but high, and all latticed with strips of black steel. Plane trees provided shade over meandering dirt footpaths, and a high, iron fence encircled the four-storied structure. It had a flat roof from which sprouted a thicket of antennas; seemingly an essential component in every military building.

Even an asylum, for that is precisely what Oxby knew it to be.

Chapter 18

Leonid Baletsky lived in a concrete-block apartment building that seemed to have been constructed with giant Lego pieces. When his wife was alive and able to bring home a small income, and his bachelor son could do the same, life in the cramped space was crowded but tolerable. Then events overtook Baletsky. His wife was institutionalized with tuberculosis and died shortly thereafter. His son suffered a kinder fate when he was suddenly struck prosperous, was married, and moved "uptown" to Tchaikovsky Ulitsa. Baletsky was far from prosperous, having received only three of his monthly pension allotments during the last six months.

Though spartan in the extreme, Baletsky's apartment had one feature that allowed him to escape the grim reality of his diminished world. It was a balcony, two by four meters, enclosed with an iron railing, with a comfortable chair and table on which he could place his glass and the cigarettes that occasionally helped drag him from his gloom. Five floors up and with an unobstructed view to the center of Petersburg, Baletsky would sit for hours, his mind slowly turning over old memories or desperately trying to conjure up new ways to cope with the inevitable shortages he would soon encounter.

It had been two days since he followed Yakov Ilyushin to the Hermitage. Two days since he took the Englishman's hundred American dollars. He emptied his pockets onto the table and put dollars in one pile, rubles in another. It was eleven o'clock, yet the evening sky was nearly as bright as an overcast afternoon. In another thirteen days the White Nights would be at their peak, but even now, there was no nighttime in Petersburg. A quarter moon had risen and hung low, directly above the Holy Trinity Cathedral, two and a half miles to the east. In midwinter, the same moon would shine like a beacon, but on June 8, it was barely discernible. He counted the money. He frowned and counted it again. There was enough to buy food for three weeks, a few bottles of vodka, and cigarettes. He put the money back into his pocket.

ᘉᕯ ᘉᕯ ᘉᕯ

Below, on the street, a car moved slowly, then pulled alongside the curb and stopped.

Galina said, "There, on the fifth floor."

Viktor aimed binoculars up to the balcony where Baletsky was sitting. "He's there, alone," he said.

They got out of the car and walked, first away from Baletsky's building past the apartment building next to it, then circled around to a narrow alleyway that ran behind all of the apartment buildings that lined the street. Pockets of wind swirled between the buildings, blowing thousands of fluffy white seedballs from the cotton grass into the air. They would settle on the hair and clothes like oversize snowflakes.

Viktor anticipated that the entrance to Baletsky's building would be protected by a massive, but typically outdated lock. When he reached the door he had a set of keys in his hand, and in less than a minute slipped the correct one into the keyhole. A fluorescent light in the ceiling hummed and cast a pale, flickering light over the windowless lobby. The elevator door was open and they got into it.

A medley of food odors greeted them, the usual cabbage and onion predominating. When they reached the fifth floor Galina was off first and went directly to the door to Baletsky's apartment. They were identically dressed in gray pants and sweaters, and only Galina's short blond wig and a trace of makeup distinguished her from Viktor.

She rapped gently, then listened for a noise inside. But the only sounds came from televisions in the other apartments on the floor. Viktor flipped on a penlight and studied the two locks. He had the tools and keys to open both; one in a few seconds, the other might take half a minute.

She rapped again. Then a third time.

A voice finally answered, "Who is it?"

"I could not come earlier, but I have brought a package for you. It is from Professor Ilyushin."

"I don't know—"

"You were with him in the Hermitage. The Englishman was with him."

There was no response. Silence. Then the locks were turned and the door opened.

As if they had rehearsed it a thousand times, Galina slipped through the opening and Viktor moved in behind her and closed and locked the door. Galina took a package wrapped in bright green paper from her handbag. She offered it to Baletsky. "This is for you."

Baletsky stared at the package, then at Galina. He was not accustomed to visitors, yet here in his apartment were two strikingly attractive young people who had come to deliver a gift from a man who was, except for a brief meeting, a total stranger. He turned toward Viktor, and in that instant his eyes betrayed the fear that suddenly had begun to sweep over him.

He moved toward the door, as if to open it and shoo away the messengers. "I was not expecting a gift," he said.

"Will you open it?" Galina said.

"Yes. Later." He tapped the package. "A book?"

Viktor nodded in agreement. "Professor Ilyushin is an old friend?"

"He's not an old friend."

"But you acted like old friends when you met in the museum. What were you talking about?"

"About nothing . . . that is . . . the museum. That was it. They are painting the outside of the museum."

"You talked about the green and gold colors? But there was something else, wasn't there?" Viktor had placed his right hand over a leather sheath that was attached to his belt above his hip. Then his fingers snapped and a knife appeared in the palm of his hand. "Perhaps your memory will improve and you will remember what you and Ilyushin talked about?"

Baletsky shrank back a step, his eyes darting from the knife to Viktor to Galina. "It was about a story he put into the newspaper. I had information. I need money and asked him to pay for it."

"What information?" Viktor asked patiently.

"About . . . about nothing you would care about."

Viktor raised the knife to give Baletsky a good view of it. It was a boot dagger; its handle was stout, heavy, and circled with ridges for a firm grip. The blade was four inches long and slightly less than an inch wide and tapered to a needle-fine point. One edge was razor sharp, the other serrated.

"What information?" Viktor repeated.

"About a Fabergé egg." Baletsky paused, transfixed at the sight of the weapon. "An Imperial egg."

Galina intruded. "How much did he pay you?"

Almost apologetically, Baletsky said, "A hundred dollars."

Viktor waved his knife. "What else did you tell him?"

"I said he could get more information from someone who—"

"The name?"

"Karsalov. Vasily Kasilov."

"And what of this Karsalov?"

"I said he was in Tashkent."

"Then what did you tell Ilyushin?"

"That is all. That is true!"

Viktor grabbed Baletsky's left wrist and twisted it sharply. "Not true! What more did you tell the professor?"

"Please, don't. I—"

Viktor sheathed his knife and got behind the older man. He took both of his wrists and pulled his arms up and across his back. Baletsky screamed.

Galina moved in front of him and slapped his cheek with the flat of her hand. "Quiet," she demanded. "Tell us everything."

"There is nothing to tell," he blurted.

Galina sent her knee into his groin. It was a hard, fast blow that doubled Baletsky over. He groaned. "No more," he said feebly. "Go away."

"We've heard enough," Galina said. "There is not much time."

Viktor straightened Baletsky and pushed him into the small kitchen. "We're going to see the view from your balcony."

Baletsky tried to break away. "Take what you want. But go."

Galina opened the narrow door to the balcony. Baletsky struggled feebly to pull away from Viktor, but stumbled awkwardly through the door and against the table next to the chair in which he had been sitting only minutes before.

"Why are you doing this?" he said in a wispy, faraway voice.

"For the view," Viktor said, taunting him. "Perhaps we will be able to see the Admiralty Tower from your little tower."

Baletsky struggled to his feet but before he could take more than a single step toward his kitchen, the heel of Viktor's hand chopped down hard onto the back of his neck. He sagged into a heap, still clutching the package. Galina retrieved it. From his pocket, Viktor took a piece of cloth and ripped it into two pieces. He wound one piece tightly around Baletsky's left hand, all but his little finger. Expertly, he sawed off the finger, then wrapped the hand tightly with the cloth. He put the finger in the other piece of cloth. Galina wrapped it in the same paper that had covered the gift that Baletsky was certain never to see.

"Will it be an accident or a suicide?" she asked.

"That will be a problem for the police," Viktor replied. "Let them argue about the missing finger."

He jammed Baletsky's bandaged hand into his pants pocket, then pulled the unconscious body to the edge of the balcony. Carefully they scanned the windows and balconies on the adjacent apartment building, aware it was possible someone might see the body fall. Viktor reasoned that suicides and accidents don't wait until the world is tucked safely into bed.

They lifted Leonid Baletsky up and over the railing. Neither was counting, but it took about three seconds until they heard a dull, hard sound.

Quickly, but carefully, they removed the spots of blood and any other hint that Baletsky had entertained visitors that evening. Then they went down the steps to the lobby. A lone reveler was returning from a boozy evening and they waited for the elevator to take him away. Only an old woman wailing tearfully as she searched for either her pet cat or dog was encountered as they retraced their route back to the car.

"You told us to call, no matter what the time," Viktor said into the phone. "Leonid Baletsky fell accidentally from his balcony approximately fifteen minutes ago. Possibly a suicide. But, as I have explained to Galina, it will be up to the police to decide."

Chapter 19

Little more than a mile north of the city's center was Kamenny Ostrov, or Stone Island, arguably the most beautiful residential area in all of Petersburg, filled with birch and elm, ponds and gracious homes protected by walls and high fences. Here lived foreign embassy dignitaries, wealthy non-Russians with an unbreakable attachment to Petersburg's cultural attractions, and a more numerous population identified as modern-day entrepreneur. Mixed among this latter group were men who had turned the meaning of capitalism on its ear. Here were former USSR officials or high-ranking operatives from the KGB who had transmogrified into the modern Russian businessman. Nearly all of them were owners or high-ranking officials of companies that operated in an economy where there were no laws to curb monopolies, and, indeed, few laws of any importance to regulate commerce. Those laws that existed were circumvented or violated with impunity.

Unlike the Mafia in America, the new Russian mafiya consisted of many nonallied business owners, each dealing in their own specialty, each with his own organization. In Petersburg, as in other major cities, single-owner cartels had sprung up, many controlling a popular commodity.

On Stone Island, on Bokavaya Alley, near Oleg Deryabin's house, was a magnificent wood and stone affair owned by Yuri Ryabov, president of North Russia Poultry Industries. Ryabov's organization monopolized the importation and distribution of 95 percent of the chickens and turkeys consumed within a hundred miles of Petersburg. The business had been built with a two-hundred-man force who met resistance to buy North Russia Poultry by torching the shop or restaurant kitchen. Each new customer was sold a package of security services, a euphemism for "protection" against the high-voltage presentations by others offering a competing package of security. Other wealthy businessmen on Stone Island included Vorotnikov in flowers, Zorkin, who controlled imported wine and liquor, Almasov, the dominant force in consumer electronics. Dealers in drugs and pornography had higher walls protecting their houses.

Oleg Deryabin's home was an architectural mixed metaphor. An exterior of Victorian turrets and gables that featured a single, glittering onion dome, and an interior furnished with fixtures and appliances that were the most modern that dollars and rubles could buy. Throughout the house were art and artifacts that contrasted eclectically; centuries-old Orthodox icons mixed with silver and enamel pieces from the houses of Saltykov, Rückert, and of course, Fabergé. Several paintings occupied a wall in the living room, undiscovered masterpieces by Russian artists whose works had been suppressed during the age of communism. The house was surrounded by an iron fence, every inch of which was under constant surveillance from television cameras mounted on towers that even a high-power rifle could not disable. The bars on the gate were doubly reinforced and attended around the clock.

In addition to four bedrooms on the second floor, there were bedrooms on the third and several more in a garage that accommodated eight people. These were the necessary facilities for the twelve men who protected Oleg Deryabin twenty-four hours a day, and every day of the year.

During Deryabin's tour of duty in Washington, he had been introduced to the Cosa Nostra by way of contacts his associates had made in the Justice Department. He attended lectures and seminars, including three days of congressional hearings on organized crime in America. He learned how the Mafia was organized and how members were recruited. He had learned about the unwritten codes by which each member participated, was rewarded, or terminated. He had been in Washington when the Berlin Wall crumbled, tensions eased, and U.S.-Russian relationships relaxed to allow cooperation between the MVD and the FBI.

As evidence gathered that *demokratiya* was about to sweep over Russia, a new cadre of businessmen were building the country's new growth industry: organized crime. Deryabin's military training had taught him to look for an enemy's weakness and it had been from that perspective that he studied the Mafia, seeking only to emulate its strengths.

He had bought a dozen videotapes of American movies that romanticized the Mafia. Even had memorized parts of *The Godfather.* And he had read. It was an enriching experience because he had learned to read and speak English. Though his accent was heavy and his vocabulary limited, it was enough. Something inside him said there would be times when he could have a unique advantage over competitors and adversaries if it were not known that he understood English. When he returned to Petersburg he polished the image by apologizing for being such a poor language student. Only the Estonian knew.

To Deryabin's way of thinking, the American Mafia was too structured, too many king's men, consiglieri, underbosses, capos, and soldiers. Too many meant a high payroll and extended communications that could break down. In his organization, the chain of command was simple: Deryabin was chairman and Trivimi Laar was his counselor. Beyond that were office workers and the inevitable security personnel. Each subsidiary business was administered by a man with the title of executive in charge.

Deryabin was alone on the first floor of his house. He stood in front of an open window, a cool, morning breeze blowing over him and sweeping away the smoke from his cigarette. Minutes before he had received an envelope from the executive-in-charge of Neva Specialty, a new and promising subsidiary. It was, ostensibly, the purpose of the small subsidiary to duplicate expensive perfumes, then ship it in liter-size bottles to Moscow, where it was poured, a quarter ounce by quarter ounce, into exotic bottles and then packaged identically to the authentic product. The envelope he held contained a note which described the newest scent perfected by Neva Specialty. When he opened the envelope the space around him was filled by the sweet floral scent of Giorgio perfume.

When Neva Specialty was not in its ostensible mode, its laboratories could be easily adapted to produce a variety of rare chemicals, compounds, and more ominously, virulent biological toxins that could be marketed through an arms dealer in Nicosia, Cyprus, and with whom Deryabin had been negotiating.

The executive in charge was Swiss and a biochemist with experience in the cosmetics industry and in the research laboratories of Hoffmann-La Roche. He went by the single name Maurice.

Chemically produced perfumes was a practical little business, one with the potential for repeat sales and growing profits. But somewhere in the system there had been a series of monumental blunders; the misspelling of Shalimar was a dead giveaway the perfume was bogus.

Chanel No. 5 in a bottle clearly intended to hold Joy brought irate customers back to the shop where the discovery of the hoax caused a flood of rejected merchandise along with dozens of demands for Neva Specialty to return payments that had been made.

Losses were mounting inexorably, and for the recent month, mistakes had cost the unseemly total of twenty thousand dollars. Clearly, New Century could tolerate no further bleeding. Yet Deryabin persisted. His vision of how sophisticated new products produced by Neva Specialty would generate huge profits shouldered aside whatever short-term problems the little perfume factory was experiencing.

☊ ☊ ☊

The Estonian drove a two-year-old Volvo, his single extravagance. It wasn't the largest model, but was comfortable and reliable. A hundred yards from the gate he tapped his ID numbers on the wireless transmitter. When he reached the gates they opened and he continued through and stopped in front of the house.

Deryabin sat at a table next to the window. He started another cigarette, then put a sheaf of papers into a folder which he placed on the table next to his chair. A minute later, the Estonian was seated across from him.

"What is the report from the twins?"

"Viktor called to say that Leonid Baletsky committed suicide."

"Give me details."

"Neighbors of Leonid Baletsky discovered his body last night, a few minutes after midnight. The district police were called. They declared it was suicide."

"How did he do it?"

Patiently Trivimi retold what Viktor had reported to him. "They carried out their instructions. They did not raise suspicions. It was done quickly."

"I'll be the judge of how well the Lysenkos performed. What did they learn of Baletsky's conversation with Yakov Ilyushin?"

"Baletsky told them that he had seen Ilyushin's newspaper article, that because he had valuable information and needed money, he wanted to be paid for his information. He told Ilyushin that Vasily Karsalov could tell him about the Fabergé egg."

"That was all they learned from him?"

"He told Ilyushin that Karsalov had been sent to Tashkent twenty-five years ago."

"What did Baletsky say about me?"

"Nothing, Oleshka. Your name was not mentioned."

"*Govn'uk!* He is a bastard and told lies to Viktor. What lies? I must know!"

"What is the difference? He is dead. Viktor threatened him, but Baletsky could only babble."

Deryabin exploded. "I hold you responsible that we know so little about Baletsky's conversation with Ilyushin. You have no control over Viktor, and again, his impulses overtook him."

"Listen to reason, Oleshka. Viktor learned all that is necessary. Early today I was in the Aeroflot offices, and explained how my dear friend Yakov Ilyushin left Petersburg unexpectedly. I gave a sad story, sweetened it with money, and the assistant manager said she would help me find where he had gone. She retrieved the passenger lists for the past three days and discovered that Yakov Ilyushin flew to Moscow and from there to Tashkent on June 7. He arrived yesterday. The 8th. With Ilyushin was his English friend, Jack Oxby."

Deryabin immediately assessed the task faced by Ilyushin and Oxby. He considered the difficulty of finding a total stranger in a strange city of two and a third million Uzbeks, Kazakhs, Tatars, and Russians. "It will take them at least three days to become oriented and work past the red tape before they find Karsolov."

"We are assuming that he is still alive." Trivimi smiled. "It would be so much simpler for us to discover that he is dead."

"We must proceed on the basis that Vasily is alive, just as this Englishman has assumed. This Oxby." He lit a cigarette. "Seven or eight years ago Vasily was put in a military hospital. A problem here." Deryabin tapped the side of his head.

"If Vasily is not so sick that he can talk, and remember—"

"Of course, that is our problem. They must be stopped. Send Viktor. Galina does not go with him. No distractions."

The Estonian pushed himself back from the table. He studied his hands, rubbing them together. "You are misjudging the Lysenkos. Their assignment in New York was only a hair less difficult than performing a miracle. You demand perfection, and I don't argue with that, but you withhold credit when it is due. They eliminated Akimov, not as quickly as you wished, but they did the best that was possible under extreme circumstances. Then, in less than the time you allotted, they have silenced Baletsky forever."

"What is this soft spot you have for the twins?"

"They are your invention, not mine. I keep them in line, that is my job. But they have begun to mistrust me because of you. They are not twins, they are husband and wife and—"

"They are the twins!" Oleg shouted. "Or should we call them the Gemini? Is Viktor half female, or is Galina more man than woman? Whatever they are, they've been trained to carry out my orders and I will accept no less!"

"There's a limit to how much you can treat them like servants. Their tempers are a match for yours."

Deryabin stared icily at Trivimi, his lips moving as if rehearsing his next outburst. Instead, he said calmly, "You have your instructions. Send Viktor to Tashkent immediately."

"It may be too late."

"And it may not be!" Deryabin shouted. He crushed out one cigarette and started a new one. "Tell Viktor to go directly to the military hospital. There will be a ward for mental patients. He is to contact us as soon as he is in Tashkent."

"Consider, Oleshka, that Viktor can not reach Karsalov in time. That his memory is excellent and he tells Oxby all that he knows about you. I don't believe Oxby has learned for certain there is an egg commissioned by Rasputin, but Vasily may tell him there is. And he could say that he lost the egg to you and believes you still have it. And, he could also say, Oleshka, that you killed Artur Prekhner."

Trivimi carefully observed Deryabin's reaction. As if the Estonian had tapped imaginary nails into an imaginary coffin with each bit of information Oxby might receive from Vasily.

Trivimi said, "What then are Viktor's instructions?"

Deryabin inhaled deeply. "Another accident. Unfortunate, but that is how it must be."

"What kind of accident?"

"Whatever the circumstances dictate. If Oxby hears what Vasily remembers, then he, too, must be killed."

The Estonian got to his feet and went to the window. He turned and faced Deryabin. "You order the death of Karsalov to stop him from talking to Ilyushin and Oxby. But if Viktor cannot stop him from talking, then you say kill them, too! This is craziness, Oleshka."

Deryabin glared at the tall man, then turned away from him. "Give Viktor his orders."

The Estonian hesitated, then went to the phone and dialed a number. He spoke, then listened, then spoke sotto voce, gesturing and imploring. His voice slowly grew louder and more forceful. Finally, he nodded and the conversation was ended.

"It was not easy to persuade Viktor to go on this assignment alone. He said he will not forget that you are dividing him from Galina."

"Did you remind him that he brought this on himself?"

"No, because you are wrong about that."

"We'll see who's right or wrong. When is he leaving?"

"This evening."

"That is settled, then. Good."

With the chore of arranging for the disposal of Vasily Karsalov completed, Deryabin's spirits rose several notches, his little smile once more in place. "I have something to show you." On the floor beside his chair was a corrugated box. He lifted it onto his lap, opened it and took out a car battery. He put it on the table beside his chair. The marking on the battery was DELCO, an American brand, one used in General Motors cars, one Deryabin said had been taken from a year-old Cadillac.

"There is a compartment in this one?" Trivimi asked.

Deryabin inserted a knife blade in a slight depression near the bottom of the battery. Carefully he pried away a two-square-inch section of the outer wall, exposing a cavity that was the size of a package of cigarettes.

"It's like one of Fabergé's Imperial eggs," he chortled. "A door you can't see and a hiding place for whatever surprise we want to put in it."

Trivimi examined the battery, marveling at how expertly the inner function of the battery had been remade to accommodate the hollow space. He replaced the little door, noting that by adding back a year's coating of dust and oil, the battery would survive the closest scrutiny.

"The battery will function the same as before?"

"Not for as long, but it will hold a full charge for several months."

"How many have been modified?"

"Only this one. When we bring the cars in from America, we will take the batteries from the cars and change them."

"Very impressive," Trivimi said. He tilted his head back and sniffed the air. "I can tell that Maurice has been here."

"He sends me a sample of each new formulation. It is Giorgio Perfume. Like it?"

Trivimi leaned forward, his hands clasped and resting on his lap. "I don't want to dampen your optimism, but I have looked at the numbers again. Neva Specialty is draining a very poor asset base and unless there is a dramatic turnaround with other divisions, you must suspend operations in Neva Specialty immediately."

Deryabin stiffened. "Reduce expenses, do whatever you must, but we will not close it down!"

Trivimi unfolded a piece of paper and placed it in front of Deryabin. "At the end of this month, New Century will have lost nearly two million dollars for the first half of the year. We will owe, in total, just under five million."

"We'll pull out of it. We always have."

"Not exactly. A year ago you were forced to sell your most promising division, the only one, incidentally, that was operating within the law."

"The law, the law. Fuck the law!" Deryabin shouted. He grabbed the Estonian's paper and rolled it into a ball.

With his voice at high pitch he said, "You can't do business in this country within the law. When I try it, someone beats the shit out of me." He threw the ball onto the floor.

"The law is one thing," Trivimi began to explain, "but money is something you can't just pretend you have. Bills don't get paid by telling some poor bastard 'fuck the law.' "

"We pay our bills."

"That's not true, and you know it."

"Don't tell me what I know and don't know," he screamed, his face nearly scarlet from both anger and fear. "You come here and show me a piece of paper that says we owe money and tell me to shut down the best hopes we've got to pay our debts and become profitable. Don't throw problems at me. Put answers on your fucking pieces of paper."

"I try, Oleshka. But you take your own counsel. I showed you the numbers a week ago. They weren't as bad then."

"What about all the other operations. Aren't they making money?"

"Income is up, but so are expenses. It costs more money to borrow money. Worst of all, we can't borrow any more. We've hit our limit."

"What limit?"

"The limit the banks have put on us. Not a single bank will lend us money."

"Zuganov will. He promised."

"No. Not Zuganov, or Lobov, or Soskovets."

"The Americans—"

"They were the first to cut us off."

Deryabin's lips moved furiously and silently. Then he said, "How bad is it?"

"We can stretch operations for three months if we cut expenses severely."

Deryabin nodded. "During that time we can bring in the cars and adapt the batteries—"

"You'll need additional money to buy the cars," Trivimi said.

"How bad is it? Deryabin asked again.

The Estonian retrieved the ball of paper. He unraveled it and smoothed out the sheets, then once more placed his financial report in front of Deryabin.

"I will explain all the numbers if you wish, but the important figures are here—" He jabbed at the rows of numbers.

Deryabin stared at Trivimi Laar's precise handwritten notations. "You didn't show me this a week ago," he said in a subdued voice.

"I didn't have all the numbers. Now everything is here."

"Five million dollars?" Deryabin said.

"You might be able to liquidate for about that much money, if you could find a buyer." Trivimi shook his head. "But I promise, you won't."

"What do I do?"

"There is a solution. The amount you need, if my research is correct, is the selling price of the Fabergé Imperial egg."

Deryabin reacted strangely, as if the Estonian's words had a ring of inevitability to them. His body slackened and for moment he was motionless. Then he rose, left the room briefly. He returned carrying a small box.

"I brought it home a few days ago. It might be safer here." He opened the box and took out the Imperial egg. He studied it for a moment. Then he said, solemnly, "No other person has seen this in thirty-five years." He handed it to Trivimi.

Trivimi turned the jeweled egg in his hand, looking with inquiring, interested eyes at the enameled surfaces, at the precision of the workmanship, at the diamonds and sapphires.

"Are you still afraid it carries a curse?" Trivimi asked.

"I thought about it, but I believe the odds are on my side."

"I will make some quiet inquiries about selling it. An auction may be difficult. I think a private sale will be best."

Deryabin nodded, then pushed a folder in front of the Estonian. Emblazoned on the cover was the word KOLESO. Beneath were the words: "Joint Venture Recommendation."

"Go to New York and show this to Mikhail Karsalov."

Trivimi looked through the pages inside the folder. "When?"

"As soon as you know Viktor is on his way to Tashkent."

Chapter 20

The dark and forbidding building Jack Oxby identified as an asylum was officially known and commonly referred to as Number 7. Inside, the walls and high ceilings of the corridors had been covered with a thin, cream-colored paint that allowed streaks of the old paint to show through. All else, doors, fans, light fixtures, was painted in a pale shade of institutional green. The unpainted and unpolished wood floor made snapping and creaking noises as it was walked over. It was a standard design, multiuse army building, probably put up some time in the mid-1930s and used during one of its incarnations as a training academy.

Until recently, Number 7 had been part of the hospital, accommodating military patients and their dependents. Now, the remaining mental patients were housed here, affording them shelter, meager food rations, and a rare meeting with a clinical psychologist who, often as not, was a nurse from the psychiatric ward in the city hospital.

Oxby and Ilyushin circled, found the main entrance, and went in. On the walls were bronze plaques and a bulletin board cluttered with notices and months-old announcements. Four recesses in the wall were empty of the busts that once had been in each, only the plaques that identified the honorees were present. Behind a sliding glass window was a small reception office. In it was an ancient telephone switchboard, a desk, chair, three fans, and no one to tell Oxby and Ilyushin where to find Vasily Karsalov.

Ilyushin discovered a button and a sign next to it that said push for assistance. A distant bell rang, but no one came. He tried again, with the same result.

"Let's see what we can find," Oxby suggested.

There were two large rooms on the first floor. One was a dining room filled with a pungent food aroma and empty of patients. A lone, heavyset woman in a dingy white uniform and cap pushed a cartful of dishes into the kitchen. The other room had tables on which were un-completed jigsaw puzzles, paper and crayons, assorted magazines less their covers, and paperbacks, also without covers. The room was empty save for two men bent over a chessboard at a table next to an open window.

Oxby approached them. "Vasily Karsalov?" he asked.

There was no answer. Ilyushin tried to engage them, but neither re-sponded.

Then a woman's voice came from behind them. "You must not dis-turb the patients."

They turned to find a young woman standing at the entrance to the room. She was dressed severely; dark skirt, white blouse with necktie, black stockings, and flat, black shoes. Her hair, a deep copper brown, was braided and rolled into a chignon.

Ilyushin spoke to her, his tone conciliatory. "No one answered the bell, and we are trying to find a patient."

"Vasily Karsalov. Is that the name I heard?"

The woman came into the room, and Oxby and Ilyushin walked to-ward her. Her face, without a trace of makeup, Oxby evaluated, was beautiful. Only that, or a word like it, described her. He answered her, choosing his words carefully.

"Yes, Vasily Karsalov. We wish to talk with him."

"Who are you?" she asked.

"I am Yakov Ilyushin. My companion is Jack Oxby. We have come from Petersburg to find Karsalov."

"You tell me your names, but I do not know who you are. There is strict policy with visitors. Do you have permission?"

Yakov waved his pass, Oxby did the same.

"Why you are looking for this person?"

Oxby attempted to answer. "It is," he looked at Yakov, "how do you say, 'family affair'?"

Ilyushin explained.

"Come with me," she said.

They followed her from the room and back to a door that opened into the reception office. She sat at the switchboard and dialed several numbers before she smiled and began speaking. After a minute's con-versation she put down the phone.

"This is a new position for me," she said. "I have not heard that name, but there is a V. Karsalov. I have asked for his file." She talked with Yakov for another minute, then grew silent and sat bolt upright, alternating fixed stares at Yakov, then toward Oxby.

"She tells me she is the assistant supervisor, but there is no supervisor at this time. And it is a new position for her. Her name is Tonya. She was born in Russia, but has lived in Tashkent from the time she was three years old."

Oxby looked at his watch and shifted impatiently in the chair. "Do you speak English, Tonya?" Oxby asked.

"Ahngleeyskee?" she said, drawing out the word. *"Nyeht."*

Oxby turned to Yakov. "Do you believe her?"

Ilyushin said he did.

"I don't think there's an abundance of efficiency in this place," Oxby said wearily. "Can you think of a way to speed things along?"

"They don't hurry in this country. Especially in the summer months."

"Perhaps she would like a nice dinner tonight. Or a few thousand of the local currency."

"You would corrupt a pretty lady by giving her a handful of sum?"

"She's too pretty to be corruptible. But, even here, everyone has a price."

Yakov shook his head. "We could lose her cooperation."

The telephone rang. A jingling, metallic sound. "Allo, allo," she said, then followed a stream of Russian sprinkled with Uzbek phrases, all of it speeding past Oxby without recognition. Some of the Uzbek was lost on Yakov.

"I have asked for V. Karsalov's file," Tonya said in her efficient way. "I cannot say how soon it will be brought to us. For now, it is not necessary." She stood, and motioned toward the door. "Come with me."

Off they went, Tonya taking long strides, leading the way to an elevator that dated to the year Number 7 was built. Making sounds Oxby had never heard, it creaked and ground its way to the top floor. Tonya spread the gate apart and walked to the middle of the floor. She stopped in front of a door with number 411 on it. She turned to Yakov.

"I do not know all of the patients, I said I have just come myself. Be aware that you and your friend may be shocked by what you find. Some patients are very ill. They may stare at you and not talk. Some will make no sense if they do. And you should know that some live in a distressful way."

Oxby understood parts of what Tonya had said. Yakov filled him in on the rest.

"Distressful," Oxby repeated the Russian word. "Interesting way to put it."

Tonya nodded, then tapped lightly on the door. A shuffling noise came from inside, but the door was not opened. Tonya tapped again. She said, "Vasily Karsalov, can you hear? You have visitors from St. Petersburg."

The shuffling grew louder, then a key was turned in the lock and the door slowly opened. The man who had opened the door stood several feet inside the room. He was dangerously thin, and though he had a full beard, the hollows in his cheeks were clearly visible. He had a full head of gray hair and with the beard it made his face seem almost tiny. Oxby noted that his eyes were clear, not rheumy as he had feared. He was average height and slightly bent forward. Oxby's initial impression was that he could be fifty or as old as seventy-five.

Tonya had been correct. The room was distressful, though disheveled and unkempt more accurately characterized its clutter and the odor of unwashed clothes.

The room, like all the others, had been a classroom. It was a large room with a high ceiling, and light fixtures that consisted of round, porcelain reflectors and clear bulbs. But half the fixtures had bulbs and apparently even those had long ago burned out. Along the outside wall were several tall windows. A tattered window shade had survived in one of them. There was the usual complement of furnishings, including a bed, chest of drawers, armoire, one large upholstered chair plus two rickety wooden ones, a floor lamp and a table lamp, shelves with books, and other odd paraphernalia.

Most unusual of all was the way Vasily Karsalov was dressed. His pants and shirt were nondescript, but in a room where the temperature hovered near a hundred degrees, he had put on a naval officer's jacket. On the dark blue epaulet that hung lopsidedly from his narrow shoulders were two and a half gold stripes and a single gold star. Oxby didn't know it, but Karsalov had promoted himself two full grades from *mladshiy leytenant* to *kapitan leytenant*.

"Here is your Vasily Karsalov," Tonya said.

"*Dobriy deyehn*," Yakov said, and held out his hand.

Vasily did not respond, nor offer his own hand.

Yakov turned to Oxby, clearly uncertain how to proceed. "What should I—"

"Tell him we are happy to find him. That we will return in the

morning. Ask him if there is anything we can bring. Brandy or cigarettes. Or food. You might also say that we can go to the hotel for dinner tomorrow if he would like."

Oxby patted Yakov's arm, urging him to translate the message. But
it wasn't necessary.

In halting, but completely comprehensible English, Vasily Karsalov
said, "I would like brandy and cigarettes." He nodded at Oxby. "I will
think of other things and tell you tomorrow."

Oxby grinned broadly. "English? You speak it?"

Beneath the heavy beard, Karsalov, too, was smiling. "Some. I will
try."

Oxby ushered Tonya and Yakov from the room and said, as he closed
the door, "This is a good beginning."

ॐ ॐ ॐ

As the elevator made its noisy descent, Yakov said, "We have come
all this way to find him, and you go away without barely saying a word.
Why is that?"

"Our first job was to find him. That, we accomplished. Second was
to determine his state of health, particularly his mind. To that, we have
a partial answer. He is articulate and, as a bonus, he has learned to speak
English."

They reached the first floor and followed Tonya to the reception office. On the desk were several folders. She sorted through them, then
handed one to Yakov.

"These are medical reports. You will see that the last completed examination was made three years ago. I cannot say what changes may
have occurred since then."

Yakov sorted through the pages. "This one, Jack. It says why it is that
Karsalov was sent here."

"A diagnosis?"

"As best I can read it. Four years ago it is dated. There was arte-
riosclerosis, and I see this; multi-infarct-dementia."

"Sounds bloody awful. Ask Tonya if we may borrow the records. Tell
her we'll return every one in the morning."

After Tonya agreed to release Karsalov's file, Oxby and Yakov went
out to find Hoja waiting impatiently. He scolded the two men for causing him to miss a meal with his family, a brief display of anger meant

to elicit a few extra dollars, not demonstrate his familial affection. On the return trip, Yakov confessed that he continued to be mystified by the way Oxby conducted their first meeting with Karsalov.

"In my business patience is most often rewarded. Vasily Karsalov has lived in that sorry room for a long time and he will be there tomorrow and the next day. I invested the hours until tomorrow to assure his confidence in us. He has tonight to think about the brandy we'll bring, and the cigarettes. And a good meal. He's lost touch with simple pleasures and now we are going to take them to him. Thirty minutes ago we walked into his room as strangers. He was surprised. Frightened, perhaps. I did not want to begin our discussions under that cloud. Tomorrow when we meet, we will be friends."

Yakov turned to Oxby and smiled. "And, you are a good friend."

Chapter 21

Viktor Lysenko went through the tedious process of working past agents and government functionaries, then took a taxi directly to the Hotel Uzkekistan in the center of the city. He locked the door to his room and phoned Trivimi Laar.

"You arrived on time, I see," the Estonian said.

"A good flight. Not crowded."

Neither spoke for a half minute, each listening for the slightest hint that Viktor did not have a secure line. Likely an unnecessary precaution, one that was taken nonetheless.

Viktor spoke first. "Galina threatened to leave. Oleg is pushing too hard. And I will say that to him when I return."

"It is his way," the Estonian said. "He bullies so you won't forget he must have his way. Quit if you want. But consider that he will not be happy if you do."

There was another brief silence while Viktor considered what Trivimi had said. "Where do I find Vasily?"

"Oleg was lucky. One of his old connections made a contact in the Uzbek government. Karsalov is in the military hospital—"

"But, where, damn it. I was told there are ten buildings in the hospital."

"Building Number 7. You know it is in the north part of the city?"

"Yes," Viktor said impatiently.

"Don't get too hot because Oleg sent you without Galina. Do your job well and he'll forget his complaints."

Viktor made a list of purchases and chores. In the lobby he exchanged dollars for sum. He was told he could buy clothes in the GUM department store, a few blocks from the hotel. He then bought a pair of jeans, a short-sleeved shirt, socks, black sneakers, and a belt. He also found cigarettes and matches.

Back in his room he changed into the clothes he had bought and approved of the way he would blend in among the other young Russians on the street.

A twenty-minute tram ride took him to a gate that at one time had been the entrance to the military grounds. The tram operator gave him directions to the hospital. It was now 11:30 and the sun was nearly overhead. The temperature would again climb to over a hundred degrees. A car passed and when it approached the building several hundred yards ahead, its red brake lights flashed and the car stopped. Two men got out and went into the building.

Viktor walked on. When he was alongside the car he saw an old sign that hung crookedly from a crumbling concrete post.

ZDANIE 7.

🐾 🐾 🐾

Oxby and Yakov went directly to the elevator and up to the fourth floor. Before they reached his room, the door opened and Vasily Karsalov stepped into the hallway.

"I was afraid you would change your mind."

"No fear of that," Oxby said. "We've been shopping."

Each carried a package and handed their gift to Vasily as they entered his room. Yakov gave him a small bouquet of yellow roses and a single, white peony. Vasily stared at the flowers, unsure what to do with them. "In case you do not have one," Yakov said as he produced a little vase made of plastic. The flowers went into the vase and Vasily gave it a place of importance on his bureau.

"That is good brandy," Oxby said. "Make it last a long time."

Vasily took the brandy and several packages of cigarettes from the bag. He opened one of the packs, took out a cigarette and lit it. The smoke made him cough, but he only smiled and inhaled deeply again.

🐾 🐾 🐾

At the path that led into Number 7, Viktor stopped and surveyed the grounds, then the building. He was close to the car that had deposited the two men and now recognized it as a taxi. He walked over to it. All the windows were lowered and the driver was slouched low in his seat, his head resting on a purple red pillow.

"Is this a hospital building?" Viktor asked.

Hoja opened an eye and looked up to find the owner of the voice. "It was, and may still be. Everything changes."

"Was that a doctor who got out of your taxi?"

Hoja's other eye opened. "Who asks?"

"I am looking for a Dr. Stolov. My father was his patient."

Hoja pulled himself up and rested his hands on the steering wheel. He studied Viktor carefully. "I don't know that name."

"There was another man," Viktor said, rummaging through his pockets. "I have the name, but can't find it. But you can help me." He smiled. "There were two men in your taxi. Do you know their names?"

Hoja watched Viktor's smile snap on, then off. He shook his head and turned the ignition key. A simple *nyeht* was his answer and he drove off.

Viktor watched the taxi disappear behind Number 7. As it did, a bus painted in camouflage colors appeared, its diesel engine clacking loudly, its exhaust exuding a stream of black smoke. It stopped in front of him and the doors opened. One by one in what seemed to be slow motion, old men began to file off the bus and proceed up the path. Viktor fell in behind a white-haired veteran, the stump of his left arm protruding from his shirt sleeve.

※ ※ ※

Out of a plastic bag Oxby took packages of cheese, biscuits, and cans of German beer. From another bag he emptied an assortment of fresh fruit and arranged it on the table. In that setting, with a soft light falling through the window, and the fruit on top of a faded brown towel, it resembled a still life by Cézanne. Vasily Karsalov watched, bemused. He was not wearing his officer's jacket, instead it was draped over the back of the chair he was sitting in. Yakov sat on the bed and Oxby pulled a straight-back chair close to Vasily, forming a tight-knit triangle.

Oxby sat comfortably, relaxed, his legs crossed, his always available notepad on his lap. "If I speak too quickly," he said in English, "please raise your hand. And stop me if I use a word you don't understand."

"It is a beautiful day," Vasily said, pointing at the window.

"First rate. That's what we would say in London."

"You are from England?"

Oxby nodded. "But I am visiting with Yakov Stepanovich, who is an old friend. He was in Petersburg during the war."

Vasily shook his head. "It was called Leningrad. It should be Leningrad today." Vasily drank some of his beer, savoring it. "Why are you talking to me? Did I do something wrong?"

"No," Oxby said. "We want to test your memory."

"It will be hot again. Yesterday was very hot."

"It is cooler if you go outside. We'll go for a walk. Would you like that?"

"I don't like to go there. They may not let me come back to my room."

"Vasily, were you in the navy when you were a young man?"

His eyes widened. "I was in the navy. It was bad. They said I killed someone." He took another sip of beer.

"I don't think so."

"Yes. They said that. It's true, you know."

"That's a reason we have come. To tell you that they were wrong. But do you remember the navy?"

Vasily nodded. "Maybe I remember."

"Can you tell us some things you remember?"

Vasily stared blankly at Oxby. "Brandy. I want some brandy."

Oxby thought a moment. "Later, Vasily. You can have another can of beer."

Vasily handed the empty can to Oxby. "There is nothing to drink in this place."

"It's a hospital," Oxby said.

"I am not sick."

"Tell us what you remember when you were in the navy."

"I was married. Anna."

"She was pretty?"

Vasily held up his hand. "What is pretty?"

"*Meelah*," Yakov volunteered.

Vasily grinned, and nodded. "*Dah.*"

"Did you have children? A little girl or boy?"

"A boy. Mikhail Vasilyovich."

"Where is your wife today? Where is Anna?"

Vasily slowly shook his head. He turned and gazed out the window.

"And Mikhail. Do you know where he is living?"

Vasily did not budge, nor did he speak.

🙢 🙢 🙢

The old soldiers filed slowly along the cream-colored corridor toward the dining room. Viktor peeled away from the procession and stopped at the window by the reception office. He rapped on the glass, then saw the button and pushed it. He pressed several times, impatiently. A door inside the office opened and Tonya hurried to the window and slid it aside.

"What do you want?" she demanded.

"I am looking for a patient. Vasily Karsalov."

Tonya could not conceal her surprise. She eyed him carefully. "Who wants to know?"

"A friend from Petersburg. I am visiting the city and said I would pay him a visit."

"Suddenly, Karsalov has many friends," Tonya said. "Two men came yesterday to find him."

"They are here?" he asked, excitedly.

"You know them?"

He nodded. "I knew some other friends might be in Tashkent." Viktor evaluated her reaction. "It is a coincidence we are here at the same time."

Tonya agreed that was so. "You must go to the building next to this one for permission to visit Karsalov. It is the rule."

She wrote on a piece of paper and handed it to him through the window. Viktor ignored the paper and wrapped a strong hand around her wrist. "I don't have time to be interviewed for a government pass." He pulled her toward him. "I think you will tell me where to find Karsalov."

She could feel his breath. "I can't."

He turned her hand over and placed several twenty dollar bills in it. Then he said slowly, an unconcealed threat running through each of his words, "It is a gift for a favor you must do for me." His grip tightened. "You understand?"

Fear spread across her face. Her eyes were unblinking and her mouth quivered when she was finally able to answer. "Yes. He is in 411."

He closed her fingers over the money, then kissed the back of her hand.

⁂ ⁂ ⁂

Oxby said, "I want you to look at a picture and tell me if you recognize it." From his shirt pocket he took two photographs and handed one to Vasily.

Vasily glanced at it briefly. "An egg?"

"What kind of an egg?"

"Easter egg?"

"When you were a little boy, did you have an egg like that in your family?"

Vasily looked at the photograph again. "Yes. Everyone did."

"Painted many colors. With flowers or the picture of a saint?"

"The flowers. But no saints. They were not allowed."

Yakov joined in. "But we had them from the old days. I think all the families in Petersburg had eggs with pictures of saints and angels. My mother kept them."

"My mother died in the siege," Vasily said. He turned to Oxby. "You know about the siege?"

He nodded. "I have read about it. Do you know what this is?" He gave Vasily the second photograph.

"Another Easter egg?"

"Yes, but anything else?"

"The top of the egg is open."

"Do you know why?"

Vasily shook his head.

"That is a picture of an Imperial egg. It is called the *Orange Tree Egg*, and was made in Petersburg by a famous man. His name was Peter Fabergé. Do you remember that name?"

Vasily crossed his arms over his chest and began to rock back and forth. He rocked ever so slightly at first, then faster and faster still. Abruptly the rocking stopped and again he stared out the window.

Oxby said, "Fabergé made special Easter eggs for the Czars. Each one had a secret hiding place. Did you ever see an egg like that?"

Vasily tilted his head and squinted, trying to pull old memories out of a brain that wasn't functioning properly.

"They were called Imperial eggs," Oxby repeated.

Vasily looked at the empty can in his hand. "More beer?"

"Not now. Eat some cheese and a biscuit."

Yakov spread cheese over biscuits and gave them to Vasily. He ate them avidly and asked for another can of beer. Oxby opened another can, urging that he drink it slowly.

Oxby got to his feet and stood next to Vasily's chair. He leaned down and put his face barely a foot away from Vasily's.

"Listen to what I say, Vasily. And try to remember." He pronounced each word slowly: "Fabergé Imperial egg. Rasputin."

Vasily's eyes were closed. He shook his head, then he nodded. He repeated the motions, searching for words, for memories, all the while mumbling incoherently.

"What's he saying?" Oxby looked at Yakov.

"He's not making sense. I think something about Anna. And Tallinn." Then suddenly, "Rasputin!" Vasily shouted. "Grigori Rasputin."

☙ ☙ ☙

Viktor made a quick inventory of the first floor; the dining room and the patients' game and social room. He found no guards or even the most rudimentary security devices. There was one elevator and one flight of stairs close to the front of the building that went to the top floor and to the basement. He found two exits in addition to the main entrance. The elevator was slow; the stairs faster. There was a fire alarm system that, in keeping with other maintenance, was probably 50 percent operable. At the end of the corridors, farthest from the stairs, was a fire escape accessible through a window.

He determined by inspection on the second and third floors that rooms 211 and 311 were approximately at the midpoint of each floor, and made the assumption that 411 would be directly above the other two rooms. His escape would be by the stairs and he would leave through the exit nearest to the adjacent building. From there he could work his way to the city streets.

It was two o'clock. Viktor began to climb the stairs. There was a landing between each floor and a window. All were sealed closed by old paint. The stairwell was like a chimney, stifling hot and hotter still when he reached the fourth floor. Slowly he started for room 411, hugging the walls to avoid making a noise on the old floorboard.

He had been sent to kill Vasily Karsalov. But there were three men in room 411. How much had Karsalov told Ilyushin and the damned Englishman? Had Karsalov remembered, and told all? If he had, what then?

He was at the door. Voices came from the other side, but he could not understand what was being said. Noiselessly he turned the doorknob. He pushed against the door. Slowly, just a thin crack.

＊ ＊ ＊

"You remember Rasputin?" Oxby said excitedly. "Was there a connection between Rasputin and an Imperial egg? Is that something you remember?"

"My father gave it to me. It was beautiful, but—"

"Yes, go on," Oxby said. Yakov was on his feet now, pleading for Vasily to remember, to say more about the egg.

"I lost it," Vasily said with finality. He stared blankly at Oxby.

"How did you lose it?"

"There was a celebration." His eyes widened as if he had made a great discovery. "It was when Kennedy was killed. In Texas. Is that right?"

Oxby and Yakov spoke in unison, "Yes, yes."

＊ ＊ ＊

Viktor opened the door cautiously until he could slip inside. He closed it and crouched low beside the chest of drawers. He expected a smaller room, but the larger one worked to his advantage. He judged he was nearly twenty feet from the trio. Karsalov was easily identified. He was seated, facing the windows. Viktor identified Yakov Ilyushin—he stood to the right of Karsalov. Then the policeman. Oxby's back was to Viktor.

Viktor made a quick assessment. He might be discovered at any instant, and his strategy was based on surprise. He must get his knife into Karsalov's chest, and have time to make a second strike. He would disable Ilyushin as he went for Karsalov; throw the old man to the floor, stun him. But he could not do the same with Oxby. To outmaneuver Oxby he must catch him completely off guard. Speed! He could not engage Oxby until he had killed Karsalov. It was a simple plan; hit fast, don't engage, run.

＊ ＊ ＊

Oxby said, "Why a celebration, Vasily. What was it about?"

"It was for my new son. For Mikhail. My navy friends came and we gave toasts to Mikhail. We gambled and I lost the egg my father gave me. Was that bad?"

"Not at all," Oxby assured him. "One of your navy friends won it?"

"I remember we were drinking. I was sick from the vodka. Then—"

"Think, Vasily. Think very hard. Who won it?"

Vasily turned his gaze away from the window. His eyes swept the room and then he saw a figure rise up from the floor and rush toward him. The man struck Yakov with a sharp glancing blow, sending him sprawling to the floor. Then Vasily saw the attacker's young face, his eyes glaring, then the knife. The knife came closer and he screamed as it was plunged into his chest. For Vasily Karsalov, the room exploded.

Oxby lashed out and jumped onto the assailant. But Viktor twisted free and lunged again at Vasily and drove the knife once more into his chest. He pulled it free, then raised his arm to strike again. Oxby rebounded, and with hands clenched together, crashed both of them into the side of Viktor's face, knocking Viktor to the floor. The knife fell between them. Oxby picked it up. Viktor rolled over onto his stomach, then pushed himself up and onto his feet. Oxby held his ground, crouched low, his legs spread wide, knees bent, his arms extended rigidly, the knife held tightly in his right hand. Viktor committed himself to fight and not run. Oxby adjusted slightly, just enough so that when Viktor plunged ahead, his head lowered, Oxby brought the knife in front of him. Viktor charged ahead, driving himself into the knife. He made a hideous and terrible yowl. The knife had pierced his right eye and was lodged there. The full length of the blade had penetrated his brain. He would never feel pain again. The heart was alive for seconds longer, then it, too, was dead.

Oxby rushed to Vasily's side. Blood had seeped out over his shirt and onto the pillows of his chair. He was breathing heavily, his eyes open.

"Yakov, go for help!" Yakov had been more frightened than hurt and went as fast from the room as only one good leg would allow.

Oxby tried to stop Vasily's bleeding but there were two deep wounds in the chest. The blade had missed his heart, but Oxby was certain it had cut an artery. He was unsure how to stanch the flow of blood other than to make bandages out of the bedsheet and press them tightly against the wounds.

As if the conversation had never been interrupted, Vasily said, his voice surprisingly strong, "I remember the gambling. There was Prekhner . . . and . . . Akimov, my good friend. Sasha knew my Anna . . . they were both . . . " His voice trailed off.

"Who else was there?" Oxby asked.

Vasily's head shook slightly. "I'm cold."

The room was a virtual oven. Oxby said, "Can you remember who won the Imperial egg?"

"After I was sent to this place I learned that he was not my friend."

"Who is not your friend?"

"They made me guilty for what he did."

"Who, Vasily? What is his name?"

"He killed someone that—"

Vasily's eyes flickered. "Tell Anna . . . and . . . Mikhail . . ."

"What shall I tell them?"

"That I am . . . sorry."

"I will tell them."

A trickle of blood came out of the corner of Vasily's mouth. Oxby wiped it away with the sheet. "Where is the egg, Vasily? Do you know where it is?"

Vasily's eyes flickered again and blood appeared again. His voice was weaker. "Are you here?"

Oxby applied more pressure on the bandages. "I'm here, Vasily. We'll have help soon."

Then Vasily died. Oxby knew the moment his heart beat for the last time. Not because his fingers no longer felt a pulse, but because he sensed that the time had come. Oxby searched the pockets of the young man on the floor. There was no wallet but he did find a hotel key. There was also money in three currencies, cigarettes, and a pocketknife that in the hands of an expert could do considerable damage.

Oxby sat on the edge of the bed and looked sadly at the blood and death in front of him. Who was the killer? There was a chance he would learn the answer. What of Vasily Nikolaiyvich Karasalov? Before, when he had spoken out, no one paid attention. Now someone would.

Chapter 22

It took twelve days, but the last balloon finally came unstuck from the ceiling in the Carson Motors showroom and floated ungraciously down and onto the desk of Georgia Gradowski at the precise moment she was closing the deal on a Cadillac Seville STS equipped with OnStar.

Above her, in his office on the mezzanine, Mike Carson was meeting with two police detectives. Peter Crowley was every bit as brash and impudent as on the day when he and Mike had met in the North Shore University Hospital ten days before. Standing beside him was Alexander Tobias, Detective Sergeant, Major Case Squad, NYPD. Tobias was experiencing the painful sight of watching a fellow officer make a fool of himself as well as destroy the hard-earned reputation deserved by most respectful and conscientious policemen.

"The guy dies from an overdose of whatever the hell it was," Crowley said as if he had single-handedly discovered the Rosetta stone. "No surprise to me. Those Ruskies don't fool around. Right, Alex?"

"Whatever you say," the older detective responded. Alexander Tobias was a man in his mid-fifties, slightly on the portly side with salt-and-pepper hair, a kind, round face plus an authentic New York accent.

Mike looked from Crowley to Tobias. He said, "Maybe one of you will tell me why both of you are here."

"I'm here to close the book on your Russian buddy, Akimov," replied Crowley. "The one that got boffed right here in this office."

"He's dead. Doesn't that close it out?"

"We'd kinda like to know who shot him. Maybe you got some new ideas on that and would like to tell me about them. Besides, Alex here is looking into the shooting of the guy that interviewed you. What's the name? Sulzberger?"

"I've told you everything I know. Right now, I've got a business to run and—"

"And I've got my business to run, too, Mr. Carson. Just 'cause you're a citizen doesn't mean you've got special rights to keep information from the police."

Tobias leaned forward, his ruddy complexion a deeper shade of red than when he had entered Mike's office. "I don't hear Mr. Carson refusing to cooperate. The facts are that a friend was killed, an employee stabbed, and a journalist shot. That's a heavy load for anybody."

"Hey look, I'm just doing my job. You asked me to meet here and turn over what I got on the shooting. So, I'm doing that. Okay?" He pitched a folder onto the table. "Copies in there of all we got." Crowley faced Mike, tilted his head, and aimed a thumb at Tobias. "You want any more, see this guy." At the door he turned, said, "See you around."

Tobias watched him leave, slapped his hands together in mock applause. "I apologize for saying it, Mr. Carson, but that is what you call a perfect ass."

"Ass, yes. Perfect, no."

Tobias said, "I know you're busy but let me tell you why I'm here." Mike was a good listener, and seemed to enjoy Tobias's gravelly voice and colorful speech.

"We're dealing with a major problem with the Russians," Tobias said. "God knows, most of them are trying to get a new start over here. But there's a bad element that's found its way into every criminal activity where they can make a dishonest buck. Right now, the FBI's got a twelve-man force working on Russian organized crime. And, hell, that's just the New York office."

There was no doubt that Mike preferred the company of Alexander Tobias to Peter Crowley. The older detective came complete with a comfort package and the clear impression he knew what he was doing. That was important to Mike. He said, "I'd like to hear what you think of the shootings."

"Pretty lousy is what I think. You mean Lenny, or the Russian?"

"Lenny's going to be all right. But Sasha's dead. "You got any thoughts on that one?"

"Don't know enough to have any thoughts worth repeating. I'll tell you when I do."

The phone rang. "No calls, Edie. I'll be tied up for . . ." He glanced at Tobias, who held up his hand, all fingers extended. "Five minutes."

"Thanks," Tobias said. He emptied Crowley's folder. "Here's a report from the Englewood PD that I received two days ago. And a copy of the Akimov autopsy that confirms everything in the Englewood report. Crowley wrote a couple of paragraphs on a close-out file." Tobias glanced at Mike. "So much for Peter Crowley.

"Let me see if I can give you an answer to your question about the shootings," Tobias went on. "No conclusions, but a fast run-through of recent events might help both of us. Twelve days ago a Russian named Akimov was shot in this office by a young woman, and minutes later one of your employees was stabbed by a man. Both were wearing Carson Motors uniforms. Three days later Lenny Sulzerger was shot by a woman with a Russian accent and his notebook was taken. Two days after that, Akimov died from an overdose of sodium pentobarbital."

"That's as simple as you can make it," Mike said, "and I think it's all tied together. Do you agree?"

"I always leave myself some wiggle room, but there's no question those events are connected. The interesting wrinkle is that we have two eyewitnesses. You saw the woman who shot Akimov, and Sulzberger saw the woman who shot him. In fact he sat next to her in a restaurant and says he smelled her perfume. Swears he could make a positive ID."

Mike said, "Akimov was transferred to the Englewood Hospital without a hitch. I saw him fifteen minutes after he arrived there. Everything seemed normal. But a few hours later, he's dead. How did that happen?"

"That one's pretty easy. The male nurse who took Akimov to the pre-op room says a nurse, or someone pretending to be one, was sweet-talking Akimov as if she was some kind of Russian Florence Nightingale. It seems she was the one who poked a needle in Akimov's IV tube and pumped a load of sodium pentobarbital into him."

Tobias shoved Crowley's papers back into the folder. "Years ago I worked homicide, but now I leave that stuff to the young guys. These days I'm usually chasing after a stolen painting or an art forger. But some guys are on vacation and they threw this crazy ball in the air and damned if it didn't land in my lap. They think I should take a whack at it because I got the experience and have pals in Treasury and in the marshal's office." He smiled. "That and a buck-fifty gets me on the E train."

Tobias took a card from his shirt pocket and dealt it across the table to Mike. "Here's my phone and fax. Give a holler if something comes up. The Englewood police aren't interested in chasing down a Russian who might have killed another Russian. It's a family feud as far as they're concerned. Nassau County has signed off because, technically, Akimov was killed in New Jersey. At least we don't have to put up with Peter Crowley anymore. The book is still open on who knifed Dennis LeGrande."

"The knife?"

Tobias smiled. "The knife is special. Our guys think it's German. Handmade for one purpose: to kill people. But no prints and no way to trace it. Another dead end."

"So, that leaves Lenny Sulzberger?"

"Poor Lenny says he missed a deadline and won't get his big check from *Playboy.*"

"I'll take care of him."

The phone rang.

Mike answered, "I said five minutes and it isn't—" His expression changed. "But I have him down for eleven." He looked at his watch. "It's quarter to ten."

Alex Tobias was edging toward the door, signaling that he would let himself out.

"Wait, Sergeant." Mike turned back to the phone: "Tell him to wait."

"It's okay," Tobias said. "You're busy."

"I've got an eleven o'clock meeting with a man who has come over from St. Petersburg. He's an hour early. There's a small chance he might have known Sasha Akimov. Do you want to meet him?"

"St. Petersburg's a big city, right?"

"Two million plus."

Tobias smiled. "I've had worse odds. You're sure I won't be in the way?"

"Not at all. This guy is looking for an American partner to ship used cars into Russia. Want to listen in?"

"Sure. I'll give it a try."

⅋ ⅋ ⅋

Trivimi Laar entered Mike's office, immediately sized up the men in front of him and nodded to Mike. "I am early for our meeting and thank you for seeing me now. You know that I am Trivimi Laar. We talked on the telephone two days ago."

Trivimi loomed tall and gaunt. He stood erect and spoke with his usual ease and soft voice. He extended his hand and Mike took it.

"I've asked Mr. Tobias to join us," Mike said. "He's with the New York police department and has been investigating some problems that cropped up around here about ten days ago."

Trivimi Laar didn't flinch, blink, or look anything but pleased to shake hands with Alexander Tobias. Tobias greeted him cordially, then backed away and took a seat at the table.

Trivimi insisted on making several preliminary statements. He assured Mike that he was grateful for the opportunity to meet, and said that he brought with him the kind wishes from the chairman of Koleso. And he acknowledged that Mike had made a brilliant success of his life in a short time and under extremely difficult circumstances. And finally, Trivimi proclaimed that Mike had greatly honored his Russian tradition.

Mike listened patiently, accepting the flattery that he recognized was half ceremony and half preamble to the sales pitch that was about to come.

Mike returned to his seat at the head of the table and motioned for Trivimi to sit next to him. Trivimi placed a thin briefcase on the table and placed a small box beside it. He took some papers from the briefcase.

"These are in Russian," he said, referring to the papers he placed on the table. "I apologize, but there was no time to make translations."

"I read Russian better than I speak it," Mike said.

Trivimi put his blue-tinted glasses on the table beside the box. "As you will remember from our conversation, Koleso is a subsidiary of New Century, which in America might be called a mini-conglomerate." He turned to Tobias and smiled. "Koleso means wheel in Russian, a name we think will appeal to our young people." Tobias smiled back, pleased to be included in the conversation.

"American cars, the big ones, are popular in our cities. We hope to bring late models to St. Petersburg. In special cases we would try to match what the buyer wants. For example, a year-old Cadillac that is black and with a sunroof."

"Isn't that happening now?" Mike asked.

"In a small way, but in all of St. Petersburg, there are not thirty places to buy a car. And for repairs, it is very difficult."

"You will have mechanics?" Mike asked. "Good ones?"

"We will get only the good ones."

"Tell me how my company fits your plans."

"You have many showrooms. And they are all located on this coast of America. Is that not right?"

"We're sitting in number 24. We go from Boston to Miami."

"I believe I know where they are." He produced a map. A red dot representing each Carson Motors dealership was spotted along the East Coast. "Is this correct?"

Mike studied the map, moving his finger from Boston south. "You have them all. Except we moved out of Washington into Virginia a few weeks ago."

Trivimi made the correction. "Just so. There are three ports on the East Coast where cars can be shipped. Newark, Baltimore, and Jacksonville."

"We've shipped cars to Europe from all of them. Plus Providence."

"We are aware of that," Trivimi said.

Mike reacted to Trivimi's comment, wondering what else he knew about Carson Motors. He said, "Who will supply the vehicles?"

"We thought of buying from other dealers, but we prefer to deal only with you."

"There will be papers and forms to complete. And every car must be prepped."

"What is this prepped?"

Mike grinned. "An inspection. To make sure the cars are in good condition."

"You will do that," Trivimi agreed. "You will also prepare the documents for the shipping company and U.S. customs."

"We must have what is called a title for every car. A dock receipt can't be issued unless the vehicle's VIN number matches the title exactly. There are customs police in the yards and on the docks. They search for stolen vehicles and look for counterfeit paperwork."

"I have heard of this VIN. It is what, exactly?"

"Every car sold in America has an identification number that contains seventeen numbers or letters. The first number is for the country where the vehicle was made. The second number is for the name of the maker, the third is the vehicle classification, and so forth to seventeen. The number is engraved on a metal or plastic plate and concealed at three different places on the vehicle. One is under the windshield, and can only be replaced or altered by taking off the glass. One may be located where it requires special tools to find it. When customs suspects a stolen car is being shipped out of the country, they will check all the VIN locations in that vehicle for a counterfeit number. From experience, I know they can be tough on cars going to Russia."

"Everything will be legal. I assure you." Trivimi referred to his notes. "Next, you will put the car on board a ship?"

"No. We will deliver the car to a stevedore contractor, along with the title and delivery instructions. The stevedore then prepares dock receipts and notarized copies of the title. Our driver will park the vehicle inside the security gates, the stevedore will tell him exactly where it is to go. That is the last time we will touch it. The vehicle will be tagged with shipping information and at a later time it will be driven onto a ship by a stevedore. The contractor charges a fee for each car. We will pay the fees and bill you for reimbursement."

Trivimi nodded, slipped off his steel-rimmed glasses and replaced them with the blue-tinted pair. He added to the notes he had been taking, then looked up. "We come to the costs," he said. "I hope that today I can give you a trial order to see how a permanent relationship between our companies can be arranged. If that order is for fifteen cars, how much will it cost?"

"What kind of cars? What model year?"

"We start with Cadillac and maybe work down from there."

"The Seville or Fleetwood or the least expensive model?"

"In the middle. Not the top, not the bottom."

Mike searched among the papers in front of him. "I can sell you a year-old Seville SLS for twenty-six thousand dollars. A little more or less, it will depend on what we've got in the system. That's an average price."

"If it is two years old?" Trivimi asked.

Mike looked at his numbers. "Five thousand less. Maybe twenty-one thousand."

"What are the other costs?"

"Prep, delivery to the port, paperwork. Another three hundred and fifty. Including the stevedore."

"For an Oldsmobile or a Pontiac. How much?"

"Eleven to fifteen. Average cost about thirteen-five. The other costs are the same."

Trivimi put a pocket calculator to work, punching in numbers, grimacing each time he hit the subtotal button. "Fifteen cars, a year old, split ten Cadillacs and five Oldsmobiles, will cost . . ." He printed the numerals, large and bold on the paper." A little more than three hundred and thirty thousand dollars."

"Add shipping costs. Those cars will have to go through Bremerhaven and be transferred to another ship into St. Petersburg. Another thousand per car should cover it."

"Three hundred fifty thousand. An average of about twenty-three thousand a car."

"How much will you sell them for?"

Trivimi smiled. "More than twenty-three thousand."

"Are you giving me an order for fifteen cars?"

"Before I leave I will tell you how many of which models we will order from you."

"You must pay all the costs before the cars are shipped to the port."

"All costs, you say?"

"We've never done business before. So I can't accept credit terms. Only full payment. Perhaps later, if we have a permanent arrangement between our companies, we can make credit arrangements through one of our banks."

"How long will it take for you to find the cars and make them ready for shipment?"

"Less than a week."

Trivimi nodded, showing a little surprise, as such a transaction in Russia would require several months and involve a half mile of bureaucratic red tape.

Mike had additional questions regarding the pending and more permanent affiliation with Koleso; nuts-and-bolts types of details. He asked about insurance and liability and said he would require a guarantee against fraud or the risk of forwarding stolen vehicles.

"We will guarantee every car we sell you to have a clean title. But understand this. When you buy expensive late-model cars on the open market, expect to find that one out of every twenty is a stolen car. It goes with the territory."

"I understand," Trivimi said. "You can expect that Koleso will have everything in correct order. We will see to that."

"Do you have a lawyer? An American lawyer?"

Trivimi searched his pockets. "The lawyer is in Brooklyn. That is New York, correct? And like you," Trivimi said with an ingratiating smile, "he is a young Russian who came to this country and is very successful." He found a business card and handed it to Mike.

"I'll have our lawyer contact him." Mike wrote out a name and phone number and gave it to Trivimi.

"I will do this today." The Estonian put his worksheets and folders in his briefcase and exchanged the blue-tinted glasses for the steel-rimmed ones. He turned to Tobias.

"What do you think, Detective Tobias. This is a good business?"

"You're out of my league. I drive a Chevy Prizm."

Trivimi said, "There will be very big profits for everyone."

"Very big doesn't mean everything," Mike rejoined. "A 15 percent return on investment, with minimum risk. That's when I get interested. When I build a new showroom, I know exactly how much profit I will make after two years, and after five."

"Russia will someday be a rich country. The richest in the world!"

"But America *is* the richest. No waiting for it to happen."

There was no arguing the point. Trivimi said, "Is there some other information I can get for you?"

"No. I'll call you if I think of something."

Trivimi put his papers back into his briefcase, leaving behind the proposal. "Now that our business is concluded, I would like to present a gift from our company." Trivimi opened the box that he had put on the table at the beginning of the meeting. From it he took a package wrapped in a luxurious gold paper. It was a small package, and Trivimi handed it to Mike ceremoniously.

Mike knew that Russians liked to give and receive gifts, and to refuse would be an insult. He took the box and placed it on top of the papers in front of him.

"Open it," Trivimi said. "I think you will be pleased."

Mike unwrapped the box and opened it. The gift was a silver and enamel *charka*, a drinking cup. The bowl was chased with miniature icons, the side straps and edges of the cup set with crimson red rubies. Mike turned it over admiringly. Indeed, he thought to himself that the cup might be worth several thousand dollars.

"You like it?" Trivimi said.

"It is much too generous."

Alex Tobias looked on, an amused expression on his sunny face. He said, "It's a beautiful gift. Is it by chance the work of Peter Fabergé?"

"How did you know?" Mike exclaimed. "Look at the inscription." He handed him the cup. "On the bottom."

Tobias studied the silverwork and the stones with a professional eye, then turned it over to see the markings.

"I've seen some bad imitations of Fabergé's work. It's much more enjoyable when I know I'm holding the real thing."

Tobias handed the cup to Mike, then faced Trivimi. He said, "Trivimi

Laar is an interesting name, but it doesn't have a Russian sound to it. Are you Russian?"

Trivimi shook his head. "My name," he said proudly, "is Estonian. It was also my grandfather's. Parts of Estonia have been governed at one time or another by every country that surrounds it. The Soviet Union, most recently. We protect ourselves by learning everyone's language. I learned to speak Russian when I was very young."

"And you speak English very well," Tobias said.

"English is the world language."

"May I ask another question?"

"Of course. And I will answer, if I can."

"Not quite two weeks ago, a young woman came through that door and shot a man who stood exactly where you are standing. We don't know who that woman was, but we do know that the man was named Sasha Akimov. He had come to America to visit Mr. Carson. Akimov survived the bullet wound, but not an overdose of a drug that was secretly given to him four days after he was shot."

Alex Tobias talked slowly, pausing between sentences, carefully evaluating every tiny reaction Trivimi made while listening to the tragedy of Sasha Akimov's first and final visit to America.

"Is it possible that you knew Sasha Akimov?"

The Estonian looked from one face to the other, settling on Alex's. He said, unblinking, "No, I did not know him."

Chapter 23

Even as the airplane gained altitude, the air that whooshed noisily from the vents in the overhead did little to relieve the oppressive heat in the cabin. Not until they had leveled out was the stale, hot air of Tashkent replaced with the cool, dry air scooped up at thirty-five thousand feet. Yakov escaped the torment by falling asleep, his head slowly listing and coming to rest against Jack Oxby's shoulder.

Oxby had not recorded the details that had filled the previous thirty-six hours and had begun to compile a chronological account of all that had transpired. An hour into the flight he put down his pen and looked down to the vast emptiness of the land below. The air was clear, not a cloud between him and the vast Muyunkum Desert in neighboring Kazakhstan.

He closed his notebook. His thoughts returned to a room in a converted military academy that had been Vasily Karsalov's haven, home, and prison. He remembered the events as if they were unfolding before him on a motion picture screen.

🦗 🦗 🦗

The burst of violence that broke out in room 411 brought death to Vasily Karsalov and, in a bizarre twist of events, the same fate to the man who had thrust a knife into Vasily's chest. When Yakov Ilyushin finally returned, he brought Tonya and a man with a thick, black beard. They stared, helpless and horrified, at the sight of Vasily slumped in his chair, covered by his own blood, wet and glistening. Lying on the floor, his head turned as if he were curious to see who had come into the room, was the dark-haired intruder. One eye was open and staring wildly, protruding from the other was the handle of the knife.

It would have been charitable to say that the man who returned with

Yakov was a doctor. But whatever his specialty may have been, it did not include traumatic injury. He stared at the dead men, blanched, spoke to Tonya, then rushed from the room.

"Nikitin is a dental assistant," Tonya said. "There was no one else to bring. He will arrange to have the bodies taken away."

Oxby went to the man lying on the floor. "Who the bloody hell is this? And who sent him?" He had stared at the awful sight until he could tolerate it no longer and got onto one knee and slowly wrapped his fingers around the heavy knurled handle of the knife. For an instant his stomach muscles tightened as if they might explode, then the nausea subsided and he pulled the knife free. Blood over the eye had begun to darken. Oxby closed the other eye. He stood, still staring at the face, a handsome face he realized for the first time.

Oxby had asked Tonya if she would report the killing to the police. Her reply was perfunctory. "This is a military hospital. The general's office will make that decision."

Oxby had not waited to observe whatever protocol still existed. "We'll look at his belongings. There may be jewelry or family mementos that should be returned to his wife. Or his son."

"The veterans who die are usually without any family. They have no possessions. Nothing to pass on."

"Will he get a proper burial?" Yakov asked.

"Sometimes yes . . . sometimes—" Tonya didn't finish.

It seemed there was little for Oxby and Yakov to account for in Vasily Karsalov's tiny empire. On the wall were prints in thin black frames and two small icons that had been valuable only to Vasily. The old furniture was worthless, and the clothes that hung in a musty armoire were tattered and soiled. In the chest of drawers they found what remained of his pathetic wardrobe. Oxby searched his pockets and found a piece of cloth that served as a handkerchief, scraps of paper neatly folded with notes scribbled in a tiny scrawl on each, a couple of pencils, and no money.

On the table beside the bed was a brass lamp with a torn shade, and a radio that dated to the 1960s. Neither appeared to be in working condition, yet Oxby discovered they both did, though the thin sound of music that came from the radio was accompanied by a high whistle. Next to the radio was a calendar. Xs had been penciled over each day through June 9, a nightly ritual Oxby surmised. Oxby X'd out the 10th, the final day of Vasily Karsalov's life.

There was also a small stack of books; a Russian-English dictionary, a few paperbacks, a thin book of poetry, and a well-thumbed anthology of the works of Mark Twain with little slips of paper marking favorite passages in *The Adventures of Huckleberry Finn.*

There was a single, deep drawer in the table. The contents were neatly separated by boxes of varying size and arranged as neatly as a museum presentation. One of the boxes contained jewelry; brooches and earrings along with a man's rings and a pair of cuff links. In another were pipes and pipe reamers, cigarette lighters, and empty matchboxes. In one were small tools including pliers, screwdrivers, and assorted small wrenches. Two boxes were filled with photographs. Two more were stuffed full with old notepads and sheets of paper clipped together and a package of postcards and letters tied with a length of thick, brown string. In one small box was a wristwatch. Oxby recognized the name. It was Bure, worth more than all of Vasily's possessions combined. Both hands pointed to 12. Noon or midnight, Oxby wondered.

Oxby emptied one of the boxes. He selected a notepad, one Vasily might have owned when he was a schoolboy. Yakov recognized it as such. A thick elastic band held it together. Its pages were smirched, a few torn, others dog-eared, and all were impossible for Oxby to decipher.

Yakov managed to read several entries in another notepad. "This one is his diary, or it was when he had something to write about. The last date I see on these pages was made six years ago. But, look here . . . it must have been written yesterday."

Yakov had struggled to make out the handwriting: "Two men came today. They will come back tomorrow and will bring brandy and cigarettes. Why have they come to see me?"

"He finally had something to look forward to," Oxby said.

Oxby untied the string around the postcards and letters. He and Yakov searched for postmarks or dates to give some idea how old the correspondence might be. The package yielded four letters written by Sasha Akimov. Anxious as Oxby was to learn what Akimov had written, the contents of all this largesse of letters, diaries, and correspondence would have to wait until Yakov could place it under a strong light and transcribe the scrawls and scribbles.

Both men sorted through the photographs. Vasily had put them in chronological order and had written notes on the margins or on the back of each one. As in the diary, his handwriting was a tiny script, impossible for Oxby to read. All of the older photographs were black and white, a few more recent ones in color. They recorded times in Vasily's life when he was a family man; a husband and father.

"Yakov, look here."

Oxby was holding a faded photograph, the blacks now sepia. It was a picture of a young woman flanked by Vasily and an old man Oxby judged to be seventy-five or perhaps older. The young woman was holding an object, looking at it self-consciously as people do when they are asked to pose. Though very small, Oxby could see bands of metal and small jewels on the object, which was unquestionably shaped like an egg.

Oxby asked Yakov if he could make out the impossibly cramped chirography. Yakov said that the old man was Vasily's father and the young woman was named Anna. Anna was holding a Fabergé egg. Yakov strained to make out the words. "Vasily's note says that Count Yusupov gave his father the egg . . . that he had worked for the count and that he was sorry that Nina could not be in the photograph. It was her camera, she took the picture."

"Who is Nina?"

Yakov shook his head. "This does not say. The diary may tell us."

Oxby studied the faces in the photograph; Vasily, his father, and his wife. He remembered their tiny embarrassed smiles. How normal. He looked long and hard at the egg, convinced that it was the egg that Rasputin had commissioned Fabergé to design, worried at the same time that it was nothing more than a cheap imitation.

Then he remembered the sight of two dead men, their blood congealing, their tragedy so terribly fresh. And he recalled the sights and smells of Tashkent, especially his introduction to *choy* and *plov*; honey-sweetened tea, and rice with boiled meat.

෴ ෴ ෴

Yakov snored peacefully. Oxby gently moved his head onto a pillow. The stewardess brought a cold bottle of beer and Oxby relished it. Tucked into his notebook was the Karsalov family photograph. He studied it. He knew their names now; Vasily, Anna, and Mikhail. The little boy was probably six when the photograph had been taken. In Yakov's search of the photographs he had found another photograph of the little boy with the name Mikhail printed on the back. "Mikhail, my little man," Oxby said, "your daddy is dead. I'm sorry."

He opened his journal and wrote:

It won't be tomorrow when I put from my mind the sights and fear I experienced during those minutes of helter-skelter in room 411. Nor will I quickly forget the terrible stench. Each man experienced an instant of terror, and, with death, their guts and kidneys leaked out. Spectacular to me that, even at the time of death, the body performs such awful miracles.

It was difficult for Yakov. But he was a good soldier, though a sick one for a while.

Viktor Lysenko. Even though he blundered badly, he accomplished his mission. Vasily is dead. He picked a fight, but with the knife in my hands he didn't have a chance. I have taught hand-to-hand combat for twenty years.

Hoja took us to the Hotel Uzbekistan. I had the key to Viktor's room. I found a wallet, airline ticket, two passports, a professional makeup kit, and his travel itinerary.

The Czech passport was in the name of Gustav Cernik. The photograph shows him to be a man of fifty. With his makeup he could make the conversion in ten minutes.

The Russian passport is likely his true identity, though not a certainty. Viktor Y. Lysenko—Age 29—student (isn't he a bit old to be a student?).

Most remarkable was the fact his passport had been stamped New York June 5. It shows he returned to St. Petersburg 6 June: 1411 hours. What was he studying in New York?

༝ ༝ ༝

There was an announcement that the air ahead was choppy and the FASTEN SEAT BELT sign was turned on. Oxby tightened the belt around Yakov, did the same for himself, then settled against the pillow he tucked against the window. He tried to sleep, but it became quickly obvious that today was one of the tomorrows he must pass through before he would be able to switch off the memory of room 411.

Three hours out of Tashkent and they were still over the flat deserts of Kazakhstan. High-level clouds obscured the ground, but had the sky remained clear he might have glimpsed the dying Aral Sea and more endless stretches of a treeless plateau.

He stared at the steel blue sky, and allowed snippets from the past two weeks to come into his head and tumble over each other in an incoherent rush. He finished the chore of recording everything that had transpired in Tashkent. Another chapter, and a tragic one, in a book he never thought he could write. Absently, he removed a piece of paper from the back of his notebook. He unfolded it and looked at three numbers, the same numbers he had copied from the note written by Fabergé's head workmaster. He had stared at the slip of paper many times, though he knew the numbers as well as his own birthdate.

"Two eleven nine," he said with intense concentration, as if demanding his brain to find a meaning for the numbers. After several minutes he put the paper back into the notepad, then slipped it and his pen into his shirt pocket.

Kip Forbes's name popped into his mind. He owed him a letter and would write from Petersburg. He would say that he had new evidence, though circumstantial, that Fabergé had indeed created an Imperial egg, one that had not been registered. He would tell Kip that his next step was to find proof that such an egg had indeed been produced. Then find it.

But there were forces that had shown a fierce determination to stop him from finding the egg. And they played a rough game. For keeps.

Chapter 24

When Viktor failed to report on Wednesday, June 10, and again on the 11th, the Estonian alerted Oleg Deryabin, who spent the greater part of a morning on the phone recruiting old contacts from Naval Intelligence and the KGB to commence a manhunt that was to reach from Petersburg to Moscow to Tashkent. An odd clash of networks intertwined; department chiefs in the Ministry of Internal Affairs spoke over secure telephone lines with crime bosses in their limousines. Then at noon on June 13, a fax was received in the communications center of New Century. A brief message stated that the body of Viktor Lysenko had been identified by a doctor in the military hospital in Tashkent, and further, while the body had been kept under refrigeration for three days, it was necessary that it be claimed immediately, or it would be buried in a public cemetery.

"Get his goddamned body back here," screamed Deryabin. "If you have to pay someone off, pay the son of a bitch. I want Viktor's body in this city in twenty-four hours."

It was, by the strictest measurement of Deryabin's tangled personality, an act of compassion.

⁂ ⁂ ⁂

At 1:00 P.M. the same day, the Estonian told Galina Lysenko that her husband was dead. She took the news, initially, with an eerily emotionless detachment.

"How did he die?" she asked.

"We have no details. It could have been an accident."

"Viktor didn't have accidents," Galina said through lips that barely parted.

Trivimi replied, "He was due for one. Acting too bold at times. I'm afraid he didn't think it was a dangerous mission. He impressed me as being overconfident."

"Viktor was the best there could be," she said, angrily brushing away the tears that suddenly erupted, crumbling her resolve not to show a weakness.

"That may be, but it doesn't change the fact that he is dead."

"He would be alive if Oleg had sent me along with him."

"I advise you not to make a war with Oleg. He, too, is angry."

"Oleg is angry?" she said contemptuously. "Oleg only cares because he has lost someone to do his dirty work."

The Estonian let the comment pass. He had called Galina to his small office; a room without a desk, the space filled with several chairs, a table, and communications gear. The walls were bare and there were no windows.

"Where is his body?" Galina demanded, her voice resolute, though she could not will away the tears. "I want to know how he died."

"You will see him tomorrow."

"Why was Viktor sent to kill the father of the man Akimov was with in New York?"

"Because Vasily Karsalov knew too much." The answer came from Oleg Deryabin, who had come into the room and was standing behind Galina.

Galina wheeled and glared at Deryabin. "We were a team. You should have sent me with him."

Deryabin approached her. "You were a team in New York, but failed to carry out your assignment promptly." His head nodded, the damned smile twisted into a smirk. "Or without causing messy complications. Now it seems Viktor made another mistake. And paid for it."

"Did you know how many people were protecting Karsalov? It was you who made the mistake."

"I know about mistakes. About lack of preparation." Deryabin drew himself up, aware that he was barely the same height as Galina. "He was not your equal. Not even close." He studied her, his bent little smile now frozen, his eyes ranging over her until they found her breasts heaving against her blouse. He took hold of her arms and tightened his grip.

She could no longer hold back the flood of tears. "You bastard! You don't know how he died." She tried to pull away from him. "It wasn't an accident. He was killed, and I want to know who killed him."

"We'll know tomorrow."

Then he tried to draw her closer to him, and as he did, she exploded. She squirmed and twisted, then pulled free. She flailed out, striking Deryabin with surprising strength. Deryabin tried to restrain her but Galina's superbly conditioned body wriggled free and she pushed away from him with an immense burst of strength. She struck Deryabin's chest with one hand and lashed out at him with the other, her fingers curled and rigid. Her hand crashed against his ear, then she dragged her nails over the soft flesh of his cheek, creating four perfect rows of blood across his face and down onto his neck.

"Shalava!" Deryabin shouted, calling her a bitch and slut, adding fuel to her rage. He ran his hand across the cuts, feeling the blood. When she came at him again, Deryabin did not err a second time. He struck her face with the flat of his hand, his blood rubbing off on her cheeks. He struck again, and again, hard slaps that put a cut beside her mouth. Her tears dissolved the dark lines penciled around her eyes, making a dark slurry that mixed with streaks of blood, transforming her face into a tragic opera mask. She cowered and retreated from Deryabin.

Slowly she straightened and gathered her poise. She wiped her eyes with the back of her hand. The two stared menacingly at each other, their mouths open, heavily sucking in air.

Then, and surprisingly, Galina called him by his familiar name.

"Oleshka," she began in a quavering voice. "I called you a bastard, because that is what you have become." She was shaking badly, but her eyes never strayed from Deryabin's. "I will stay with you, but only if you promise to help me have revenge on whoever killed Viktor."

"Revenge can be dangerous," Deryabin said. He pressed a handkerchief against his cheek. "If you remember that I give the orders, you can stay with me."

Chapter 25

After four days of rice and over-cooked beef, Oxby looked forward to a simple breakfast in Yakov's kitchen; yogurt, hot cereal, and hard-as-nails bread on which he heaped a mound of strawberry preserves. Both men had slept late, proof that their Tashkent experience had taken its toll.

Oxby cleared the table and then put his notebooks on it, along with dictionaries, a *Blue Guide* to St. Petersburg, two magazine articles covering the arts highlights in the city, a detailed city map that included bus and subway routes, and, not at all incidentally, an envelope with the balance of the expense money advanced by Christopher Forbes.

"I want you to pretend," Oxby said gravely, "that this kitchen is what we call in Scotland Yard the 'incident room.' It is where we bring our files and case information so that a group of specialists can concentrate their activities on a major crime. Such a room has several phone lines, its own fax receivers, a computer terminal, and of course access to support facilities such as fingerprinting, forensic labs, medical examiner, Interpol databank, et cetera. Can you imagine such a room?"

"I will try," Yakov said good-naturedly.

"You must try very hard, because I plan to pursue the investigation into the Rasputin Imperial egg, and your kitchen will be my incident room. With your permission, I shall deputize you to be my assistant and ask you to carry out certain assignments."

Oxby leveled his gaze at Yakov. "Before you commit yourself, I must remind you of two items that may have great significance once we begin the investigation. First is this—" Oxby placed the broken *matryoshka* doll on the table. "Second—" Next to the doll he put the knife used to kill Vasily Karsalov, the weapon that also destroyed Viktor Lysenko.

"In a very short time, you have seen two men die. I can't explain why, and I have no idea who is behind it. But, obviously, someone doesn't want us poking around. So, consider your answer carefully. Are you in this with me, or do you want out?"

"Of course I am with you. I have half my legs, but twice the desire to help."

Oxby said, "We were a perfect team in a strange country. Here in your home city, you will be invaluable."

Yakov nodded. "I know Petersburg as well as anyone," he said. "I can be guide and translator. Besides, without me you will never know what is in Vasily's diary or the letters from Sasha Akimov."

"How long will it take for you to transcribe them?"

"It will take a little study at the beginning, but not a long time."

"Good, then. We'll shake hands on it."

Yakov smiled and the two men shook hands vigorously.

"We are not starting with many advantages," Oxby said. "On the table I've put our entire anemic arsenal. To that I'll add the diaries and photographs left by Vasily Karsalov. And the correspondence. Also two passports, courtesy of Viktor Lysenko." He then pulled a single sheet of paper from the pile. "This is our assignment. You've heard it before, but it bears repeating." In his neat hand, Oxby had printed the following:

Premise: Peter Carl Fabergé was commissioned by Grigori Rasputin to design and make an Imperial Easter egg intended as a gift for Czarina Alexandra.

Objective: prove the premise, determine if egg still exists. Then find it.

"Vasily Karsalov said that his father gave him a Fabergé Imperial egg and we have photographs showing Vasily with his father and the egg. Leonid Baletsky told us he, too, had seen the egg. They told us about a celebration in 1963, at the time of JFK's assassination. There was gambling, and Vasily lost the egg. Baletsky stopped talking after a hundred dollars. Another hundred might get him talking again."

"But Rasputin," Yakov said. "Have we proved there is a connection?"

"Not directly. Though Vasily blurted out his name. We might not be able to prove that Rasputin commissioned an egg unless we find the bloody thing. I suspect it will have the usual information inscribed on it; dates and workmaster's initials. I'll wager that Fabergé added some kind of mark to indicate that Rasputin was involved."

Oxby got to his feet. He went slowly to the middle room in the little apartment, taking an inventory, inspecting each room, keenly noting the location of doors, windows, and electrical outlets in a way he had not previously observed. As he did, concern began to show in his eyes and the set of his mouth.

"We have a problem," he said, "possibly a very serious one. I thought of it on the plane, and I wrestled with it last night before I let myself get some sleep."

Yakov looked quizzically at Oxby. "What is this problem?"

"This apartment is the problem. They—whoever in bloody hell they are—know we are here. And by now, they've figured out who I am. At the least they know I've been with Scotland Yard. When they conclude that we are going ahead with our search for the egg, we automatically become very vulnerable. Yakov, my good Russian friend, you have but one door. We come in by it, and we leave by it. There are three small windows that neither of us could climb out of, but each one is perfect for throwing something in—such as a fire bomb or canister of gas, the kind that makes you laugh, cry, or fall dead."

Oxby circled the table, then came back to his chair. "I'm not certain there is any place where we would be completely safe, and frankly, the two of us cannot protect ourselves. We need help, someone to provide protection for us. Do you understand?"

"Yes. This protection you talk about, it is called *krysha*. We read it in our newspapers, about these *mafiya* people we have."

"Is it possible you have a friend who imports food? I'm quite serious, someone who brings frozen chicken or fruit to Petersburg."

"You want something special to eat?"

"No. The companies that import food or, I suppose, nearly any commodity, must have protection against the crime bosses who want to break into their monopolies. You understand?"

Yakov said that he did. "But chickens? No," and he laughed, shaking his head. "I know someone. He is Kinsky. He has a business with his son and brings food for pets into the city."

"That's bloody damned good. Lots of pets in Petersburg."

"We had a cat, when my wife, Valentina, was alive. It made me sneeze. But it was my wife's family who knew Kinsky." Yakov sighed. "Now he lives in a fine apartment and I see him in a big car. I am not sure he will remember me. Sometimes money helps them forget their old friends. The same where you live, Jack?"

Oxby nodded. "The same everywhere. Get Kinsky on the phone.

Explain that we need what you call *krysha*. Ask for the name of the people who take care of his company."

Yakov searched and found the number and then, to his surprise, was put directly through to Kinsky. They spoke for several minutes, Yakov calling his old friend Misha, obviously delighted that he had been remembered. Yakov nodded as he wrote out the information. "*Spahseebah, spahseebah.*" He thanked Misha the obligatory half dozen times, his head bobbing, then finally put down the phone and turned to Oxby with a victorious grin.

"I have the information," he said, pointing to his notes.

"Call them and tell them we have an urgent problem . . . ask if they can come here today."

Yakov learned quickly that a professional crime organization can be superbly efficient, yet numbingly impersonal. A meeting was set for two o'clock that afternoon. Yakov was told to expect a phone call shortly before that hour. No names were given.

Oxby proceeded to refine his action plan, placing special emphasis on assignments he felt Yakov could handle without close supervision. First, he wanted Yakov to explore the bureaucratic jungle inside the offices of the deputy commander for personnel, Naval Forces, Baltic Fleet Operation. He was to locate and make copies of the files for Vasily Karsalov. Vasily Karsalov had also mentioned a man named Akimov. No first name, just another player in the poker game. Still, worth checking.

"Karsalov was exiled to Uzbekistan for a murder he said he did not commit," Oxby said. "There could be a problem with that. Most criminals go to prison screaming their innocence. See what you can find in the Military Tribunal offices. They'll throw plenty of red tape at you, but you might be lucky."

"I could write a volume on red tape. It is, after all the color of the Soviet flag and I worked under that stifling system for more than half my life."

"I want a list of every Leonid Baletsky and Viktor Lysenko in Petersburg. I particularly want to meet Leonid Baletsky again. Normally, I would start with a phone directory, but there isn't one. Where do you suggest I begin?"

"Our Central Telephone Exchange has every name and you can try with them. It will cost money."

"Not surprising," Oxby said. "While you are searching the naval records, I'll go to the exchange."

Until noon when the two men nibbled on fruit and cheese, Yakov
worked the phone, preparing the way for his visit to the naval personnel files. Oxby wrote a brief letter to Christopher Forbes.

> St. Petersburg
> 13 June
> Dear Kip:
> As I don't wish to have this letter exposed to prying eyes, I shall not
> cable or fax it, relying on what I am told is a dependable private mail ser-
> vice via Helsinki. The past fortnight has not lacked for excitement. Nor,
> exactly, have I been glued to one spot. Details must come at a time when
> I can personally share them with you. For now I shall pass on the fol-
> lowing. Subject to finding one or two corroborating pieces of evidence, I
> am confident that Fabergé produced an Imperial egg that has heretofore
> been excluded from the official records. I cannot say with certainty that
> the egg was commissioned by Rasputin, though circumstantial evidence
> suggests that it was. I believe we will have answers to all these impon-
> derables once I have located the egg. In that regard, I shall keep you ad-
> vised of my progress.
> With sincere respects,
> J. Oxby

🐝 🐝 🐝

At five minutes to one the phone rang. Yakov answered, listened for
a moment, then put down the phone.

"It is our *krysha*," Yakov said, not knowing how else to identify the
group that had called. "They are here. First they will inspect our building, and call to tell us to unlock the door."

"A good sign," Oxby said.

Ten minutes later the phone rang again, this time to announce that
they were at the door to Yakov's apartment.

"They are here," Yakov said. He pulled away the chain and turned
the heavy bolt in the door. He opened it and three men entered the
apartment. The last one closed the door and inspected the chain and
locks.

Two of the men, including the lock inspector, wore light summer
shirts and dark blue jeans. They were in their early twenties and powerfully built. They had short-cropped hair, and expressions of complete

indifference. One was swarthy, his face marked with small scars over one eye, the other had fair skin with yellow hair and blue eyes, and was, eerily, the more intimidating of the pair. Oxby studied both and made an imperceptible nod of approval. He watched their heads move in little jerks, their expressions blank, their eyes gathering in the details of the room and the rooms beyond. They disappeared, moving on to complete their examination of Yakov's apartment.

"Are you Ilyushin?" The man who asked the questions was well dressed, wearing a suit, tie with cuff links that glittered, and holding a cellular telephone in his hand, one he had used minutes before to announce his presence. He was young, thirty perhaps, and his face was only slightly more animated than the young *byki* who had come with him.

Yakov acknowledged that he was. "What is your name?"

"Ivan," the leader said, and handed a card to Yakov and one to Oxby.

Ivan wanted to know about Yakov's neighbors, about electric lines and fuse boxes and windows and where the telephone wires entered the building and came into the apartment. There were more questions, several minutes' worth. The two muscle men returned. One stood at the door, the other took his position alongside Ivan.

"Ivan knows my friend Misha Kinsky."

"Good," Oxby said. "Ask him if his men will be on duty around the clock, and how many men will there be."

Yakov relayed the question. "Ivan asks how long will they be needed and how much will you pay."

Time and money, Oxby mused, always time and money. "God save me if it takes more than a week. Explain to Ivan that I've never hired protection in Petersburg, London, or anywhere else. How much does he want?"

Questions and answers went back and forth for as long as it took to resolve all the issues. As part of the give-and-take, Oxby learned that Ivan was part of a collection of small businesses that were engaged in the mixing and delivery of concrete, trucking, moving and storage, and, as Oxby decoded Yakov's translation of Ivan's descriptions, insurance. Ivan called himself an insurance manager. He sold insurance, but there were no written policies and no schedule of claims benefits. But there were premiums (fees), payable in advance. It was a hard currency business. English pounds or American dollars. The insurance that Ivan would provide for Oxby, Yakov, and Yakov's apartment would be put in force with the payment of six thousand dollars. That would buy a week's insurance. This translated to four men on duty at all times, each with a phone.

Ivan explained, "If you want a man to go with you when you are away from the apartment, that will reduce the number of men surrounding the apartment to three. If you both are away with one of the men, the number guarding the apartment shrinks to two."

"Can Ivan supply more men if we need them?" Oxby asked.

Yakov translated and Ivan smiled as he answered. "Yes, of course. For additional money."

The how much and how to make arrangements ended the negotiations. Oxby counted out the money. Half in pounds, half in dollars. He asked Yakov to repeat his instructions so as to avoid any misunderstanding. Yakov pointed to his watch and said that the insurance was in effect as of 3:00 P.M. on June 13 and would remain in force until 3:00 P.M. on June 20.

Chapter 26

While Yakov's apartment was converted into a fortress, there became, by mid-afternoon, a vastly improved feeling of security about the little place. A Mercedes station wagon was parked across from the building and inside it was a young bull who sat hunched forward with his thick arms curled around the steering wheel. He watched the traffic and the walkers, and paid particular attention to loiterers. He was connected to his three associates by phone and whenever man, woman, or child entered the apartment, he flashed the information. It was a boring job, one that served as entry-level into a career where, with a bare-bones education, he could become a well-paid operative by wearing a pistol and having no qualms about using it.

Another member of the team was in the back of the building, on foot, and carrying a sort of rake that he occasionally used to sweep a weed-filled patch of grass. At night, his post became the cab of a pickup truck that carried a small arsenal of rifles and handguns. Two others roved through the neighborhood. They took turns going into Yakov's building and climbing up to the top floor where they had a hooded-crow's view of the street below.

One of the rovers, the head man of the day shift, was the one with the intimidating eyes and straw-colored hair. Each time he inspected the interior of the building, he would stop to visit briefly with Oxby and Yakov. His pale blue eyes rarely blinked, and he would flex his thick shoulders in a rolling motion, as if were trying to shrug off a buildup of nervous energy. High up on his chest, to the side of his thick neck, was a scar that was the result of a gunfight during which he had taken three bullets, small perhaps, but honest-to-god bullets nonetheless. Two had been removed, one still lay deep beneath the scar. For this he had earned the name Poolya, or Bullet.

Oxby had placed a call at nine o'clock New York time to Alexander Tobias. They were friends as well as professionally acquainted, having

179

worked cases in both New York and London when they chased after
faked da Vinci manuscripts and a crazy pharmacist who had made a
nasty habit of destroying Cézanne's self-portraits. He was told that Tobias had gone off for a long weekend to his camp in the Adirondack
Mountains. His exact whereabouts and phone number could not be
given to anyone except, and under extreme circumstances, the mayor of
New York.

"He said that?" Oxby asked.

"No, but it would be like him," the officer who answered the phone
said with a little chuckle. "You have a choice if you want to get a message
to him before he gets back. Voice mail, e-mail, or fax. Got a preference?"

"This is Jack Oxby, Detective Chief Inspector with Scotland Yard.
Does that get me any preference?"

"Sorry, Inspector. Alex left a short list of people we can give his
phone number to and your name isn't on it."

"Give me the voice mail number," Oxby said.

Oxby thought of Alex Tobias in his lakeside cabin on Big Moose
Lake. He had promised to take Oxby there, and under the circumstances, there was no other place on earth he would rather be at that
moment. Oxby dialed the number with the hope that Alex would call
for his messages before deciding to take an extra few days to empty Big
Moose of all its small-mouth bass.

"Alexander, this is Jack Oxby. I know you're on the lake, and they
won't give me your number, so I shall trust to your disciplined spirit to
call in and hear what I've got to say.

"I'm on leave from the Yard, sorting out my personal fortunes and future, and not incidentally, currently involved in a fascinating assignment
that has suddenly and absurdly turned completely around. To sum it up,
I've fallen into a great deal more danger than I'd bargained for. So much
so, that I've engaged several bodyguards to put, as they say so quaintly
over here, a 'roof' over my head. Never thought I'd be in league with the
Russian *mafiya*, but I am, and with mixed emotions, quite happily, too."

Then, briefly and precisely, Oxby told Tobias about the assignment
he'd received from Christopher Forbes and about St. Petersburg and
Tashkent, and Yakov, and the deepening mystery surrounding
Rasputin's Imperial egg. "Initially I didn't believe the rumor about such
an egg. Now I think it's quite possible. Of course I also didn't believe
that murder would be committed over such an erudite rumor.

"I've a special favor to ask, Alex. You told me once you would like to know more about Fabergé's work, so here's your chance. Make a date to visit with Christopher Forbes. He's there on Fifth Avenue where you can see their Fabergé collection. He likes to be called Kip and, knowing both of you, I think you'll get along splendidly.

"When you see Kip, give him my best regards. While you're at it, you might also plan a visit with Gerard Hill. He's Sotheby's expert in charge of Russian icons and decorative arts. You might ask him what he knows about the Rasputin egg. He'll likely laugh you out of the building, or, God knows, show you a file an inch thick.

"Oh, and a final thought. What do you know about that section of New York where so many Russians flocked to over the years? Can't think of it right now. But I know there are some old-timers who went there after the revolution and may have passed on stories about Rasputin. It's a long shot, but you might have a piece of luck.

"Alex, I hope you don't mind my rambling on like this. All these suggestions are long shots, as it's one of those nothing-ventured sorts of things.

"I'll call when you're back in the city. Early Tuesday morning, your time. Cheerio."

Chapter 27

Clouds flowed in from the west and with them a light morning drizzle. Oleg Deryabin stood at the window in his office, a phone in his hand. Thin scabs had formed over the scratches on his cheek and the skin around the four neat rows was inflamed to a hot pink. Trivimi Laar was sitting in one of the chairs in front of the big desk, leaning forward, making notes. Deryabin held his phone, listening, and whoever he was listening to had monopolized the conversation for the last minute, far longer than Deryabin usually allowed an underling to speak without interruption. Deryabin was angry and perspiring. Then it was over and Deryabin clicked off the phone without an acknowledgment.

"Fucking bastard." He said it as if it was all he was going to say about the unsatisfactory conversation he had just held with the Russian-American lawyer who was representing Koleso in New York and who had submitted a purchase order for fifteen cars to Carson Motors. He pulled back his chair and sat in it. He stared across the desk to the Estonian, waving the phone. "You didn't tell me that Mikhail wanted a deposit. Not some puny amount, but twenty percent of the total cost of the transaction. Do you know how much that is?"

"I told you we must pay a heavy deposit. I didn't tell you how much because I didn't know how much Mikhail would ask for. If you will nudge that convenient memory of yours, you will recall that I said it would be substantial."

"Twenty percent is too goddamned substantial."

"Seventy thousand dollars," Trivimi said evenly.

"And you lecture that I spend too freely."

"I explained that if we make severe reductions in expenses, we can survive through October. From there, it will be week to week until we can turn matters around. There is still the debt, and before the end of the year, we must begin to pay down on it, or we'll have a roomful of creditors screaming for everything you own. Including your home and every possession you haven't sent out of the country. In that case, only a miracle will keep New Century alive."

Deryabin looked plaintively at Trivimi. "Is there enough to make the damned deposit?"

"I've accounted for that. Don't let it slip that convenient mind that Mikhail will demand the balance before he ships the cars."

"Tell me more about Mikhail. What is he like, what kind of questions did he ask?"

"He was businesslike, and he asked businesslike questions. He knows automobiles and how to sell them." Trivimi gathered his papers. "I didn't mention that there was a detective with him. A man named Tobias."

"We've got a fucking detective meddling in our business in Petersburg. Now there's one in New York? What was he doing with Mikhail?"

"You forget, Akimov was shot in Mikhail's office. One of his employees was stabbed."

Deryabin's eyes flashed. "I haven't forgotten."

"The police would like to know who shot the writer, the one Galina shot to get his notebook."

"The strange writing in his notebook was not so strange after all. I have the translation. There is no mention of my name."

"I'd like to read it," Trivimi said. "What else was in the notebook?"

"Akimov talked to Mikhail about the old days, and about the celebration that took place when Mikhail was born, and how everyone made toasts to Kennedy's assassination. Mikhail described the woman who shot Akimov, and except for the color of her hair, he described Galina perfectly. He told the reporter that Akimov would probably die."

"Did Akimov talk about the poker game, or the egg?"

Deryabin shook his head. "Read it before you fall asleep tonight." He pushed the typed translation across to the Estonian.

Trivimi stared at the report, then put it in his pocket. He said, "During my meeting with Mikhail I never used your name. I referred to you only as chairman of New Century."

"What are you getting at?"

"The important fact that Mikhail has no idea who you are. I strongly believe that Akimov never mentioned your name."

"Are you certain of that?"

"No. But remember that Akimov was an old man telling old stories and making toasts to Mikhail's family. If he planned to tell Mikhail about you, he waited too long. You see, Oleshka? The circumstances are exactly as you want them. Mikhail Karsalov and his father never communicated with each other and now the father and Akimov are dead."

As Deryabin listened, he opened and closed his cigarette case, the clicks as steady as a metronome.

Trivimi said, "But if you have any fear that Mikhail will discover a reason to stop the negotiations, then make your contract with another company. There are hundreds of automobile dealers in the eastern states."

Deryabin learned forward and crossed his arms over his chest. "There are no other dealers who have showrooms where Mikhail has put his."

"Then go to New York. You can meet with Mikhail and develop a good relationship. Perhaps he will invest in Koleso. That way you will have the money to build your first showroom."

"I'll think about it," Deryabin said perfunctorily, then got to his feet and stretched. He looked gaunt, as if he had lost weight. That, and his face with the scratches and redness, gave him the appearance of a man who had gone sleepless for half a week. He opened a bottle of mineral water and poured a glass, then drank it in a single swallow. He returned to his chair and stood beside it.

"The detective. Tobias you called him. He asked questions?"

"He asked was I Russian. I explained. He asked about your gift, the *charka*, and was it Fabergé? I said yes. After Mikhail told us about the shooting, Tobias asked if I knew Akimov. I said I did not."

"That is all?"

"I said it was a terrible thing to have a man shot in front of your eyes. And I said goodbye."

"If I go to New York, I will be able to tell Mikhail who I am." He looked inquiringly at the Estonian. "You are saying that?"

The Estonian nodded.

Deryabin's little smile lengthened. "When I meet him I can say that I knew his mother and father, and that I first saw him when he was a baby. And I will tell him Akimov worked in our company but that he became old and could not carry out his assignments."

"Will you tell Mikhail that Sasha Akimov saw you win the Fabergé egg from his father?" The Estonian leaned forward. "And will you tell him you are responsible for his father's exile. That you ordered his execution?"

"What are saying, bastard Estonian? Fat prick of all time!" Trivimi had become a master at insinuating into their conversation the topics that would inevitably cause Deryabin's emotions to crash. Deryabin ranted on, "You push too far." He reached across the desk for Trivimi's arm, then yanked the Estonian toward him until their faces were inches apart. "I will send you back on the street. You hear? On the street where you will be nothing again!"

The Estonian pulled away. "Don't threaten what you can't deliver, Oleg." He had dropped the familiar Oleshka, and was glowering even more fiercely than the furiously angry man across from him.

"It will be better when you are able to share with Mikhail all the relationships you had with his father. You stand alone too much of the time, shutting others from your life." He stood, looming over Deryabin. "I have not forgotten what I learned when I was young, when I was made to go to our family's church. I didn't like it, but I learned about a power that is greater than I shall ever be, a power that gives strength and takes away fear. You lived in the Soviet where power was government. No God, no faith, only the State.

"Now, you believe you have gained some kind of supreme power and can do no wrong. But you know that is not so. Whatever sins or crimes you committed still control you, and someday, when you are not prepared, when you least expect it, those unrepentant sins will destroy you."

Deryabin had never heard Trivimi speak with such feeling. He stared at the tall figure, moving his mouth but uttering no sounds for a full, seemingly endless minute. He snapped open the lighter and held a shaking flame beneath a new cigarette.

"What pious bullshit," he finally mustered. "Since when have you become a model of sanctimony?"

"I do what I must," Trivimi said. "I hope for change and share what I was taught." Trivimi turned to the window and inspected the gray sky and the light rain that continued to fall. "I am taking Galina to the airport this evening. The plane with Viktor's body arrives at seven. Will you go with us?"

Deryabin nodded and said that he would.

*   *   *

Deryabin remained in the limousine while Galina and the Estonian located the baggage handlers who would deliver the coffin. Galina had insisted on making arrangements for the burial and a black van waited inside the gate. The rain had picked up and gusts of wind blew miniature waves over water that had pooled on the tarmac.

They could hear the engines before they saw the jet drop below the clouds, land, and taxi to the terminal. Galina went out to the plane and stood in the rain, waiting for Viktor's coffin to be offloaded. Her head was covered with a scarf and her hands were buried in the pockets of a raincoat that reached below her knees. She waited a long twenty minutes, never wavering, staring at the hole in the plane out of which came suitcases, packages, cartons of furniture, and finally a coffin.

She went over to it, the Estonian at her side. As was tradition, the coffin was covered with a thin layer of zinc and had an eight-by-ten-inch window located directly over the head of the deceased. Beneath the thick glass was Viktor's face. The rain collected on the glass and Galina wiped it away. The lights, bright as they were, did not shine on Viktor's face and she could see only a dim, pale visage. She lowered her head and began to speak softly.

"I don't know what happened, but you weren't prepared. Why did you rush? Like always you said you could not lose." She wept. "If I had been with you . . ."

She turned to Trivimi. "Have you learned any more? How he died?"

"I don't have all the pieces, but we believe that the Englishman and Ilyushin were in the room with Karsalov when Viktor arrived at the hospital."

"Then, it was the policeman who killed Viktor?"

"I said there are missing pieces. But it is possible."

"His name is Oxby?"

"Yes," the Estonian replied.

"Where is he now?"

"In Petersburg. With Ilyushin. We have the address."

Deryabin approached, holding an umbrella. "What can I do?"

"Bring Viktor to life?" Galina said, snapping off the words. "You can do that?"

"A bad joke, Galina. I will help if I can. Money?"

"Yes, a lot of money. And whatever I will need to repay the Oxby bastard."

"I am getting more information," Deryabin said. "You will do nothing until we have all the facts. Even if you are justified in taking your revenge on Inspector Oxby, you will do it when I give the order."

The van pulled alongside and two men lifted the coffin into it. Galina climbed in and sat on the wet floor, her head leaning against the casket. The doors were closed and the van was driven away.

Deryabin was still holding his umbrella, the usual smile gone and replaced with a disagreeable frown. Viktor's body had not been embalmed, nor had it been chemically treated in any manner. Though the coffin had been sealed, an intense, fetid odor of death hung in the damp air.

"We are left with a half of the twins," Trivimi said.

Deryabin replied, "By far, the better half."

Chapter 28

Two weeks had slipped by since Lenny Sulzberger had been so ignominiously inconvenienced. He was not quite fully recovered, still carrying an inflatable pillow with a hole in the middle because his left cheek hadn't healed as well as his right thigh. Always the creative punster, he had invented several "half-ass" jokes and had played them out ad nauseam. *Playboy* had extended the deadline for his profile on Mike Carson, and Monday the 14th was both Flag Day and the day Lenny would interview Mike Carson and replace the notes that had been surrendered on that painfully regrettable evening. In fact, Lenny had two interviews scheduled. Alex Tobias had called him on Sunday and said it was important that he meet with him, that it wouldn't take a lot of time, and would he stay around after his interview with Carson. The detective said he was flying into La Guardia from upstate New York, and was 2:30 okay.

Lenny shifted his interview with Mike Carson to 1:30. He asked the same questions he asked during the first interview, except he slipped in a few extra ones he felt had been earned on account of being shot a couple of times. Lenny sat on his doughnut cushion, occasionally standing when it became more comfortable to do that.

"Still hurts, damn it. I'd like to punch out that Russian broad, except she'd probably beat the shit out of me."

Mike was amused that Lenny could speak his mind, no matter about what, or who was listening. "Another week and it will all be a memory," he said, hoping to soothe the writer's feelings as much as his slow-healing wounds.

"Yeah. I could read for ten minutes at a stretch on my stomach," Lenny complained, "so there wasn't much I could do for a week except watch soap operas and try to remember what earth-shattering news you gave me in our first interview that was worth getting two bullets in my backside." Lenny shifted uncomfortably. "But, damn it, I was shot! Why?"

Lenny's tale of woe evoked both commiseration and a good laugh. Mike Carson said, "As a guess, I'd say that whoever shot you and took your notebook was under the impression I had important information. Either about the business, or about me. What other reason can there be?"

"There's Akimov. Did he bring any secrets, any inside information?"

"Who would bother about Sasha? And who would know he was in America, let alone in one of my showrooms? What little I learned from Sasha I kept to myself."

"Are you going to tell me now?"

"Maybe later."

ॐ ॐ ॐ

Alex Tobias was on time. Precisely. He impressed people early on that he was also the sort who was completely reliable in other ways. And not in your face about it.

"Thanks to both of you for changing your schedule," he began. "I received a phone call from a fellow police officer. He's an old Scotland Yard friend and it prompted me to ask for another meeting with the two of you."

He took a seat at the conference table. Mike sat across from him, Lenny stood, holding his arms crossed over the pillow and held tight against his tummy like a security blanket.

"Now, then," Tobias began, "when I was last in this office, a man by the name of Laar was here, making a proposal for a joint venture between his company in St. Petersburg and Carson Motors." He looked at Mike. "Any further developments on that?"

"We're getting the lawyers together," Mike said.

"I think the idea of importing used American cars into Russia seems like a reasonable business proposition. Not the kind of deal that causes murder, least not as I heard it being discussed between you and that Estonian fellow. What's more, you're paying lawyers to sweat the details and keep you out of trouble."

He went on, "That's what I was thinking, but then I said, wait a minute. An old man is murdered. And you, Mr. Sulzberger, you get roughed up so they can steal your notes. So I ask myself, what the hell's that all about?"

"Yeah, what the hell is that all about?" Lenny echoed. "There wasn't a damned thing in my notes except how a young guy from Russia came to America and made it big-time."

"But they thought there was more," Tobias said. "Follow me on this." He looked at Mike. "Your old family friend, Mr. Akimov, surprises you with a visit. He didn't take the train up from Philadelphia that morning, he flew in from St. Petersburg, Russia. Maybe it's a coincidence, maybe not, but he comes just when you're negotiating a big contract with a company from St. Petersburg."

Tobias moved forward on his chair. "I learned from Mr. Sulzberger that you and Akimov were together for approximately ten minutes before he was shot. And during that time he told you that he knew your mother and father, and that the last time he saw you was when you were ten years old."

"That's right," Mike said,.

"I think he said more than that," Tobias said. "Some news or information you didn't include in your interview with Mr. Sulzberger. Am I right?"

Mike turned from Tobias to Lenny. "I can't remember precisely what he said."

Tobias said, "I don't want to pry into your personal life, Mr. Carson, but I'd appreciate it if you would tell me anything Akimov said that could help us learn who killed him."

"He talked mainly about my father, who I never really knew. He was out of my life when I was just a kid."

"You lived with your mother?"

Mike nodded. "And an aunt, until I was eleven or so."

"Is your mother still living?"

"This is the personal stuff I didn't want to get into with Lenny. I think she is, and I feel like hell admitting that I don't know."

"Your aunt?"

"Same."

"What did Akimov say about your father?"

"He said that my father threw a party to celebrate the fact I'd just been born . . . this was November of '63. After all the drinking, my father gambled away what you'd call a family heirloom, something my grandfather gave him. Akimov said it was a Fabergé Easter egg and worth a lot more than what he owed in the poker game."

Tobias became rigid. "Wait a minute. Did he say it was an Imperial Easter egg?"

"We spoke in Russian, and mine is pretty rusty. I recall he said it was a jeweled egg, made by Fabergé, and was worth a lot of money. That's pretty much how he described it."

"You'll excuse me, but that's an incredible story." Tobias shook his head as if he were coping with an extra discharge of endorphins. "Why do you suppose he came all the way to New York to tell you about a Fabergé egg?"

"He had more to say on personal matters that I don't want to talk about." Mike smiled, or perhaps it was more of an embarrassed grin. "I told him that if my father had stupidly lost the egg, then it wasn't mine."

"What did he say to that?"

"I don't think he gave a direct answer."

"Why do you suppose he was tracked down to your office and murdered? There had to be more to it than the fact he knew your father lost a Fabergé egg in a card game. Do you agree?"

"It wasn't just about the egg," Mike said. "He told me other bits about my father." He paused. Mike was clearly troubled. "This gets to the hard part—"

"Do you want Mr. Sulzberger to hear this?"

"It's all right, but no notes. And none of it gets into the article."

Tobias glanced at Lenny. "Did you hear that?"

"Yeah. It's off the record."

Mike looked from one to the other, and seemed to gather himself before he said, "I was told that my father was accused of murder. This was in the early 1970s. I might have been nine or ten when it happened."

"Tell us as much as you want," Tobias said. "Or say nothing."

"There's not much to tell. My father was still in the navy and was transferring supplies like meat and liquor to a civilian partner who warehoused and sold it on the street. Sasha said the partner had been cheating, that he was found dead, his throat slashed. My father was accused of killing him. There was a trial, but it was secret, and a rumor he confessed. He was sent to some place in Central Asia. Sasha believes he's been there ever since."

Lenny jumped in. "So why does this guy come over with all this negative crap and give you a hard time about your father?"

"I think he was about to explain all that. Then the woman and the gun and Akimov's got a bullet in his throat."

Tobias said, "Can you think of anything else he said. Names, places, dates. Anything at all?"

"Though he never actually said it, I think he knew that someone was following him. A couple of times he went to those windows and stared down at the crowds on the showroom floor."

Tobias said, "If we're going to figure out the riddle, you'll have to remember every word, every detail, every gesture, every change of expression that Akimov made during those minutes when you were together. We'll never know of course what he had planned to say to you, but we might be able to speculate on why he went to such a huge effort to try."

Lenny opened his notebook, "Does that mean I can—"

"I'm sorry, Mr. Sulzberger. From now on it's just between Mr. Carson and me."

Chapter 29

Since bringing on the crew of body-guards, and accepting the need to make himself as small a target as possible, Oxby had surrendered to the claustrophobia of Yakov's tiny apartment. Sunday had been particularly stifling, and not until after he had put the message on Alex Tobias's voice mail, and Poolya gave assurances the neighborhood was clean, did Oxby and Yakov take two of the men and drive across the city to a Ukrainian restaurant.

Now, it was Monday, Oxby's first opportunity to begin his investigation. Yakov along with Mikki, his designated bodyguard and arguably the most sullen-looking of the lot, had been sent off to the Naval Offices to find the personal records of Vasily Karsalov. Oxby gave himself the chore of obtaining the addresses of all the Leonid Baletskys in Petersburg. Because he had found Viktor Lysenko's passport, along with an address, it seemed unnecessary to get a list of every Lysenko. Or was it? Oxby had found a second passport, and it seemed likely that a man in Lysenko's line of work might have a dozen passports, none of which might have any bearing on who he was or where he lived.

No matter how skilled Poolya might be at detecting trouble, it was unlikely he could single-handedly fend off an organized assault on the streets of the city. He and Oxby were about to spend most of the day roving through the city in search of the homes of Baletsky and Lysenko, going God knows where. Oxby could handle a pistol remarkably well, but he had not brought one. Poolya offered him a choice. A Glock-17 semiautomatic, or a CZ-75 compact autopistol. Both 9mm, both held ten rounds. The Glock, made of polymer, was lighter by ten ounces. He chose the Glock and a hip holster.

Instead of driving directly to the address bureau, Oxby instructed Poolya to go first to St. Isaac's Cathedral. The familiar urge had come over him and it was time for a few moments of quiet time. So his day began in hushed surroundings, though the symbols and art were

changed from those of his haunts in London. He stood in front of a
stained glass window that depicted Christ looming twenty feet tall, covered in a brilliant red robe edged with gold braid. Above Oxby was a
mammoth painting, *The Virgin Majesty*, high up in the central dome of
the church. On either side of him were giant pillars made of bronze and
clad with perfectly matched pieces of malachite. St. Isaac's Cathedral
could hold fourteen thousand worshippers, all standing, of course. For
seven decades the communists showed it off as a museum, and now in
the atmosphere of a new enlightenment, services were again being performed in the church inspired by Peter the Great.

Here, beneath the icon wall, in one of the most famous holy buildings in the world, Jack Oxby lowered his head and prayerfully announced his presence. This was not a display of piety; Oxby had never
declared his dedication to one religion or another. But it was Oxby's
way of acknowledging that a Supra Power had created man and man's
inventions, including lasting, beautiful art in all its forms. Now he could
add St. Issac's to the long list of great cathedrals where he had, as he put
it, "borrowed a little space," so that he could speak to whatever Power
would listen.

His message delivered, he searched for Poolya in the crowd and
waved to him. They met at the great south door, twenty tons of bronze
and oak, then went out into a warm sun. Poolya had a car, a small, ancient Peugeöt, likely owned by a long departed member of the French
consulate. The two men were getting on, not forming an intimate relationship, but communicating through their minimal understanding of
each other's language. Their conversation was laced with "uhs," grunts,
and a few words strung together. Occasionally Oxby pointed to a word
in his dog-eared dictionary.

In a city without telephone directories, it is possible to obtain the address of a resident by applying at an *adresnoye byiuro*, or address bureau.
But these leftovers from the Soviet Union are anachronisms; out-of-
date, slow, and of questionable accuracy. Such a bureau is located in
each of Petersburg's twelve districts, and usually can be found three
steps below street level in a windowless room with dark green paint on
the wall and red linoleum on the floor. Behind a small window similar
to a currency exchange booth, a *bahbooshka* receives the written appli-
cation, then commences her tedious look-up in a tome-like ledger. The
setting and the process might have been devised by Franz Kafka. Prov-
identially, there was an alternative.

In the manner in which things have changed, the incentive for profit helped create a more modern method, though still not in any measure as practical, efficient, accurate, and so utterly prosaic as a telephone directory. To Oxby, it was inconceivable that in a country where the government had, over a span of three generations, devoted huge resources to capturing information on its citizenry, facts ranging from sexual preferences to secret religious leanings, that only mere dribbles of the data had been permitted to become public knowledge.

Oxby's collection of guides and references yielded the names of two private companies that, for a price, would find the address of a name the customer supplied. The most expeditious way to obtain an accurate address was to submit a full name; first, middle, and last. The very old and very young might also have a saint's name appended. Though Russians take personal pride in their names, in a city of five million, there would be more than one Leonid Baletsky. Provide a phone number and the accuracy of the address improved to nearly 100 percent.

The address bureau at 6 Liteyny Prospekt got Yakov's recommendation on the basis that it had the best address. Poolya parked close to the building. Sheltering Oxby in a professional manner, he rushed him into the building. The address bureau was on the third floor, and in the front overlooking the street. It pleased Poolya, as he could keep an eye on his car.

A row of windows lined an inside wall, and resembled, it seemed to Oxby, a bank. Three of the windows were attended and Oxby chose one he hoped would move quickly. An idle hope in Russia, as he was soon reminded. After thirty minutes he had moved to the front of the line and placed the names Yakov had neatly printed on a glass counter. Fingers with painted nails picked it up. The young woman gave Oxby a bored, but nearly friendly smile and entered the names into a computer.

Oxby was told there were seven persons answering to the name Leonid Baletsky. Included along with the address was a middle name. Interesting information, though of dubious value.

When the search for Viktor's address was made it confirmed that a Viktor Y. Lysenko lived at 9 Kubansky Street. Oxby asked for information for all the other Viktor Y. Lysenkos. There were five. He bought them.

For the twelve addresses he was asked to pay 550 rubles, or about two dollars an address.

"We'll locate Baletsky first," Oxby said, handing the names to Poolya and suggesting that they begin their search at the farthest point from the Winter Palace, the epicenter of Petersburg as reckoned by the locals.

Poolya studied the street names, said he was not familiar with two of them, but said he had a city map in the car. Though he had watched his car carefully, he approached it cautiously. Oxby smiled admiringly as Poolya checked the little pieces of clear tape he had put on both front doors. If either had been opened, the tape would be broken. They were intact and Oxby was waved into the passenger's seat.

Poolya drove south from the city to a long line of apartment buildings that had been built in the 1960s. There was an inevitable sameness to the architecture, the exterior walls either curved or severely straight. Along Varshavskya Street the buildings rose fifteen floors, and whether the exterior was covered with a stuccolike finish, or a smooth brick, each high rise had a boring similarity to the one next to it. Only the color varied; pale yellow or pale gray. Every apartment had one small balcony, some had two. On the balconies were pots of flowers or laundry pinned to a line, both adding little spots of much needed color.

They made their first stop. Poolya took charge and said they would wait until someone went in or came out through the locked entrance. In ten minutes an elderly woman approached the door, burdened with a plastic food bag in each hand. Poolya jumped at the opportunity to help and, taking the bags, ushered the old lady inside, Oxby following.

Leonid S. Baletsky's name was printed on the mailbox numbered 66. The *bahbooshkah* had held the elevator door open, waiting for them to join her. Then they rode together to the sixth floor and the men got off and were wished a smiling *dah sveedahneeyah*.

Poolya pushed a button at the door. A chime sounded and soon the door was opened by a trim woman in her mid-forties. Her hair was combed neatly and she wore jeans and white sneakers. She held the door tightly and asked who was inquiring about Leonid Baletsky.

Oxby strained to understand her, but he could not. In no more than a minute he saw that the conversation was over and the door was about to be closed.

"Wait," he said. "What did she tell you?" he asked Poolya.

"She said Leonid Baletsky is her father. A very old man."

"How old?"

Poolya waved his hand as if guessing the old man's age. "Seventy? I don't know. He sits at the television all day."

No, Oxby confided to himself. That wasn't good enough. "Ask her if we can see her father. Say it will take only a few seconds."

Poolya turned back to the woman and spoke to her, pointing at Oxby, who smiled and wondered which Russian word for "please" was appropriate and decided he'd try all he had learned if it came to that. It would not have mattered, as she pulled the door toward her and invited Oxby into the apartment with a wave of her hand. It was, except for a woman's touch, very similar to Yakov's apartment. The front door opened on to a small central room with doors to bedrooms, to a kitchen, and to a room in which an old man with flowing white hair sat in a large chair. He stared blankly at a silent performance of *The Flintstones*.

Oxby looked at the man, turned to the daughter and thanked her, then nodded to Poolya and they went to the elevator.

Poolya referred to his map and said their next stop was on the Obvodny Canal. The traffic thickened as they moved past rows of kiosks, and neighborhoods of small factories. The apartment building was an old affair that might have been built a hundred years ago as a private home. A strong odor of stagnant water and engine fumes lifted up from the canal. A steady stream of small boats moved noisily, ferrying women with shopping bags and tourists with cameras.

It required all of Poolya's resources to gain entrance, and once inside it was difficult to locate the apartment in which a Leonid Baletsky lived. There was no response to Poolya's rapping and shouting, but it did attract a neighbor who said Baletsky usually returned to his apartment for lunch each day at between five and ten minutes after noon. It meant an hour's wait but Oxby agreed to sit it out.

The man who returned for his lunch answered all the questions that were put to him with both politeness and patience. But Poolya, educated to Oxby's thoroughness, demanded proof. The man produced a registration and driver's license as evidence that he was Leonid Baletsky, reacting just short of outrage that there might be some doubt.

Even if there were a hundred Leonid Baletskys in Petersburg, only one had followed Yakov and Oxby into the Hermitage. This was not that man. Again Oxby expressed his thanks with now familiar words. Poolya checked the car once more, then they got into it.

In the home of the third Leonid Baletsky, the identification was determined quickly and convincingly. Leonid was aged fourteen and at that moment was in the Polytechnical School. His mother showed Oxby an album of family photographs and pointed to her son, proudly proclaiming, "Leonid skiing . . . Leonid birthday . . ." the mother was pretty and Oxby could not refrain from using his favorite all-purpose word, with a superlative tossed in for good measure: "*Spahseebah. Bahlshoeh spahseebah.*"

The fourth location was on Zagorodny Prospekt. They arrived at two in the afternoon following a stopover to feed Poolya. It was another high rise apartment, in a dull, faded yellow. As he had been able to do on their first stop, Poolya waited until the main entrance was opened, then slid inside as if he were a longtime resident who had misplaced his key. But a surprise awaited them when they reached the mailboxes and searched for Leonid Baletsky's name. It wasn't there.

The elevator door opened. A man and a woman walked out of it and started for the exit. Poolya stopped them.

"We do not find the name Leonid Baletsky." He spoke in Russian. "You know him?"

"He is dead," the man said. "He killed himself."

"What is it, Poolya?" Oxby asked.

Poolya explained.

"Ask how he did it, and when? And did the police come?"

Poolya quizzed the couple, who showed little interest in talking about a suicide. They halfheartedly answered a few of Poolya's questions, then would take no more. Oxby watched them go off.

"They say he jumped from his balcony."

"Not pushed?"

"They say he jumped."

"Police?"

"The police were here."

"What floor?"

"Five."

"Let's go."

On each floor were three apartments, all opening off a rectangular-shaped room illuminated by a window and a single ceiling light. An open door led to the staircase. In front of one apartment entrance was a child's tricycle. On the floor in front of all three doors was a thick, fiber mat. There was a number on each door, no names.

Oxby pushed the button at the door with the tricycle. No answer. He pressed the button again with the same result. He tried the next door. The third try brought a response.

"*Dah?*" a man's voice said from inside.

"We are looking for Leonid Baletsky," Poolya said.

The door was opened by a man who Oxby imagined was an Olympic heavyweight wrestler, as he literally filled the doorway. He pointed.

"In there," he said. "He's dead, you know."

Poolya turned to Oxby. "You understand?"

"Yes," Oxby said firmly. "Can he describe Baletsky for us?" Oxby threw the question out, expecting Poolya to shape it into Russian. To their surprise, an answer came from the wrestler in a mix of Russian and English. His description matched up with the man Oxby and Yakov had seen in the museum.

Oxby inspected the locks on the door to Baletsky's apartment, fully aware neither he nor Poolya could get past them. And with a man the size of a small mountain residing across the hall, he wasn't about to become involved in breaking and entering. Perhaps it was time to introduce himself to the local constabulary.

"Where is the nearest police office?"

The word "police" caught Poolya by surprise, but the big man answered again. The words had strange sounds, but Oxby understood perfectly that the precinct station was less than a kilometer away on Moskovskiy Prospekt.

❧ ❧ ❧

Oxby had noted his bodyguard's reaction to the thought of paying a visit to the police, even though Poolya had vigorously claimed that he was not currently in violation of the law. He argued that many of the police were pigs because they ran the biggest extortion racket in Petersburg. "They bodyguard the ones with big money. Politicians, too," he grumbled.

"Stay in the car and smoke your bloody cigarettes," Oxby said. "I'll handle this myself."

There would be an officer on the force who could speak English. Follow the money and you'll find someone who speaks the language, Oxby reasoned. He was right. Within five minutes he was sitting with the precinct deputy commandant, an ice-cold Coca-Cola in his hand.

Bureaucracy changes slowly, and in Russia, progress is perceptible only to those with keen eyesight and immense patience. In Petersburg there was a police office, or precinct station, in each district. The precinct police were called the militia. But there was another police authority known as the procurator. Also uniformed, the procurators traced their origins to Peter the Great and were responsible for investigating major crimes, leaving all else to the militia.

"You are from Scotland Yard?" the commandant said respectfully. "I have read much about your system. Very good, you think?"

"Very good, indeed," Oxby replied, restraining the urge to unburden his complaints to a fellow policeman. He would gladly discuss the Yard, but would resist any invitation to reveal the true purpose of his inquiry into the death of Leonid Baletsky. The commandant, Oxby observed, was named Yuri Safarov. His name appeared on a bronze plaque on the door, and on official-looking business cards stacked on his desk.

There was a considerable amount of dark stained wood in Safarov's office. The room had a high ceiling and thick casement windows, and a worn parquet floor. The furniture bore the scars and cigarette burns of hard use. The chief was well worn, too. He was fifty, wore glasses, had unruly gray hair, and wore a white shirt that was not very white and in its third day without a wash.

"This Leonid Baletsky," Safarov began, "fell from his balcony and there was no way to say it was an accident or if he committed suicide. Or that he had been pushed. We conclude he did not fall by accident or from the Green Serpent that causes old people to kill themselves."

Green Serpent, Yakov had explained, was the euphemism for vodka. If not suicide or accident, Baletsky had been murdered. Oxby asked the commandant if he thought that was so.

"We believe he was pushed off his balcony, but have not the proof. So strange about this one," Safarov went on and held up his left hand and wiggled the little finger. "This was missing when the body was examined. Perhaps that hand had scraped against the side of the building or he fell onto that hand when he hit the stones. We searched for the finger and could not find it." He shook his head. "Nothing."

Oxby thought about the missing finger, that it was a queer notion. "Is there a superstition about such a thing?" he asked.

"Not one that I know about," the commandant answered.

"Did he have a family?"

"A son." Safarov leafed through some papers. "No wife. The son claimed the body at the morgue."

"I would like to talk to his son. Do you have his telephone number?"

"Explain, please, why you are searching into this death, and wish to see Baletsky's son. Is it official business?"

Oxby smiled. It was the broad, warm kind of grin that could melt the most obstinate levels of officialese. "I recently became acquainted with Leonid, and had looked forward to seeing more of him. Mutual friends, common interests . . . that sort of thing. And so, I should like to pass on my condolences to the son."

Safarov listened, his face expressionless. He pondered Oxby's question, then nodded. "I will give you that information."

Oxby then asked a series of questions that would come naturally in the investigation of a suspected murder, though couching each question in the character of his recent friendship with the deceased. What was the condition of Baletsky's apartment? Describe the balcony from which he fell or was pushed. Was an autopsy performed? Were there witnesses? What time did it happen? On and on. The commandant enjoyed the skill Oxby displayed, confessing on several occasions that his own people had failed to develop certain facts. Oxby recorded the answers in his always available notebook. When he completed the interview he handed Safarov his card, insisting that he contact Oxby on any future visit to London.

"I will show you how we chase our criminals," Oxby said, and held out his hand. "Then I promise to take you to one of our very best pubs."

🐞 🐞 🐞

There were uncertain consequences connected to chasing over the big city to find Viktor Lysenko's apartment. But that was precisely what Oxby planned for the remainder of the afternoon. Poolya claimed they weren't being followed, an opinion, not necessarily a fact. And Oxby knew it. There remained dangerous possibilities and questions that required answers: Who hired Viktor to kill Vasily? Did he live alone? With another professional? Did he have another life with job and family?

If Oxby could get into his apartment, he might find the answers. Answers that might lead to the Fabergé egg.

The possibilities were endless, and became somewhat more problematic when they stopped in front of 9 Kubansky Street. It was the first address of the five Oxby had purchased. It was a bakery shop.

They had no luck at the second, third, and fourth addresses. Oxby was ready to declare that Viktor Lysenko had been a phantom. Hired killers he had known were that way.

The fifth address was near St. Petersburg University on Vasilievsky

Island, the largest of all the city's islands. The apartment buildings were attached to each other in a long row, and every one showed scars from the heavy German artillery shelling during the long siege in World War II. Every third building had been destroyed and rebuilt to its original specifications. There were two apartments on each floor, and according to Oxby's list, Viktor Lysenko's apartment, *kvartyra 2,* was on the second floor. Poolya leaned on the button. They heard a bell ring and reacted to the simultaneous loud report from a truck's backfire. Poolya pressed again. Oxby glanced at his watch. It was 7:30 and fatigue was setting in. Oxby pressed the button, waited half a minute, then sought help from the occupants in the other apartment on the floor. No sound came when the button was pushed, so they rapped repeatedly on the heavy wooden door. Still, no response.

"Enough for today," Oxby said, and preceded Poolya out to the street and the car. The bodyguard examined his strips of tape while Oxby leaned against a tree and gazed up to the windows where, according to the list of two dollar names he was holding, a man named Viktor Lysenko was supposed to live.

Staring down at Oxby from behind heavy, crocheted curtains was a young woman dressed in black pants and sweater. Her blond hair was combed severely back and tied with a black ribbon. She was tall and slim. She wore no makeup. Galina Lysenko had stood at the window waiting quietly and patiently for the doorbell to stop ringing. Her lovely features were marred by a dampness and slight puffiness around her eyes. A telephone was pressed to her ear.

"Describe him," Galina said.

"I've never seen him," Trivimi said. "I've been told he's average height, light brown hair, mid-forties. I can't give you more."

"I know it's Oxby," Galina said. "He was at the door. Ringing and ringing. What is he looking for?"

"Information," Trivimi said.

"Has Oleg learned how Viktor was killed?"

"We've heard nothing."

"It doesn't matter," Galina said too softly for the Estonian to hear. "I know who killed Viktor."

"I can't hear you."

They're getting into the car."

The Peugeöt pulled away from the curb.

"They're leaving," Galina said.

Chapter 30

The sky had cleared and at 9:30 in the evening it was brighter than it had been all during the wet, gray day. Occasional bursts of fireworks punctuated the evening air, early signals that the summer solstice and the official onset of the White Nights was six days off. The pyrotechnics were probably the work of early celebrants, themselves ignited by too much high-voltage vodka. After their meal, Yakov's kitchen once more assumed its role as an incident room.

"You've been quiet," Yakov said "I'm beginning to understand your moods. You haven't told me the news about Baletsky."

"Bad news I'm afraid. We found the apartment all right, but not Leonid. He's dead. Murdered, the police are saying."

Yakov stared blankly for a moment. "Now three are dead."

"Not a pleasant number. Of course one is too many."

"What happened?" Yakov asked.

Oxby related his conversation with the precinct chief. "There was no suggestion of a robbery. They believe he was pushed off his balcony. He could have jumped, but there wasn't a note and his son told the police he doesn't think his father would commit suicide." Oxby turned toward Yakov. "Sons and fathers try desperately not to think ill of each other. But, whatever caused it, a drop from the fifth floor onto concrete is a bloody long, hard fall."

"You talked to the son?"

"No, but I plan to. I've got his phone number, compliments of the police. In spite of negative reports to the contrary, I find your police very cooperative."

"To you they might be. You are like a brother."

Following his visit to the Naval Records Office, Yakov had continued to translate Vasily's diary and the letters he had received from Sasha Akimov.

"Once I put the diaries under a magnifying glass I could see more clearly how Vasily formed his letters. Then I was able to understand his handwriting and could transcribe nearly everything he wrote. Fortunately, Sasha Akimov wrote very neatly. He was my age, and we learned our penmanship at the same time. It makes a difference when you are writing in Cyrillic."

"Start with Vasily. Based on his diary and notes, do you have the impression he was rational or did he ramble on without making much sense?"

"I thought his insights were very rational, not at all what I expected after so long a time away from home and the last years in that dreary asylum. Though toward the end, he seemed to lose interest and would go on without much purpose. When I pieced together the dates, it was obvious that many pages and perhaps entire tablets were missing. He listed several names, ones he was convinced were stealing from him. Some years ago he was writing a diary, adding a little every day. But in the recent years, there was nothing to write about. So he added an occasional note and inserted a date only now and then."

"Were you struck by anything unusual?"

"Yes, very much."

"What was that?"

"Let me say that the earliest date I could find was ten years ago, and that appeared about a quarter of the way into the diaries that we found. I imagine the stolen notebooks he refers to cover the years before that time. He wrote on many occasions about a military trial in which he was involved, and how he had never been allowed to prove his innocence."

"Convicted criminals go to their grave protesting their innocence," Oxby said. "They all do it, and sometimes they're right. If he claimed he was innocent, he must have had a good idea who was guilty. Did he say?"

"Not directly." Yakov referred to his copy of the translation. "He was obsessed by the fact he could not get the court to grant his appeal for a new trial. He repeated this same thought several times. And always pointing a finger. Here is a typical entry. It's not dated, but he says it is Sunday: 'They deny my appeal again. They are cowards. Stupid asssucking bastards. Sasha tells me in his letters that Deryabin gains power with the committee. He says I must continue to write. But letters are a waste. I should kill Deryabin.'"

"Steady, mate!" Oxby said anxiously. "Show me where he wrote that. And your translation."

"It's here, at the top of a page ten." He passed over the pages to Oxby.

Oxby read it and the pages before and after. He looked intently at Yakov. "Think hard. Have we heard the name Deryabin?"

Yakov pondered. "No, this is the first time."

"Does Vasily refer to Deryabin again?"

"Yes, quite a few times."

"How many? Ten? Fifteen?"

"No, no. I think four or five."

"That's enough. His nemesis was Deryabin. I bloody well would like to read what he wrote in all those missing pages."

"I am not a psychologist," Yakov said, "but I can see a great amount of anger and guilt in Karsalov. It is most clear in his recent notes, as if he were aware that he would die soon and wanted to absolve himself by writing about his shortcomings and his failures. I saw this in the strange way he wrote, as if his cramped little words would disguise his confessions. In other places he seemed pleased to get these troubling thoughts off his chest. He says very clearly that he deeply regretted the way he had treated his wife and son."

"Is it so clear from what he wrote, or is this Yakov Ilyushin reading these sentiments into the diary?"

"When you read the translation, you will find for yourself that this is true."

Oxby scanned several pages. "I see that he makes numerous references to Sasha Akimov."

"They were friends. Apparently they worked as a team before all of his troubles. I suspect they served in the navy together."

"What other names are repeated?"

"He mentions his son frequently, the name Mikhail appears more than any other. Then his wife, Anna, and his sister, Nina. He rarely put a first and last name together but of course these were very personal notes, and these were people he knew intimately. For example, he writes about Leonid and Prekhner and Artur, but I can't determine if that is two or three different people. He also wrote about his father, Nikolai, from time to time."

"Prekhner," Oxby repeated the name. "How is it spelled?"

"It is there, in my translation."

"He mentions Baletsky?" Oxby asked.

Yakov nodded. "Yes, and a judge that he wrote the words *yab tvoyo-mat*, which I will only say is a terrible obscenity. And he wrote about a doctor a number of times because I think he liked him."

Oxby flipped to the last page. "Bedtime reading." He smiled. "Excellent work."

"Thank you, but it is not all. I have the letters of Sasha Akimov." He gave Oxby four pages, each a summary of the correspondence.

"What are the dates?" Oxby asked.

"Old, I'm afraid. The most recent I am estimating was written more than four years ago. I have numbered them in sequence. I think I have done it correctly."

Oxby placed the pages side by side in front of him and began a slow perusal of each letter.

"Akimov wrote to Vasily many times, I see."

"Yes, but most of those letters were thrown away or stolen. Who would steal a letter?"

"Hmmm, yes," Oxby said absently, not answering the question. "He writes about Anna. You say she was sick, but I don't understand the word you use."

"It is like a pneumonia that will not go away. I don't know the English word for it."

"Consumption? Or tuberculosis?"

Yakov shrugged. "I think something like that."

"A sick lady, no matter what it was. Do we know if Anna is alive?"

"In the diary Vasily hopes she is well. That could have been written two years ago. Then, she was alive."

"Can you ask some of your friends to find her?"

"It will be difficult, but yes. I will try."

"In this letter—" Oxby pushed it to the side. "Akimov tells about the appeal for a new trial. 'There is a new judge,' he tells Vasily, and writes his name. 'You must write to him.'"

"That is the letter where he mentions Deryabin," Yakov said, "but it is confusing what he writes."

" 'I have met with Deryabin,' " Oxby quoted, " 'and may have a position in his company. Then I will have the chance to learn the truth.' "

"There was nothing more. No more letters after that one," Yakov said.

Oxby read the last letter again. "It's about politics and Yeltsin. He says 'democracy means a few get rich and the rest of us don't get our pensions.' He says '*mudozvon.*' What is that?"

Yakov laughed. "It is a word I cannot accurately translate. He means all the politicians were talking shit. We have many words like that. Some very much worse, I fear."

Oxby gathered the letters and put them aside. "Good work. Now tell me what you discovered in the Naval Records Office."

Yakov was a willing and energetic investigator who possessed a natural talent many police investigators would kill for. Earlier in the day, he had entered the labyrinthine halls of the Russian Naval Offices, Baltic Division, and in two hours had charmed his way into the office of the official in charge of personnel records. It took until late in the morning for him to be assigned to a clerk who led him to a room with several computers. He had been put in front of one of the machines and shown how to search the files, select a name, then bring up a complete dossier on the screen. He was shown how to create a hard copy of the information.

"At noon I was prepared to bring up Vasily's file, but was told that it was the meal hour and that I must come back after 1:30. I ate my apple and waited. At quarter to two I was back in front of the computer and here is what I was able to find." He smoothed out the curled facsimile copy and his own notes.

"Because I had met Vasily, and had been with him in that awful place where he died, I was most interested in finding his records. So, I typed in Vasily Karsalov's name. In all those records of tens of thousands of Soviet and Russian navy servicemen, I was able to sort him out from others with the same name. Years ago, the record keeping was incredibly voluminous. You will see that Vasily attended the Nakhimov Naval Secondary School and the St. Petersburg Naval College. You can see that he achieved average marks and considerable criticism for disciplinary problems and underachievement."

"What did you learn about his trial?"

"That he had been charged with the murder of a civilian named Prekhner who supplied nonmilitary provisions to the base where Vasily was stationed, and where he was senior procurement officer of navy stores. Vasily was also charged with stealing property from the State and accepting bribes from Prekhner. The court found him guilty of bribery and theft, but the murder charge was reduced to self-defense."

Oxby said, "Vasily told me before he died that he didn't kill Prekhner."

Yakov lay the papers down. "You must realize that during the time when the Soviet was trying to appear progressive and benevolent, justice was not meted out with the same heavy hand as in earlier times. In those terrible days, Vasily would have been hanged or put immediately in front of a firing squad. As it was, he was transferred to a permanent post in Uzbekistan."

Oxby tried in vain to read the copy of the official file, finding the military and legal jargon beyond him. "Tell me, Yakov, how did he plead?"

"Vasily pleaded innocent to all the charges. He testified that he had been invited to Prekhner's apartment, along with—the name is blanked out—and that he drank too much and went into the bedroom and fell asleep. When he woke up several hours later, he found himself lying next to Prekhner's body, a knife in his hand. He swore he had not killed Prekhner. He insists that—again the name is blanked out—was the murderer and had made it appear that Vasily was guilty. 'Why would I kill Artur Prekhner? He was my good friend.'"

"When was the trial?"

"November 1972. On the 25th and 26th."

"When was Vasily sent to Tashkent?"

Yakov turned to the last page of the transcript. "January 7, 1973."

"You said a name was blanked out of Vasily's testimony. How could that be?"

"I can not answer such a question, but you can see that there is only an open space in the transcript." Yakov pointed with his pencil at the blank spaces in the report. "It was blanked out on the original file and transferred to the computer in that same way."

Oxby studied the report, frowning as he tried to read the words that appeared before and after the blank areas.

"How many letters were eliminated?"

Yakov studied the printout. "Here," he pointed to the first instance of an open space, "I count twelve spaces. But the blank spaces are shorter after that. In those I find seven spaces."

"Twelve, then seven." Oxby mulled over the numbers, then wrote them down. "Twelve . . . then seven. Suppose that initially the first and last name had been inserted in the transcript, and then, in succeeding references, only the last name was used. That would be a normal practice in English. Would that be a normal practice in Russian?"

"Who can say what is normal practice?" Yakov asked. "Names are important to Russians, and the normal practice might be to use the first and the patronymic name before the familiya, or last name. But in military records, who is to say what is correct? I would think with only twelve letters, the patronymic name was eliminated and there were the first and last names as you suggest."

Oxby's frown deepened. "If what you say is correct, and I fear it is, then my suspicion that the missing name is Deryabin has evaporated."

Yakov's face wrinkled into complete surprise. "Deryabin? How is it you select that name?"

Oxby forced a weak smile. "I was working on an obscure theory known as Occam's razor that allows the possibility of identifying the person whose name was deleted from the transcript of Vasily's trial by applying facts we know, and arriving at an answer in an uncomplicated way. We know that Vasily Karsalov was tried for murder, but he claims he was innocent. He also tells us a person named Deryabin had influence with the committee that could grant an appeal of his conviction. He writes in his diary, 'I should kill Deryabin.'"

"And those facts lead you to believe it was Deryabin's name that was deleted from the transcript?"

"Yes, until you calculated that there were a total of twelve characters deleted in the first instance, and seven thereafter. If I'm correct, the missing character has a first name containing four and a last name with seven characters. I assume there was a space between the first and last names."

"It would be that way," Yakov said, trying to be helpful.

"But then I wrote Deryabin's name. It contains eight characters."

Yakov took the pad on which Oxby had written the name. "In English, you are correct," Yakov said. "But not when the name is spelled in Russian. Then it has seven characters. Like this . . ."

Дерябин

"You see we have one letter that does the work of two English letters."

Oxby smacked his hands together. "Bloody good, Yakov. My hunch is still alive. Now let's see if it holds up."

"How will you do that?"

"*We* will do it. The first step we'll take is to return to the Naval Offices where you will find the records of a man named Deryabin who served alongside Vasily Karsalov and has a first name that contains four letters."

Chapter 31

"These toxins are elaborated by soil bacteria," the bearded, slight little man intoned in a manner that might resonate in a biochemistry classroom. He held two bottles in his hand. They were two inches square and three quarters of an inch thick and made of heavy glass. They were sealed closed with a heavy cap over which was a molded, clear plastic overwrap. He handed one to Oleg Deryabin, the one that contained a small amount of a gray powder.

"Anthrax," he said solemnly. "The activity is at the limits of our laboratory's capability, but exceeds by a wide margin the specifications we were supplied. We have found excellent sources for the bacteria, most especially in the farm country along the Volkhov River south of here. Three bottles of the size you are holding could, depending on the method of dispersion and density of the population, disable ten thousand people."

Oleg eyed the contents respectfully, then gingerly placed it next to the second bottle on a table that was in the center of a "clean" room, one of four rooms that comprised the premises of Neva Specialty, the little enterprise which produced perfumes that paralleled the high quality of the world's most famous fragrances. The division employed two laboratory technicians, led by the biochemist Maurice, who was skilled in duplicating *haut parfum*.

The room was windowless and the ceiling, walls, floor, and table were covered with a glistening white vinyl. Though the air was scrubbed and filtered, an unmistakable hint of a delicate odor came from the ceiling vents. Deryabin sat, motioning for Maurice and Trivimi Laar to join him. All three wore pale blue coveralls as well as hoods and goggles, and their shoes had been replaced with cloth boots laced tight below the knees.

Deryabin fidgeted with an unlit cigarette he was dying to put a match to. He said, "Time is important, as well as the purity of the toxin."

The Estonian reached toward the two bottles, not sure of which to pick up, then, thinking better of it, pointed a long finger at the bottle next to the one that contained anthrax. "Are there *Clostridia* toxins in this bottle?"

Maurice pushed the jar in front of Trivimi. "That bottle contains ten grams, or a third of an ounce of a mixture of *Clostridium botulinum*, type A and B toxins, and I will warn you, it is potentially an overwhelming amount."

"How much can you produce in a week?" Deryabin asked.

"A problem," Maurice said. "Our equipment is only sufficient to produce sample quantities. It is slow and hazardous work to make larger amounts."

"I asked how much you can produce in a week," Deryabin said impatiently.

"As much as that bottle will hold. Thirty grams."

"Only that?" Deryabin asked.

"This laboratory is designed to make small quantities of perfume, not toxins of such virulence." Maurice drew himself up, and said proudly, "It is a major accomplishment to produce these toxins in any quantity."

"Can you produce thirty grams each week until October 1? That would be fifteen weeks, or about 450 grams. A little less than half a kilogram."

"I cannot promise that. It would be too dangerous. And we could not make perfume during that time."

"How much can you promise?" Deryabin insisted.

"We will do our best to make thirty grams a week. But, week in, week out? I cannot promise that much. We do the best we can."

Deryabin pulled off his hood and slapped it against his thigh. "What would it take to bring in larger equipment? The kind that would let you make five kilograms by October 1?"

"There's no money for new equipment," Trivimi said.

Deryabin shut the Estonian off with a glare and eyed Maurice. "How much?"

"Expensive," Maurice said. "Then it must be shipped and installed."

"How much and how long?" Deryabin persisted.

"There is a source in Zurich that can supply what is needed for, I will guess, a hundred thousand Swiss francs. To ship and install would take six weeks."

"Leaving nine weeks to produce five kilograms of *Clostridia* toxins. You could do that?"

"Please, this is not boric acid we are making." Maurice picked up the bottle and held it uncomfortably close to Deryabin's face. "I cannot describe the risk. The very slightest breath of what is in this jar can mean a horrible sickness. Or death."

Deryabin glared at his chemist. "I pay you to solve problems, not whine about them. I ask again. With more equipment, can you produce five kilograms in nine weeks?"

Maurice put up his hands in mock surrender. "It would be possible to produce a half kilogram a week."

The answer, which Deryabin computed to mean four and a half kilograms, satisfied him. He relaxed and seemed about to adjourn the meeting when Trivimi spoke up. The Estonian had listened patiently and had heard the unspoken caveats that Maurice had been bullied into letting go unsaid.

Trivimi said, "As we are unable to spend a thousand Swiss francs for new laboratory equipment, it is impossible for us to spend a hundred thousand."

"Find the fucking money!" Deryabin shouted. "I will not let this opportunity go past us."

Trivimi responded, "You are ahead of yourself, Oleshka. No price was set on the toxins, and we agreed only to ship a trial quantity. Five kilograms was your idea. Half a kilogram would be more than enough, that is somewhat more than a pound. Am I correct, Maurice?"

Maurice nodded and said that it was.

Trivimi continued, "If the sample quantity is approved, we will receive a larger order and demand partial payment in advance. Then Maurice can order his new equipment."

Deryabin flicked on his lighter, then extinguished the flame with his thumb. Nervously he did it a half dozen more times before snapping the lighter closed.

Trivimi said, "Maurice has told us he can make thirty grams a week with his present equipment. Maybe a little less, but I believe that is all right."

Deryabin bit on his lip. "Then get on with it."

Maurice stared first at Trivimi, then at Deryabin. "Monsieurs, you must know that while I said it was possible to produce a half kilogram of *Clostridia* toxins, you must also know that there will be a great risk in using only laboratory instruments to accomplish it."

Deryabin rose from his chair. "You repeat yourself too much. Your responsibility is to assure me that no mistakes are made."

Maurice nodded, but not enthusiastically. "I make no promises. Remember that until October, we will not make any perfumes."

"We will survive," Deryabin said.

"You asked for an empty bottle," Maurice said, and pushed one in front of Deryabin.

"Is it absolutely empty and clean?" Deryabin roared. He inspected the bottle minutely, but without touching it. After Maurice assured him that the bottle had, in fact, been sterilized, he picked it up, and walked from the room, leaving the bewildered scientist alone at the table wondering what sort of mad person he was dealing with.

The Estonian joined Deryabin and both removed their coveralls and boots.

Deryabin handed the bottle to Trivimi. "You see the size, and the shape? It will fit exactly into the battery."

The Estonian wrapped his long fingers around the bottle. "Excellent," he said. Then he added, "You gave Maurice a difficult assignment. If it is too much for him, there could be trouble."

Deryabin slipped on his shoes. "It is my job to give Maurice his orders. It is your job to make certain he carries them out."

Chapter 32

Oxby chose to use a telephone in the Grand Hotel Europe rather than risk calling Alex Tobias from the phone in Yakov's apartment. Odds that a tap had been put on Yakov's phone were reasonably high, and so the inspector felt more comfortable aligning himself on the side of caution.

There were other benefits; the Grand Europe served rare African coffee, was private, and he could bill the charges to a credit card. He could also have a lunch of smoked salmon in the Brasserie, better even than a rare indulgence in the Grill Room of London's Connaught Hotel.

Yakov, along with Mikki, had gone early to his district office, a kind of municipal government agency that was a holdover from the old days, and where now a new breed of civil servant plied their trade in the same old obstinate ways that prevailed under the Soviet. He was appealing for his back pension payments, and permission to book entry into the polyclinic. The stump on his leg had become uncomfortable and he was due for a replacement prosthesis. From the district office, Yakov would continue on to the Naval Records Office and join Oxby.

Oxby placed the call at 7:00 A.M. New York time, confident that Tobias would be shaving or on to his first cup of coffee. Wrong.

"I've been up for over an hour, read the paper, and had made up my mind to go off to work whether you called or not."

"How were the fish?"

"God knows I spent the weekend with a hammer in my hand. What's with you, Jack? You gave me plenty to worry about."

"Sorry, I might have laid it on a bit thick. My real problem is that I can't see who or what I'm up against. I began to think I should consult the local police."

"Why the hell don't you?"

"In this country the police come in two flavors, and I'm not sure

214

where I'd be welcome. They've got the militia and the procurator, and if you don't know your politics, you don't know which one to see."

"Can you get help from your British consulate?"

"They'll tell me to get my nose out of the mess."

"Aren't you staying with a national? A homegrown Russian native?"

"Yakov's Russian, all right, and an intellectual who doesn't trust the police either."

"I thought the days of the evil empire were over."

"Replaced by what they loosely refer to as free enterprise. I'm playing it as safe as I can."

"I got back to the city on Monday and had a meeting that generated a little news you might be interested in."

"You saw Kip Forbes?"

"Afraid not. He's in Colorado. I did better than dig up some dry, old information about Fabergé's eggs."

"How's that?"

"It's your nickel, so listen carefully. Before I went up to the lake, I was asked if I'd help out on a nutty case that involved a guy who got shot in the TriBeCa section of Manhattan. He's a writer, a little loopy, but I like him. He got a hell of a scare along with getting shot a couple of times. Took a hit in a thigh and another in his right buttock where it hurts like hell, so right now he's nursing a couple of bad sores. At any rate, I thought I was through with this sort of thing, but schedules are screwed up with guys on vacation. So I said okay and first thing you know I'm in a brand-new Cadillac dealership talking to a young Russian who's got more smarts than any ten car dealers I'd ever met."

"A young Russian?"

"How about that? Told me he left St. Petersburg when he was a kid. Went to London, learned to speak English, then New York where he put himself through school. That's when he got into selling cars and today he's got a couple dozen showrooms up and down the East Coast."

"What's his name?"

"He changed it to a good old American name. Would you believe Mike Carson? Not bad for someone selling automobiles, don't you think?"

"That's what I think, Alex. Go ahead."

"Well, it seems there's an outfit in St. Petersburg that wants Carson to buy and prep late-model American luxury cars—mostly Caddys and Olds—and ship them to St. Petersburg."

"It's getting better. Go on."

"The guy that was doing the negotiating for the St. Petersburg outfit is Estonian. Last name's spelled L-A-A-R. His company is called Koleso. If you don't know, that means 'wheel' in Russian."

Oxby was getting a language lesson from his friend in New York. He smiled. "Move along, Alex, remember it's my nickel."

"Two and half weeks ago Carson had a surprise visit from an old gent named Sasha Akimov. Akimov was—"

"Hold on!" Oxby exclaimed. Say the name again?"

"Sasha Akimov."

"Okay. Akimov paid a visit to Carson. Go on."

"They were having a discussion when a woman burst in on them and put a nine millimeter in Akimov's throat."

"Kill him?"

"No, that didn't kill him. He died a few days later after a nurse with a Russian accent needled him with sodium pentobarbital."

"Russian nurse? Are you being serious?"

"I think it was the same woman who shot him, but we don't have evidence to prove it. And I know damned well we couldn't find her if we had any. I'll say that whoever it was went to hell of a lot of trouble to finish the job."

"Why did Akimov go all that distance to see Carson?"

"He knew Mike's family, claimed he first saw Mike when he was a day old. He was going on about the family and the old country, then bang!"

"What was Carson's name before he changed it?"

"I got it here . . . Karsalov. Mikhail Karsalov."

"Incredible," Oxby said, "bloody incredible. What's this got to do with the shooting in TriBeCa?"

Alex gave an abridged version of the Lenny Sulzberger saga.

"Do you know if Carson's mother is alive?"

"Mike said he wasn't sure, but thought she might be."

"What else did Akimov have to say?"

Tobias retold Akimov's story of the card game, and how Mike's father gambled and lost a valuable Fabergé egg, and more tragically, how Vasily Karsalov had been accused of murder, presumably confessed to it, and had been sent to Central Asia.

Oxby did not respond, he was making notes and digesting all that his friend had told him.

Tobias interrupted the silence. "Jack? You still there?"

"I'm here. A little stunned, trying to put all this in perspective. What you've told me is something damned close to a miracle."

Alex laughed. "It's that good?"

Immediately after Oxby finished speaking with Alex Tobias, he and Poolya drove to the Naval Records Office. Waiting in his car, alone, was Yakov.

"Where's Mikki?" Oxby demanded.

"Your associate," Yakov said to Poolya, "asked if he could go to one of the shops over by the metro station. I felt safe in front of all these buildings filled with military people, and said that he could."

"How long has he been gone?" Poolya asked, bridling his fury that Mikki had violated instructions.

"Twenty minutes."

Poolya parked alongside the Lada. He carefully examined Yakov's relic, then applied his tape to both cars.

Yakov spoke to an officer at the reception desk, pointing first to Oxby, then Poolya, jabbering as best Oxby could determine about relatives and loved ones. A ten dollar bill appeared in Yakov's hand , one of several Oxby had given him, and the officer, without changing a bored expression, waved all three toward an elevator. Yakov led the way to a series of rooms on the third floor and to a counter where he immediately filled out a two-page form. He asked for an attendant by name, and when she appeared, handed her the form and another ten dollar bill appeared.

Minutes later they were seated in front of a computer and Yakov was entering the search information he had learned during his previous visit.

Oxby handed Yakov a page from Karsalov's diary and pointed at the name.

Yakov typed in Cyrillic: DERYABIN.

The computer began a name search. After half a minute, the first of sixteen names appeared, all with a first and middle name or initial. The names appeared randomly, not by age, dates served, or alphabetical order. Yakov called up each name in the order it appeared, searching for one who had served during the period 1961 to 1973.

Oxby struggled to read the first few lines of each file, but could not keep up with Yakov, who scanned the information as quickly as he might grab the headlines in the morning newspaper. He would glance at it, then delete it and enter the next name. Twenty minutes into the search Yakov waved to Oxby.

"Come around here, Jack. This might be it."

Oxby moved in front of the monitor and studied the Russian letters. "Damned right! That's our man. Say the name, Yakov."

"Oleg Vladimirovich Deryabin."

"Where was he stationed in 1963?"

Yakov read off the critical dates. "In June of that year he was transferred to the naval base in Tallinn."

"That should cinch it," Oxby said. But to assuage his sense of caution, he instructed Yakov to run a check on all the Deryabins on their list. "It's no time to rush into a mistake."

Oxby stared at the monitor as Yakov called up the records of the remaining naval veterans with the name of Deryabin. None had a four-letter first name, and none matched the dates of service.

"Bloody damned good." Oxby beamed. "Let's get a print out of his record."

That accomplished, the trio departed. Mikki was not in sight, and a small crowd was gathered to the side of the building, near to where they had parked their cars. Poolya ran ahead and pushed away the curious throng that was gaping at the broken driver's side window on Yakov's Lada. Oxby joined him and stared past shards of glass at the large paving stone that had caused the damage. Along with countless bits of glass, the stone was on the front seat and next to it was a green box tied with pale green ribbon.

Yakov arrived, stunned to discover that his faithful old automobile had been senselessly damaged. He swore volubly, venting his frustration, asking one or two gods to strike dead whoever had done the deed. He reached for the door handle.

"Wait," Oxby said. "We've had company, and they've got terribly bad manners. Let's look about and make certain they haven't left any more surprises."

He and Poolya checked the tape strips and examined both cars carefully. Poolya probed under Yakov's car with a pole that had a mirror attached to its end. For good measure, he checked under his car. Only then did Oxby open the door and allow Yakov to brush out the glass and retrieve the green box.

"What have they sent this time?" Yakov asked.

"I'll open it," Oxby said, taking the box and feeling its weight, ever suspicious that little packages can pack a deadly wallop. He untied the ribbon, then set the box on the pavement, found a stick and edged the top up and off the box. Inside were loose strips of paper, and nestled in the paper was another small package.

"I wish to say, Jack, these people have little imagination. It is like the first parcel they sent, wrapped in the same cloth. You remember?"

"I remember, but this time it's not a doll," Oxby said. He held the little package, kneading it gently, feeling its contours. "I'm afraid I know exactly what it is."

He began to unravel the cloth. "Be prepared," he said. "It will not be a pleasant sight."

When he took away the last of the cloth wrapping, Oxby was holding in the palm of his hand a folded piece of paper and next to it a human finger. Yakov recoiled at the sight of the white skin and blue fingernail. It had been cleanly severed from the hand, though blood had clotted and turned black and scabbed over the bone.

Poolya stared at the finger with professional curiosity. He said, if Oxby understood correctly, that he hoped the poor bastard was unconscious or dead when the finger was lopped off his hand.

Oxby unfolded the note and handed it to Yakov. He read it and unlike his response to the previous warning, showed new resolve. He put the words into English.

> *Stop your search at once. We can eliminate your protection in a minute's time. This is the last warning.*

Oxby showed the note to Poolya. He said, "They can stop you from protecting us? Is that what they are saying?"

"It is a game. You hire me to protect you, they hire someone to kill me." Poolya grinned. "But we hire more people to protect me."

It was like a Ponzi scheme, Oxby thought, only the stakes were murderously high.

🐝 🐝 🐝

Oxby helped Yakov clear his car of the glass. They got into it. "Follow me," Poolya said. "When I wave my arm, turn right at the next street. Circle the block and come back to where you made the turn. I want to see if you are being followed."

It was a strategy that won Oxby's approval. To Oxby's trained eye, it appeared obvious they were not followed. But Oxby was learning that in Russia the obvious was often too subtle to detect.

It was evening when they returned to the apartment, the sun now shining. Poolya reported to Oxby. "I was surprised that you were not followed."

"You're surprised, and I am pleased. I had hoped that Mikki might be following us. Can you guess where he is?"

"Not in the city. He'll be away until he's spent his money." He shook his head. "He'll never work with us again."

"You will replace him?"

"Tomorrow there will be a new man."

Oxby wondered if it was as simple as Poolya was trying to make it. Poolya had called it a game. "Like a round-robin. Even if you lose, you can still compete."

After supper, Yakov took the papers he had collected that day and placed them on the table. He began translating Oleg Deryabin's naval records, reading aloud portions, making occasional comments to himself. Oxby reviewed his journal and made additional notes. For an hour neither spoke, each absorbed in the work at hand. Oxby pushed away from the table. He sat quietly, staring at his friend, his expression ranging from amusement to deep concern.

"You have acted bravely in the face of several intimidating experiences today. In fact, you have acted with extraordinary courage through all of these two weeks we've been together. Now your life may truly be in danger. I cannot allow you to remain at risk."

"You are going to leave my apartment?"

"Not only shall I leave, but I will make it abundantly clear to all who will listen that I am the one who is searching for Rasputin's egg. Not you."

"If you are concerned about my safety, put it out of your mind. You have brought some excitement into my life and I don't want to go back to boredom and feeling useless."

"We are having a language problem," Oxby said. "Listen carefully to me. You are in danger of being killed. At the very least, you may be seriously injured. I can't make it any plainer."

"My English is thoroughly competent, thanks to you. I wish to say that I fully understand the danger, and find in some perverse way that

I like it. I'll make a small bargain with you. Pay for a new window in my beloved car, and I will continue in my role as your deputy assistant investigator." Yakov rose and found a bottle, two glasses, and slices of dark bread. He returned to the table and poured a golden brown liquid into each glass. "This is Tutovka, a cognac from Karabakh." He beamed. "In the Caucasus Mountains. You will like it."

He gave Oxby a glass, then raised his. "Shall we agree? We will see this through and no more talk of your leaving?"

"I have a small bargain, also," Oxby said. "You shall never, ever go out of my sight without permission."

"*Davay chokhnymsya,*" Yakov said, inviting Oxby to clink their glasses. The cognac was strong and it burned Oxby's throat. He drank all of it, then broke off a piece of the bread and ate it, chewing slowly, considering if his decision to stay in Yakov's apartment was the right one. He watched Yakov return to his task. Fifteen minutes passed and Yakov announced that had completed translating all of the papers that comprised Deryabin's naval records.

"Besides the four pages that make up his service record, there were nine additional pages," Yakov reported. "Three were letters, five were copies of transcripts that dealt with some part of his activities, and one is a portion of a court proceeding. From what I have seen, Deryabin had a successful naval career."

"In what way?" Oxby asked.

"He was a *kapitan tretyego ranga* at the time of discharge. That would be the same as commander in your navy. A very high rank for someone so young. I wish to say he was awarded enough medals to cover half his chest, also very special because when he was active there were no hot wars to fight."

"How many years did he serve?"

"A long time. I think seventeen. Yes, he entered in 1961 and was discharged in May of 1978. But more important, he was transferred to Tallinn in July of 1963. Later he was in Tehran and Cairo. Then to Petersburg in 1971. He was sent to Washington in June of '73 . . . appointed adjutant to the senior military officer in the Soviet embassy."

Oxby thought about the Washington assignment, concluding that about that time, when he was thirty-four, Deryabin's career began to blossom.

"Jack, this will interest you." Yakov handed Oxby a page. "It is a summary of Deryabin's testimony at Vasily Karsalov's murder trial."

Oxby read the translation. "Interesting isn't quite the right word. This confirms that Deryabin and Vasily served in the navy together, and according to Deryabin, they were friends. He says that Vasily was a man of good character, but that alcohol was a constant problem for him."

"Why would that page be in his record?" Yakov wondered.

"To make it appear he had been a loyal friend. Let me see Vasily's records and your translation of his diaries. I'm putting two and two together and coming up with five."

Oxby sorted through the paperwork Yakov handed him and made several neat piles. "I'm looking for the transcript that you found in Vasily's personal records. The original, not your translation."

Yakov shuffled through his own growing mound of papers, selected several sheets, and handed them to Oxby.

"Come around and look at this," Oxby said. "Does the name Oleg Deryabin fit here where the first blanked-out area appears?"

Yakov said that it did. "And just the last name would fit in all the other blank spaces."

"I can't go to court with it, but what I see tells me that Vasily Karsalov didn't commit murder. But Oleg Deryabin did."

"I wish to say, Jack, that under the Soviet, such tampering with official records could take place only on orders from a high authority. Under the new enlightenment, an underpaid government clerk will perform the same tiny miracle for a carton of Camel cigarettes. Besides, if the name had not been blanked out, it would be Vasily's word against Deryabin's."

"And Deryabin wins that little skirmish." Oxby sat back and read all the pages Yakov had translated. "Every entry in his file was put there to add more gloss on a service record that reads like fiction. No one's that perfect," he said. "He was given flawless performance evaluations and awarded several dozen commendations. With every bloody commendation he got another medal and a ribbon. Right down to discharge '*with distinction.*'"

"There's one thing more," Yakov said, handing Oxby a letter. "It is a copy of a letter Deryabin sent to the commandant's office in which he acknowledges receipt of his pension statement. You see that in spite of all his medals, he will not receive a large check each month. But you can also see that it was dated five months ago and includes Deryabin's personal and business addresses and telephone numbers."

"First rate!" Oxby raved. "I will give you odds that the address bureau cannot supply that information and even higher odds that Deryabin paid to have his name permanently stricken from those records."

"Why?" Yakov asked. "No one lives in secret. And see?" pointing to the letter, "he lives on Stone Island where the tour buses show tourists our most expensive homes."

"Men like Deryabin are like children playing hide-and-seek," Oxby said. "They believe if they can't see you, then you can't see them."

Chapter 33

Gino's Ristorante, with its mystifying Italo-Russo cuisine, had not quite made it as a tourist mecca. It was on the Fontanka Embankment, but on the wrong side of the Nevsky Prospekt, west of the great boulevard by more than a mile. The room was dark, illuminated by candles stuck into stout chianti bottles, the kind that had never held wine, the kind with the straw wrapping that had been made in Thailand. To its credit, garlic and oregano were in the air. The little eatery was quiet, the atmosphere unhurried. Little wonder. It was, except for two tables, empty.

At a table by a window sat a mother, father, and daughter speaking in German. Galina Lysenko sat at a table next to an inside wall beneath an Alitalia Airlines poster. She stared out from behind sunglasses at the entrance, waiting. A waiter poured water in a glass and put the bottle on the table. He gave her a menu and went away. She looked at her watch, then at the family, and back to the entrance. The door opened. A man entered, spied Galina, and walked directly to her table.

It was Poolya. He was dressed as he had been earlier in the day when he accompanied Oxby to the Naval Records Office. His pale blue eyes seemed to pop out from his face, his skin a deep olive in the luteolous candlelight. His shirt was damp and smelled of his sweat. For the hard work he had put in that day he had obviously rewarded himself, for his breath stank from a cheap, sweet wine.

"You're late," Galina said impatiently.

"I went to the Moscow train station and mixed into the traffic. Then I came here." He hailed the waiter and ordered a bottle of Italian wine.

Galina took off her glasses and leaned forward. "Has Oxby talked about Tashkent? Has he admitted that he killed Viktor?"

"They don't talk about it in front of me. If I ask how Viktor was killed, they will say how do you know that he was dead?"

"You can say that half of this city knows about Viktor. And knows that he was killed in Tashkent. You can tell them that."

Poolya laughed. "The half who know are like you and me. Oxby and Ilyushin know because they were in Tashkent when it happened."

Galina stiffened. "We are wasting time waiting for proof that Oxby killed Viktor. I have all the proof I need."

"What proof?"

"Inside here," she rubbed both hands over her breasts, then down and across her stomach. "I feel it all through my body." She lifted her face and pointed to the sores on her face. "See these? Put there by Deryabin, who tells me Viktor caused his own death. Lies."

"He went to Tashkent because of Deryabin," Poolya said. "He's as much to blame as anyone."

"I told Deryabin we were a team."

"Then why did he send Viktor without you?"

"It was his way to come between us. He expects us to follow his orders without a mistake. Without a complaint."

Poolya's wine came. He poured a glass for Galina, then drank straight from the bottle. He took several long swigs, then said, "I say again that I am sorry about Viktor. He was my good friend, too."

Galina said, "Did Oxby and the old man like the gift we gave them?"

"Ilyushin was angry as a wounded cat that the window in his car was smashed. But they weren't frightened when they saw the finger. Oxby tore the message into a hundred pieces."

"These are silly games Oleg insists we play." She sipped the wine and made a face. She pushed her glass in front of Poolya.

Poolya said, "You can tell Deryabin that Oxby has a copy of his navy records."

"How did he —"

"At the Naval Records Office. Give a name and put it on the computer. Anyone can do it."

Galina said, "What else have they been fishing for?"

"Oxby made a phone call to New York this morning. I don't know who he called or what he said."

"Have you tapped the phone yet?"

"They said the lines were old and mixed with a hundred others. It should be completed tomorrow. But Oxby suspects and uses the phones in the hotel."

Galina put an envelope in Poolya's hand. "Here is half of your price. The other half comes when Oxby has paid everything he owes me."

The abbreviated smile on Galina's lips collapsed into a cold glare. "I'll give you some advice." She leaned forward. "Talk to Oxby like he is a lost brother. Ask him to tell you about London and about Scotland Yard. Stay close to him. Get inside the apartment and listen to what they say. Tell me everything. It's your job."

"Saturday is the last day for us."

"You didn't tell me this. What will they do after Saturday?"

Poolya leaned back in his chair and drained his glass. "They don't talk about it."

"Talk to Oxby. Learn what his plans are."

"I'll try." He emptied Galina's glass. "Who's replacing Mikki?"

"I chose Boris. Ivan will call Oxby tonight and say Boris will be at the apartment in the morning."

"I don't trust Boris." Poolya finished off the bottle. "Get someone else. Boris is not a team worker."

"I picked Boris," Galina said firmly. "He begins tomorrow morning."

"Boris does what's good for Boris. It is a bad mistake."

Chapter 34

At a quarter of ten, Wednesday morning, Oxby dialed Poolya's cellular phone and instructed him to bring the car to the front of the apartment. Accompanied by Yakov, Oxby climbed in back and gave instructions for the Hermitage.

St. Petersburg traffic had grown considerably thicker as the season of the White Nights approached. In each row of tour buses parked off Palace Square behind the Winter Palace were over thirty of the behemoths. They were lined up three abreast; more than a hundred of them, some from as far away as Madrid.

They passed the General Staff building behind the museum, Poolya searching for a parking spot. "So today we have culture," Poolya said. "We wear out our feet while our brains become smarter. Is so?"

"Is not so," Oxby said. "Today, Mr. Ilyushin and I will soak up the culture. You will stay with the crew and keep a sharp eye on the apartment."

"What is 'sharp eye'?" Poolya asked.

Yakov explained, but Poolya wasn't buying. "I must find a place to park so I can come with you. I am paid to protect you."

"Not today, Poolya," Oxby said. "Take us to the entrance."

Poolya grumbled, but edged the Peugeot ahead, behind a line of cars curled around the side of the great museum. He turned onto the embankment road and stopped at the main entrance, a stone's toss to the Neva River.

"Pick us up at this precise spot at four o'clock," Oxby said. They went inside. Oxby stayed by the door, watching until the last of the Peugeot went from sight. He took Yakov's arm and they returned to the street and to the south end of the building where the taxis were gathered. Several of the drivers scurried toward them, hoping for a fare. Oxby chose the car in front. The driver, a middle-age man wearing a leather cap, grinned widely and noticing the older man's limp, took Yakov's arm and helped him into the cab. A small gesture designed to improve his tip.

"Zagorodny Prospekt," Yakov instructed. "Eighty-six."

It was a twenty-minute ride that took thirty, and when they arrived it was shortly before noon.

"Ask him to wait," Oxby said. "I'll make it worth his time."

Yakov spoke to the driver, who asked how much and agreed to the offer Yakov made. Yakov had become expert and generous when dispersing the American dollars Oxby handed him.

It was a familiar setting to Oxby. A row of tall apartment buildings with a patch of green overrun with cotton grass in front of each one. Here and there were scraggly bushes and even more disappointing flowers. Before the entrance to number eighty-six was an alder tree that seemed to have been sliced perfectly in half from top to bottom, the half remaining leaning as if pushed by a persistent wind. Then the high, pale gray building itself with its balconies serving as refuges from the cramped living spaces inside. Standing near the entrance was a man in his mid-thirties with thinning brown hair and wearing a heavy wool suit with white shirt and maroon necktie. He looked uncomfortably hot in spite of a gentle, cool breeze and air as dry as an old bone.

"That should be our man," Oxby said.

Yakov approached and said, "I am Yakov Ilyushin. Are you Pavel Baletsky?"

The man smiled self-consciously. "*Dah*," he said simply.

Yakov shook his hand and introduced Oxby. Oxby tried his Russian and Pavel responded in English. Though he was a Russian language neophyte, Oxby was a master at identifying English dialects and idioms.

"Your English is excellent," Oxby said. "I detect one of our London schools. Which one?"

"The London School of Economics." Then, with an embarrassed smile, he said, "Is it so obvious?"

"Only to someone who loves his language as much as I," Oxby said. "It's like a hobby. I congratulate you for choosing an excellent school."

Pavel unlocked the door and they entered the lobby. The elevator creaked its way to the fifth floor. Pavel produced two more keys and unlocked one of the apartment doors. He stepped back and let Oxby and Yakov go inside before he followed and closed the door behind them.

"Am I correct in saying that you once lived here with your father?" Oxby said.

The young man nodded. "When my mother died it was the two of us."

Oxby recalled meeting the elder Baletsky in the Hermitage and was struck by how much they resembled each other. Both shared the same features, even to the same chestnut brown hair. They were the same height and their voices were remarkably alike.

They were in an all-purpose room, small, with odd pieces of furniture. A sofa, chair, the inevitable television on a table angled into a corner, another table. On the walls were prints of country scenes and photographs in thin, black frames. Suspended in wire frames attached to the wall were colored globes that held philodendron plants that had spread across the wall in spidery patterns. A door inset with colored glass led to a bedroom. Then, two narrow doors to the bathroom and toilet. Through an opening was the kitchen with a window and door to the balcony.

"I am happy you agreed to meet with us," Oxby said. "I know it is a difficult time, but you may have information that could help us understand what happened to your father."

"Thank you," Pavel said. "Let me put water on to boil. We can have tea while we talk."

The prospect of tea was, as usual, anathema to Oxby. He grimaced, then forced enthusiasm into a response, "Splendid idea. There is something special about Russian tea that I must describe to my friends when I return to London."

As the water was heating, Oxby drifted into the kitchen and from there to the balcony. The railing was high and argued against an accidental fall. There were no hanging plants, nor anything else Baletsky might have reached for to cause him to lose his balance. The balcony was also a place to store boxes and odd household items like an ancient pair of snowshoes and skis, and a suitcase and box stuffed with old cooking pots and chipped plates and cups. A plant stand with an ivy plant that needed water. It had been Baletsky's getaway; the single chair with an ashtray next to it seemed ideal for a nap or a few hours with a book. A place for a drink and a cigarette and a view of Petersburg's skyline.

The space was cluttered but orderly and showed no evidence of a struggle. But Oxby had not seen the balcony the morning after the discovery of Baletsky's body. He searched the floor. It was a reinforced

concrete slab cantilevered from the building. The surface was smooth
and splotched with splatterings of grease and other droppings of food
that had been brought onto the balcony for alfresco dining. He kicked
at a piece of bread or cake and a small bone that might have been the
drumstick from a chicken. Then he dropped to one knee and ran his
finger over three smudges, each the size of an old sixpence coin. Each
had the distinctive color of dried blood. Oxby knew blood when he
saw it, whether it was fresh and glistening or old and the color of
dried mud.

"Can't tell how old it is," he murmured softly to himself, "or where it
came from. A piece of meat, a bloody nose. Or the blood that spills
when a finger is lopped off."

He joined the others. A cup of tea awaited him, served in a mug with
the Olympic symbol on it. He added the prerequisite six spoonfuls of
sugar and sat between Yakov and Pavel at a round table in the kitchen.

Oxby chattered easily with Pavel. Pointing to his mug he asked if his
young host had attended the Olympics in 1980. Pavel said he had, that
his father had taken him, that he was a teenager at the time and wished
he could have been a champion sprinter. Oxby's skill at interrogation
was enhanced by his natural gift for setting a stranger at ease. His open
face concealed nothing, his smile was genuine, his eyes always warm
and unthreatening. Yet Oxby missed nothing. He read volumes from
vocal inflections, body shifts, and eyes that the owner could not prevent
from shifting or turning away at precise moments of indecision or at the
telling of a small, careless falsehood.

"If I ask questions that are the same as the ones you have been asked
before, please forgive me. Is it true that you lived with your father until
a short time ago?"

"Yes."

"When did you move away?"

"In January when I was married."

Oxby beamed. "Well, then. Congratulations are in order. During the
months since January, did you see your father often?"

Pavel lit a cigarette. "No, not as much as I would like. My wife has
family, too."

"Loyalties are difficult, aren't they?"

"Yes."

"Did you see him once a month, or less often?"

"Each month, at least that often."

"Did you notice any change in your father? His health, or how he felt?"

"He didn't like living alone. He wasn't eating regularly."

"An unhappy circumstance," Oxby said. "But not an unexpected one. Was your father employed? Even on a temporary basis. Or was he retired?"

"He wanted to work, but he complained that his arthritis had became very painful. He had a pension, but the checks were late."

Yakov cleared his throat at the mention of missed pension payments.

"Were you able to help your father?"

"He was proud, but near the end he accepted some money I gave him."

"Did he have many friends?"

"Most of them had died or moved away. Some were in hospitals."

"Any friends at all?"

"A few. They would get together each month or two."

"Can you think of anyone your father didn't like?"

Pavel smiled ironically. "There was one."

"Who was that?"

"His oldest friends were the ones he met when he was in the navy. It was one of those men that he didn't like very much."

"Did you meet any of these navy pals?"

"I believe there were four of them." He nodded. "And I met them all." Pavel stood. "There is a photograph—" His voice faded as he went into the next room. He returned and put an opened photo album on the table. "There is a date: May 10, 1964."

Oxby looked closely at the four young officers. Though the photograph was three inches square and slightly faded, each face was in clear focus.

"Can you tell me their names?"

"On the back my father wrote their names." He took the photo out of the plastic sleeve. "This one was Karsalov." He pointed. "Vasily was his first name. I was told that he killed a man, but my father thought it was an accident. I never knew the full story. He was sent to Kazakhstan or Uzbekistan, I'm not sure which."

Pavel handed the photo to Oxby and pointed to another face. "This one is Sasha Akimov. He was the oldest and he was like an uncle to me. He was my favorite."

"You have good memories of Akimov?"

Pavel nodded and smiled. "He was funny and brought me a gift every time he visited us."

"Do you ever see him?"

"Yes, he came to the wedding. And once after that. When he was with us we had a good time."

Oxby inspected the faces carefully. "That accounts for three of them, including your father. What about this one?"

"I'm not sure if my father disliked him, or was frightened of him." He considered what he had said, and added, "Both, I am sure."

"Who is it?" Oxby urged.

"Oleg Deryabin."

"Why do you think your father might have been frightened of him?"

"He was the one who was most successful. He was in the KGB after the navy."

"Is that a reason for your father to dislike him?"

"My father thought that old friends should help each other. The KGB changed Deryabin. My father didn't want charity, just a chance. When my father asked him for help and said he would do whatever his legs allowed him to do, Deryabin all but laughed at him."

"What happened?"

"Deryabin stuffed two hundred dollars in his pocket and walked away from him."

"When was that?"

"Not long ago. Two weeks I think."

"Do you recall hearing your father talk about a Fabergé egg?"

Young Baletsky thought for a moment, then shook his head. "No."

"When was the last time you saw your father?"

"Ten days before he died. He came to my apartment. It was my wife's birthday."

"Did he enjoy himself?"

"A little."

"The commandant explained that you did not think your father committed suicide. Is that how you feel?"

Pavel stared at Oxby as if he were looking for an answer. He blinked, the involuntary blinks that come with tears. "I have thought about that many times since he died. He had changed and was unhappy. But I can't believe he would kill himself." He wiped his eyes. "And I can't allow myself to think someone was so cruel and pushed him to his death."

"I'm afraid," Oxby said, his voice lowered, "that someone was that cruel."

Pavel's face showed an odd combination of sadness and surprise. "You know who it was?"

Oxby nodded. "I'm certain that I do."

"You'll tell the police?"

"The person who killed your father is dead."

"I hope he died painfully."

Oxby bit on his lip and nodded.

"Why would anyone want to kill my father?"

"That's why I'm asking you these questions. When I have the answer, I will tell you. That's a promise."

🐜 🐜 🐜

They were in the taxi, headed toward the center of the city. Oxby was making notes while Yakov silently watched him. Oxby folded his pad and slipped it into his shirt pocket. "What did you think of Pavel?"

"That he's a very unhappy young man who doesn't think well of Oleg Deryabin."

"So far, no one does. I plan to make my own evaluation."

"You are going to meet him?" Yakov said excitedly. "I will go with you."

"No. Though I don't expect a surprise visit will cause a problem, there is the chance that it will."

"No, Jack. I insist."

Oxby gave Yakov a reproving glance. "And so do I."

🐜 🐜 🐜

After Poolya had deposited Oxby and Yakov at the entrance to the Winter Palace, he had continued along the embankment road and past three adjoining buildings. The four combined were what the world knew as the Hermitage, and as he reached the fourth and last building, he had suddenly wakened to the realization that Oxby had tricked him. Dulled by the excess of wine the night before, Poolya believed that he, along with Oxby and Ilyushin, would tramp through the museum's galleries and corridors for the better part of the day. He had even allowed himself to become elated when he was excused from the torture. Instead, he had been eased out of the way so that Oxby could be free to roam the city unobserved.

Poolya had turned at the first opportunity and, after an argument with a driver and his crew, parked in the shadow of a giant moving truck waiting its turn to move to the loading docks. Then he had run back to the entrance with the faint hope he would find them. Neither *bah-booshkah* at the ticket booth recalled seeing Ilyushin or Oxby, nor were they to be found in the book and souvenir shop. He returned to the street and saw the gathered taxis, their drivers milling about. He jogged over to them and described both Ilyushin and Oxby.

"They went with Lipkin ten minutes ago," one of the drivers said.

"They drove west," said another, helpfully.

"They went east, you idiot!" a third chimed in.

"Which way!" Poolya asked a driver who struck him as the most reliable out of a poor batch. "What kind of car . . . what color?"

He was told Oxby was in a black Volga. A terrible car, Poolya thought, prone to breakdowns. He hoped he would find it pulled to the curb with its hood up. But after an hour's futile search he concluded that Oxby and Ilyushn had been delivered to wherever they were going. He stopped at the entrance to a metro station and found a kiosk that sold fruit ades, liquors, and vodka made from pure ethanol. He bought two bottles of beer and drank both. He thought of calling Galina but lit a cigarette instead.

"Fuck Galina," he said, accompanied by a roar of stomach gas, loud enough for the women queued at a bakery kiosk to react with black, scornful stares. He glared back at them, "Fuck all of you, too."

He drove back to the Hermitage, found another spot to put his car. He roved between the street and the rooms immediately inside the museum for the next several hours, expecting that when four o'clock arrived, both Oxby and Ilyushin would arrive at the main entrance in yet another taxi. But at two o'clock, and unknown to Poolya, Yakov had led Oxby into the museum's administration offices located a block away and also accessible from the embankment road. While Yakov had rested his leg, Oxby had had free run of the museum. Then at the appointed hour, both men appeared.

"You enjoyed?" Poolya asked.

"Very much," Oxby said.

"You have been here since I last saw you?"

Oxby gave one of his disarming smiles and said, "Where else do you think we might have been." It was a statement, not a question.

Chapter 35

"God but this place spooks me," Lenny Sulzberger said. He was at the long stretch of glass in Mike Carson's office, looking down on the tops of sparkling new Cadillacs and Georgia Gradowski trying to sell one of them. He gave Patsy Abromowitz a sideways glance. "You feel that way?"

"No, I love it. I like all of Mike's showrooms."

"Maybe spook is the wrong word, but everywhere I look I see a memory that's eerier 'n hell."

"Hey, I was here when Akimov was shot. In fact I'm the only person who heard gunfire. I didn't know what it was, but I heard it, and I saw Dennis, too. Christ, there was a lot of blood."

Lenny drifted over to the table and eased himself into a chair next to Patsy, wincing perceptibly. He opened his shoulder bag and pulled out a pile of papers and put them on the table.

"I made a copy of the article for you and one for Mike. I think it's damned good."

"If you do say so yourself."

"Yeah, I say so. Read it and applaud. Hey, I hope we're not going to go through this line by line. I'll make changes within reason, but I'm damned if I want to prowl through it another time."

"If it's as good as you say it is, that won't happen. I'll suggest to Mike that he take it home and spend a little time with it."

"Yeah, I like that." He gave Patsy her copy and put one on the desk in front of Mike's chair. "You said you might have another project for me. What's up?"

"Mike's joint venture with the Russians. You heard him talking about it."

"I didn't know how serious he was. It's a done deal?"

"It's not that far along, but Mike's going to try it out. If it looks good, he'll sign a contract."

"The Russian angle will make a hell of a story."

"Only the business part of it. The personal stuff is still off limits."

Lenny opened his notebook. "You know the story that really fascinates me is how Mike's grandfather came to own a Fabergé Imperial egg, and how Mike's father lost it in a card game. Then Sasha Akimov turns up, an old guy who can't speak English worth a lick, tells Mike all about his family and says he ought to take back his egg. You got to agree, Patsy, that's goddamned hot stuff."

"Sounds like you're trying awful hard to tell a part of the family saga. I told you to forget it." She gave him a hard look. "That's a goddamned order."

"What's an order?" Mike had joined them, unobserved, and was standing by his desk, sorting through his messages.

"Lenny thinks you come from an interesting family and wants to write about it. I told him to forget it."

"Patsy's right," Mike said. He dropped the notes on his desk and took his seat at the table. "What's this?"

"Lenny's piece on you. I haven't read the final-final, but I think the draft is great."

"Am I supposed to read it?"

"Not this minute, unless you want to. Take it home, spend some time with it. If you spot a mistake, make a note. I'll do the same, then Lenny will put it all back together and send it to the magazine."

"What else we got?"

"The world wants to know what's been going on inside Carson Motors during the past few weeks."

"We're busy, that's what's going on."

"They seem to think it's more than that."

"Who's they?"

"I got a supermarket tabloid on my e-mail every day. Then I get queries on my voice mail and fax and occasionally I even have an old-fashioned telephone conversation.

"They all smell a news story and the more I say I don't have anything, the more messages I get."

"Maybe we'll have something soon," Mike said. "The top man from Koleso is coming to New York in a few days. That means, Patsy, that if everything goes smoothly, you can cook up one of those press conferences you're so good at."

Chapter 36

Oxby's first impression of Boris was that he was like the others; thick-chested, thick-muscled, and nearly mute. But both Yakov and Oxby discovered the comparisons ended with physical similarities. Boris's youthful face belied the fact he was past thirty, older than the others, including Poolya. He had graduated from one of the institutes and had trained to be a member of Gorbachev's personal security force. He had survived the putsch in August of 1991. All was well in his world until December 25, 1991, when the man he had sworn to protect announced the end of the Soviet Union.

Boris lacked Poolya's limited command of English, but could understand, if Oxby spoke slowly. Yakov interviewed Boris and when their talk ended, he shrugged and said that Boris appeared to be reliable, but confessed that he had felt that way about Mikki and had a man's finger to show for it.

Yakov had been issued the papers that would permit him to be fitted for a new leg. He had been through the procedure before and knew the lines would be long and slow-moving. Immediately after Yakov and Oxby had vetted Boris, Yakov and his new bodyguard drove off in the Lada. The window had been replaced by an enterprising neighbor who had a reputation for repairing mechanical objects that had a motor, or made a noise. Yakov put a thermos of his tea brew and some apples in a string bag and took along a book to help pass the time.

"I'll come by to see how you're getting on," Oxby had promised.

"You won't like what you will see," Yakov had warned. "But come if you wish. It is the Kuybyshev Hospital."

Immediately Oxby lifted the phone and as he was about to dial Poolya, he heard a weak, but distinctive crackling noise in the receiver. It was the sound of a phone tap made with an outdated piece of equipment. He pressed the switchhook and listened to a fresh dial tone. The sound remained. He tried a third time with the same result. He called Poolya and ordered him to meet him in thirty minutes.

🐜 🐜 🐜

"Put me off over there," Oxby said. He was pointing to the entrance to the Astoria Hotel.

Poolya swung the car to the curb and stopped. "You will go to the hotel?" he asked.

"It's one of the places I'm going today. I will need two hours." He looked at his watch. "Meet me here at one o'clock."

"But you are alone," Poolya said, showing his annoyance that Oxby had not told him his plans for the day. Now, as on the day before, he indicated that he would again be off by himself.

Oxby was on the sidewalk. He closed the door and peered through the open window at Poolya. "It's the way I want it," he said, then he turned and walked briskly into the hotel.

Poolya slapped the wheel in frustration, and made an abrupt U-turn, nearly sideswiping a bus and a taxi. Ahead, cheek by jowl with the Astoria, was the five-story building that housed the offices of IBM and New Century. He grabbed his phone, but before he touched the last number, he switched off the instrument and dropped it back in its cradle. In those few seconds since he had watched Oxby walk into the hotel, Poolya had had a revelation. The bright blue eyes that had been dimmed by too much wine the night before seemed to clear. He slapped the steering wheel again, but this time he was smiling, as if he had put a nagging problem behind him. He pulled away and merged into the traffic.

The inside of the hotel was a hive of activity. Tourists and turbaned businessmen paraded back and forth across the long, narrow lobby. Tour directors assembled their flocks, and mothers looked anxiously for teenagers who had fearlessly taken sightseeing matters into their own hands. Oxby purchased a copy of the English language *St. Petersburg Times*. He went into the dining room and to a table where he ordered a reasonable facsimile of an English breakfast. While his four-minute eggs were simmering, he went to the phones in the lobby and dialed the number Yakov had discovered in Oleg Deryabin's personnel files.

"New Century," a female voice said in Russian.

"Do you speak English?"

She did, she said, though not well. "May I help you?"

"Please give Mr. Deryabin a message. Tell him that Jack Oxby will come to his office at 11:30 this morning."

"Please repeat?"

Oxby did, then asked the operator to read back the message. She repeated it correctly and he put down the phone.

The breakfast was not up to the standards of London's Stafford Hotel, but the coffee, particularly, was a rewarding break from Yakov's powerfully scented tea.

❧ ❧ ❧

At 11:30, Oxby stepped from the elevator. He paused in front of the company logo and read the list of subsidiaries. Then he went through the door into the reception room where he felt as if he was in the hall of mirrors on Brighton Pier by the sea. Surrounding him were dozens of his own image. Standing in front of a mirror, rigid and unblinking, was the security guard with his left hand jammed into his suit pocket. He was speaking into his right hand, which he held to his mouth. In the center of one of the mirrors, Oxby located a face looking at him.

"My name is Oxby," he said. "Jack Oxby. I do not have an appointment, but I phoned earlier to say I would be here at this time. Is Mr. Deryabin in his office?"

The receptionist, pretty, with dark red lipstick, stared back. The answer came from behind him. From a voice that belonged to a tall man who stood next to a mirror-covered door.

"Mr. Deryabin is not in the office today," Trivimi Laar said. "Perhaps I can help you."

Oxby turned and walked toward the Estonian. "Forgive me for coming on short notice, but I am anxious to learn if Mr. Deryabin would be available to help me locate a valuable piece of art made by Fabergé, an item that I believe he knows something about."

"Fabergé?" Trivimi shook his head. "We are not in the art market."

"My questions for Mr. Deryabin are not related to his business. They are personal."

"Either for business or personal matters, Oleg Deryabin is not available."

"I'll wait," Oxby said, and took a step toward one of the chairs next to a table with magazines stacked on top of it.

"You misunderstand. Oleg Deryabin is not available at any time for a discussion of his personal affairs."

"Perhaps I can persuade him to make an exception."

"There are no exceptions," Trivimi said firmly.

Oxby had been sizing up the tall man, whose English was, to his practiced ear, very acceptable. And though he had but a rudimentary knowledge of Russian, of stress and inflexion, he could detect twists in the accent and knew it differed from Yakov's, a well-educated son of St. Petersburg.

Oxby said, "May I ask your name? I don't believe you introduced yourself."

Reluctance showed on the Estonian's face. He paused, then said as if he were in some distress, "I am Trivimi Laar."

Oxby produced one of his warm smiles. "I am delighted to meet you, Mr. Laar." He extended his hand.

Oxby's behavior seemed to baffle Trivimi. Reluctantly he put out his hand and discovered that the smaller man's hand was both large and strong.

"Mr. Laar." Oxby lowered his voice as if he were about to hatch a conspiracy. "Can you attach any significance to the name Vasily Karsalov?"

Oxby's smile and powerful grip had diverted Trivimi's attention for the tiniest fraction of time before he said the name. But it was sufficient. Trivimi's mouth twitched. He instantly ran his fingers across his lips, aware himself that he had flinched.

"Karsalov?" Trivimi repeated the name. "I probably know someone with that name, but—"

"Vasily Karsalov?"

Trivimi replied, his face implacable, "Probably not."

"But Mr. Deryabin knew a Vasily Karsalov," Oxby persisted. "I believe they served in the navy together."

"Come in my office," Trivimi said, motioning to the guard, who stepped back from the door. "I have ten minutes."

Oxby eyed the guard warily and followed Trivimi past the door and to the Estonian's small office, the room without a desk or windows. "Ten minutes." The time limit was repeated and the door closed.

Trivimi said, "What are you looking for?"

"I believe you know the answer to that," Oxby said. "I came to this city to search for the truth to an eighty-year-old rumor and for reasons I cannot explain, three men have died. Can you possibly imagine why?"

The Estonian said, implacably, "No."

"Because you don't know? Or because, how should I say, it would be bad business?"

"I said I can't answer," Trivimi snapped.

He took out his blue-tinted glasses and exchanged them for the steel-rimmed pair. Oxby watched, unaware the glasses were a ploy Trivimi Laar used when he was in serious negotiation, but very much aware that the opaque lenses gave shelter. It was effective, as it denied Oxby the opportunity to read the eyes of the man who was sitting a mere seven feet away from him.

"What is your interest in this egg?" Trivimi asked.

"You must know that I am on leave from Scotland Yard . . . am I right?"

"If you say that you are."

"I was retained to explore the possibility that Grigori Rasputin commissioned Fabergé to design an Imperial egg for Czarina Alexandra. An intriguing speculation. Yes?"

"Perhaps so."

"While exploring, I have uncovered information that connects Oleg Deryabin's name to the egg."

"I had never heard that was so."

"You can bloody well believe that it *is* so," Oxby said solemnly. "The particular Fabergé egg I refer to changed ownership during a card game thirty-five years ago. At that time the egg became the possession of Mr. Deryabin, and unless he has sold it or given it away, he continues to own it."

"Only Deryabin can speak to that."

"When can I meet with him?"

"I don't know."

"Tomorrow, perhaps. Or the next day?"

"At this moment he is preparing for a trip to New York."

It was surprising news to Oxby but he concealed his joy. "Perhaps I can visit with him when he returns. When is he going to New York?"

"On Saturday." Trivimi got to his feet and gave every indication that the conversation was fast approaching an end. "If you leave a phone number, it is possible an appointment can be made."

"But you already have my phone number. Correct?"

Trivimi wagged his head. "No. You did not give it to me."

It was a fact that Oxby had not given Trivimi the phone number, and while it missed the point, he decided not to press the issue. He said, "Perhaps it is a coincidence that Mr. Deryabin is going to New York. I say that because I understand you were recently in that city."

Trivimi shifted in his chair. "I have not been—"

"Please, Mr. Laar." Oxby's smile returned. "I am not conducting a deposition, though I urge you not to commit perjury. I learned of your visit to Carson Motors from an associate who attended a meeting at which you were present. It's an undeniable fact, as quite plainly, there were witnesses."

"We are having confidential negotiations and don't want competitors to know of our plans."

"I assure you that neither my friend nor I have the vaguest idea who your competitors might be."

Trivimi looked at his watch. "You have one minute. I have appointments."

"Of course," Oxby said. "Please understand the problem I am facing. If I had tried to make an appointment you would have refused. Police work can sometimes lead to bad habits."

"You are wasting time."

Oxby had surveyed Trivimi's office, searching for microphones, or a miniature closed-circuit television camera. He hoped the room was wired, as that would assure that there would be no slippage between what he said and what Trivimi could remember. The most likely place to conceal a microphone was in the telephone, which in this case was a modernistic affair that resembled a miniature flying saucer. It was in the middle of the table that separated them.

"A man named Akimov was shot in Michael Carson's office. This, too, was reported to me by my associate. You were asked if you knew Akimov."

"And I said that I did not know him."

"Oleg Deryabin knew him. In fact Akimov was an employee of New Century at one time. You stand by what you said? That you did not know him?"

"It's possible that I met him years ago and have forgotten his name. There are many employees. They come and go."

"Akimov came and went and was killed." Oxby could feel Trivimi glowering at him from behind his glasses.

"Has your company concluded its arrangements with Carson Motors?"

"You must leave now."

Oxby edged forward in his chair as if he were about to get to his feet. Instead, he turned his gaze up to the Estonian and said, "My client may wish to buy the egg. He is a serious collector with considerable resources. A private sale is quick and the money would be transferred immediately."

Trivimi was at the door. "You must know that a public auction for such a rare item would bring the highest price."

"A sound observation, but auctions for a piece of decorative art of this importance occur infrequently. The Sotheby's auction was early in June, and there won't be another for a year. There are high expenses, also commissions and fees."

"I commented only for the sake of argument."

Oxby had obstinately remained in his chair. "I must ask one more time. Will you confirm that the Fabergé Imperial egg is in Oleg Deryabin's possession?"

Trivimi pulled the door open. "You have no more time."

"And will he take it with him to New York?"

"I repeat. There's no more time. Go before you are forced to leave."

The Estonian seemed outwardly calm, but Oxby, superbly expert in detecting tiny defections others fail to observe, realized that Trivimi Laar was at the brink of losing his temper.

"Leave!" Trivimi roared.

"I think you are serious about this," gathering himself as if to rise, "and I shall take your advice. Except for one last question." He turned quickly, leaned into the strange-looking telephone and said, "There are strong suggestions that a crime of murder, of which Vasily Karsalov was accused, was actually committed by Oleg Deryabin. How do you or Mr. Deryabin respond?"

On saying the last word, Oxby was on his feet and in three strides reached the door and went through it. He did not wait to be escorted to the reception area, but walked past the guard with the earplug and the mini-microphone and the bulge in the left side of his jacket.

* * *

Oleg Deryabin was behind his desk, tapping the sharp end of a letter opener into the polished wood. No lights were on and the draperies had been pulled, except for a slim shaft of bright yellow sunlight that shone over the rug, across the desk and against the wall directly behind the chairman of New Century.

The Estonian came and sat in his usual chair. "You heard?"

"Every fucking word."

"How could he learn so much in so little time?"

"Because he's good. Too damned good."

"He asked about the murder. He meant Prekhner?"

"He was fishing. That's how they do it. Scotland Yard wrote the book on it."

"Only fishing?" The Estonian exchanged his glasses once more. "What if he knows?"

Deryabin grasped the letter opener and, holding it like a dagger, he stabbed at the leather inlay in his desk. He struck again and again as if the destruction of a beautiful piece of furniture would turn every wrong into a right. "If he does, he can't prove anything."

Trivimi was undisturbed by the outburst. He said calmly, "Now that we know what Oxby is up to, what do we do about it?"

"Kill him! Kill the son of a bitch now!"

"How do you suggest it be done? With a gun? Blow up the apartment?"

"No, you fool. An accident."

Trivimi was well aware that Oxby's death must be planned carefully and carried out in the same way. He was also aware that planning was the easy part, the execution much more difficult.

Trivimi said, "Viktor was the expert. He's gone."

"Work it out with Galina. She has her own reason for killing him."

❦ ❦ ❦

Poolya had gone into the hotel and when he returned he found his Peugeot squeezed between a bus from Germany and one from Sweden. The German bus was a double-decker affair and one of its young tour guides was amused by the problem Poolya faced. The guide might have posed for a 1930s poster extolling membership in the Hitler Youth. His hair was pale yellow, his eyes were a perfect blue, and his skin was as fair as milk. It was like a movie set and he had just come out of the makeup trailer. He scowled at Poolya, who scowled back. In a street fight, smart money would have been on the Russian.

Oxby got into the car. "The Kuybyshev Hospital. Fifty-six Liteyny Prospekt. Do you know it?"

Poolya moved the car forward and back in the tight spot until he was finally able to turn away from the curb. "Two months ago my job was to take a doctor to Kuybyshev. I have been there many times."

"I will stay with Mr. Ilyushin and return to the apartment with him."

"You will be alone again. That is not good."

"Boris will be with us."

"He is not a *byki*," Poolya said derisively. "He's never guarded anyone."

"He'll get on-the-job training. Best kind."

"Is the worst kind. What is more, Boris is dishonest."

Oxby smiled at the irony. These were all petty crooks. No one of them to be trusted more than the next.

He said, "Drop me, then go back to the apartment and keep an eye on things."

Poolya remained silent, but drove on disconsolately, a cigarette dangling from his lips.

There were no parking garages near the hospital, and no lots, paved or dirt, to put the new population of cars that had sprung up in the city. Cars of every size and age were parked along the street and over the curb. Taxis carrying sick patients were hooted out of the way. Poolya was forced to stop in the middle of the street. Oxby jumped out.

"Cheerio," he shouted, and in a second melded into the crowd.

Once inside the hospital, Oxby instantly realized that he faced a real challenge. Asking for information that would lead him to Yakov was problem enough, but finding someone to ask was an equally formidable task. Either mismarked, or because he couldn't interpret the signs, he spent the first minutes locating the equivalent of a registration desk. When finally he did, he patiently waited his turn to ask where the prosthetic cases were handled.

The orthopedic wing of the hospital bustled with mostly ambulatory patients. Many were accompanied by family or a friend, and a few had the gaunt look of someone in the throes of extreme discomfort. He found Yakov, sitting peacefully in a room filled with patients missing an arm, a leg, or worse, and half doing what Yakov had come prepared to do; read or compose a letter. Yakov shifted in his chair, offering half of it to Oxby, who refused.

The time had edged on and it was quarter to three. "Where are you in scheme of things? Have you been fitted, or what?"

"I was in luck. Now they take an impression and four hours later they have made the socket. They tell me I will have it before the day is over."

"When is the day over in a place like this?" Oxby wondered aloud.

"Tonight, until nine o'clock. Time enough, but I have eaten my apples and am hungry again."

"I'll take you to dinner to celebrate your new leg," Oxby said, then eased himself down onto his haunches. "Where is Boris? Don't tell me another one ran off."

"He hadn't eaten and I sent him off to find something. Poolya said it was his first assignment. Called him a baby."

"Poolya's as trustworthy as a convicted spy. Your phone is tapped. They spliced into your line last night."

"Yakov Ilyushin!" a speaker boomed. "Yakov Ilyushin report to room 14-B."

"Come with me," Yakov said. "They are breaking speed records today."

ᏗᏗ ᏗᏗ ᏗᏗ

"I feel like there is nothing from my knee to the floor!" Yakov exclaimed. "It is the new plastics. So light."

"Is it comfortable?"

"I have soreness from the old leg. It will take time for that to go away."

Yakov walked in a circle for a few minutes and pronounced that all the joints flexed smoothly. Two white-cloaked therapists checked him a final time, then asked that he sign the requisite releases and forms. Yakov looked at his watch. "Twenty after five." It had taken less than seven hours. "A Russian miracle," he said.

ᏗᏗ ᏗᏗ ᏗᏗ

But Oxby found no miracle in the fact that Boris, on the job for less than forty-eight hours, had not returned. If Mikki, and now Boris could not be trusted, what faith could he have in Poolya and the other bodyguards that had been since the first day, silent, blank-faced hulks that hovered around the apartment. They waited an additional forty minutes. Still no Boris.

"Where's your car?" Oxby asked.

"I learned to park away from the hospital. It is on the road three streets away."

"You have the keys?"

Yakov pulled the keys from his pocket and shook them. He said, "Maybe Boris went ahead of us."

"Don't count on seeing Boris again today," Oxby said. "I'm of the impression that when these men go, they go for good."

They turned the last corner and Yakov pointed to the opposite side. "There it is," Yakov said. "You are correct. No Boris."

"I promised you dinner. If Boris is still on our team, he'll find his way back to the apartment."

The neighborhood was a mix of high-rise and low apartment houses. At the corner were two kiosks; one sold detergents and household items, the other stocked hardware and hand tools. Commuters carrying plastic shopping bags were on their way home, and kids on Rollerblades were attempting to skate over a street pitted with ruts and holes.

They were in the middle of the road when Oxby saw Poolya running toward them, coming from the opposite end of the street they had just entered. Then came shouts and after that the unmistakable sound of gunfire.

Poolya was waving his arms frantically, veering quickly to his left, then his right.

"Deerzhi! Deerzhi!"

Oxby knew Poolya was shouting for them to stop. He also knew that Poolya, dodging and weaving as he ran, was evading the shots being fired.

When Poolya was abreast of Yakov's car there was a loud THUMP! accompanied by streams of blue and white flames from under the Lada. The hood was blown straight into the air where it hovered, then fell back on top of the car. Poolya had been lifted up by the concussion and tossed hard against the road. He lay there, motionless. Oxby ran to him. There was blood on Poolya's shoulder and on his face, which had scraped against the graveled road. Oxby lifted him and carried him off the road to a scruffy patch of grass.

Yakov stood nearby, silhouetted against a fire that had erupted inside his precious automobile, beginning to engulf his keepsakes and memories. He slouched, a pathetic figure, then went slowly to where Oxby was attending Poolya.

"How badly is he hurt?" Yakov asked.

"He's been shot," Oxby said. "In the back. He's alive. Find someone who can take him to the hospital."

A ring had formed and Yakov pleaded for help. A woman with a broad, mature face, and the body of a young middleweight boxer said she owned a taxi and would help. The gas tank exploded. But it was a bang no louder than a giant firecracker. Yakov added gas sparingly and the tank contained more fumes than fuel.

The taxi came. Poolya was put in the back seat, stretched flat, newspapers put under the bleeding shoulder.

The inside of the Lada continued to burn, with as much black smoke as red flame spilling out the windows. Yakov stared at his reliable old friend until they turned the corner. Then his car and everything inside of it became a memory.

Chapter 37

Poolya lay against a pillow looking as if he were a badly wounded Pünjabi, with yards of white gauze wrapped around his head like an oversize turban, and more bandages on his back and over his shoulder. Deep scratches on the right side of his face had been slathered over with a glistening clear gel, the eye puffed closed. His right hand and lower arm were bandaged and rested limply on his lap.

It was three in the morning and though the shades had been pulled over the windows, light seeped into the long, narrow ward from an eastern sky that was preparing for a reappearance of the sun. There were ten beds on each side of the room. Beside each bed was a table and next to it a single chair.

Yakov sat in the chair beside Poolya's bed. Oxby stood next to him.

"In spite of all, you had good luck," Oxby said.

"The bullet was a little one," Poolya said bravely, his voice no more than a whisper, his words slurred and thick from the heavy sedation.

"Little ones kill," Oxby responded. "It depends where they hit you. This bullet got you in the shoulder, but they got it out." Oxby held the bullet in front of Poolya. "They want you to have it for a souvenir."

Yakov said, "Some bones were chipped. That is why there is so much pain."

Poolya nodded. "They gave me something, but it's not enough."

Oxby sat on the edge of the bed. "We'll ask the nurse to give you another dose."

"He might try again," Poolya said.

"Who might try?" Oxby asked.

"Boris."

Yakov leaned closer. "He is like Mikki, a traitor?"

"It's the business. We all do it."

"Do what?" Oxby asked.

"Take money from both sides."

"Did you?"

"Yes. But it was a mistake."

Oxby was puzzled. "What was a mistake?"

"To spy on you and take their money."

"I'm learning that's the way it's done over here," Oxby said. "Was Boris hired to kill us?"

"Boris is hired to kill. He killed my best friend. An accident he said. He lied."

Killers lie and some are good at it, Oxby thought, and wondered if Poolya was. "Is that why you warned us away from Yakov's car?"

"I wanted Boris to look foolish. If he kills you he is a big shot again." He shook his head. "I want him to suck shit."

"Obviously you are not one of Boris's fans, but suppose Professor Ilyushin or I had been injured. Or killed, perhaps. Would that matter to you?"

Poolya closed his good eye. No answer.

"Has someone paid Boris to kill me?" Poolya's head was nodding, but he did not respond. "Answer me, Poolya, or I'll see that the nurse forgets to give you a painkiller."

"*Dah*," he said. A muttered sound that was barely audible.

"Who's paying you to spy on us? And tap the phone? Who?"

Poolya blinked, his only response.

"Who is it?" Oxby persisted.

Poolya said proudly, "I saved your life. I warned you."

"No, Poolya. You were playing a game with Boris. You don't give a damn about me, only if I pay you money."

"You are wrong," Poolya said, shaking his head.

"Who paid you?" Oxby asked again.

Poolya turned away.

Oxby turned to Yakov and spoke to him with all the authority he could put into his voice, "I will stay with Poolya, while you explain to the district police that it was your car that blew up. Tell them that we are holding the person who planted the bomb."

Poolya stiffened. "No." He turned as if trying to get out of the bed, but a child's hand on his chest could immobilize him.

Oxby said, "You're not going anywhere. Not until you do some explaining." Oxby lowered his head so he was inches away from Poolya's hot and glimmering face. "Who paid you?"

"Galina Lysenko."

"She is related to Viktor Lysenko?"

"Her husband. He is dead."

Oxby nodded. "We saw it happen."

"Galina said you killed him."

"I was a witness," Yakov said. "Inspector Oxby didn't kill him. Viktor caused his own death."

"Galina will never believe that."

"How long have you known Galina?"

"Two years. I knew Viktor before that."

"For how long?"

"A long time. I don't remember."

"He was your friend?"

"A little. He was a killer."

"And you are not?"

Poolya, in spite of his bull neck and thick body, lay helpless, a pitiful sight. He looked up to Oxby. "I am not a killer," he said, the words coming with as much strength and clarity as any he had spoken since Oxby had come to his bedside ten minutes earlier.

Oxby nudged Poolya gently. "We'll let you sleep, but I want an answer." Poolya's good eye opened partially and he began breathing noisily.

Oxby stared down at Poolya and said softly, "You say Galina paid you. Who paid Galina?"

"The Estonian. Trivimi Laar."

"And who paid the Estonian?

"Oleg Deryabin."

Chapter 38

Deryabin was holding court, pacing before the wide casement windows in his stronghold on Stone Island, puffing furiously on a cigarette. He was in a black, angry mood. "Tell me again. Who is this deceiving bastard Poolya?"

The question was floated out to whoever chose to answer, either Galina or Trivimi Laar, both standing a safe distance from the storm, waiting for the man's hot wrath to cool.

Galina answered. "One of Ivan's men."

"Ivan is connected to Misha Kinsky," Trivimi added.

"Kinsky is the worst of all! With the stinking dog food he brings to Petersburg, he will kill every animal in the city. And you took one of his *byki*?"

"Kinsky approved," Trivimi said. "He said he might want help from us in the future."

"Another lie. What did it cost?"

"Nothing to Kinsky. Ivan shared three hundred dollars with Poolya."

Galina stifled her surprise. Poolya had deceived her as well as the Estonian.

"Who planned the car bombing?"

Trivimi answered. "I brought Ivan to my office. I explained that Oxby was a problem to us, and asked him to come back with suggestions for getting rid of him."

"You blame Ivan for the bombing?"

"Yes," Trivimi said.

"You're all a bunch of amateurs," Deryabin said. "I gave instructions to get rid of Oxby in an accident that would not raise suspicions. But what have you accomplished? A bungled car bombing as if we are fighting a stupid guerrilla war."

Galina pleaded, "If Poolya had not turned against us—"

"But he did!" Deryabin exploded. "The district police will dig into this. If Oxby had been hurt, even so slightly it couldn't be seen, your goddamned car bomb would be a case for the procurator's office."

"Why are you frightened of the procurator's office?" Trivimi asked.

"Because we have no influence there. The young zealots would say this case is about a police investigator. That Oxby is one of theirs. They would be relentless."

"But Oxby wasn't hurt," Trivimi said. "In the end, that is the best news."

"Come and sit next to me," Deryabin said to Galina. "This blunder about the bomb has caused me to think deeply about Inspector Oxby. He came here to find a Fabergé Imperial egg as a private individual, not sent by his government or Scotland Yard. Yet he is a trained police detective and has learned more than is good for him." Deryabin turned from Galina to the Estonian. "Oxby must be disposed of, but not with a goddamned bomb that tells all of Russia that he's been killed, and with pictures on television every night and newspaper reporters asking who did it and why. A bullet for Akimov was correct. He was nobody and nobody cares that he died. Not so with Oxby. When Oxby dies there will be many who care. They will demand an investigation."

He looked solemnly at Galina. "And so I come back to the reason Oxby came to Petersburg." As he was speaking he reached for the presentation box that was on the floor next to him. He picked it up, turned a brass fastener, and raised the lid. He took out the egg and instructed Galina to extend her hand, palm up. He placed the egg in her hand, and then he pushed against the largest of the rubies and the top sprang open. From the hidden compartment he took out the tiny easel and put the equally tiny portrait of Nicholas and Alexandra on it. Galina touched the gold basket on top of the egg, then she turned the egg slowly to see the diamonds and sapphires. Deryabin took it back and reassembled the pieces.

"This is what brought Oxby to Petersburg. If the Imperial egg leaves the city, Oxby will follow it."

"How do you benefit from that?"

"Because the egg will be with me. Oxby will follow me. But at the same time, you and Galina will be following Oxby."

"That will be difficult."

"It is your job," Deryabin said. "There's been enough blundering. I won't tolerate any more."

Deryabin returned the egg to the box. "One of you will keep Oxby

under surveillance. When the time is right, I will meet with him."
Deryabin was taking great pleasure in presenting his scenario. "I predict
that he will not waste precious time and will demand that I show him
the egg. And I will insist that he introduce me to his client."

"And if he refuses?"

"He won't. He's risked his life to find the egg. And his client has
risked a lot of money. I'm not sure which one is more anxious to see it."

There was doubt on Trivimi's face. "You would sell it directly?"

"Possibly."

"But you agreed that an auction would bring a higher price."

"How will I know what is the highest price? If I ask for five million
and he will pay it, who can assure me I would get that much if I put it
into an auction? Less the commissions and fees." Deryabin beamed.
"And it is done. No waiting."

Trivimi said, "Not long ago you gave the order to eliminate Oxby.
Now you want him to take you to his client?"

Deryabin drew heavily on the cigarette and slowly exhaled a stream
of smoke. He turned to Galina. "What are your thoughts?"

"Use him for whatever he can do for you, but—" Galina paused, then
said defiantly, "He can never go back to London. He must pay for what
he did to Viktor."

Deryabin gave Trivimi a knowing glance. "There's your answer."

Trivimi said, "I am troubled by one detail. When Oxby was in my office I never said that you owned the egg." He shook his head. "How
would he know that you are taking it to New York?"

"You told him about my travel plans. Now I count on you to complete the job." Deryabin rose from his chair. At the door he turned.

"You have his phone number."

Chapter 39

Aeroflot flight 003 connected St. Petersburg to New York through Shannon. It was due to arrive at Kennedy at 3:55 in the afternoon and was close to being on time. In the first-class cabin, in a forward row, sat Oleg Deryabin and Galina Lysenko. Their seats had been secured by World Travel, the once profitable subsidiary of New Century, now struggling to remain in business after being told to turn a profit or shut down. No easy accomplishment. When World Travel opened for business six years earlier, the competition came from what remained of the Soviet-operated Intourist. Today in Petersburg there were nearly as many travel agencies as drugstores.

Trivimi Laar had taken the same flight the day before and would be waiting in the International Arrivals Building.

To the casual observer, Deryabin and Galina were husband and wife, though most would agree that they were oddly matched. He, a bit old and round through the middle, she, a trophy wife with a knockout figure and face to match. It was an arrangement demanded by Deryabin, but acceded to by Galina only after her own demands for the accommodation were satisfied. Deryabin, his hand lightly touching the scratches that were neatly healing, turned to speak but found that she had fallen asleep, her head slowly dropping until it rested against his shoulder. He kissed her hair, inhaling the familiar odor of her body. He was aroused and wanted desperately to put his arms around her. To pull her close to him and kiss her. For a rare instant, Oleg Deryabin was a man possessed by feelings of genuine affection.

Galina slept for an hour. When she wakened she went to the lavatory to freshen up. She returned and Deryabin watched her settle into her seat.

He said, "Trivimi will take us to the hotel. Then he will return to the airport to meet Oxby's plane. I want you to go with him. It will take two of you to follow Oxby. If it's necessary to have another car, then rent it. Do what's necessary, but I want to know where Oxby is staying. No less than that."

"The Estonian doesn't have any training." Galina frowned. "It's not like working with Viktor. Trivimi will be a handicap."

"Your orders are to work with Trivimi," Deryabin said firmly. "He's had more experience than you realize. I expect that Oxby will be met by one of his detective friends, and if they suspect they're being watched, they'll lose you faster than you can blink. It's their city, not yours."

Galina stared past Deryabin, to the empty sky beyond the window. She said, "Why is it so important to know where Oxby's staying? You said he was following you, that he would call you."

"Don't you want to know where to find him? Or do you expect he'll show up when you snap your fingers?"

"I will find him," she said with complete conviction. "It doesn't matter how big the city is, or if he tries to hide from us. I will find him."

"Good," Deryabin said, and put his hand on top of hers.

"How can you be sure that someone will meet Oxby?"

"For some reason he wants us to know. When he discovered the phone in the apartment was tapped, he began using the phones in the Europe Hotel. When Trivimi told him I was going to New York, he made his own plans. But that same night he called from the apartment and gave his flight information."

She pulled her hand away from his. "You wait until now to tell me all this?"

"What would you have done if I had told you before? It doesn't change matters, it's still your job to work with Trivimi." He tried a smile, but showed only insincerity and a mouthful of yellowed teeth. "And you must work with him."

The steward stopped to say he was taking last-call orders from the bar. They passed.

🕮 🕮 🕮

Oxby looked again at his watch: 7:30. Eleven hours since departure from St. Petersburg. He had slept, but in snatches, and was wakened by a brilliant sun that was low in the western sky and sent a blaze of gold-colored light through the windows. His seat was on the aisle, the seat next to him unoccupied. In the seat next to the window was a teenager curled into half a circle. Her face, sweet and innocent, lay against a pillow, in profile. A blanket had slipped from around her shoulders and Oxby put it back, then he leaned across her and lowered the shade. The Air France flight had made a stop in Paris and the layover extended a half hour because of the heavy summertime traffic. But headwinds were light and they had made up the lost time and ten minutes more. They would arrive in New York at 8:55. He looked at his watch. It was now eighty-two minutes until touchdown.

On the empty seat beside Oxby was his travel bag. In it a couple of magazines, several guidebooks, a 35mm Pentax camera, a paperback of LeCarré's *The Russia House*, and his notebook. During the morning flight to Paris, he had written:

20 June. Saturday.

Yakov does well with his new leg. I shall worry about him, but he is a wise man and promised me he would leave his apartment and stay in a friend's dacha near the Finnish border.

We found a replacement car, one very similar to Yakov's late and lamented Lada. It was remarkably cheap, undoubtedly stolen off the street five hundred miles from Petersburg. It all but extinguished my funds.

Poolya is recovering rapidly and will leave the hospital as soon as he can recruit some trustworthy friends to get him away safely. I fear trustworthiness among Poolya's acquaintances is rare. I wish him good fortune.

Telephoned Alex Tobias from the apartment. Difficult to detect if the tap was still on, though I suspect it was, and rather hoped so! I am curious to see who may be lurking in the shadows.

I look forward to seeing Alex, and staying in his home. Helen is delightful company, besides being a first-rate cook.

The pitch of the engines dropped and the plane began its descent. Oxby felt a twinge of anxiety, a minute surge of adrenaline. If fatigue was about to overtake him, it went away.

He took his pen from his shirt pocket, and as he did, the little piece of paper with the numbers on it tumbled onto his lap. He hadn't yet elevated the significance of the three numbers to the level of a mystery, though it continued to frustrate him. He spoke the numbers aloud in the unlikely event that Divine Intervention would strike and their meaning—if there was one—would be revealed.

"It's all bloody stupid," he said softly, then repeated the numbers. "Two, eleven, nine."

He stuffed the paper back into his shirt pocket, and took up his pen:

It is 8 P.M., eastern daylight time. We land in an hour. I shall not bore myself by recounting an uneventful twelve hours of travel in this age of speed. Suffice it to say, it remains a miracle that I rose in the morning from my bed in Russia and on the night of that same day I shall go to sleep in a bed in America.

As I write these notes, it is three o'clock in the morning in St. Petersburg, Sunday, June 21. It is the day of the summer solstice, the longest day of the year, the first official day of the White Nights.

Sadly, I shall miss it.

Chapter 40

Oxby's young seatmate uncurled herself and looked anxiously down to her first glimpse of America. Their flight heading was south over Boston and Providence, then over water and a turn west for a direct line into Kennedy.

"Below is Long Island," Oxby said in his flawless French. "We will be on the ground in fifteen minutes."

The sun was setting, a fire-red ball descending below a broad band of purple and magenta clouds stretched across the horizon. The land directly below was in shadow, dotted by a million lights for as far as the eye could see.

"C'est beau!" she said in a loud whisper that was brimful of great wonderment and expectation.

There was nothing for Oxby to add to her little statement. He sat back and watched the delight spread over the youngster's bright face.

Ed Parente became a New York City cop after graduation from City College, intending to earn a law degree at night and let it become his ticket into big business and big money. But he got married, had his first son, and joined the New York–New Jersey Port Authority police. After twenty-one years he had the same wife, two more kids, and had risen to the rank of detective lieutenant, which meant he was head of more than half of the Port Authority's team of one-hundred-plus detectives. There were few veterans in the fourteen-hundred-man police department who could match Parente's familiarity with Kennedy airport, and perhaps none who had his extensive contacts among airline and ground support personnel and the nearly dozen other police and security organizations. It was rumored that Parente knew what was behind every door in the vast airport complex, and more important, knew how to get on the other side of each one whether it was locked or not.

Ed Parente and Alex Tobias met the year Parente was a rookie cop and Tobias made lieutenant. Though separated in age by a half generation, they had become close friends. Years earlier they had worked a number of cases together, but with time they'd gone their separate ways. Now they were a team again. They met in a small office inside the arrival building. Alex had described the circumstances surrounding Oxby's visit.

"Jack told me that two men and a woman came in from St. Petersburg during the last two days. He said that when we catch up with them that I'll recognize one of them. The guy's Estonian, not Russian, as if that mattered. But if he's in the terminal tonight it's because he wants to follow Jack to wherever he's staying. I'm not too keen on that because Jack's staying with Helen and me."

☙ ☙ ☙

Outside the terminal, in a rented car close to the taxi line, was Galina. She had given in to Deryabin's orders to team with the Estonian, happy she had relented because while the airport was familiar territory, she had not imagined the vastness of it, nor the impossibility of freely moving about whether by private car or taxi. Without Trivimi's help, she could not possibly trail Oxby from the customs hall to the street, retrieve her own car, and follow him. While Trivimi Laar was stiff and unpleasant, he was wily and resourceful. And though she had gained a level of confidence during her recent experience in New York, the circumstances were now vastly changed.

She pulled off the dark wig and ran her fingers through her blond hair. The wig was hot and she rolled it up and jammed it into her purse. Trivimi would be angry, but that would be his problem. She inspected herself in the rearview mirror. She wiped off the gray eye shadow and applied the red lipstick she loved. Nothing more was needed. Her hand reached inside her purse and found the Semmerling pistol. She rubbed the stub barrel, then gripped it, her finger against the trigger. Her eyes closed, and she smiled.

☙ ☙ ☙

Trivimi Laar leaned against the side of an advertising kiosk, trying to shrink his tall body, but at the same time be able to see over the heads of a milling congregation waiting to greet a friend or relative. As passengers from Air France flight 8 began appearing, Trivimi retreated a step and all but disappeared behind a brazen advertisement extolling the joys of a weekend at the Trump Casino in Atlantic City.

⁂ ⁂ ⁂

"Meet Ed Parente, Jack. He waves magic wands around here and genies pop out of the luggage carousels."

"I've heard about you," Oxby said, "courtesy of Alex." He put out his hand. "Thanks for the help."

"Happy to do it," Parente said. He put himself between Oxby and Tobias and took each by the arm. "Got any other bags?"

"Just this." Oxby hoisted up a carryall.

"Good. We'll take a shortcut."

Oxby tugged on Tobias's arm. "Did you tell Ed there might be a small welcoming committee looking for me?"

"We're all set for you," Parente said. "I've got a man at customs and another waiting in a car out front. Right now we're going to see a miracle worker who will waive all the red tape. Let me have your passport."

They went through a door that had a number on it, down a narrow passageway to a second door, and into a small office where two men sat at a table staring at a wall covered with rows of closed-circuit television monitors. Parente opened yet another door and led Oxby to a uniformed woman seated behind a desk and in the act of completing a phone call.

She looked crisp and efficient, then on seeing Parente gave a warm greeting. "Hi Ed. What brings you here?"

"One of Scotland Yard's finest." He handed over the passport. "Meet Detective Chief Inspector Jack Oxby."

The woman stood and offered her hand. "I'm Kathy Harris. Welcome to the land of the crazy. You know you're in fast company?"

"I know," Oxby grinned. "I rather like it."

Agent Harris was black, efficient, and could read a stranger like an old, familiar book. She flipped through Oxby's passport, pausing on the page with stamps from St. Petersburg and Paris. She said, her eyebrows arched, "Didn't I read where everyone's going to St. Petersburg this time of year and here you are coming away from there?"

Oxby said, "My business suddenly became urgent. I mean no offense to New York, but at this time of year, I'd far prefer to be in St. Petersburg."

"You don't offend me," she said, putting a stamp in the passport and handing it back to Oxby. "If you think there's anything I can help you with, give me a call."

Oxby smiled appreciatively. "I collect cards from anyone who offers to help. Do you have one?"

She took one from a card wallet. "You got it."

"Thanks, Kathy," Parente said. "Okay if Inspector Oxby takes a look at the television monitors? He's expecting someone."

They returned to the room with the wall of television screens. Parente asked for the pictures coming from the cameras positioned outside the customs hall. One of the agents hit a few buttons and pointed at monitors 7 and 9. Oxby stared at one screen, then the other. The cameras were in a fixed position and were trained on what had become a large crowd of family, friends, and limo drivers holding up homemade signs with names written on them. One camera was aimed at the passengers exiting customs, the other caught them as they proceeded into the terminal. It was the picture coming from the second camera that interested Oxby.

The images were in black and white, the foreground pale and overexposed, the figures in the rear of the picture in shadow. "Look, there, Alex, next to the advertising sign. Who do you see?"

"Trivimi Laar."

"You guys agree?" Parente said.

Oxby nodded

Parente moved close to the screen. He opened his cell phone and dialed the detective sergeant posted in the area outside customs. He was out of camera range, but Parente described the figure near the kiosk. Then Parente nodded. "Let's go," he said.

ᓚ ᓚ ᓚ

An elderly woman shuffled alongside a porter and the Estonian feared she was the last straggler from the Air France flight. New faces came to meet new arriving passengers, the old ones gone with whoever had come to meet them. Had Oxby slipped past him? He edged slowly away from his shelter, a frown of disappointment on his face. Then he spied Oxby, alone and walking briskly, his folded carryall slung over his shoulder like a golf bag. Trivimi fell in behind and trailed him through the terminal and out to the taxis. As Oxby waited, Trivimi searched for Galina, then found her moving ahead slowly in a line of cars picking up new arrivals. He ran to the car and got into it.

"Did you lose him?" Galina said accusingly.

Trivimi pointed. "He's there, waiting for a taxi."

She pulled out of line, then slowly advanced until they saw Oxby get into a cab. She continued, holding her distance. At the first exit sign the taxi turned. Galina followed.

"This is good," Trivimi said. "Not so many cars that we lose him, but enough to hide us."

"Don't crow so soon. It is a long drive to the city."

A half mile before they would leave the airport road, red and blue flashing lights appeared beside them. Then a siren and a signal to pull to the side of the road.

"What is this?" Galina said. The intimidating lights, bright and relentless, flooded into the car, reflecting off glass and chrome and Galina's hands that tightly gripped the steering wheel. She had no choice except to turn off the road and stop. The cruiser came in behind her, its lights continuing to flash. Both she and the Estonian looked ahead to watch Oxby's taxi sail smoothly away from them.

🐜 🐜 🐜

Oxby watched the flashing lights through the rear window, and when he could no longer see them, he instructed the driver to pull off the road and stop. The man at the wheel was not a homegrown product, as was suggested by the maroon fez on his head and the chains around his neck. His working knowledge of English was apparently limited to ordering gasoline and asking for his fare. He hunched his shoulders and held both hands up in the gesture that said he didn't understand Oxby's request. He continued on.

Oxby abbreviated his request: "Turn! Stop! There!" he bellowed, pointing for emphasis.

The driver hesitated, then followed instructions. As he was getting from the cab, Oxby dropped several bills on the seat next to the driver.

He closed the door and stepped back. The taxi lurched forward and was immediately replaced by a gray Accord.

"Want a lift?" Tobias said.

Oxby tossed his carryall in the back and climbed in. "Everything come off as planned?"

"Without a hitch."

"I'm confused by one detail," Oxby said. "Trivimi Laar was waiting for me in the terminal and it's not possible that he could have followed me alone. Am I right?"

Tobias had pulled back onto the road. "You are. There were two of them. A woman was driving."

"Did you see her?"

"A glimpse. I can't describe her. Parente will have all that."

"I saw them get pulled over."

Tobias smiled. "Ed will work them over pretty good. He knows just how far he can go. He'll get them out of the car, then one of his guys in the cruiser will get a dozen shots on high-speed film. Be nice if they got some video but don't count on it."

"I want to see photos of the woman," Oxby said. "I suspect she's Viktor's wife."

"Viktor?"

There was a pause before Oxby answered. "You'll think I am making this up, but it is as true as we are driving to . . . where in bloody hell are we driving to?"

"We're on the Belt Highway on our way to Bay Ridge. You could say Bay Ridge is to Brooklyn what Paddington is to London."

"About Viktor. I met him in Tashkent, though pity for him, we didn't get to know each other. He ran into a knife I was holding. Blade went through his eye. Killed him."

"Come off it, Jack. That's Hollywood crap."

"I couldn't invent a story like that. That's exactly what happened. Viktor had a wife. I haven't seen her, but she's been described as blond and very beautiful. Would that describe the woman you saw in the car this evening?"

Tobias frowned. "I didn't get a good look at her. Blond hair, I think. Her face was—sorry, Jack. I don't have a good ID."

Both were silent for a moment. Oxby yawned. "Sorry. I got a few hours' sleep on the plane, but I'm on Russian time." He watched the thick traffic that was moving in both directions. "Where are we?"

"Those are the Rockaways over there, and Coney Island after that. You've heard of Brighton Beach? Just ahead."

Oxby repeated the name. "That's the name I couldn't remember. The Russian community."

"An old one, too. They started coming before the Second World War. The Russian mafia operated out of there, and a few of the old boys are still around. But the new ones, they're young and the Beach isn't posh enough for them. This Mike Carson got his start in Brighton Beach."

"Tell me about him."

"Bright. Successful. Young. That enough?"

"Is that a cop's description, or one from Alex Tobias?"

"Both. I've been around too long to get tangled up with all the jargon. I think you'll like him."

"I met his father."

"When?"

"I'll never forget the date. June 10."

"St. Petersburg?"

"I told you about Viktor Lysenko. I didn't tell you that a few minutes before he ran into the knife I was holding, Viktor used it to kill Mike Carson's father."

Tobias turned quickly to Oxby and the car swerved. He straightened. "Holy shit, Jack, what the hell is this all about?"

"It's about this crazy search for an Imperial egg I've been on." Oxby settled back in his seat and peered ahead to a looming structure, aircraft warning lights flashing high up in its towers. "At the risk of repeating some details I may have passed on to you over the telephone, I shall begin at the beginning."

And he did. He recounted every essential fact and date commencing with his meeting with Christopher Forbes to the moment Tobias greeted him at Kennedy Airport. The account was succinct and delivered in Oxby's inimitable manner. After he concluded and after a short pause, he pointed to what he recognized as an immense suspension bridge.

"That's quite a bridge, Alex. What's it doing here?"

Tobias didn't hear the question, his mind was still riveted to the story Oxby had related. They drove on, now under a long, sweeping ramp that led up the bridge.

"What's the bridge, Alex?" Oxby repeated. "It's positively monstrous."

Chapter 41

Only the coffee from the tray of food had been touched. Deryabin lit a cigarette and pushed aside the cart. He sat facing a television set tuned to a Sunday morning kiddie show. The clock in the VCR read 7:42. Over his boxer shorts he had put on a white terry cloth bathrobe, one that had come courtesy of the Hilton, one that made him look like an over-the-hill light heavyweight. The room was cool, but he was sweating profusely. Simultaneous with the sound of chimes, the door opened and Trivimi Laar entered.

Deryabin rushed toward him. "Did you find him?"

"I haven't been looking," Trivimi replied. I told you it would be impossible."

"It's not, goddamn it! Get your ass moving and find the son of a bitch. Call every fucking hotel in the city. He's in one of them."

"He's not in a hotel." Galina had joined them. She was wearing the mate to Deryabin's bathrobe, except on her it was as if she had stepped out of an ad for *Victoria's Secret*. She was brushing her hair, her head tilted.

"How do you know?" Deryabin asked.

"Because it's how I feel." She fixed a cup of coffee and went to the window and looked down to the Sunday morning traffic moving along Sixth Avenue. "When I thought about last night I realized that Oxby planned every detail perfectly. Even to staying where he can't be discovered."

"All the more reason it was so fucking important for you not to lose him."

"We saw him get into a taxi. We followed him. Then the police came. What should we do? Shoot them?"

"They took photographs. Damn you, listen to me!" He spun her around causing her coffee to splatter over his bathrobe. "They've got

266

videos of you." He grabbed a handful of her hair. "Without your wig. Why did you take it off?"

She pulled free. "I was hot."

Galina exchanged glances with Trivimi, each waiting to see which way the unpredictable Deryabin would pounce.

Deryabin's wild glare subsided. Slowly his head tilted forward and his shoulders sagged. He said, "I'll accept that you can't find Oxby. But the police followed you to this hotel and now the fucking bastard knows where to find us." He looked up at the Estonian. "He knows I have the egg with me. Am I right?"

Trivimi nodded. "I phoned him. I said that you had instructed me to confirm that you would take the egg to New York."

"What did he say?"

"He said it wasn't necessary to call. That he knew."

⁂ ⁂ ⁂

Helen Tobias was executive chef and chief executive of 73 86th Street in Brooklyn's Bay Ridge. She had welcomed Oxby with a snack of cold chicken, potato salad, and iced tea, and sent him to bed with one of her brownies and a glass of milk. Helen was the rare, perfect mate for a cop; tolerant of his late night shifts and patient on her lonely weekends. It helped immeasurably that Helen and Alex were each other's best friend and that on their thirtieth anniversary they were able to say "I love you" from their hearts. Their home was typical of the neighborhood; narrow, long, two floors, with a game room in the basement. The house and driveway was crammed into a thirty-foot-wide lot. In the back was a single-car garage, a sundeck, and a garden where Helen raised tomato plants and roses.

They were up early on Sunday morning, though Oxby, still eight hours out of sync, was the first. He saw the *Times* being tossed onto the driveway and took it to the deck and read until Helen came out of the kitchen with an ice-cold glass of fresh orange juice. Ten minutes later she placed a tray with his favorite breakfast on the table. Waffles and Vermont maple syrup with country sausages. Tobias brought his tray and they had breakfast together.

At nine o'clock a black Mercury was in the driveway. Ed Parente, dressed in shorts and a golf shirt, delivered an envelope that contained the photographs taken the previous evening.

"I told my guys to concentrate on the woman." He smiled. "Take a look and you'll see why I didn't have to tell them twice."

Two 35mm cameras with long lenses had caught Trivimi Laar and his companion vigorously protesting to the police. Most of the photographs were of a stunning blonde who seemed even more erotically beautiful because of her frustration and anger. The four-by-five prints, nearly forty of them, were sharp and in color.

"They got a video," Parente said. "Maybe all of five minutes. But it's like a snapshot that moves. Not as good as the photographs."

Tobias stared long at the blonde. "This is who's chasing you, Jack? I think you should let her catch you."

"She'd scratch his eyes out," Helen offered.

"We couldn't develop a hell of a lot of information. There wasn't a violation so we gave them a lot of hot air, and stalled until we got the photographs, then let 'em go. We got their names and saw the rental agreement. Here's a copy of the report we filed. That's about it."

Oxby took the report and read a two-paragraph account of the incident, as it was officially referred to. "Did you see their passports?"

"They claimed they weren't carrying them, and we didn't have warrants to search."

Oxby went over each photograph carefully. He knew how to use them, especially when there were more than a few snapshots. It was not uncommon for Oxby to deduce from a photograph that a suspect was left- or right-handed, or had a limp, or was shortsighted.

"She's every bit how my Russian bodyguard described her." He turned to Helen. "Her name is Galina Lysenko. How old do you suppose she is?"

Helen reviewed the pictures carefully. "Young, of course, but old enough to have some hard edges. Thirty. Thirty-two maybe."

"Not important," Oxby said. "Though it's sometimes useful to know how long people like this have been around. How street-smart they might be."

Oxby looked at Parente. "You tailed them into the city?"

"To the Hilton. Want the room numbers?" Parente was holding a piece of paper.

Tobias reached for it. "I see you haven't lost your connections." He slipped the paper into his shirt pocket. "You playing golf today?"

"Mass at seven, Tobias at nine, on the tee at 11:26."

"Should be a great day for it," Oxby said.

Parente beamed. "Hot, but that's okay. We're playing the Black Course at Bethpage. Took some horse trading to get a starting time."

"I'm jealous," Oxby added.

"Next time, maybe." Parente shook hands, kissed Helen's cheek, and was off.

Helen took away the trays and returned with a hot pot of coffee. "I know you two are going to talk, so here's your coffee before one of you comes asking for it."

Oxby made a concoction of coffee, milk and spoonfuls of sugar. He stirred it, then sat back. Tobias watched him, amused, waiting for his guest to give the tiniest hint that he had relaxed. It came.

"What are you thinking, Jack?"

"That I'm a bloody damned fool."

"Why do you say that?"

"Because a Russian named Deryabin would like to add me to his casualty list. Not exactly the sort of list I want to be on."

"You're not in harm's way."

Oxby sipped his coffee. He selected one of the photographs and flipped it onto the table. "Galina Lysenko is employed by Deryabin. And not as a beautiful empty-headed decoration. Her husband also worked for Deryabin as his enforcer. A hired killer. What do you make of the fact these two were married to each other?"

"That it was more than a coincidence. They were a team?"

"That's what I'm thinking," Oxby said. "We've got a few facts about Galina that we can use for starters. She's tall, and bloody damned good-looking. Her natural hair color is blond. Age thirty, give or take a couple of years. Mike Carson saw the woman who shot Akimov. How did he describe her?"

"The report quotes him saying she was beautiful—and tall."

"Who else was shot by a tall woman?"

"Lenny Sulzberger. But he said the woman who shot him was on the heavy side and older. He thought she was at least forty-five."

"But tall. Right?"

"Right."

"Then the nurse. The one who put the needle in Akimov and finished him off."

Tobias nodded. "The male nurse—name is Nick—wheeled Akimov into intensive care. He said the nurse who came on duty that evening was on the heavy side, and spoke with a thick accent. Russian, he thought, but couldn't be positive. Like Lenny, he said she was in her forties."

"I'm not concerned about how old these women appeared. Learning to use makeup comes naturally to most women. It's likely Galina had training, and knew how to use stage makeup. Look at that photograph. Scrub the face, broaden the nose, add some lines around the eyes, then put on a plain, gray wig and she's her own mother."

Tobias nodded. "Add some padding. Easy enough."

"We've got three witnesses who saw three tall women. Two of the women had gray hair, one was dark. The gray-haired women appeared to be forty or older, and the one with dark hair was young. The older ones spoke with Russian accents. We don't know about the younger one."

"I might have that covered," Tobias said. "I got a phone call from one of the Englewood guys who found a uniform shop that sold a nurse's outfit to someone they guessed was Russian. The date matches up with the Akimov death."

"Will you be able to show the photographs to Mike's salespeople tomorrow?" Oxby asked.

"If I don't, someone will. And I want Mike Carson to see them," Tobias said.

"That's even more important. How soon can you arrange a meeting?"

"I've got his private phone number, and he insisted that I call when something urgent came along."

Oxby twirled the spoon in his coffee. "Do we dare call him Sunday morning?"

Tobias rose. "Worst that can happen is we talk to a machine."

Tobias went into his house and returned with a phone. He dialed, expecting to hear a recorded message, but was surprised. "Hello Mike, it's Alex Tobias. This a bad time?"

Mike was just leaving his apartment. He was meeting bigwigs from General Motors for brunch. They were taking him to a Yankee game, the pleasure part of new contract negotiations. But he could meet later, at seven, in his apartment.

"Suppose, Alex, that Mike and the uniform people are able to match Galina's photographs with the woman each one saw a few weeks ago. What could you do with that information?"

"I suppose I could get a warrant. But we couldn't keep her long."

"Even if they saw Galina in a lineup and made a positive identification?"

"Mike said the woman who shot Akimov had dark hair. In these photographs, Galina has blond hair. Beyond that we don't have the weapon, we don't have a corroborating witness, and I doubt if we've got a motive. Besides, I don't know who has the energy to prosecute. There's even a jurisdictional snag because Akimov was wounded in Nassau County, New York, and, technically, was killed in Bergen County, New Jersey. Lenny Sulzberger would give his left testicle to find the woman who shot him, but I doubt if he can make a positive identification."

Oxby was rubbing his chin, absorbing the unique reality of the quandary Tobias faced.

Tobias said, "I answered your question, now you answer mine. What will you do if Mike identifies Galina?"

"First off, it won't matter if he can or cannot identify her. As far as I'm concerned, Galina shot Akimov, administered the needle to finish him, then shot Sulzberger. But I don't have to arrest her and bring charges against her. In keeping with the adage that it is wise to know thine enemy, I shall proceed on the basis that Galina Lysenko is as dangerous as she is young and beautiful."

"But you still want to see Mike Carson?"

"Bloody damn right! I've looked forward to meeting him ever since that terrible hour I spent with his father in Tashkent."

"You'll get your chance this evening."

"Another question, Alex. Where's the knife that was used on the football player?"

"Tagged and bagged and in a locked file."

"Any prints?"

Tobias shook his head. "The handle was gnarled and rough. Not good for prints, but great for grip."

"Describe it."

Tobias did, in detail. "I know something about knives, and this one was handmade for a single purpose. If Dennis LeGrande had been carrying less fat, he'd have been killed."

"Dennis LeGrande?

"Ex–football player. Works for Mike."

"Have you talked to him?"

Tobias nodded. "Poor witness. He remembered the yelling and screaming, then he was stabbed and he says everything went blank until he woke up in the ambulance."

"An identical knife was used to kill Mike Carson's father," Oxby said. He got up and went to the railing that surrounded the deck. He leaned against it, his arms crossed over his chest. "Alex, I sometimes think I'm living in a crazy, foolish dream."

"I'll tell you straight out, you're not dreaming."

"Then help me understand a few facts that need to be dealt with. I'll start with Oleg Deryabin. Deryabin ordered the death of three men for fear one of them would spill the beans to Mike and explain how Deryabin cheated his father out of an extremely valuable Fabergé Imperial egg. And far more tragic, how his father paid a horrible price for a crime that Deryabin committed."

"That's a good start," Tobias said helpfully.

"Then, incredibly, Deryabin comes to New York to enter into a partnership with the very son of the man he destroyed."

"I've seen a lot of slime in this business, but that's as repulsive as it gets," Tobias said.

"That single, defiant action explains the man. You might define him either by the absence of a single redeeming virtue, or the presence of a hundred heinous character defects. I prefer to list his evil defects, it reminds me who I'm dealing with."

"Which leads me to ask where you figure in the equation."

"Obviously, where I chose to fit, not where Oleg Deryabin wishes. He didn't plan on my entering into his world, but chance put me there, and now both of us are dealing with the consequences."

"You have the advantage. He doesn't know where to find you. Are you going to call him?"

"I have some thoughts about a meeting with Deryabin and I'd like Mike to arrange it."

"And the Fabergé egg?"

"It's very strange about the egg, I know he has it with him because I got an alleged anonymous phone call just hours before leaving Petersburg. Deryabin, or his sidekick, Trivimi Laar, got someone who spoke flawless English to tell me Deryabin would take the egg to New York with him. I suppose Deryabin figured it would be a good time to test the market and see what price it might bring. And he knows I might have a buyer for it."

Oxby gave Tobias one of his knowing glances. "If there was the tiniest suggestion that he possessed a redeeming quality, I might guess that he's brought it along as a peace offering to Mike Carson."

Chapter 42

It was noon. Deryabin's expectation of a call from Oxby had not materialized. Each phone—the one in the bedroom, the one in the sitting room, and a third in the bathroom—had remained silent, though the Russian had glared menacingly at each one as if commanding it to ring. At twenty-minute intervals he had called the hotel switchboard demanding to know why a call of "overwhelming importance" had not been put through to him.

"I know he's calling me!" he shouted at the bewildered operators, "why do you lie?"

"There have been no calls, Oleshka," Trivimi said in an attempt to mollify him. "No conspiracy. Galina was correct to say that Oxby had been able to put a plan together with his friends. Be patient, I promise the phone will ring."

Deryabin redirected his glare from the phone to Trivimi, reluctantly accepting the Estonian's assessment. He lit another cigarette and crushed out the one that still burned in the ashtray.

"Fucking Sundays in this country are like funerals," Deryabin fumed. "Nothing happens."

"No different from Petersburg," the Estonian said. "Watch the television. They have fifty channels. Something will pass the time."

"Where's Galina?"

"You wouldn't let anyone touch a phone. I told her to use the one in my room."

"What does she want a damned phone for?"

"She didn't tell me."

"Ideas get into her head, then nothing stops her." He glared at Trivimi. "Find her."

೫ ೫ ೫

Galina made one phone call from the Estonian's room, then called for her rental car and went to the lobby. She bought a road map that covered a radius of fifty miles from Columbus Circle in Manhattan at dead center. It included nearby portions of New York state on both sides of the Hudson River. At 12:30 the sun was directly overhead and it was as stifling hot as only New York can become on the first day of summer. She opened the top buttons on her shirt but she was still too warm in clothes meant to be worn in the cool air that blew across the Gulf of Finland.

The parking attendant told her to drive west to the Hudson River, then north on Route 9, beyond the George Washington Bridge to the Tappan Zee Bridge.

She found her way onto the bridge, crossed it, and took the exit to the town of Nyack, a residential community with antique shops and colonies of artists and writers. There was another colony; one comprised of the descendants of Russian émigrés who had fled Russia in the 1910s and 1920s. Though most were second- or third-generation, a few still came from the new Russia, searching after, they would say, the American dream.

She stopped at a motel in the center of town for directions, referring to the notes she had made during her earlier phone call. She was told how to get on the road north from Nyack. She followed it over the low hills that sprang up from the big river below, continuing for three miles until a sign directed her onto a road leading to the village of Valley Cottage. There, on her right, she would find a campuslike setting with rows of white frame houses and small cottages. She had been told to look for a small, white church topped by a gold onion dome and a cross rising above it.

There it was. Near the road, a small building, unmistakably a Russian Orthodox church. It was a reminder of home that, for an instant, sent a touch of excitement through Galina. But to have any feelings surprised her. In her entire twenty-nine years she had been in two churches; a Lutheran church in Petersburg where as a teenager she went swimming in a pool installed in the sanctuary by the Soviets when it proclaimed the church as State property. And once when she and Viktor were completing their training and had been sent to follow a doddering old doctor who went each day to his church for prayers. She turned into the parking area and stopped beside a sign. It read: TOLSTOY FOUNDATION.

She knew that Tolstoy was a famous Russian author, yet knew little about his books. What was this place? The little cottages and the houses had been converted to tiny apartments. Beyond the church was a large house, and beyond that, more buildings. Weaving among the trees were paths that crisscrossed the campus and on the paths were men and women. She noticed they were elderly, every one. They walked slowly, many carrying a cane.

The passenger door opened and Pavel Rakov slipped in beside her. They had seen each other less than three weeks before, but in that time Galina's life had been tortuously twisted and forever changed. Pavel wore sunglasses that resembled two green, luminescent reflectors. His shirt was a bright blue and red plaid, his dark hair was graying and cut short. He took off the glasses and they eyed each other familiarly.

He said, "Hello, Galina, you are as pretty as ever."

Galina acknowledged the compliment with a nod.

"You found your way all right?"

She continued to stare at him. Not answering.

"How is your friend Oleg Vladimirovich?" he said icily.

"He is not my friend," she snapped. "He pays me for what I do."

"How much did he pay you for Viktor?"

Her gaze hardened. "What do you know about Viktor?"

"We learn quickly over here. The news comes to us from all over, including Tashkent. When a stranger dies in that city and no one pays to send him home, there is only a box for the body and a hole in the ground to put it in. But someone paid all the people who had their hands out, and for a zinc box and space on the airplane to take it to Petersburg. My friends learned Viktor Lysenko was in the zinc box. It was Oleg Deryabin who paid."

"If I had been with Viktor, he would not be dead."

"I am sorry." He tried to smile. He opened the door. "It's hot. Let's walk. I want to show you something," he said, and took her arm. He guided her onto a path and toward the church.

"No, Pavel. Not there."

"It's all right," he said gently. "Nothing will bite you," he smiled. "I promise not to tell anyone you went inside."

"I feel odd about it."

"Come." He urged her ahead and they entered the church.

Somehow it seemed larger inside. One room, square, its ornately painted ceiling thirty feet above, and directly in front of them an icon wall with a fresco of Christ and his disciples painted in bright colors. A man with a full beard was at work on a side wall, working his brushes over a mural that had been water-damaged in the spring.

Galina was subdued, her head bent forward as she turned to face each wall. She tugged on Pavel's arm. "Can we go?"

Pavel nodded, and they went back out into the sun. They walked on the path and to a bench that was in the shade of a cluster of birch trees. They sat. Neither speaking.

Pavel broke the silence. "How long will you be here this time?"

Her head shook. "When I've done my job. Maybe two or three days."

"What kind of job?" he asked.

"Moy zadanie?" she repeated. "The same as before."

"Who will you kill this time?"

She lowered her eyes. "A man."

"What man?"

She didn't answer immediately. Then she brought her gaze up and said, "The man who killed Viktor."

"Do you know the man?"

"I don't know him. I've seen him. He's English."

"I was told that Viktor fought with an Englishman in Tashkent."

"Viktor was tricked. I don't know all that happened, but he was outnumbered, ambushed."

"The Englishman is here in New York?"

"His name is Oxby. He is with Scotland Yard, but is on a private assignment. Oleg was told that Oxby killed Viktor. That is all I know."

"Who told Oleg?" Pavel asked, his tone doubtful. "He has friends in Uzbekistan?"

"He has friends everywhere. From the KGB."

"You said this was a job. Is it really, or is it your revenge for Viktor's death?"

"Oxby has meddled in Oleg's business. He can make trouble."

She was staring at a long scar above Pavel's left eye, the result of a wound he had received a year after they met. There were the welts of flesh, remnants from a knife wound that had nearly destroyed that eye, and had taken away all but traces of hair in his eyebrow. It was a horrible irony, she thought.

He said, "Viktor was my friend, too."

Galina studied the whole face. A face she knew as intimately as Viktor's. Galina had fallen in love with Pavel when she was eighteen and he was twenty-seven. She was a student, he was a teacher. She wanted to be an actress, he wanted Russia to be a capitalist superpower overnight. The reforms moved too slowly for Pavel and he found his way into a company owned by communist retreads, but run by intimidation and murder. A business that took the life of a close friend. That friend's young brother was Viktor Lysenko.

Fatefully, Pavel introduced Viktor to Deryabin. A year later Galina and Viktor met. After five successful years, Pavel met with a string of failures and was summarily evicted from the company. He scrambled for some IOUs, found a few that were owing from old cronies in the government, then received a visa and moved to America.

"What is this place?" Galina asked. "And the church—"

"The church is called St. Sergius of Radonezh and all that you can see is a home for old people. Old Russians who escaped from the Soviet."

"There is no Soviet," Galina said. "It is Russia now."

"And still they come. I have friends here. They are old, but good people."

"Your friends are here?"

"It is not so strange, Galina. I have many friends here. And more in the city where I live. I have a good life."

She turned and looked intently at her friend. "And you are married?"

A little smile crossed his lips. "Yes." He nodded. "And I have a son."

Slowly her eyes shifted away from him. Her response was silence. Pavel watched her carefully and waited patiently for her to speak.

"You have a son." There was a sweetness to the way she spoke the words. And envy.

She spun around, her eyes flashing. "I have no one."

Pavel wrapped his arms around her and hugged her tightly. "You have friends," he said, kissing her forehead. "I am your friend."

She buried her face against his shoulder, holding him tightly. She cried. But only for a moment. She pulled free, her face wet from tears that rarely came. Now she was staring at Pavel's familiar face, at the scar above his eye, at his lips that had kissed her so many times. A good face, in all. She spoke softly, "You knew that Viktor and I were—" She rubbed her fingers across her lips to smother the rest of her sentence.

Pavel said, "How much longer are you going to be Deryabin's assassin?"

"As long as he needs me. And pays me."

"Without Viktor, he might decide he doesn't need you any longer."

"That could happen."

"If he cuts you off, he'll have you killed."

Galina felt herself take a short, deep breath. "He wouldn't do that to me."

He snapped his fingers. "Like that. He might want you around if you'll go to bed with him."

"I'd rather be fucked by a dog."

"Then leave. Go to Moscow. Get a visa. Come here and start over."

She looked at Pavel, her face wreathed in sadness. "I can't," she said quietly. "I can't."

⁂ ⁂ ⁂

The breakfast cart had been replaced by another. This one with plates mounded with sliced beef and cheeses, salads, and a huge bowl of fresh fruit. But like the food on the first cart, it had been scarcely picked at. Deryabin was alone, still in the bathrobe, still unshaven, still hot with anger. He mumbled, a kind of gibberish laced with vile obscenities. He tore open a fresh package of cigarettes, took one and lit it, then went to the window and stared down at the broad avenue below. The door opened. It was Trivimi Laar.

"Where the fuck is she?" Deryabin roared.

"Gone. With the car. They said she asked for directions to the Tappan Zee Bridge. Have you been there?"

Deryabin said he had, that it was north of the city. That the bridge went over the Hudson River.

"Can you guess why she went there?"

Deryabin blew a stream of smoke. "How the hell would I know? Maybe she's trying to find Oxby."

Chapter 43

The cables and towers of the George Washington Bridge were sharply silhouetted by a hot, orange sun that would set in an hour and half, which would be, on this first day of summer, 8:31 P.M.

Tobias turned into the right lane. "We're going over there," he said, pointing to a row of high rises on top of the Palisades. "Mike Carson's in one of them."

Oxby shifted in the seat for a better view of the western side of the Hudson River. His thoughts moved forward to the impending introduction to Mike Carson, aka Mikhail Vasilyovich Karsalov. There were intensely private portions of Mike's life that he knew, and now, the realization he was about to meet him caused a sudden rush of anticipation. In his mind flashed the vivid sight of the room in the asylum in Tashkent when Mike's father died in his arms. That indescribably tragic incident served to bond Oxby with the son even before the two men laid eyes on each other.

"You're big on bridges," Tobias said. "If you go by the traffic count, this one's a real workhorse. But the Verrazano, the one you asked about when we came in from the airport, she's my favorite."

Oxby considered, fleetingly, whether a bridge was masculine or feminine, concluding that, as in French, bridges were masculine. While Alex may think of the Verrazano as a lady, the GW was a man.

Once on the Jersey side, Tobias took a series of loops and turns and guided his car onto Palisades Avenue. He proceeded slowly until he spotted the sign in front of the Atrium Palace. At 7:00 P.M., promptly, the lobby attendant rang Mike Carson's apartment, and the two men went up.

"Mike, this is Detective Chief Inspector Jack Oxby, pride of Scotland Yard and an old friend of mine. Jack, this is Mike Carson."

The two shook hands, each taking the measure of the other.

279

"I've been looking forward to this," Oxby said. "And ignore the formalities. I'd like for you to call me Jack."

Mike smiled. "And I'm Mike," he said simply. "Come in. I finally got rid of the painters and funny little people who've been trying to make this place look presentable. Hope you like it."

There was nothing not to like. They entered a large room furnished with modern sofas, chairs, and side tables, the colors muted, the lines soft and flowing. In sharp contrast were three large paintings, each in vivid colors. One, on the inside wall, was a Stuart Davis landscape in turquoise, blue, and a yellow sky with setting sun. Oxby moved to the windows, scanned the view from north to south, then turned and admired the room, which still held the scent of fresh paint and polyurethane.

"Spectacular view," Oxby said.

"They charge extra for it," Mike said. He was standing at an opening in the wall, a wet bar behind him. "If you'd like something cold, come help yourself." A few minutes later they were seated, each with a drink.

"How was the ball game?" Alex asked.

"Boring," Mike replied.

"Yankees win?"

Mike smiled. "I was with the sales manager of Cadillac and he roots for Detroit. Though he's from Chicago, he . . ."

Oxby settled back into a thick cushion and listened to Mike and Alex, a die-hard Yankee fan, discuss baseball. Mike's Americanization had not included a love for the national pastime, but he made it clear he enjoyed the football season and his favorite team was the New York Giants. Oxby observed Mike closely, listening to him speak and hearing evidence that he had learned English in London, then had skillfully attuned to the American idiom. Mike and his father were not look-alikes, but there was a resemblance. Mike was blessed, Oxby determined, with a natural ability to put a stranger at ease. He projected sincerity and complete trust.

"...and so the Yanks won and my friend was very quiet after the game."

"Detroit took the series; two out of three," Tobias said. "Can't complain about that."

Mike turned to Oxby. "So, you're with Scotland Yard."

Oxby smiled. "I'm on what the we British call a busman's holiday."

"You've been to Russia," Mike said. It wasn't a question, but a flat-out statement. "What cities did you visit?"

"Only one, in Russia. St. Petersburg." Oxby watched Mike carefully when he said, "And three days in Uzbekistan. In Tashkent."

Mike never wavered, but frowned, thoughtfully. "Tashkent," he repeated the name. "It's been in the news, something about oil and natural gas. Major cotton producer, right?"

"They seem to be stuck with cotton," Oxby said. "In fact there's talk of making automobiles from cotton. I read somewhere that they're planning to convert cottonseed oil into a tough polymer plastic."

"I know something about automobiles," Mike said. "They better think twice before getting into that business. But why Tashkent? What made you go there?"

"I am going to share with you some of my experiences in Petersburg and Tashkent. But I must warn you that some of what I will tell you will be difficult for you to hear. Fair enough?"

Mike glanced at Alex, then back to Oxby. "Go ahead."

"Mike, it was never my intention, but while I was on leave and conducting what I thought would be a pleasant, but challenging investigation, I uncovered some extremely personal information about you and your family. I want to be very clear about this. Whatever I know I have treated as privileged and have shared it only with Alex and Yakov Ilyushin, an old friend who I lived with during the time I was in Petersburg. A good man who has my complete trust."

"Before you go on, does what you are going to tell me have any relationship to the death of Sasha Akimov?"

"Yes," Oxby said. He waited while Mike considered his answer. Mike moved to the windows, where he stared down to the cars and trucks whizzing across the bridge. He turned and faced Oxby.

"What have you learned?"

Oxby had carefully prepared for this moment. He began by describing the challenge he had accepted, and how the opportunity came at a time when he felt a need to take a leave from his duties at Scotland Yard.

"I considered it a marvelous opportunity to visit St. Petersburg, and I was fascinated by the rather astounding proposition that Grigori Rasputin had commissioned Fabergé to create an Imperial Easter egg for Czarina Alexandra."

He then told his odyssey. He could see beyond Mike to the bridge, and the mellowing light of the setting sun against the high towers. As his tale unwound, and the sun fell low in the sky, shadows slowly climbed up the towers until, when he completed his story, the sunlight had completely disappeared.

A long silence followed, then Mike spoke. "You said my father was not in pain before he died. Was it that way, or did you want to spare me from the truth?"

"His wound was mortal and I suspect there was pain, but only for an instant. He went into shock very quickly."

"His diaries and photographs, and the other odds and ends he left, have they been put someplace where can I claim them?"

"I have all the diaries and a box of photographs. I will send them to you. His other belongings were put in safekeeping."

"My mother. Did you learn about her?"

"I wish I had a better answer. But, no. We read about her in your father's diaries, and in Sasha Akimov's letters. I've asked Yakov Ilyushin to try and locate her."

"Sasha gave me her address. I gave the information to a friend in Brighton Beach who has a Web site and communicates by e-mail with his contacts in many Russian cities. So far he hasn't found anyone who knows my mother." He grinned sheepishly. "It is time for the prodigal son to go home."

"I'll put you in touch with Yakov. He'll treat you like a son."

"I had planned to go over on business. Now it will be a personal visit."

"You and Deryabin have several issues to settle."

"Oh? What are they?"

"First is his joint venture proposal. He'll want to push ahead on it."

"I put nearly a half million dollars' worth of cars in Port Newark and planned to ship them to St. Petersburg as soon as I was paid. That deal is dead."

"The cars?"

"We'll take them back." Mike shoved his hands deep into his pockets. "What are the other issues?"

"The Fabergé egg. It belongs to you."

"I said before that if my father was stupid enough to gamble it away, it doesn't belong to me."

"But it does, Mike. There were five men playing cards that night. They're all dead except Deryabin. Doesn't that say something?"

"It says Deryabin's a son of a bitch, but it doesn't prove I own the egg."

"There may be no law that says you do. But there's an unwritten law of equity I like to invoke in situations like this."

Oxby approached Mike. "Look at me," he said firmly. "Forget the poker game, though you can be sure your father was cheated. The egg belongs in your family."

"What do I do about it?"

"First, let's clear up the other issues I believe you must deal with. Foremost is the fact that your father paid a terrible penalty for a crime he didn't commit."

"You're absolutely certain of your facts?"

"While your father was in the navy he was also running a business with Artur Prekhner. I explained how Deryabin became involved and how he pinned Prekhner's murder on your father."

Mike pointed toward the Manhattan skyline. "He's over there, isn't he?"

"In the Hilton Hotel with Trivimi Laar. And with the woman who I suspect shot Sasha Akimov in your office."

"That's a nasty combination."

"I would agree that Deryabin is as bad as they come. It takes a twisted mind to meet face-to-face with the son of the man he destroyed."

"I asked before. What can I do?"

"You told Alex that you have an appointment with him tomorrow morning in your office. Is that still on?"

"Yes. Ten o'clock."

"I'd like for you to meet him outside of your office. In the open. In one of the parks, for example. Got an idea, Alex?"

"Mike said he put some cars in Port Newark. I'm familiar with that operation. How about meeting over there? It's anything but a park, but it's wide open."

"What do you think, Mike?" Oxby asked.

"Hell of a big place to have a meeting," Mike said. "Be hot, too."

"What about security and locked gates, that sort of thing?"

Tobias said, "There are gates and guards, and customs police patrol it, but we know the right people. That won't be a problem."

"All right, let's do it. What's a good time, Alex?"

"It's busy in the morning. I suggest mid- or late afternoon."

"Four o'clock. That agreeable?"

Mike said, "Who tells Deryabin?"

"You do it. You can tell Deryabin you've got the cars he ordered and this would be his chance to see them before you ship them over."

☙ ☙ ☙

Deryabin had been looking at every timepiece in sight throughout the afternoon and evening. When nine o'clock came and went, he was certain he would not hear from Oxby and any hopes of a call from Mike Carson also expired. But at ten past nine, the phone rang.

Trivimi Laar answered it. Deryabin went hurriedly to listen on the bedroom extension.

"It is good to hear from you, Michael," Trivimi said. "Has everything gone well since I saw you?"

Mike assured the Estonian that, indeed, all had gone well, and that he had a message for Oleg Deryabin. "Please explain that something urgent has come up and I can't meet until the afternoon."

"What time?"

"At four. But we will not meet in my office. I have gathered the cars you ordered and I want you to see them."

"A pleasant surprise," Trivimi said. "Where are they?"

"The cars are in New Jersey, in Port Newark. It's a short drive and shouldn't take more than forty minutes from your hotel. I will send instructions."

Then Mike rang off, saying he looked forward to meeting Trivimi again.

Deryabin returned to the sitting room at the very moment Galina unlocked the door and joined the two men.

"Where have you been?" Deryabin demanded, his tone sharp and challenging.

Galina went to the cart and put a pastry and fruit on a plate. Without turning to face him, she answered, "I went for a Sunday drive. Someone told me it's an old American custom."

Chapter 44

It was ten miles, as the crow flies, from midtown Manhattan to Port Newark, New Jersey. By car, the distance increased but not by much. The port was located on the western shore of Newark Bay, which in turn was connected to Upper New York Bay by the Kill Van Kull, a narrow stretch of water through which the big ships passed as they came from or went out to the Atlantic Ocean. The docks and the huge warehouses were in the center of a fifteen-square-mile region packed solid with a variety of industry, commerce, trade, and transportation. To the west, and separated by the New Jersey Turnpike, was Newark International Airport. North and south of the port area were specialty chemical plants and petroleum production factories, plus soccer-field-size yards filled with small mountains of squashed automobiles, or giant-size construction equipment. The odors in the air changed with the wind and factory schedules; from the acrid and pungent to fragrant concoctions of spices and sweet-scented disinfectants. Heavy trucks spewed up lung-blackening streams of diesel exhaust.

Cargo of every kind came through the port each year. Of note were a half million vehicles, shipped in specially designed ocean freighters, some rising twelve stories above the water-line. Most were passenger cars with names like Volvo, SAAB, Hyundai. After each vehicle was driven off the ship, it was inspected, logged in, and parked at a predetermined space in what was known as the Field. No grass grew on the Field, for it was a gigantic expanse of asphalt with a cross-hatching of white painted lines.

Most of the vehicles were factory-fresh and from Scandinavia or Seoul and came in their traveling clothes; hood, roof, and trunk covered with a protective skin of white, tough plastic. Newly minted American-produced cars were in the same protective cover, and marshaled in sections of the Field set aside for exports.

There were nearly ten thousand new cars and miscellaneous vehicles on the Field, their combined value easily exceeding a quarter of a billion dollars. Yet not one of the cars was locked. Immense as it was, the Field had but two gates. One was for the long car carriers that moved out every few minutes with their heavy burden, the other for car dealers or individuals who came to ship or receive a car from overseas. The gates were guarded by a combination of the New York–New Jersey Waterfront Commission and private security forces. During hours of operation, usually from 8:00 A.M. to 6:00 P.M., the Field was patrolled by armed members of the U.S. Customs Service.

In a designated section of the Field, several hundred feet away from what was known as the Doremus Avenue Gate, were an assortment of vehicles waiting to be exported. Here were privately owned cars being shipped abroad for use by families on extended personal visits or business assignments. Also, there were small groups of vehicles being shipped by entrepreneurs and independent automobile dealers. Mike Carson fit the latter category, and the fifteen cars he had assembled for shipment to St. Petersburg were gathered here.

Mike chose nine Cadillacs, four Oldsmobiles, and two Pontiacs. Each car had stickers on the front windows and a bright yellow tag dangling from the rearview mirror. One of the stickers read Bremerhaven, and beneath the name of the port, a printed message rendered with a bright red Day-Glo pen: "*Do not load pending authorization of Carson Motors, Inc.*" On the passenger seat was the car's manual and two sets of keys.

Surrounding Mike's fifteen cars was an eclectic collection of vehicles, including a ten-year-old white Lincoln Continental stretch limousine with a windshield sticker indicating it was on its way to Southampton. Next to the Lincoln were two Hummers, one black, the other dark blue. Strange-looking, even menacing with their low-slung profile and small windows, Hummers were the king of the recreational vehicles, designed for safari or a beach party and immediately convertible to military action. Appropriately enough, these two were the property of a Kuwaiti sheikh.

There was an oddity about this field filled with so many automobiles. Or perhaps it was a contradiction. These were modern machines meant to move at high speed, and to those who walked the Field, the row upon row of stilled power was an incongruity. One could sense the bridled energy straining to burst free.

ભ ભ ભ

Deryabin stirred first on Monday morning. The bed next to his was empty, the cover had been turned down but it had not been slept in.

"Where are you, bitch?" he said, pinching out the words. "Galina!"

He stormed into the sitting room, then flung open the bathroom door. He was alone. There was a blanket and pillow on the sofa. He took the pillow and punched it. He kept at it, hitting the pillow with the anger and frustration of a little boy. He threw the pillow to the floor, then picked up the phone and called room service and soon another cart of food appeared. This time he ate ravenously. He watched a morning television host go on about vacation travel. He flipped off the set, then tried to make sense out of the business pages of the *New York Times*. He heard the door open and close. It was Galina.

She came into the room and the two stared at each other, neither speaking. She poured coffee and sat in the chair where her view was to the Upper West Side of the city. Deryabin watched her, frowning. "Aren't you going to eat?"

She didn't look his way, but shook her head. "*Nyeht.*"

"When did you go to bed? I didn't hear you."

She ignored his question.

He raised his voice a notch. "I asked when did you come to bed?"

"Is it important? You were making so much noise I came here."

"I told you that if I was asleep to wake me."

"Why should I wake you?"

"I wanted you."

"I didn't want you, Oleg. That was our bargain. You want to fuck, get a whore. They have very good ones in New York."

"You slept here?"

"On the sofa. It is comfortable. And quiet."

He poured more coffee and sat in the chair opposite from her. "You said you went for a drive yesterday. Where did you go?"

"North of here. The Tappan Bridge, I think."

"Tappan Zee."

"Yes."

"Why did you go there?"

"To get away."

"Away from here? From me?"

"Don't start a fight, Oleg. I was bored."

"You have a job."

"It's not my job to sit in this room waiting for the phone to ring."

"You do what I tell you."

"I know what I have to do. And I'll do it my way."

ఇ ఇ ఇ

Mike Carson walked into his kitchen, a phone crooked to his ear, a mug in one hand and a sheaf of papers in the other. He put more coffee in his mug and went back to the living room just as Patsy came through the door he had left open for her.

"Hi, boss," she said, and put a paper bag on the coffee table.

Mike signaled to her with two fingers, talked another half minute on the phone, then clicked off. He took a sweet roll from the paper bag and bit into it. There was something ritualistic and familiar about the way Mike and Patsy joined each other, as if it happened exactly this way every morning. On every Monday morning at nine o'clock it did.

"You've got a date with the Russians at eleven," Patsy declared. "Everything copacetic?"

"It's been put off until four."

"Oh?" It was an utterance that conveyed assorted concerns and at least one question. "Somebody got a problem?"

"Not exactly a problem. More like a strategy."

"Changing the time is a strategy?"

He took another bite of the roll and sipped on his coffee. He wasn't looking at her, trying, it was becoming obvious, to sort out his thoughts and explain what he was trying to say.

"Two men were here last night. One you know, Alex Tobias. The other from London. Interesting guy named Jack Oxby. With Scotland Yard. "

"What did they want?"

"Oxby's been in Russia. Brought some news about my family."

"Good news, I hope?"

"Some good, some bad. It's been so long—" He caught himself. "They asked me to change the time of my meeting with the Russians."

"Any reason?"

"I'll tell you—but not now."

Patsy cocked her head and gave one of her I-know-something's-up looks. "Anything I can do?"

He shook his head and said there wasn't. "Unless you want to get me another Danish . . ."

‰ ‰ ‰

It was getting hot. As in sizzling hot with the thermometer outside the Tobias kitchen reading 97 at 11:45 A.M. The air was heavy and there were no clouds, except for a few to the south that appeared threatening and that might bring a storm if they stayed on track. Alex Tobias saw the clouds. He had turned to the Weather Channel and had seen the satellite pictures. A fast-moving front coming from the southwest would hit the New York metropolitan area between 2:00 and 4:00 P.M. and would be "accompanied by rain, heavy at times with winds expected to gust to 40 miles per hour." Then it would clear, but would remain hot and humid.

"We don't need a rainstorm, Jack."

"Know how to stop it?"

Tobias smiled. "You're right. Maybe we can make it work to our advantage."

"I'll work on it," Oxby said.

‰ ‰ ‰

An envelope with the Carson Motors logo printed on the front was delivered to Deryabin's suite at 11:35. Inside was a map with the route from the hotel to Port Newark highlighted in yellow. Trivimi estimated that it would take thirty or forty minutes to make the drive. There was also a note:

> Mr. Deryabin:
>   Enclosed you will find a map that will guide you to the location of your meeting this afternoon at 4:00 P.M. The guard at the Doremus Avenue entrance will show you where to park inside the gate. He will give you directions onto the large parking area where the cars you have ordered are located and where Mr. Carson will be waiting for you.

The unsigned message was typed on company stationery with Michael Carson's name printed near the top of the sheet. Trivimi handed the map and note to Deryabin, who looked quickly at both, then stared at the map for several long seconds. He held up the pieces of paper, and as he did, his eyes closed and his face twitched as if every part of him was about to unravel into a horrible rage.

"It's Oxby. He's behind this." Then he crumpled the papers into a ball and threw it across the room.

Galina retrieved it and separated the pages. She studied the map, then gave it and the note to the Estonian. She went to the door and opened it.

"Where are you going?" Deryabin said.

"To the lobby for something to eat."

"We've got food. All you want, right there."

"I want to eat alone."

ᘓᕯ ᘓᕯ ᘓᕯ

Mike Carson went for a drive. Alone. He drove over the GW Bridge and continued on the Cross Bronx Expressway, over the Throgs Neck Bridge, and on to the Long Island Expressway. A left turn would take him to Roslyn and his new dealership, but without hesitation, he turned right and followed familiar highways and streets that eventually led him to a wide parkway that ended in the Brighton Beach section of Brooklyn. He was, in a manner of speaking, home.

He parked and got from his car and began to walk. He rolled up the sleeves of his shirt and wiped the sweat from his neck with a handkerchief. How long had it been since he had walked on Brighton Beach Avenue? Old memories were difficult to bring into focus because they competed with new memories from the previous evening. The ones put there by Jack Oxby, who had met his father and seen him die. He had put Russia and his family out of his life. Or, thought he had. But it wasn't so. There was the photograph of his father and mother and his grandfather. Now, the knowledge that he was the son of a man who paid a price for a crime he didn't commit. The son of a mother he must discover and love.

At the least he was confused. He was lonely and angry and he felt that he had lost the privilege to have selfish feelings.

He passed the markets with their odors of fish and old food rotting in buckets set out at the curb. The clothes shop with jeans for the family and shoes for infants. Book stalls on the sidewalk and tables heaped with old magazines and paperbacks in Russian and Greek. He stopped in front of a nightclub that advertised exotic dancers including photographs of a bare-breasted showgirl fresh from her hit appearance in Minsk. He went inside and though it was the lunch hour, it was nearly empty. He sat at a table and ordered a bottle of soda and a salad. It was a room in greens and black with clusters of ceiling lights. At the far end was a small stage festooned with decorations left from last night's anniversary party, the music stands and chairs disarranged as they had been left. A man, a patron or maybe a musician, got onto the stage and tapped life into the microphone. He sat at an electronic keyboard and began to play. He sang a Russian folk song, haunting and sad.

The salad came and Mike ate a little of it, then paid and went back into the heat. Shadows were no longer sharp, but dulled by a hazy sky. He walked to the boardwalk and saw the dark clouds on the southern horizon far across the water of the Atlantic Ocean.

He looked at his watch: 1:50. In a little more than two hours he would meet Oleg Deryabin. The feeling that gnawed inside him was foreign; part of it anger, a part he recognized as fear. It was an alien feeling that he was slowly beginning to recognize as his newfound compulsion to atone for abandoning his family. It was also the feeling of a growing hatred toward the man who had destroyed his family.

He bowed his head. Tears came. They were a purgative, uncomfortable at first. Then they renewed and refreshed him.

🐝 🐝 🐝

"Let's remember that when Mike Carson and Oleg Deryabin last saw each other, Mike was a little boy and his name was Mikhail Vasilyovich Karsalov."

"Mike's a big boy," Tobias said. "He'll handle it."

"I hope he does," Oxby said. "Until last evening, he might have guessed Deryabin was just another crooked Russian businessman. I gave him a lot to think about."

"You took the guesswork out of it. Now he knows the bastard's a crook."

"And much more. That's what I hope he can cope with."

Tobias smiled. "You're both the playwright and director of this reunion." The smile faded. "Are you having second thoughts?"

"Not exactly. Except I am getting one of those bloody hunches of mine."

"What's it telling you?"

"I'm getting mixed signals."

"What kind?"

"The kind that tell me I should have taken something from that gun collection of yours. Chances are I won't need it. But—"

"I'll have one with me. And look." He tapped his watch. "It's just two o'clock and I can get Ed Parente to send over a couple of his guys. I like Mike too much to have anything happen to him."

"No, Alex. Mike Carson's not in any danger. Deryabin doesn't go after people who can put money in his pocket. It's the ones that can expose him that he wants to get rid of." Oxby tapped his chest. "Like me."

૨⅃ ૨⅃ ૨⅃

"It's time," Deryabin grumbled. "Where's Galina?" Nothing would appease Deryabin short of the sudden appearance of Galina. He opened the door and stormed into the corridor. He went to the elevator, then returned to the room, trailing a stream of Russian obscenities behind him.

"Where is she, you fucking Estonian bastard?"

"Don't blame me that you can't control Galina," Trivimi roared back. "She went to eat."

"I pay her for a job. I pay you to make sure she does it."

"You don't need Galina to help you look at fifteen automobiles and sign a contract. Is that her job?"

"Make a copy of the instructions and put it where she will see it. Tell her to find a taxi, or whatever gets her there."

Trivimi proceeded calmly to check the papers in his briefcase. Then he tucked it under his arm and went to the door and opened it. He said, "I don't have to leave a message for Galina. She knows where to find us."

૨⅃ ૨⅃ ૨⅃

Mike put Brighton Beach and an assortment of memories behind him and drove through the downpour to New Jersey by way of the Verrazano and Goethals bridges. He tuned in to a weather forecast and learned the rain would end before the rush hour traffic, but all motorists were admonished to use extreme caution and be prepared for flooding in the usual low-lying sections of the city and suburbs. The announcer intoned the time: 3:19. Mike was on the Turnpike, south of Newark

Airport. He would get off at the airport exit. From the toll booth it would be five minutes to the Doremus Avenue gate. Beyond the gate was the Field. He agreed to meet Oxby and Tobias at quarter to four. The traffic was getting thicker and moving more slowly. He figured he would just make it.

ठ‍ ठ‍ ठ‍

Tobias turned onto Doremus Avenue. Several hundred feet ahead was the gate and the guard station nestled against the fence. He parked beside a year-old Jeep Cherokee with Ohio plates. The driver, a twenty-two-year-old redhead with a gold earring and T-shirt with the Bud-weiser logo printed front and back, was trying to detach a Harley-Davidson motorcycle from the Jeep's tow bar before he was drenched to the skin. The rain had intensified and the wind had picked up. The guard, covered with an orange slicker, came from his shed, opened the door to the Jeep, and tossed a gate pass and an envelope on the shelf above the dashboard. He hurried back to the shed.

Two more cars arrived. One parked ten feet from Tobias's car, the other stopped abreast of the Jeep. The drivers, one with an umbrella, the other running, went to the guard's shed. A few minutes later, the one with the umbrella returned to his car and drove off. The other got back into his car and waited for a gate pass.

The young driver pushed the motorcycle close to the shed and let it rest against its kick stand. Then he got into the Jeep and drove through the gate, where he parked in front of a low, one-floor, wooden building. He disappeared inside. This was the final checkpoint before driving onto the Field. License and title would be confirmed, along with proof that shipping charges and fees had been paid. When the driver received his final clearance, a second gate would be opened and he could drive onto the Field and put the vehicle in its assigned space. This done, he could return to his motorcycle and begin his drive back to Ohio. In view of the weather, he might wait out the rain.

Tobias was familiar with the procedure and explained it to an always curious Oxby. As the Jeep Cherokee disappeared, Mike Carson pulled in next to them.

"Wait here," Mike said. "I'll get our gate passes." It took several minutes, and when he returned he got into the back seat of Tobias's car. He handed a pass to Tobias.

"I've got one for Deryabin." He looked squarely at Oxby. "Who's going to wait for him? Not me."

"Alex will," Oxby said. "Both of us know Trivimi Laar, but I might be a lightning rod." Oxby added, "I think you and I should be together when we meet Deryabin."

Mike said, "Have them follow you through the gate and park over there next to Building 1. Go inside and ask for Sam Salzano. Sam expects you as well as the others. He can't let you drive onto the Field, but he'll get you past the gate at the far end of the building." Mike pointed. "Sam will show you where the cars Deryabin ordered are parked. It's about a four-hundred-yard walk."

Oxby got into Mike's car and they drove through the gate, parked, and went into the building. Mike didn't visit the Field regularly, but Sam Salzano knew him and the two chatted briefly. Then Mike waved for Oxby to follow him. They left the building through a back door. A gate directly ahead of them led onto the Field. The rain had lightened to a fine drizzle, the air still heavy and hot.

As he walked, Oxby took in the scene, impressed as Mike had predicted at the sight of row upon endless row of automobiles.

"Up ahead," Mike said. "The cars with red streamers on the rear windows. Those are ours."

🐜 🐜 🐜

Tobias recognized the car that was bringing Deryabin and Trivimi when it was a hundred yards away. It was the same car that had been driven by a beautiful blonde two days earlier. But no blonde was at the wheel this time. Five after four meant that Trivimi had negotiated the trip far better than he expected.

Tobias got from his car and walked to the driver's side window and leaned down to get his first look at Oleg Deryabin, who inclined his head and said nothing.

"Hello," Tobias greeted Trivimi, without offering his hand. "You made good time."

"Yes," Trivimi said. "But is this a strange place to meet?"

"Not if you're in the automobile business. Isn't that why you're in New York?"

"But why are you here?" Trivimi asked. "Are you now in the automobile business?"

"I get mixed up in lots of different businesses," Tobias said. "Occupational hazard."

"I don't understand," Trivimi said.

"Inside joke," Tobias said. "Put the car over by that building. I'll meet you there."

The rain had stopped, but in the heat, Tobias had taken off his seersucker jacket and was carrying it over his right arm so that it obscured the butt end of the pistol that protruded from his hip holster. It was a twenty-year-old Smith & Wesson that Tobias could use expertly. Trivimi and Deryabin stood by the car.

"Are you Mr. Deryabin?" Tobias asked.

Deryabin nodded, but Trivimi replied. "Oleg, this is Detective Tobias."

That brief exchange constituted the introductions.

They went up the steps and into the building. Sam Salzano was waiting. He instructed them out to the Field.

"There's a ship just come in," Salzano said. "You can't miss it. Go right for it and you'll find the others."

They filed out, Tobias leading. There, a quarter of mile across the Field was the *Atlantic Companion*, one of the largest car freighters that could be moored in Port Newark.

Dead ahead of Tobias stood Oxby and Mike Carson.

🐜 🐜 🐜

"Are you ready for this?" Oxby said.

Mike nodded. "I hope he is."

A hazy sun poked through and reheated the asphalt that had been briefly cooled by the rain. Tobias slowed and moved to the side. Deryabin was now in front. At fifty yards, Mike could see his face; his pink skin and thinning hair. At twenty yards he saw the red lines across his cheek. With each step, another of his features became clear until, when he was fifteen feet away, Mike saw the strange little smile that seemed, immediately, to be both ingratiating and indulgent. Deryabin's arm went out, his hand fully extended.

"Mikhail," the deep voice rumbled out. "I am Oleg Deryabin."

Mike ignored the hand and said, "I know you are. Those cars," he pointed, "were ordered by your company. A deposit of seventy thousand dollars was paid to us."

"Yes," Deryabin replied, "that is right. And you will be paid the balance before they are put on one of those ships."

Tobias had moved next to Oxby, who had taken a position ten feet from Mike. Trivimi stood beside Deryabin. Mike, alone, faced Deryabin. The five men seemed to have formed a triangle and they were all within a few strides of the Cadillacs, Oldsmobiles, and Pontiacs. To the other side of them was the stretch limousine and the pair of Hummers. And also the Jeep Cherokee that had just been delivered by the young man who was by now on his motorcycle and whizzing his way back to Ohio.

"They're not going anywhere," Mike said.

"There is a problem with the cars?" Deryabin said.

Mike made a gesture toward Oxby. "Have you met Inspector Oxby?"

"What has he to do with our business?" Deryabin asked.

"With our business?" Mike repeated. "Nothing. It is my family."

"He has told you lies, Mikhail."

"Not lies, Deryabin, and the name is Mike. He told me everything that Sasha Akimov wanted to tell me, but couldn't before you had him killed. And my father who spoke the truth before he died. You killed him."

"You can not believe the lies. You hear me? They all lied!" Deryabin screamed.

The rear door to the Cherokee opened and Galina stepped down. She took a step toward the group, the Semmerling raised.

"Galina," Deryabin said, pointing at the Jeep. "I'm happy you are here, but how—" His voice trailed off.

"I am paid to know how."

Oxby and Tobias faced her and each felt cautiously for their pistols. Mike could do nothing but stand rigid. Trivimi held up a hand as if to halt whatever Galina planned next.

"Don't get in the way, Estonian," Galina said.

Deryabin said, "Put the gun down."

Galina stared defiantly at him. Her lips parted, as if to speak. Instead, she squeezed the trigger and put a bullet precisely where she had aimed it. High in Deryabin's leg, inches from his groin.

"You bitch!" he shouted and sank to his knees. "Shoot that one," he pointed at Oxby. "He killed your Viktor."

"You always point the finger away from yourself. But no more can you do that. It was you. You killed Viktor!"

"Don't do it, Galina," Oxby shouted. "Another killing won't solve anything."

"Don't try to stop me," she said, warning off Oxby with her pistol. Then she turned it on Deryabin and fired again, this time striking his other leg. He sprawled onto his stomach, writhing on the hot, wet pavement.

"Bastard prick," she shrieked, and took aim again.

Deryabin rolled over and came up facing Galina, holding his own gun and firing wildly at her. He emptied the clip.

Galina shot twice in the exchange, and hit Deryabin high in the chest, not a kill shot. Only one of Deryabin's seven shots hit Galina, but that one caught her in the temple on the right side of her face. The bullet, a heavyweight .38, transformed her truly beautiful face into a horrible mass of bone, blood, and silky blond hair.

Chapter 45

"Why?"

The word floated out and hung tantalizingly in the air for a half minute. Oxby broke the silence. "I don't have a good answer, but I'll do my bloody best to come up with one."

He sat next to Mike Carson. Across from him was Kip Forbes seated in front of a painting that filled the wall behind him. Oxby recognized the picture, an immense portrait of Empress Eugénie, wife of Napoleon III, surrounded by her ladies-in-waiting. On the adjoining wall was a bookshelf crammed with museum exhibition catalogues, biographies, and references covering the life and production of Peter Carl Fabergé. Oxby made a professional appraisal of Kip's office, concluding that the room with all its paintings, sculpture, and hundreds-year-old furniture belonged in the Louvre Museum in Paris, not in one of America's great publishing companies.

Oxby continued, "I didn't know what either one looked like, until yesterday. My alleged bodyguard gave me some sketchy bits about Galina, including the fact she and her husband Viktor Lysenko were Oleg Deryabin's enforcers."

Kip shot a wide-eyed glance at Oxby. "Then why in God's name was she going to kill him?"

"That's what I don't have an answer for. Maybe nothing more than the fact that Deryabin was a mean son of a bitch who deserved all the bullets she could put into him. What I know about Deryabin I learned from his naval records and fifteen minutes with Trivimi Laar. He's a *pakhan*, a crime boss. One of the businesses he owned is a delivery service that he planned to expand into a chain of automobile showrooms. Deryabin said he was going to sell American cars. Expensive ones. That's one of the reasons he was in New York. To work a deal with Mike."

"But buying and selling American cars isn't a crime," Kip said.

"No, but Deryabin intended to export the cars to Cyprus—to an arms merchant with clients throughout the Middle East. Inside each car would be a quantity of a deadly biological toxin."

Kip exhaled a low whistle, "That could mean big money."

"Risky, too. Deryabin was having the stuff made in another of his little companies, one with a chemistry lab he set up to duplicate expensive perfumes. A harmless dishonesty, I suppose. They switched from making perfume to *Clostridium botulinum*. A drop of that can kill a dozen people."

"That doesn't explain why they were shooting each other," Kip said.

"When Galina popped out of the Jeep I fully expected her to shoot me."

"You said you'd never seen her. Why would she want to hurt you?"

"She thought I had killed her husband."

"You're going too fast," Kip said, incredulously. "You killed Galina's husband?"

"I had no choice."

"What in God's name happened?"

"You've heard this, Mike. Do you mind hearing it again?"

"Not at all."

Oxby relished telling his tale again, sharing his impressions of his friend Yakov, of Poolya, of Tashkent and Mike's father, Vasily Karsalov. And about the Hermitage, the broken *matryoshka* doll, and watching an aged Lada he was supposed to be sitting in explode into flames. Kip Forbes listened, enraptured, rarely letting his eyes stray from Jack Oxby.

Mike also listened attentively. "I didn't make the connection the other evening. Are you saying it was Galina who came in my office and shot Sasha Akimov?"

"Bloody right. She was also the nurse who finished off Sasha with sodium pentobarbital. And she was the woman who shot the writer."

"Lenny Sulzberger. He'll be angry that he can't have his own revenge."

"Revenge is what this is all about," Oxby said. "And this—"

He reached for a plastic shopping bag that he had put on the floor by his chair.

When Kip saw Oxby remove the distinctive pale brown presentation case, he edged forward. "Incredible," he said, anxiously anticipating his first view of what he hoped would become the most famous of all the Fabergé eggs. "How did you get hold of it?"

"After we put Deryabin in an ambulance, we let Trivimi consider his new circumstances inside a holding cell in a New York City precinct station. We told him to cooperate or else. The or else being that he would be charged as an accessory in the murder of Sasha Akimov, and as an accomplice in the death of Galina Lysenko. He told us that Deryabin had brought the egg to New York with the intention of finding a buyer for it. In fact, you were on his list of prospective buyers. I told him that the egg belonged to Mike Carson's family, that it would be to his advantage if he would show me where Deryabin had put it. He did, and here it is."

Oxby placed the egg in front of Mike. "It belongs to you, Mike."

Mike studied it for a moment, then, timidly, picked it up. He lifted the egg off the golden hands that held it. He touched one of the diamonds. "Beautiful," he said, as if saying it only to himself. He looked at Oxby. "But I can't take it."

"Think again, Mike. I told you that your father paid a heavy price for a murder Deryabin committed. If you refuse to take the egg, does that mean you want Deryabin to have it?"

He shook his head. "Hell, I don't know what I want."

"I have a suggestion," Kip said. "Suppose you don't return the egg to Deryabin and suppose also that you don't take it. Suppose further that we have it appraised by three experts and average the prices. I will pay you that amount plus five percent. The money will be placed in an escrow account which you will designate. It can then be apportioned out to your family, to a charity, or for whatever purpose you choose."

"That's fair all around," Oxby said. "How does it sit with you, Mike?"

Mike cradled the egg. He looked squarely at Oxby and said, "How many people are dead because of this?"

"I counted six, though I suspect there were more."

᱿ᱽ ᱿ᱽ ᱿ᱽ

Kip Forbes was no stranger to the outpouring of decorative arts from the workshops of Peter Carl Fabergé. He had moved to his desk where he was evaluating the egg; studying each of its precious stones, the basket with its flowers made of small but beautiful jewels, and the brilliant blue enamel surface. He made accurate copies of the engraved marks on the bottom of the egg, and the scratched markings that had been incised into a silver band that encircled the egg.

Oxby was making his own evaluation of Kip Forbes's office, admiring a unique collection of paintings, portrait busts, and Staffordshire pottery figures, all portraying Napoleon III or members of his family. The furniture, including Empire and Biedermeier, was from the same period. Opposite the large painting of Empress Eugénie was a life-size portrait of Napoleon III. Oxby was in front of it.

"You're a fan of Louis Napoleon. How did you choose him?"

Kip grinned. "I discovered long ago that old Louis hadn't been shown the respect I thought he deserved, so I began to build a little collection around him. Like it?"

"I do." He spun to face the Empress and her ladies. "Especially Eugénie."

"I like her, too," Kip said, then turned his attention back to the Imperial egg.

"What do you think of it?" Oxby asked.

"That it's an authentic Fabergé, dated 1916, the last year Fabergé made an Imperial egg. I predict that when this one is catalogued it will be known as the Final Fabergé. The workmasters made peculiar scratches on certain items. Like these—" He showed Oxby the marks he had duplicated. "These scratches were like a code and were copied into Fabergé's record book. One of the marks might tell us if Rasputin commissioned the egg."

"Where's the record book?" Oxby asked.

Kip laughed. "Sorry. It's been missing since the communists closed the Fabergé shops in 1918."

"Any other surprises?"

"If you're asking if there's a surprise compartment, I'm sure there is."

"I'll be in St. Petersburg during the second week in September," Oxby said. "Yakov assures me the weather will be pleasant. Any chance either of you can meet me there?"

Mike had been quiet, preferring to listen. He responded enthusiastically. "I've decided to go."

"And you, Kip?" Oxby asked.

"I've got an impossible schedule coming up, but I'll try. If I can make it, where do I reach you?"

Oxby flipped through his notepad for one of his cards. The piece of paper containing the numbers fell out. He put it in front of Kip.

"I copied these numbers from the note that was left behind by the old woman in Schaffhausen. The translation doesn't explain what these numbers mean. Got an idea?"

Kip Forbes glanced at the piece of paper. "Two—eleven—nine." He shook his head slowly. "They don't mean a thing to me. Not now."

"Hold on to it." Oxby gave one of his knowing, warm grins. "I have a hunch they might mean something important."

☙ ☙ ☙

When they reached the lobby of the Forbes Building, Mike turned to Oxby. "I owe you something for all you've done for me. Trouble is—"

"You don't owe me a thing," Oxby said. "I've been paid doubly with memories and new friendships."

"Except for you, Deryabin would still have the egg."

"And if I hadn't meddled, your father might still be alive."

Mike pressed Oxby's arm. "You can't blame yourself for that. From what I've learned, my father was a dead man breathing."

Oxby smiled at Mike's eerie oxymoron. "I very much want Yakov to find your mother."

"Not more than I do."

"I'll show you St. Petersburg," Oxby said with a perfectly straight face. "I'm practically a native."

"Okay, you're hired." They shook hands, each acknowledging the beginning of a friendship.

"Can I drop you somewhere?" Mike said.

"Thanks, but I want to see the collection Kip helped put together. I'll call before I leave."

There was an awkward pause. "So long," Mike said, sounding as American as the flag he walked past on his way out to Fifth Avenue.

Oxby watched until he was gone from sight. Then he crossed the lobby and went into the Fabergé Galleries. He had just reached the first display case when a familiar voice came from behind him.

"How'd it go?"

Oxby turned and faced Alex Tobias. "You're a bloody scoundrel," he blurted out. "It went splendidly, but I wanted you with me."

"I couldn't. I had two Russians to baby-sit."

"Correction. One Russian, one Estonian."

"They're all the same to me."

"How's Deryabin?"

"Better than he deserves. He tried getting help from the Russian cunsul's office, but they weren't interested."

"And Trivimi?"

"The DA's cooperating, but they can't hold him for more than a couple of days."

"Would Lenny Sulzberger like to interview Deryabin?"

"Why would he want to?"

"Because it would make a bloody good story. There's a good chance it would be picked up in St. Petersburg. The procurator's office might get interested and suddenly Deryabin would have a lot of explaining to do."

"Lenny will do anything to extract his pound of flesh."

"Then arrange a meeting. Lenny's the only one in this mess I haven't met."

"I'll do it." Tobias took a newspaper clipping from his shirt. "I meant to tell you about this. Interested?"

Oxby was reading about an art auction scheduled for that evening in the Sotheby Galleries.

"Want to go?"

"It's all modern," Oxby remonstrated.

"There'll be some good stuff. Motherwell. Calder. Andy Warhol."

"Should be an interesting crowd."

"Lots of young people with plenty of money."

"I'd like to see the Warhols. Anything interesting?"

"His *Orange Marilyn*, for one," Tobias said. "Know it?"

"Oh, indeed." Oxby grinned. "As you Americans say—that one is *Big Time!*"

Glossary

privyet	hi (friendly, informal greeting)
prospekt	avenue
shalava	bitch, prostitute
Skola?	How much?
Spahseebah (bahlshoeh).	Thank you (very much).
sum	Uzbek currency
ulitsa	street
Vahsheh zdahroveh!	To your health!
Vor v zakanye	Godfather of crime gang
yab tvoyo mat	vile obscenity
zdanie	building

Acknowledgments

To Christopher Forbes I extend a special thanks, not only for generously sharing his knowledge of Fabergé and the incredible Imperial eggs, but for allowing me to include him as an essential character in the story. I salute Margaret Kelly Trombly and Robyn Tromeur of the Forbes Magazine Collection for their invaluable assistance. Gerard Hill of Sotheby's also shared his extensive knowledge of Fabergé and Russian art and icons.

My wife, Barbara, and I were in the home of Joseph and Marina Wolfson in Moscow and that of Nelly and Viktor Obukhova in St. Petersburg. We were warmly received and learned firsthand about the wrenching difficulties the Russian people face as they make the move toward a capitalistic society.

Jane Lombard provided additional insights into modern-day Russia, and Laryssa Lysniak proved to be expert at choosing Russian phrases. To Laryssa I owe a special *spahseebah*!

Nina and Leonid Bazilevich, native to St. Petersburg, read the manuscript and shared their intimate knowledge of the culture and traditions of the people. I was lucky to spend time with Iouna Zeck in the State Hermitage Museum.

Carl and Ann Klemme were the accurate eyes and ears for Tashkent, Uzbekistan.

My thanks to Dick Welch for his great knowledge of guns, and for John D'Andrea's equally informative knowledge of personal knives.

Always generous with their time were library researchers Barbara Simmonds and Barry Devlin.

FBI Supervisory Special Agent Raymond Kerr and Special Agent Joseph Valiquette revealed the inner workings of Russian crime in the New York area.

I am indebted to Stuart Stearns for describing biological agents and his compelling explanations for the reasons we must keep all such lethal toxins tightly sealed. And to Jim Coyne for his medical acumen.

Helping me understand the little mysteries surrounding the preparation and forwarding of automobiles from America to foreign ports were John Rozema, Sam Salzano, Robert Forsyth, and Brian Maher. Also my thanks to Officer Pat Caputo for showing me some, but not all, of the ways our U.S. Customs Service prevents stolen vehicles from leaving port.

As always, I thank Pete Wood for his dedication and unswerving loyalty. He remains my favorite reader and uncompromising critic.

About the Author

Thomas Swan has chosen the sometimes bizarre and frequently surprising world of art as the backdrop for his thrillers, and is the author of *The Da Vinci Deception* and *The Cézanne Chase*. He has served as secretary and member of the board of the Mystery Writers of America, and is a past president of the New York chapter of MWA. Having retired from a thirty-plus-year career in the field of advertising and marketing, Swan now writes full time, and lives with his wife Barbara in Short Hills, New Jersey.